PENGUI

PITCHER

Ira Berkow, a sports   w York
Times, was born in Chicago in 1940 and was gradu-
ated from Miami University (Oxford, Ohio) and the
Medill Graduate School of Journalism, Northwest-
ern University. He is the author of nine books,
including *The Man Who Robbed the Pierre: The
Story of Bobby Comfort* and the best-selling *Red:
A Biography of Red Smith*. He lives with his wife in
New York City.

IRA BERKOW

Pitchers Do Get Lonely

And Other Sports Stories

PENGUIN BOOKS

PENGUIN BOOKS
Published by the Penguin Group
Viking Penguin, a division of Penguin Books USA Inc.,
40 West 23rd Street, New York, New York 10010, U.S.A.
Penguin Books Ltd, 27 Wrights Lane,
London W8 5TZ, England
Penguin Books Australia Ltd, Ringwood,
Victoria, Australia
Penguin Books Canada Ltd, 2801 John Street,
Markham, Ontario, Canada L3R 1B4
Penguin Books (N.Z.) Ltd, 182–190 Wairau Road,
Auckland 10, New Zealand

Penguin Books Ltd, Registered Offices:
Harmondsworth, Middlesex, England

First published in the United States of America by
Atheneum, a division of Macmillan Publishing Company 1988
Published in Penguin Books 1989

1 3 5 7 9 10 8 6 4 2

Lyrics from "Mrs. Robinson," © Paul Simon 1968.
Text copyright © 1981-1987 by The New York Times Company.
Reprinted by permission.

LIBRARY OF CONGRESS CATALOGING IN PUBLICATION DATA
Berkow, Ira.
Pitchers do get lonely, and other sports stories/Ira Berkow.
p.   cm.—(Penguin sports library)
ISBN 0 14 01.2045 9
1. Sports.   2. Newspapers—Sections, columns, etc.—Sports.
I. Title.   II. Series.
GV707.B45   1989
070.4'49796—dc19   88–37993

Printed in the United States of America
Set in Trump Mediaeval

For Joe Vecchione and Sandy Padwe,
who opened a door

Contents

A CLUSTER OF STARS

EARLY STAGES

BUMPY ROADS

THOSE YESTERDAYS

A SOUPÇON OF SAVVY

STRICTLY PERSONAL

Foreword

All newspaper writers have heard that the stuff they compose today has an excellent chance of being used to wrap tomorrow's mackerel. This is no doubt a fact of life, though I have never personally seen anyone sartorially improving a deceased fish with a sports column of mine. I probably just don't frequent the right places.

One morning, though, I learned of another use for my column.

I had left my Manhattan apartment and was walking up 31st Street, occupied with thoughts of the column that appeared in that day's New York Times. As I recall, it was an especially difficult column to write, though most generally are for me. I had struggled to arrive at a cogent idea, had struggled to dig up the necessary background information, and struggled to lay the words and spelling down on paper in a way that would keep the Times's sports copy editors from overworking themselves and keep the Times's editors interested in retaining my name on the payroll.

I was also going through the usual postpartum pang—was the piece as good as I thought (one moment) or was it as bad as I thought (another moment). At this moment I was feeling rather pleased with myself. And my step had taken on a decided little spring to it.

I now saw a woman whom I didn't know and don't ever want to know carrying that morning's Times in one hand and her schnauzer on a leash in the other. It happened that when I drew closer the dog stopped to take care of business and the business was conducted on, of all things, my painstakingly wrought column.

So I am thrilled now to have some of those Times columns in book form. They are harder for dogs to get at.

That's one reason I am interested in the publication of this book. Why should anyone else be? Why should anyone want to read newspaper stuff—and sports pieces at that, considered the most perishable of all newspaper writing—that go back several years?

Perhaps, as a sportswriter once said, it is part of the record of our time, and sports and athletes regularly reflect the hopes and expectations, the dreams and fears, the disappointments and exultations in a more clearly defined and easily apprehensible form than most other activities.

It is all there in the 10 seconds of a dash, or 60 minutes of a football game, or seven months of a baseball season. And, in the best of all possible worlds, in the 900 or so words of a sports column.

As a sports columnist—I've been with the *Times* since 1981, starting as a sports feature writer, and, for nine years before that, wrote a sports and then a general column for Newspaper Enterprise Association—I've traveled to many points on the compass, and usually am afforded a pretty good seat in the press box to observe man in motion.

There is, however, much that doesn't meet the eye directly, and there are things going on inside the man, or woman, and behind the scenes, that the writer/observer/commentator strives to comprehend, and describe.

The issues and problems of sexism, of racism, of nationalism, of community, of labor-management relations, of individual and constitutional rights, and arrant knavery as well as practiced idealism, are all involved in the modern-day sports scene. Some of all of this is included in my sports columns and feature articles for the *Times*, though not all are represented in the following pages. The reason is that I've attempted to include only those that retain what seems to me some aspect of timeliness.

Particular issues change swifter than men do, which is why we can enjoy Shakespeare with as much benefit now as the Elizabethans did some four hundred years ago. The point is simply that, though the world around us may change drastically, people basically don't.

And so it is for me that people prove the most intriguing element of my work, a kind of work that is seen in different ways, as I've come to understand, by different people. At the season opener in Yankee Stadium a few years ago, I met Richard Nixon, a sports buff on the highest order.

"You must lead a very exciting life," he said to me.

"Not as exciting as yours, Mr. President," I replied.

It made me smile to think that after all that that politician had gone through, he could imagine anyone else's life being exciting. But he did—I assumed, at this stage of his career, he wasn't just hustling my vote—and others believe it exciting too. And in fact, mine is, in many instances. Though it remains difficult to convince many of this, the job's not always a day at the beach.

About 40 years ago, John Lardner, one of the finest writers on sports, published a collection of his pieces with the title *It Beats Working*. This was a kind of joke, since Lardner labored over his stuff, though, as art must be, the effort never showed through. All of us—the knights of the keyboard, as Ted Williams would twit those who sat in judgment of him—go at it in our own way. Some more successfully than others, to be sure.

Years ago in New York there was a sportswriter—to be known here as "So-and-so"—who on a daily basis fought a losing battle with the language. In the press box one day, someone mentioned to Jimmy Cannon, the acerbic and highly regarded sports columnist, that So-and-so's house had burned down the night before.

"Must've been an English professor," said Cannon, without looking up.

For some of us, the struggle to get it right, to do it well and to realize at least a small portion of our dreams never ends. Like sports.

Uncommon Conditions

Vince's Story

New York, December 25, 1986

When the holiday season rolls around and talk of miracles is in the air, Mickey Lolich remembers a boy named Vince.

In fact, the thought of Lolich was triggered by the arrival recently of the ballot for the Baseball Hall of Fame. One of the names on it for the third straight year—he has received only a modest number of votes in the past—is Mickey Lolich, who pitched for 16 years in the big leagues, mostly with the Detroit Tigers.

Besides having won 25 games in one season, and having started, completed and won three games in the 1968 World Series—in the seventh game he defeated Bob Gibson and the Cardinals, 4–1, and was named the most valuable player in the Series—besides all that, Mickey Lolich stood out because, from the neck down, he looked like Santa Claus in a baseball uniform.

Six feet tall, and weighing as much as 225 pounds in his playing days, Lolich sported a pot belly ("Got it from home cooking," he said; "I rarely drank beer") but still threw hard and well and long.

He could hit (he had a home run in the World Series) and he could field. "That belly of his never seemed to get in his way when he was on the mound," said Rod Carew. "But I always marveled at how well this chubby guy bounced off the mound after bunts or taps. I always thought that the fatter he got, the faster he got. He seemed to defy the law of nature."

"The fatter you get," Lolich said recently, with his easy laugh, "the faster you get in perpetual motion. I'd come off the mound to field a bunt and just let my weight propel me. But I pitched a lot—one year I threw 376 innings—so you can't tell me I was out of shape."

Lolich now earns a living from—perhaps not surprisingly, given his penchant for munching—the Mickey Lolich Donut Shop in Lake Orion, Mich., some 50 miles from Tiger Stadium, the scene of many of the triumphs.

Lolich was someone many guys in the stands could relate to. "People used to say to me," Lolich recalls, " 'Hey, it's nice to see you in the major leagues. You look human, and not like all those Golden Gods.' "

But Lolich and his teammate Al Kaline were gods to Vince, who in 1977 was 14 years old. Lolich and Kaline ran a one-week baseball camp for boys, in Ypsilanti, and Vince was one of the campers.

"He was a black kid who lived with his mother, was overweight for his age, and retarded," said Lolich. "He didn't know how to put a key in a door. He was confused about things like that. When he put on a T-shirt, he put it on backwards.

"We didn't know about Vince, and just accepted applications and let it go at that. We really didn't notice him the first day at check-in, but we discovered on the second day that basically he could do nothing in the way of sports."

Lolich and Kaline became "quite concerned" that Vince might get hurt, and their attorney suggested that Vince be sent home.

The attorney called Vince's mother, and she broke down in tears. She said Vince idolized the Tigers, and that he worshiped Al Kaline and Mickey Lolich. Vince would sit in front of the television set and watch ball games wearing his Tiger cap and baseball glove.

"He lives and breathes the Tigers, and exists only for baseball," she said. She said she was a cleaning lady and living on that and welfare. Vince had never been to a Tiger game because she couldn't afford it, and she had to take odd jobs to come up with the money to send Vince to the camp.

"It would be the greatest blow to him if he were sent home," she said. "I don't know what effect it would have on him."

"When Al and I heard the story," said Lolich, "we said, 'What choice do we have?' "

So Kaline and Lolich called a meeting of the 90 or so campers—all but Vince, who was taken for a walk by one of the counselors. "Al and I explained the situation to the kids, who had been teasing him and calling him 'Fatty' and 'Stupid,' the ways kids can be cruel when there's someone different among them," said Lolich. "We told them it was Vince's life dream to be here, and we'd appreciate it if they could accept him and try to help him.

"They did immediately. They helped him get dressed, and put

food on his tray at each meal, and took him to the ball field. A couple of kids would stand around him to protect him in case of a line drive. It was really something to see. He couldn't play, but he coached first base, and he cheered hard. Vince was a great cheerleader. He was in his glory, he was having the time of his life.

"On the last day, I pitched to all the campers, and Al and I decided to let Vince bat. He had tremendous problems making contact with the ball. Al was on the on-deck circle, and called advice: 'Get your hands up, Vince, get your bat back.' And he'd walk over and show him.

"I had moved in, but I still threw overhand. The first pitch was a strike down the middle, and the umpire naturally called it a ball. Vince swung at the next pitch and missed. And then, lo and behold, on the next pitch, the miracle happened. Vince hit the ball! He tapped a slow roller to the shortstop.

"Vince chugged to first, and the shortstop—God bless him, I wish I could remember his name—juggled the ball on purpose, and threw to first just as Vince was one stride from the base. Vince beat the throw, and both teams were jumping up and down, yelling and screaming.

"Later that night, there was an awards banquet, and Vince got the award for most improved player.

"Vince was given a standing O, and he put his arms around Al and me and gave us a big hug. He said, 'I'll never forget this as long as I live.' And that's when Al and I both cried."

The Yankees and Dr. Freud

New York, May 2, 1985

Sigm. Freud, as the good doctor signed some of his correspondence, departed from this vale of tears nearly half a century ago. Yet his wisdom in many matters lives on. Recently, Dr. Peter Berczeller, who, like Dr. Freud, was born in Austria, and who now practices medicine on, and follows the Yankees from, Second

Avenue, wondered aloud what Sigm. might have cogitated about the latest undertaking of the principal owner of the Yankees, the fantastical Herr S.

A clue, perhaps, may be found in the newly published *The Complete Letters of Sigmund Freud to Wilhelm Fliess, 1887–1904.* An interview follows that uses this text. The answers were chosen with careful selectivity by this typist, but the words, whether they would have been approved in the context or not, are Sigm.'s.

Q: Dr. Freud, how are you feeling now after Herr S.'s firing of Yogi Berra and his hiring for the fourth time of Billy Martin?

I have not yet really overcome my depression. . . . On my side of the tunnel it is quite dark.

Q: Sorry to hear you're so ill over the recent events.

My state of health does not deserve to be a subject of inquiry. . . . There was a recrudescence of the suppuration of the left side, migraines rather frequently, the necessary abstinence is hardly doing me much good. I have rapidly turned gray.

Q: Could you guess at how Met fans are feeling about this?

The sun and the stars are shining.

Q: Have you given much study to the case of the principal owner?

I shudder when I think of all the psychology I shall have to read up on the next few years. At the moment I can neither read nor think. I am completely exhausted by observation.

Q: Did you have any idea that Herr S. would make this move?

So my premonition of something ominous turned out to be right.

Q: You mean that Yogi was fired only 16 games into the season?

I find it sad that the interval is so short.

Q: Yankee fans appear to be deeply depressed. Any words of advice for them?

I seem to remember having heard somewhere that only dire need brings out the best in man. I have therefore pulled myself together. . . . A basket of orchids gives me the illusion of splendor and glowing sunshine; a fragment of a Pompeiian wall with a centaur and faun transports me. . . .

Q: On the subject of Herr S., it seems to most laymen that he has a compulsion or fixation or obsessional idea or some other oddball thing that they can't quite put a finger on in regard to firing people, particularly managers. He hadn't fired a manager in over a year until last Sunday. Can you relate to such an itch as Herr S.'s in any way? What about your quitting smoking?

After seven weeks . . . I began again. . . . From the first cigars on, I was able to work and was the master of my mood; prior to that, life was unbearable.

Q: Does that mean that firing people, like smoking for you, makes him feel better?

It is a question of psychic mechanism that is very commonly employed in normal life: transposition, or projection. Whenever an internal change occurs, we have the choice of assuming either an internal or external cause. If something deters us from the internal derivation, we naturally seize upon the external one.

Q: Does that mean, Doc, that he has to blame people other than himself?

In every instance the *delusional idea* is maintained with the same energy with which another, intolerably distressing, idea is warded off from the ego. Thus they love their delusions as they love themselves. That is the secret.

Q: Are you saying that this is the answer?

That is the material we have. No one really has a clear picture. . . .

Q: But?

The whole business is uncanny.

Q: Many Yankee fans and some local journalists have advanced the notion that Herr S. should sell the Yankees and stick with his shipbuilding business. Your thoughts?

I vaguely sensed something I can express only today: the faint notion that this man has not yet discovered his calling.

Q: But if he continues as principal owner, what might this mean for Yankee fans?

Gloomy times, unbelievably gloomy.

Q: What do you foresee for the Yankee fans in the near future?

Fathomless and bottomless laziness, intellectual stagnation, summer dreariness, vegetative well-being. . . .

Q: Even for you?

In times like these, my reluctance to write is downright pathological.

Q: Granted that you are not a prognosticator as such, but how do you think the Yankees will do this year?

Fluctuat nec mergitur.

Q: Pardon?

"It floats but it does not sink."

Q: I think I follow, Doctor; Floating is not sinking, but it's not sailing, either. In other words, no pennant in the offing?

Pour faire une omelette il faut casser des oeufs.

Q: Oh?

"To prepare an omelet, one must break eggs."

Q: Yes, yes, eggs plural. There has to be more done than just a changing of managers. And the bottom line, then, is that you're still down at the mouth about all this?

Life is miserable. Life is otherwise incredibly devoid of content.

Q: Well, how do you plan to spend the rest of the baseball season? I notice you are packing. Are you going someplace?

Italy . . . the journey will take in San Gimignano-Siena-Perugia-Assisi-Ancona—in short, Tuscany and Umbria. I am seeking a punch made from Lethe—the dead drank from Lethe, the river of forgetfulness, upon their arrival in the underworld. . . . Here and there I get a draft.

Q: Thank you, Doctor. Many of us would love to drink a draft of forgetfulness with you.

The LaMotta Nuptials

Las Vegas, November 20, 1985

Neither of the Las Vegas dailies, nor, for that matter, the *New York Times*, reported in their society news sections the wedding of Jacob (Jake) LaMotta, 63 years old, erstwhile pugilist, and Theresa Miller, younger than the bridegroom and decidedly prettier.

Perhaps it was determined in some editorial conclave that to cover one of Jake's nuptials is to cover them all, for this is the sixth time he's tied the knot. But to Jake, each, of course, is unique. His first wife divorced him, he says, "because I clashed with the drapes." Another one, Vicki, complained about not having enough clothes. "I didn't believe her," LaMotta says, "until I saw her pose nude in *Playboy* magazine."

The betrothal of LaMotta, the former world middleweight champion, to Miss Miller (this was her second trip to the altar) took place last Sunday night in Las Vegas at Maxim Hotel and Casino in a room stuffed with a wide assortment of beefy people with odd-shaped and familiar noses. They included such ex-champions as Gene Fullmer, Carmen Basilio, Willie Pep, Joey Maxim, Billy Conn, José Torres and, the best man, Sugar Ray Robinson, plus a potpourri of contenders, trainers and matchmakers, all of whom were in Las Vegas to attend the Hagler-Hearns world middleweight title fight the following night.

For LaMotta, having Robinson as the best man was a sweet and perfect touch. "I fought Sugar six times," he said. "I only beat him once. This is my sixth marriage and I ain't won one yet. So I figure I'm due."

Both the groom and the best man wore tuxedos with white corsages in their lapels. The bride was radiant in a white dress with mother-of-pearl-and-lace design, and a garland of baby's breath in her auburn hair. The wedding party assembled under a white lattice arch in the corner of the room as District Judge Joe Pavlikowski of Clark County presided over the ceremony.

Despite the loud, happy chatter of the guests, the judge began a recital of the vows. "Quiet, please," a man shouted. "Quiet." When that didn't work, the man stuck two fingers in his mouth and whistled. That got their attention.

The judge continued. He asked Jake and Theresa if they would love and obey. They said they would, and Jake kissed the bride.

"Wait a minute," said the judge. "Not yet."

Jake looked up, and Theresa smiled. The judge coughed.

In another corner of the room, a phone rang.

Jake looked around brightly. "What round is it?" he asked.

The room broke up. Theresa, laughing, said, "I've changed my mind!" Then she hugged Jake, who smiled proudly at his bon mot.

"We've got to finish," said the judge. The room settled down somewhat. ". . . With love and affection," continued the judge, speaking quicker now. In short order, he pronounced them "Mr. and Mrs. Jake LaMotta."

Applause and cheers went up, and the couple kissed again, this time officially.

"Jake's ugly as mortal sin," observed Billy Conn. "He's a nice guy, though."

Shortly after, Jake and Carmen Basilio argued about who was uglier. The issue wasn't resolved. Steve Rossi, the comedian, who was performing at the hotel, was the master of ceremonies at the wedding. He brought the fighters onto the stage, where they talked and laughed and feinted and hit one another with friendly jabs and hooks.

When all the fighters were onstage, Rossi said, "Let's all go eat before the platform collapses."

Teddy Brenner, the matchmaker, asked Joey Maxim, "Who was the only white guy to beat Jersey Joe Walcott and Floyd Patterson?" Maxim said he didn't know. "You, ya big lug," said Brenner. They both laughed. The story gleefully made the rounds, varying a little with each telling, until finally, ". . . and so he asked Joey, 'Who was the only white guy to beat Louis and Ali?'. . ."

Someone asked Fullmer how many times he had fought Robinson.

"Three and a half," he said. "The second fight I asked my manager, 'How come they stopped it?' He said, ' 'Cause the referee counted to 11.' "

Basilio said he had recently retired as a physical education instructor at Le Moyne College in Syracuse. Someone asked if he had a degree.

He smiled and brushed the ashes from his cigarette off the sports jacket of the person he was talking to. "I got a degree from H.N.," he said. "The school of hard knocks."

Billy Conn, who lives in Pittsburgh, was telling about the time that his brother Jackie, a nonconformist, visited Conn on a Thanksgiving Day. "We were having the Mellons over and I told Jackie that we wanted everything to run smoothly, so here's 50 bucks and go buy a turkey for yourself. But he kept the 50 bucks and took the two turkeys we had in the stove."

What did the Conns and the Mellons eat that night?

"We didn't eat," he said, "we drank whiskey all night. Oh, Jackie was a character. Jackie's dead now."

Roger Donoghue, once a promising middleweight from Yonkers, and now a successful liquor salesman, was recalling the television-fight days of the early 1950s. Basilio came over and handed Roger a small camera and asked him to take a picture of him and his wife.

"I got hit in the head a lot," said Roger, looking at the camera, "but I'll try."

The doors of the room were opened and the clanging of slot machines was heard from the adjoining casino. People wandered in and out of the wedding party.

Jake was explaining, "You wanna go through life with someone, and she's a great kid, a great kid."

"This one," said Theresa, "is going to last until we die."

Now, Jake and his bride stepped onto the dance floor. A trio, headed by a piano player wearing a black cowboy hat, played "The Nearness of You."

Joey Maxim removed the cigar from his mouth as he watched Jake dance with his new bride. "Ain't that nice?" he said.

"Hey, buddy," said a man who walked in from the casino, "you know where a fella can get two tickets for the fight?"

A Kiss Is No Crime

New York, April 7, 1984

John Thompson is not against hugging, so why is he rapping kissing?

After Coach Thompson's Georgetown Hoyas had attained an insurmountable lead late in the National Collegiate Athletic Association basketball championship game last Monday night in the Seattle Kingdome, the television cameras panned to the bench and picked up Thompson's victory embrace of Fred Brown and Patrick Ewing, two of his players.

Madly and sweetly they exulted. And with cause.

The coach particularly. The son of an illiterate laborer and a domestic, he took a losing basketball program at Georgetown University and worked assiduously and skillfully, rose to the top of his profession on merit and in the process became the first black coach to win the NCAA basketball title. And this after having lost in the final in the last seconds of play two years before.

Coach Thompson has also been criticized by some in the press for what has been termed "overly physical basketball." That is, roughneck stuff. Sometimes a Georgetown game resembles a hockey game.

But college basketball is a rough business, and the teams are playing for high stakes: each team in the Final Four, for example, earned $614,000. And the object, obviously, is to win.

So Coach Thompson retaliated, and said about the press, "The most physical thing they've done is kiss."

Now, it's true of some reporters that, as it has been said, when they feel an urge for physical exercise they lie down until it passes.

But kissing, as Thompson so sagely noted, is an exercise they engage in. One reason, perhaps, is that it can be effectuated *when* lying down.

By his condemnation, are we to presume that basketball coaches don't kiss? If that is so, then if they could tear themselves away from watching game films for a while, they might find it not so bad a thing.

Even boxers kiss. When Archie Moore was light-heavyweight champion of the world, someone asked if his wife minded kissing him with his beard. "No," Archie said, "she's more than happy to go through a forest to get to the picnic."

On another level, Thompson may be faulted for stereotyping the press. There is at least one ink-stained wretch who jogs. There is at least one other who plays recreational basketball. And there probably have been at least as many members of the press who served in military combat as there have been basketball coaches.

One would think that Coach Thompson, who has rightly resisted and been sensitive to labels, would be the last person to cast a stereotype.

He has also been protective of his players, often shielding them from the press. Sometimes rightly, sometimes wrongly. Anyway, the aura created by Thompson has been called "Hoya Paranoia."

He recently responded by criticizing the role of the press, and said to reporters, "You're making a living off a kid who's playing for free, basically."

Somehow, Coach Thompson makes it sound as if the press—which surely has its faults, as even some basketball coaches do—is performing evil work.

Does he mean that the press shouldn't cover college basketball? And by press it is assumed he also means television. Shall we allow college basketball to return to the anonymity it once enjoyed in peachbasket days? How would the Georgetown president feel about having $614,000 less than he has now?

And it follows that if the press didn't cover college basketball, there would be a de-emphasis of that extracurricular activity, and that would mean a loss of scholarships, and, in many cases across the country, a loss of cars and television sets and other perks for athletes, many of whom are not playing for free, basically.

And Thompson is not Mother Teresa. He, too, is making a living off a kid who's playing for free, basically.

Thompson earns about $65,000 a year in salary from Georgetown University; that is nearly triple the average salary of professors on the main campus. And his is a revolving three-year contract, which means that if he is dismissed, he gets paid for two-plus years.

Thompson talks about motivating youth and building character, and he may succeed in those aims. But he is still not Mother Teresa. John Thompson lives in a $300,000 house with a large pool in a swanky area in Washington. He was provided this house by the Alumni Association when he used an offer to coach at Oklahoma as leverage to improve his position at Georgetown.

Because he implies that he is not living off a kid who's playing for free, basically, he was offered and accepted a basketball sneaker endorsement worth $50,000. He also runs a summer basketball camp from which he earns about $50,000 more.

Thompson also makes numerous speeches, some for charities he does gratis, some for businesses for which he charges a fee. Now, Jim Valvano, who coached last year's NCAA champion, North Carolina State, commands $3,500 an engagement. Thompson need ask no less than that. And 15 of those speeches give him about another $50,000.

Thompson, who proudly admits to making a good deal of money during his decade or so at Georgetown, will conceivably earn in the vicinity of a quarter of a million dollars this year—plus living in a $300,000 house that he hasn't paid for.

But never mind that. What rankles here is his put-down of the press for what he considers, and, it must be admitted, with justification, its predilection for smooching.

Our defense? Who needs a defense? Our position, though, was advanced most nobly and cogently by Robert Herrick, a 17th-century scribe, who wrote:

Give me a kiss, and to that kiss a score;
Then to that twenty, add a hundred more;
A thousand to that hundred: so kiss on,
To make that thousand a million.
Treble that million, and when that is done,
Let's kiss afresh, as when we first begun.

Denny McLain's Star

New York, March 24, 1985

It was 1968, and the nation's sports fans followed Denny McLain's stirring quest to win 30 games.

"How did McLain do?" people asked.

"Won again," came the usual answer.

"Again!"

He pitched the Detroit Tigers to the American League pennant that year, winning 31 games and losing only 6, the first pitcher to win 30 or more games since Dizzy Dean 34 years before, and no one has done it since.

McLain was then 24 years old. He would be one of the best-paid players in his time. His future looked glorious.

Four years later, plagued with personal problems, his weight up, his arm sore, his fastball gone from the express to the local, he pitched his last game in the major leagues.

On the surface, this would seem the stereotypical, and perhaps melancholy, case of the star athlete who burst across the scene like a shooting star and then falls into oblivion. But there was more.

For some time, McLain did recede from public view. But early this week he surfaced in Tampa, Fla., where he has been living. He was charged in a federal indictment with racketeering, conspiracy, extortion, possession, and distribution of cocaine, and conspiracy to import cocaine. Two days ago, he surrendered to federal marshals, then was freed on $200,000 bond. McLain who will be 40 years old next Thursday, the day of his arraignment, will face up to 90 years in prison if convicted of all charges.

This was not, as the baseball world knows, the first time that McLain had gotten into serious trouble.

After the 1969 season, in which he won 24 games and for the second straight season won the Cy Young Award as the best pitcher in the American League, the commissioner suspended him six months for gambling activities. Specifically, he had been a bookmaker and had made betting phone calls from the Tiger clubhouse.

Later, in the 1970 season, he would be suspended from baseball again, for carrying an unregistered gun.

McLain's problems with illegitimate elements apparently began around 1967. He had suffered a mysterious foot injury in the heat of the pennant race, after having won 17 games that year, and the loss of him was one factor in the undoing of the Tigers, who finished one game behind first-place Boston. He said he suffered the injury when he tried to walk after his foot had fallen asleep. Then he changed his story: He had kicked a clubhouse door in anger.

The truth, it turned out, was that a Detroit hoodlum whom McLain was dealing with had stomped on his foot to emphasize how important regular payments were.

One evening during his first suspension, McLain was visited by a reporter at his home in Lakeland, Fla.

The discussion turned to heroes. McLain said that the man he most wished to be like was Frank Sinatra. "Not only is he a great entertainer," said McLain, " and has fans and friends and money by the millions, but he also has power. That's what I want."

Apparently, McLain sought power through underworld associates.

"I was not quite twenty-six years old," he wrote in his autobiography, *Nobody's Perfect*, written with Dave Diles and published in 1975. "I had a beautiful wife and three lovely children. I was making at least $150,000 a year and maybe a lot more because I just couldn't keep track of things. I was the finest pitcher in baseball. I had a successful night club act, a paint company, a flying service, I was getting into the organ business, land deals, sporting goods and a game company.

"I had a lot more, too. . . . My wife, the FBI, the Internal Revenue Service, the commissioner of baseball, eighty-six creditors, and a few other vultures were on my back—all at the same time. On the outside I was happy. Inside, I was dying. I owed more than $446,000!"

In business, he would declare bankruptcy.

In baseball, he went from the Tigers to the Senators, where, in 1971, with a 10–22 record, he lost more games than anyone else in either league. He would pitch the following year for the A's and the Braves.

The next season, in the summer of 1973, McLain was pitching for a semipro team in London, Ontario—the last time he pitched anywhere—and was photographed on the mound. He looked pear-shaped. In his prime, the 6-foot-1-inch McLain had weighed about 190 pounds. He would balloon to 300.

"I can't believe it," he said at the time. "I can't believe I can't help a single major-league team."

He bounced from job to job, catching on as a general manager of a minor-league team for a while, then getting involved in businesses from public relations to selling large television screens to taverns.

None of it seemed to work out.

Referring to his days as a major-league ballplayer, he once said, "When you're used to going first-class, you can never turn back."

Dennis Dale McLain grew up on the South Side of Chicago and, as he would recall, dreamed great dreams of glory. He was a star pitcher at Mount Carmel High School and was signed to a contract by the White Sox right after graduation, in 1962. He was sent to their farm teams in Harlan, Ky., and then Clinton, Iowa.

McLain jumped both clubs several times. "I knew they couldn't cut me," he said. "I was winning."

He was 18 years old, and cocky, and wrong. The White Sox put him on waivers because of his disregard for rules. He despaired, his dream of pitching for the hometown White Sox crushed. But the Tigers happily picked up this talented though possibly quirky kid, who soon began a 10-year big-league career that ended at age 28, and much too quickly.

Now McLain has been indicted, but not convicted, and so he is innocent until proved guilty. What seems beyond doubt, though, is that the days since his big-league career ended have been difficult ones, especially so for one who dreamed and realized great dreams of glory, who once went first-class, and who was ambitious for something that he perceived as power.

McLain was convicted and received a 23-year sentence. He served 28 months before being released on judicial error in his trial.

A Snorkeler's Tale

New York, November 11, 1984

When the landslide reelection victory for Bill Bradley as United States Senator from New Jersey was apparent last Tuesday evening, one of the television commentators discussed the Senator's style.

He spoke of the great respect that the tall, dark-haired man with the oddly upturned left eyebrow had earned from both sides of the aisle in the Senate, of how hard he had worked to gain a firm grasp of issues and of the tremendous popularity he had attained in his state. The commentator also mentioned that Bill Bradley's speaking voice was rather flat, though he had been endeavoring to improve it, and that his sense of humor could be wooden.

Dave DeBusschere and his wife, Gerri, smiled when that last point was made. That's not quite the Bill Bradley they know.

"He's not a joke teller; some people just aren't," said Gerri DeBusschere. "But Dave and I enjoyed his kind of wacko sense of humor, especially when he was with the Knicks."

Dave DeBusschere, now the Knicks' executive vice president and director of basketball operations, was Bill Bradley's roommate on the road when they played together, from 1968 through 1974.

"I remember when a man began writing and calling Bill at hotels," said Gerry, "and Bill would whisper to the guy on the phone, and they'd have meetings in coffee shops. Dave finally asked Bill who the guy was. Bill said, 'He thinks I'm not Bill Bradley. He thinks I'm really an Albanian spy.' And Bill encouraged him."

On the road in basketball, Bradley, the Princeton graduate and Rhodes scholar, also involved himself in such issues as prison reform, the economy and foreign affairs. Unlike most of the other players, who were dapper, he seemed to have little time for sartorial concerns. He would sometimes forget to bring extra socks and would borrow DeBusschere's, and when a button broke on his shirt he'd replace it with a paper clip. His raincoat was generally wrapped up in a ball and carried under his arm. On seeing it, Dick Barnett would make a sound like a foghorn, an esthetic appraisal of sorts.

After the 1974 playoffs, the DeBusscheres, Bradley and his wife, Ernestine, and another couple, the Nick Kladdises of Chicago, went to Greece on vacation. Gerri DeBusschere recalls that everyone except Bradley took at least one suitcase—the DeBusscheres had one suitcase just for their scuba-diving equipment. "Bill came with a little gym bag," she said. "He didn't even have a bathing suit. He swam in his Knick practice shorts."

The three couples rented a cabin cruiser and embarked from the port of Piraeus for a two-week trip around the Greek islands. They lay on the deck and watched the islands go by, and Dave and Bill, particularly, would don snorkeling masks and flippers, drop down and explore the Aegean. From the boat one afternoon, they saw a church on a hill of a tiny, isolated island. They decided to get a closer look.

The island was so small that there was no place to dock the boat, so it remained about a quarter of a mile out to sea. Bradley and

DeBusschere swam to shore. DeBusschere came up first, and saw a man sitting on a beach chair, reading a book.

DeBusschere took off his mask, and the man jumped up, his book dropping out of his hands. The man's mouth was agape, and he pointed frantically at DeBusschere.

DeBusschere thought that there might be something wrong with him, or that he was frightened that someone who was 6 feet 6 inches tall was suddenly rising from the sea.

"Then," DeBusschere recalled, "the man stuttered, 'You're, you're you're Dave . . . Dave . . . Dave DeBusschere!'"

DeBusschere was surprised that anyone on this little island could speak English, let alone recognize him.

"Then Bill came out of the water right behind me," DeBusschere recalled. "The guy says, 'Oh, my God! Bill Bradley too! I can't believe this!'"

The man sputtered that he had season tickets under the basket, and that he had been postponing his vacation until after the playoffs, and that he was on this island because he had been so overworked that his wife had said he needed to go to a secluded place for a rest.

"And to see you guys here is—"

"Sure," Bradley said with understanding, " and Willis Reed will be here in a minute."

"The whole team is coming up," said DeBusschere.

The man said, "Wait, wait right here. I've got to get my wife. She'll never believe this. Oh, my God!"

The man flew off down the beach, screaming his wife's name.

Bradley turned to DeBusschere and said with a grin, "Let's leave."

DeBusschere nodded. The pair clamped on their masks and disappeared back into the water.

Gerry DeBusschere happened to be watching this from the deck of the boat. She sees the man now racing back along the beach, dragging his wife by the hand.

He returns to the spot where his chair is, and where his book is lying in the sand. Otherwise, the beach is deserted.

He goes to the water's edge, looking around and pointing. Meanwhile, Bradley and DeBusschere have returned to the boat and are hiding in a cabin below deck. Nick Kladdis revs up the motor, and the boat heads farther out to sea.

On the beach, the man is waving wildly, while his wife is looking at him and then looking at the receding boat.

Bradley and DeBusschere never saw him again. The next season, they looked for him under the baskets at Madison Square Garden, but he wasn't there.

"The guy's wife probably thought he had flipped," said Gerri DeBusschere, "and he never came up to Bill or Dave and said, 'I saw you in Greece.' He was probably too embarrassed. He probably thought he hadn't really seen them, and that he was just suffering from being overworked."

Is That All There Is?

New York, May 21, 1986

Something's missing. Chris Evert Lloyd, in an article on her in the most recent issue of *Life* magazine, revealed a part of her private life as a tennis champion and the wife of the British tennis player John Lloyd: "We get into a rut. We play tennis, we go to a movie, we watch TV, but I keeping saying, 'John, there has to be more.' "

This is no dreamy department-store clerk in cosmetics or bathroom accessories. She is Chrissie, a world-famous personage, a glittering star in the glitzy firmament of country clubs and television commercials and gossip columns and championship trophies.

And when she gets low, she can go out and buy a chocolate milkshake and not have it make much of a dent in her $3-million-a-year income. Or she can move the furniture around in her townhouse in Kingston, England, or hang new pictures in the condo in Rancho Mirage, Calif., and, soon, she'll be able to rattle around the four-bedroom house she and John are building in Boca Raton, Fla.

But she believes that fame, fortune, and 146 professional tennis championships, the record, are not enough.

In the background of her life one may hear the strains of the song, "Is That All There Is?"

She has tried separation from John, she has, she admitted, tried affairs—"I'm no angel," she says. (She discovered that John was more important to her than she had realized.) And she has even considered quitting tennis, not only because Martina Navratilova has forced her to second spot in the rankings, but because, well, "there has to be more."

Chrissie—which is the title of the *Life* piece—is 31 years old. An old 31, a young 31. Old in that she has been a nationally known tennis star since she was a ponytailed lass of 16. Young in that the narrow focus of tennis, the countless hours of rapping, rapping, rapping a tennis ball has in some ways confined her to within the lines of the tennis court, thereby retaining in her a quality of the ingenue. Call her present state burnout, maybe. Call it middle-age crisis, possibly. Call it human.

She says, "I've had enormous success, but you have to find your own happiness and peace. You can't find it in other things and other people. I'm still searching."

She seems now somewhere between Alexander the Great and Cinderella before she lost her shoe. At the top of his game, Alex plopped down on a rock and bawled, so frustrated was he that there were no more worlds to conquer. Ella, meanwhile, tended to her cinders and wondered what else was out there.

But it's not just charwomen and tennis greats who yearn for more.

Joe Namath comes to mind. He was once the world's most renowned bachelor. Namath was the kind of guy who surely had the world and all the women he wanted in the palm of his hand.

In fact, an article in 1969 stated that the night before he was to play in the American Football League championship game he was seen wearing a mink coat and clutching a bottle of Scotch in one hand and a lissome blonde in the other, headed in the general direction of his motel room. He denied this fervently, "I wasn't wearing a mink coat," he said.

One evening a year or so later, Namath sat in his Upper East Side duplex with his small book of phone numbers in his hand.

He dialed one number, there was no answer. He dialed another number. No answer. Then he shut his book and sighed. "There's only one girl in the world I want to be with tonight," he said to a visitor, "and she's not home."

At that moment, he wasn't Broadway Joe, but Joe Namath, a kid from Beaver Falls.

A number of years ago, Al Kaline, now in the Baseball Hall of Fame, was talking to a reporter about whether there was, as Chrissie wonders, "more."

Kaline then was 34, and had been a big-league baseball player for 17 years (this is Chrissie's 16th year as a tennis professional). "Sometimes I wonder what I'm doing," he said, "if I've wasted my time all these years. And sometimes I think I have.

"I would like to have done more to contribute to society. I don't know, maybe have been a doctor. Something where you really play an important part in people's lives."

He said that sometimes he sat in the dugout and looked out on the field and wondered what good it's all done, this "thinking about me, me, me, my batting average, my fielding average. Oh, sure, you care about the team. You have to. But in the end you're worried about you."

He said that he then had to think of himself as an entertainer. "Maybe kids can draw an inspiration from what I do," he said. "Maybe people who come out to the park can forget their problems for a while by watching me play."

Kaline, like Chris Evert Lloyd, devoted his young adulthood to the pursuit of a ball, and neither had much formal education beyond high school. And despite all the trappings of glamour in their professions, their lives, it seems, were both oddly insular.

After dinner one night about a year ago, she was asked by Murray Olderman, a sportswriter for Newspaper Enterprise Association, what she plans to do when she retires from tennis.

"Travel," she said.

"Travel?" he asked of this world traveler.

"I'd love to see things like the Berlin Wall," she said.

"But haven't you been to Berlin?"

"Yes," said Chrissie, "but whenever I travel I just play tennis. I never see anything."

One for Eli Yale

New York, November 23, 1985

For the 102nd annual Harvard-Yale game at the Yale Bowl in New Haven this afternoon, the weatherman said there was a chance of rain, but not necessarily a torrent. It seems unlikely that it would be anything like the 1932 Harvard-Yale game, which was played in one of the worst rainstorms in New Haven history. It rained so hard for so long that even Babe Ruth left the game early.

The *New York Times* of November 20, 1932, reported the details of the game, a 19–0 victory for Yale, highlighted by Walter Levering's touchdown runs of 45 and 55 yards. Following the account of the game, there appeared a small item, which read: "Babe Ruth sat in the downpour with Mrs. Ruth until even his massive physique could not stand it any longer. He left in the fourth quarter totally unnoticed. He was just another bedraggled figure heading for the exits."

Someone who will never forget that game, and keeps that clipping among his Yale memorabilia, is Milton White, professor emeritus of English at Miami University in Oxford, Ohio. He was a 17-year-old freshman at Yale in 1932.

He remembers the days leading up to the big game, and the excitement. "I wasn't a great sports fan, but, after all, this was the Harvard-Yale game, and there would only be two that I could go to as an undergraduate," he said. "I didn't think I could attend the two at Harvard. I mean, it was the Depression, and I was very poor—destitute, I guess you'd say—and my father, who was a merchant-tailor in Springfield, Mass., had saved hard to send me to Yale. I thought I'd never be able to afford to go to Boston for the game."

Freshman White was supposed to have a date for the game. A girl he knew in Springfield was going to come down for it, and earlier in the week he had arranged with a woman who worked for a local florist to buy a white chrysanthemum for 35 cents. "But my date conked out at the last minute," said White. He had also planned a double date at the game with his roommate and his date, but they decided to stay indoors because of the rain. He gave the chrysanthemum to his roommate for his girl, and young White went off to the game alone.

He had never known it to rain so hard. Wearing a yellow slicker and a yellow rain hat to match, he waited in the rain for a trolley, and dodged the spray of taxicabs. Finally, the trolley clanged into view and he boarded it to the Yale Bowl.

On the way, he saw parties going on in the warmth of rooms in dormitories and apartments. Those people were simply not going out in this rain. But Milton White was determined to attend the game.

When he arrived at the Yale Bowl, he trudged through puddles and sloshed down the aisle to a seat near the 30-yard line.

"I remember that the stadium looked pretty empty," he said.

He sat down on the soaking bench. The rain had dripped from the collar of his slicker down the wool jacket he wore underneath and made him uncomfortable.

"I've always hated the smell of wet wool," he said.

Most of the people at the game were huddled around the 50-yard line. "I was too shy to go there at first, but after a while I said 'Oh, why not?'"

So he moved down and took a seat closer to the 50-yard line, a solitary figure in the pouring rain. He had been sitting there only a moment or so when he felt someone tapping him on the shoulder.

"You don't want to sit alone," the man behind him said. "Come sit with us."

The man was with a woman and they were sitting "sort of off to the side," recalled White. The couple held a large strip of linoleum to protect them from the rain. White, even through rain-streaked glasses, recognized him immediately. "I know you, you're Babe Ruth!" he said.

"He had a wonderful smile," White recalled, "and he introduced me to his wife. I was aghast. She said, 'Come on under, you don't want to get wet.'" The couple shifted the linoleum in order to extend a part of it to cover the dripping student.

At about this time, the Yale and the Harvard teams came sloshing onto the field, and the small crowd cheered. The Yale Band struck up "Boola Boola."

"The game was just about to begin, and Babe Ruth lifted a gallon jug from under the bench," said White. "He poured something into a paper cup for himself and he poured one for me. They looked like whiskey sours.

"He handed me a cup.

" 'To Eli Yale,' he said.

"My hand was shaking. 'Eli Yale,' I said.

"Babe Ruth grinned at me. We raised our cups and drank.

"I remember that he seemed somehow to understand my loneliness, and I wondered if he was lonely, too, even being so famous. But I never dared asked him anything like that. In fact, I don't really remember anything else about the game, except that Yale won."

He said he didn't even recall when he left, but it was probably when his companions departed in the fourth quarter with their strip of linoleum that had protected the three of them against the rain.

After White's freshman year, his father died and he was forced, for financial reasons, to leave Yale. White never attended another Harvard-Yale game, and never shared another whiskey sour with Mr. and Mrs. Babe Ruth.

Invitation to a Locker Room

New York, July 18, 1983

The political columnist George Will, it was recently reported, took part in the Ronald Reagan rehearsal sessions before the debate with President Jimmy Carter in 1980. Mr. Will was supposed to have helped coach the Republican presidential candidate, and then to have commented favorably on national television about Mr. Reagan's performance. He has been criticized for a conflict of interest. In defense of his presence at the rehearsal sessions,

Mr. Will said, "It's like being invited into the locker room for a sportswriter."

It came as a surprise to this reporter to learn that locker-room invitations have been profferred to certain members of the press. Well, in the traditional phrase of politicians, I asked, "Where's mine?" This reporter had been under the impression that access to the locker room—equal access—comes only with the proper credentials accorded all bona fide members of the news media.

I waited for a week to see if the Will statement had galvanized the Yankee front office, and expected an invitation in the mail, or at least a phone call. Nothing happened.

So as soon as the Yankees returned from their road trip, I went to Yankee Stadium and entered the clubhouse as I always do, uninvited. I had always thought that the clubhouse was where a reporter gathers information, not gives it. I had been going into clubhouses for years, and never realized that the ballplayers, like some politicians, were looking for advice from the likes of me.

I was more than happy to oblige.

Of course, it wouldn't be the first time that I, or other reporters, had helped a ballplayer or a manager. But it is usually done from a discreet distance, six or seven miles away, in the newspaper office, at the typewriter.

I approached a famous Yankee pitcher who had been having some control problems recently.

"Hi," I greeted him, "how's the old soupbone?"

He didn't look up as he pulled on his sanitary hose.

"You know, Lefty," I said, "I've noticed that in your follow-through you aren't bringing your—"

He looked up. His teeth were set tightly and shone fiercely in the light. And a strange noise rumbled from his throat. Perhaps this is the way people from his part of the country show appreciation, but I decided not to finish my sentence, and moved on.

I saw the team's slugger buttoning his uniform top. I strolled over.

"What's happenin'," I said blithely.

"Grrfllmmmpp," he replied.

I rather expected this response, since I actually knew what was happenin'. An 0-for-15 slump.

"I've been watching you closely, Swish," I said to him, "and it's my considered judgment that you're holding the bat too high. If you'd—"

He reached into his locker and grabbed one of the bats and raised it over his head with two hands.

"Like this?" he said, stepping forward.

I took several swift steps back, to get a better perspective.

"Kinda, but let's talk about it later," I suggested.

I turned and bumped into an infielder in front of his locker. Just the man I wanted to see. He had been fielding with the effectiveness of a torn fishnet. Here was a guy who needed my assistance. He looked at me and rammed his fist into the pocket of his glove. The sound echoed in my ears. I'd see him later.

Next, I strolled into the manager's office. He is a man whose gentle disposition has made him a national treasure. Oh, he's had a few rare flights out of character, such as kicking dirt on umpires, going nose-to-nose with one of his outfielders and declaiming against his owner, but these have only emphasized his competitive zeal. In the analytical aspects of baseball he is a scholar of purest ray serene.

I was wondering why, in the last game, he hadn't changed pitchers in the sixth inning when there were two outs and the next batter was—

"Did you ever play baseball?" he asked. Obviously the man was of philosophical bent and seeking intellectual dialogue.

"A little stickball, some softball and the Springfield Avenue Squirrels—"

"I can see then how this qualifies you to be an expert on major-league baseball."

"But what does this have to do with your not taking the pitcher out in the sixth, when—?"

"'Look, stupid," said the manager wittily, "do you know how Lefty had done against that batter in the late innings in the previous five games? And did you know how the two healthy pitchers I had in the bullpen had done against him in the same situations over the past two years? Do you know how well that guy hits in the late innings, period?"

"Yes, which is why I thought you should change. Also, it's

apparent that there should be a switch at shortstop, and one in center, and—"

The manager, his mustache twitching with what I took to be delight over my acuity, bent down under the desk. I paused in my recitation and looked over. He was gnawing on the edge of his desk.

I figured that he had suddenly decided to partake of his pregame meal, and since I hadn't been asked to join, I'd graciously take my leave.

I walked out into the main locker-room area. The left-handed pitcher saw me and smiled that steel-trap smile. The slugger took notice of my presence and reached again for his bat. The infielder raised a fist.

I decided that I had done all I could for the ball club this day, and departed the locker room.

The Yankees went out and won.

Another day, another sportswriter helping the guys in the locker room. Just like the political beat.

Frenchy is Alive and Swell

Detroit, August 20, 1981

Whatever happened to Frenchy Fuqua's glass shoes with goldfish in them?

Whatever happened to Frenchy Fuqua's white musketeer hat with red, white and purple ostrich plumes?

Whatever happened to Frenchy Fuqua?

"The mad Frenchman!" said John (Count Frenchy) Fuqua. "The true and only and original black count! He's alive and still doin' swell."

He sat behind a desk, with a sign that read "Communicate," in his glass-paneled cubicle in the *Detroit News* office, where he has, he says, the longest title in the company: carrier recruitment sale crew supervisor. That is, in charge of delivery boys and girls.

Frenchy has laughing eyes and a handsome beard. He has been at this newspaper job in his hometown since he retired as a running back with the Pittsburgh Steelers in 1977, after playing nine years in professional football and winning two Super Bowl championship rings and numerous dress-offs, or haberdashery clashes.

"Pittsburgh was destined to be a championship team when I was traded there from the Giants in 1970," he said, "but what they needed was a touch of class. And that was my contribution. I put a new trend in.

"I was awesome. One outfit that wowed 'em was the Pancho Villa, with a big black sombrero and black skintight jumpsuit and knee-high white moon boots. My caveman outfit floored 'em, too: red jumpsuit, fur poncho and a hell of a little bow tie to go with it.

"Pretty soon everybody started getting into it. The better we dressed, the better we played. Even Chuck Noll, the coach, got into it. One day he wore white shoes."

Frenchy laughed. "Then I get a call from a friend. 'Frenchy,' he says, 'I got somethin' real sweet for you.'

" 'What is it?'

" 'How would you like some shoes you can put goldfish in?'

"I said, 'Hey, I got an outfit for it.'

"It was my count suit, with the musketeer hat and gold cane and lavender cape, and my valet, which was Franco Harris, who carried the cape and never let it touch the ground. And, oh yes, my wine-red knickers. That's why I switched from goldfish to tropical fish. The tropical-fish colors went better with my outfits.

"The shoes were actually fiberglass clogs with three-inch heels. I had two fish in each shoe. They were a little slippery to walk in, being glass, so you'd have to hold on to a rail when you went down stairs. But my biggest problem was that the fish kept dying. I kept running and adding water, and that just got my socks wet. I experimented with a small pump that ran up my pants, but that was uncomfortable. Finally, I gave up the fish but kept the shoes—and put in a terrarium.

"I remember when I tried on my caveman outfit," he said. "I said to my wife, 'Doris, will this one blow their minds?' She said, 'John, you done blew mine already.' She was afraid to go out with me with some of those outfits.

"But I was the dress-off champ, she couldn't deny that. We had these contests in the locker room. One was on local TV in Pittsburgh. I went up against L.C. Greenwood and Chuck Beatty and Lee Calland. A sportscaster announced it like a fight: 'L.C. breaks out with hot pants, but Frenchy counters with fringed briefs; Beatty slugs back with a sock; Calland whips out a shoe.'

"But it was no contest," Frenchy said. "I won every dress-off. Once, a defensive back for the Dolphins named Henry Stuckey challenged me. It was on the beach in Miami. I come out and see he's in a pink fur coat. I refused to compete. I said, 'A fur coat? If he can't dress for the season, I want no part of this.' "

Frenchy touched the knot of his quiet red tie, against a subdued peach-colored shirt. He wore black pin-striped suit pants. "Now I have to wear more conservative clothes," he said. "But sometimes when things aren't going too swell I'll go to my garage, where I keep my old clothes and artifacts, and think about those days. You got to have a little Walter Mitty in you to get through some days, right? But not long ago I wore my count outfit to a party and I made the mistake of bending down for a drink of water. Instant ventilation."

He will wear his Super Bowl rings when he recruits for delivery personnel in junior high schools.

"I was fortunate—to be a pro football player, to play in the Super Bowl and to play on two winners," he said. "That's double the pleasure. When I make my pitch, it'd better be fast and good, because kids don't have a long attention span, *and* they don't want to work unless you can inspire them. Well, I say, 'Hey, any of you want to be pro football or basketball or tennis players?' Naturally. Then I go straight to the blackboard. I say, 'Did you know that every year 250,000 college kids are eligible for the pro draft but only 1,600 are drafted? And that only about 180 make the teams?' They say, 'Wow, is that all?'

"I say, 'I don't refer to football as a career. It's a stepping stone. I know too many ballplayers who were lost when opportunity didn't knock on their door.

" 'But there's a way to prepare yourself. Now.' Now they're quiet, listening close. 'Start off learning a little something about business—and you can do that with a *Detroit News* route! You'll freeze your butt, you'll get mad when some people don't pay—but you're your own boss.' Then I destroy 'em with the prizes and gifts they can win. Sometimes I get so many applications I can't handle 'em all.

"It's challenging, it's fun. There were adjustments to be made after football—you're off the pedestal, the money takes a big drop. I know a lot of guys who've had grievous problems after they retired. But I've landed darned good. You know, I wrote a poem about my life."

And he recited:

"I swam the ocean and didn't get wet,
A mountain fell on me and I ain't dead yet,
Horses and elephants trampled my hide,
A cobra bit me and crawled off and died.
I hitchhiked on lightning, rode with thunder,
Made people wonder. Whoa, whoa.
Yes, I'm a man of some ability, with much more agility,
Often imitated, but never duplicated."

Frenchy Fuqua, the true and only original black count, smiled, leaned back and loosened his tie. It had been quite a long journey.

Cus D'Amato's Gym

New York, November 11, 1985

Nighttime, and the walk up the poorly lit, steep, narrow wooden staircase to the shadowed area on the third floor seemed long. The street noises grew muffled and the creak of the stairs became louder.

The climb Tuesday night in this old building at 116 East 14th Street to the Gramercy Gymnasium at the top of the stairs—quiet now, because it is just past closing time, 8 o'clock, and the punching, skipping, snorting fighters have gone home—brought to mind the words of Cus D'Amato.

"Any kid coming here for the first time who thinks he wants to be a fighter, and who makes the climb up those dark stairs," said Cus, "has it 50 percent licked, because he's licking fear."

Cus D'Amato, the sometimes strange, usually sweet, often suspicious, invariably generous teacher and philosopher and boxing manager and trainer, owned this gym for some 30 years, and, when young, slept in a cot in the back with a police dog for a companion. Printed on the front door was the name "Gramacy," misspelled by the painter.

It was here that one returned to recall the celebrated days of D'Amato, when he was the most successful handler of fighters in the world.

It was here that D'Amato, short, thick-chested, bushy-browed, nearly blind in one eye from a childhood accident, did battle with the mob-controlled elements of top-level boxing in the 1950s and '60s. It was here one time that a pair of head-knockers with sideways noses approached D'Amato about one of his talented young boxers. "We're in," one of the visitors told D'Amato, declaring themselves his partner.

D'Amato looked at them and stuck out his hand. "You can start here," said D'Amato, hacking one hand at the fingers of the other, "and you can cut off my hand piece by piece—but you're out."

The head-knockers and their sideways noses retreated down the stairs.

It wasn't just that D'Amato didn't want to share his fighter with creeps, but D'Amato believed he could not show weakness to his fighters. He had to set an example. He was also motivated by his hatred of the corruption that was inherent in professional boxing.

Inside, the large room is like a small barn, containing two boxing rings with drooping ropes. There are a few heavy punching bags hanging from the ceiling, and resting on a rubbing table is a medicine ball with blue stuffing oozing out, a medicine ball that D'Amato might have slammed into a fighter's stomach 20 years before.

The smell of sweat in the gym seems embedded in the woodwork. On a bulletin board, yellowing newspaper clips. There is, however, a freshly penciled notice on lined paper. It reads: "Cus D'Amato. Funeral Services Thursday, 8:30 A.M. Catskill, New York." It went on to give driving directions.

Cus D'Amato died Monday night of pneumonia at Mount Sinai Hospital in New York City. He was 77 years old. And in his old gym the legacy of Cus D'Amato is seen with the medicine ball, with the odd shriveled speed bag that is filled with sand and hangs from the ceiling so that a fighter must learn to slip and dip as he walks by, or get conked, and Cus's legacy is felt through his accomplishments.

"His memory is still alive here," said David Bullock, a caretaker of the gym, who now sleeps here as Cus once did. "Look at what he done. He took two of the boys who came up those stairs and made champs out of 'em—world champs."

He referred to Floyd Patterson, who became the youngest man to win the heavyweight championship, at age 21, in 1956, and José Torres, who won the light-heavyweight title in 1965.

D'Amato and Patterson had developed a father-son relationship that was even closer than the close relationships D'Amato had with most of his fighters. Then came an estrangement.

In later years they reconciled. And last year Patterson said that he would change nothing in his life except the time he was apart from D'Amato. "It turned out," said Patterson, "that whatever Cus said worked out to be true."

D'Amato had insight into human nature. "People who are born round don't die square," he said, denoting that the basic character of someone doesn't change. He asserted, "No matter what anyone says, no matter the excuse or explanation, whatever a person does in the end is what he intended to do all along." And he said, "Heroes and cowards feel exactly the same fear. Heroes just react to it differently."

D'Amato had some odd ways. He rarely revealed his home address because he feared snipers, and he never married because he believed a wife might be duped by his enemies into doing him in. But he was principled to the teeth, and so honest that the strangest thing that could befall a fight manager befell Cus. He filed for bankruptcy in 1971. Historically, it is the fighters who go bankrupt and their managers who walk away flush. But there is no record of any of his fighters having problems while he was handling them. Torres, in fact, recalls that he earned close to $1 million in his career, "and Cus never took a penny."

As Cus got older, and had fewer fighters, he began to spend more time in the mountains, where he loved to fish. About 10 years ago he moved to Catskill, where he opened a boxing club for teenagers.

One troubled youngster who found his way there, Mike Tyson, had talent. He and D'Amato became so close that D'Amato became his legal guardian. Tyson, now 19 years old, credits D'Amato with changing his life, and he is now one of the brightest lights among rising heavyweights, with a pro record of 11–0, and 8 knockouts. Developing a fighter like Tyson, D'Amato said not long ago, "makes me excited, makes me feel like a young fella."

D'Amato always worried more about the well-being of his fighters than anything else. Once, shortly before a big fight, José Torres, normally a model citizen, was arrested and was taken to the precinct house, where he phoned D'Amato at the Gramercy Gym.

"Cus," said Torres, embarrassed and apologetic, "I'm in the police station. I got into a street fight."

"José," said D'Amato, with concern in his voice, "did you keep your chin down?"

At Issue

One Definition of a Winner

New York, March 19, 1983

In between running a baseball team and operating a shipbuilding company, George M. Steinbrenner has also found time in his busy schedule to assist lexicographers.

He recently was of invaluable assistance to them in adding to the definition of the noun "winner."

In *Webster's New Collegiate*, "winner" is defined as "One that wins; **a:** one that is successful esp. through praiseworthy ability and hard work **b:** a victor esp. in games and sports."

Steinbrenner generously has added to this: "**c:** one who wears a World Series ring. That is, a member of a team that has won the World Series."

The definition may have come to him in a dream, or perhaps it was arrived at after long hours at a desk while wetting meditatively the tip of a pencil. No one is quite certain. The ways of the wondrous are strange, indeed.

Steinbrenner referred specifically to one of the laborers on his baseball team, Dave Winfield, an outfielder.

"Until you wear one of these," Steinbrenner had said, pointing to a ring he wears from the 1977 Yankees' world championship, "you are not a winner. Winfield is almost there."

Winfield, upon hearing this a few days later, said about Steinbrenner, "He bought a team that won. Hey, the clubhouse guy's got a ring. The ticket guy's got a ring. Think about it."

Winfield is in his third season as a Yankee, after playing the first eight years of his career with a poor club, the San Diego Padres. In Winfield's first season with the Yankees, he helped them get into the World Series, in which they were defeated by the Dodgers.

Last year, the Yankees did not make the World Series. But Winfield had a very fine season. He led the Yankees in most offensive categories, batting .280, with 106 runs batted in, 37 homers (third in the American League) and a slugging percentage of .560 (second in the league). His 17 assists were tops among the league's outfielders, and he won a Gold Glove for fielding excellence.

But Winfield has yet to be on a team that has won the World Series.

Forget his individual achievements, forget that a team consists of 25 players. By Steinbrenner's definition, Dave Winfield is a loser.

So is Ty Cobb.

So is Ted Williams.

So are Nap Lajoie, George Sisler, Harry Heilmann, Paul and Lloyd Waner, Gabby Hartnett, Wee Willie Keeler, Sam Crawford, Early Wynn, Luke Appling, Joe Cronin, Hack Wilson, Babe Herman, Chuck Klein, Ted Lyons, Robin Roberts and Ernie Banks, among others—each a member of the Hall of Fame and each of whom never played on a team that won the World Series, though some played in the Series.

The boob Cobb could do no better than a record .367 batting average with a record 4,191 hits over a 24-year major-league career.

The wretched Williams, the last man to hit .400—.406 in 1941—could muster only a .344 career mark and 521 homers.

Cobb was on three pennant winners, and Williams one. Neither ever a winner. But talk about losers, Ernie Banks never was on a team that even got into a World Series! You wonder how he ever played 19 years and hit 512 home runs and was twice named Most Valuable Player in the National League.

Now there are many players who have won World Series championship rings, and some of them, of course, are in the Hall of Fame as well.

But some aren't.

George William Zeber wears a World Series ring; in fact, from the same team that Steinbrenner wears his.

Perhaps not many remember Zeber. He was an occasional infielder on the 1977 Yankees, and on the 1978 Yankees, who also won the Series. But he played in only the '77 Series, against the Dodgers, pinch-hitting twice and striking out both times.

His career totals are: 28 games, 71 times at bat, a .296 batting average, 3 doubles, 0 triples, 3 home runs, 10 runs batted in, 0 stolen bases. In contrast, Winfield's career record is: 1,362 games,

4,924 times at bat, 735 runs, 1,399 hits, 228 doubles, 48 triples, 204 home runs, 800 runs batted in and 149 stolen bases.

But, as defined by Steinbrenner, Winfield is a loser and Zeber a winner.

Some people confuse George William Zeber with William Henry Zuber, another winner. Zuber was a pitcher for the Yankee team that beat the Cardinals in the 1943 World Series. Zeber didn't get into a single game, but Zuber, like Zeber, got a ring.

And like Zeber, Zuber would get into one World Series game when, with the 1946 Red Sox, he pitched two innings and gave up three hits, one walk and one run.

There was also Rollie (Bunions) Zeider. But in contrast to Zeber and Zuber, Zeider was a loser. In the 1918 World Series, he was a replacement at third base in the late innings in two games for the Cubs, who lost in six to the Red Sox.

The next time the Red Sox were in the World Series was 1946—it was the team of Ted Williams and William Zuber—and they lost to the Cardinals. One of the winners on St. Louis was a catcher named Clyde Kluttz, who did not get into even one of the seven games. But he got his ring. It is a curious point of history in that 31 years later, Mickey Klutts, an infielder with the Yankees, would emerge as a winner.

Like Kluttz, Klutts didn't get into a game, either. But Kluttz and Klutts, like Steinbrenner, all wear World Series rings without ever having appeared in a World Series box score.

Steinbrenner also has a ring from the 1978 Series, as do performers named Brian Doyle, Gary Thomasson, Ken Clay, Fred Stanley, Cliff Johnson and Mike Heath. All except Steinbrenner and the clubhouse guy and the ticket guy played in that Series.

Meanwhile, Dave Winfield is in spring training with the Yankees to try once again to earn a World Series ring and finally become a winner, a winner, that is, as defined by George Steinbrenner, the owner of a team that last season finished in fifth place.

Batgate: The Gun Doesn't Smoke

New York, July 26, 1983

The smoking gun in Batgate—exhibit A—was wrapped in yellow paraffin and delivered to the American League office on the third floor of 280 Park Avenue yesterday morning.

The smoking gun is 34½ inches long and weighs 32 ounces. But it is not a gun nor does it smoke. It is a baseball bat, made of white ash. It is the now-notorious bat used by one George Howard Brett Sunday night when he hit the home run into the right-field seats at Yankee Stadium that counted for the last out of the game.

"The bat arrived in the office about 10 o'clock, maybe a little before, I really can't pinpoint the time," said Tess Basta, a secretary in the office.

It had been due an hour earlier. When it finally came, it was brought in by a man wearing jeans and a shirt, "or whatever," said Tess Basta. "Neatly dressed. I don't know his name, but he works for the Yankees."

Bob Fishel, assistant to Lee MacPhail, the league president, had been told by one of the umpires in the crew Sunday night that it would arrive at 9 A.M. He was also called at home by Dick Howser, manager of the Royals, and told that the Royals would appeal the game.

The league office would await the physical evidence—the bat—plus the reports from the umpires. Then MacPhail would check precedents and history and decide on whether to uphold or overturn the umpires' ruling.

As the world now knows, Brett came up in the top of the ninth with one man on and the Royals losing to the Yankees, 4–3, and hit a home run. However, Alfred Manuel Martin, the field brains behind the Yankees, rushed out and said Brett had been using an illegal bat. He claimed that the pine tar on the bat exceeded the legal limit of 18 inches from the knob.

The umpires measured it, and the plate umpire, Tim McClelland, gave the signal that upheld Martin's protest.

The two-run homer was nullified, and it became the third out, and in an instant turned a lead into a loss. It also turned Brett into a rather unhappy person, and about 25 men were needed to keep him from the umpire's throat.

Fishel, in his office yesterday morning, waited about 15 minutes more for the bat and then went out for breakfast.

When he came back, still no bat.

Shortly after, Tess Basta informed him that it was here.

Fishel came out, took the bat and then went into his office and closed the door. He would later testify to a reporter that he took the bat out of the wrapping and checked it over.

Reporter: Were there any fingerprints on it?

Fisher: I didn't see any.

Reporter: Are there any now, after you held it?

Fishel: Not mine, I can tell you that. I held it by the ends.

Reporter: As if you were eating corn on the cob?

Fishel: Sort of, but without the margarine.

Reporter: Margarine?

Fishel: Butter's high in cholesterol.

Reporter: Yes, well, where's the bat now, Mr. Fishel?

Fishel: It got stashed.

Reporter: In the office?

Fishel: Not saying. I don't want to sound mysterious about this, but Lee MacPhail is out of town and won't be back until tonight. I don't want anyone to see it until he does, so he can determine for himself about the appeal.

Fishel said MacPhail would probably not rule on it for "at least another 24 hours."

The appeal, as he understands it, will contend that the rule was interpreted too strictly, and that the pine tar on the barrel of the bat in no way aided the distance or the direction of the ball.

"We're going to check every facet of it that we can," said Fishel. "There may have been a reason why the pine tar was up so far on the bat."

At 10:50, Murray Cook, the general manager of the Yankees, arrived in Fishel's office with a video tape of Sunday's events.

Simply amicus curiae, of course. Cook, this impartial friend of the court, thought it was nonsense that the Royals had anything to appeal.

Reporter: Why?

Cook: You can't have foreign substances going all the way up the bat. Say you want to bunt, the ball would stick and aid the batter.

Reporter: But his ball didn't stick, it flew.

Cook (shrug, smile): Strange, isn't it?

Following up on Exhibit A, a call was placed to Hillerich & Bradsby in Louisville, makers of the Louisville Slugger. Brett's bat, said Rex Bradley, a vice president for the company, is a T-85 Marv Throneberry model.

Reporter: Marvelous Marv Throneberry? The Mets' legend, the guy who did things like hit a triple and miss both first and second base?

Bradley: One and the same.

Reporter: Why is a hitter like Brett using a Marvelous Marv bludgeon?

Bradley: I once asked George the same question. Apparently he picked it up in spring training one year, liked the feel of it, and had us make some for him. It's been about five years, I'd guess. He's used 'em ever since.

Reporter: Any distinguishing characteristics about the bat?

Bradley: There's no finish or lacquer on it. We turn it, brand it, sand it and send it. George doesn't wear a batting glove, you know. He likes raw skin against raw wood.

The pine tar, Bradley added, is put on the bat so that Brett can touch it to get a good grip. A hitter like Brett, who doesn't get jammed regularly and often gets good wood on the ball, breaks relatively few bats. A bat may last him as long as a week. And as he touches the pine tar, the substance creeps higher on the bat.

Brett said that the bat was a particular favorite. "It's a seven-grainer," he has noted.

Most bats, according to Bradley, have five grains. "Each grain or ring indicates a year's growth of a tree," he said. "We don't like to think that there's any difference in a seven- or five-grain bat. As long as the weight is evenly distributed and the rings have grown evenly, it's a good bat."

Five grains or seven grains, it has become for the league office one big migraine.

Meanwhile, Bill Guilfoile of the Baseball Hall of Fame called Fishel to ask for the bat.

Fishel said not until MacPhail sees it. And probably not after that, either.

Someone else requested it first. He lives in Kansas City.

"I want my bat back," the person said. "I like it."

Henry Aaron and Dedication

New York, January 15, 1982

On the afternoon of April 4, 1974, a sports talk show was being taped in a television studio in Manhattan. Suddenly it was interrupted. A note had been passed to the host by a producer, and the guest, a sports reporter, waited.

"There's a bulletin," the host said, looking up from the note. "Henry Aaron has just hit a home run for the Atlanta Braves to tie Babe Ruth's career record."

A feeling of relief passed over the guest. In the last decade or so, when a program was interrupted by a news bulletin, it invariably meant that something tragic had happened.

Now it celebrated an individual triumph, one that could be achieved only by the highest dedication to sustained excellence—at that point, it was Aaron's 21st season in the big leagues.

The scope of the accomplishment went beyond the ball park and beyond that television studio. It touched the nation, which had been following Aaron's pursuit of the record—the home run mark was generally considered the most unreachable in team sports and was held by Ruth, the most revered American athlete in history.

It touched some negatively, to be sure. Some simply did not want to see Ruth's legendary record broken—a small but malicious number of others did not want to see a black man do it. Soon, some of Aaron's mail—he was getting nearly 700 letters a day—was being screened by the FBI.

Four days after he hit the homer that tied the record, Aaron belted the 715th of his career and broke the record that had stood for 47 years.

Last Wednesday, Henry Louis Aaron was voted into the Baseball Hall of Fame, and not solely because of that lifetime home-run record—755 by the time he retired, in 1976.

"Henry," said Monte Irvin, of the baseball commissioner's office, "owns the National League record book." Not quite, but the records he holds are numerous, including most runs batted in, most total bases and most extra-base hits.

But it is home runs No. 714 and 715 for which he will be most remembered.

Ruth's record was broken by an unassuming man whose power was recognized early but whose professionalism and dignity over a period of 23 years came to be widely appreciated only gradually.

"The thing about Hank," said Eddie Mathews, Aaron's onetime teammate with Milwaukee and Atlanta, and later his manager, "is that he does everything so effortlessly, so expressionlessly.

"He runs as hard as he has to, for example. His hat doesn't fly off the way Mays's does. Clemente ran, and he looked like he was falling apart at the seams. Pete Rose runs hard everywhere and dives headfirst. Aaron runs with the shaft let out, but you'd never know it. Yet when the smoke clears, he's standing there in the same place as the others."

His teammates, when he came up to the Milwaukee Braves in 1954, called him "Snowshoes" because of the slow way he seemed to drag his body.

But he swiftly demonstrated that he was anything but lethargic. His bat, as they say in baseball circles, was quick.

"Trying to sneak a fastball past Hank Aaron," the pitcher Curt Simmons once said, "is like trying to sneak a sunrise past a rooster."

From the start, Aaron seemed to defy convention. When he entered pro baseball with the Indianapolis Clowns—a black team—as an 18-year-old out of Mobile, Ala., his form seemed wrong: he swung with his weight on his front foot instead of the back one; he held his bat in the palms of his hands instead of in the fingers; and, oddest of all, he batted cross-handed, like someone's aunt at the family picnic.

Only the last would be changed. The rest remained—but who can account for genius. "I may have looked like I was leaning at the plate," he said, "but my bat was ready."

When the bat no longer was, when he couldn't "pick up the rotation on the curve anymore" and his eyes "began playing tricks," he retired at the age of 42.

In his last several seasons, Aaron, who had been a quiet man not prone to controversial or colorful remarks, was given a forum by the press, who seemed to have discovered him at last. And Aaron did not shy away. He began to speak his heart. And what he said surprised many.

He criticized the baseball establishment, for example, for not hiring blacks in management, and he also said blacks were not getting a fair shake as players, either. "You know, we're considered supergiants on the field, but when we come off the field we go to the back of the bus, again."

Aaron had great respect for Jackie Robinson. "Before Jackie died," Aaron said, "we had long talks. I will never forget that he told me to keep talking about what makes me unhappy, to keep the pressure on. Otherwise, people will think you're satisfied with the situation."

The Braves, upon his retirement, offered Aaron the job of vice president in charge of player development. "I thought I could make a contribution to the organization, and I said I'd take it, but I don't want to sit in an office and stare at the four walls. I want to make decisions." He has, and he still holds that position with the Braves.

But wherever he goes, he is still reminded of the home runs that broke Babe Ruth's seemingly unbreakable record.

"The funny thing is that I never saw them," said Aaron. "Whenever I hit a home run, I'm too busy concentrating on touching first base to watch the ball." He said he developed the habit in Class C ball in Eau Claire, Wis., in 1952, where he played after the Braves signed him from the Negro League.

"I was on the road to realizing my dream of making the major leagues," he said. "And when I hit my first home run there, I was so excited, I missed first base and was tagged out. From that day on, I decided if I hit the ball into the stands, I'll know about it, and then I can go into my trot."

Rubbernecking on Billy Day

New York, August 11, 1986

"What are you doing today?" a friend asked.

"Going to Yankee Stadium."

"Who's playing?"

"The Royals, and it's Billy Martin Day. They're putting a plaque of Martin in the outfield."

"You're kidding."

"No, it's true."

"They're putting a plaque of Billy Martin out there with the plaques of Ruth and Gehrig and DiMaggio and Mantle and those guys?"

"Yeah."

There was a pause on the phone. "It's, it's sacrilegious," the friend said. He wasn't aware that there were also two plaques commemorating the visit to Yankee Stadium of two Popes. "I mean," he continued, "why are they honoring this man?"

"I'm not sure," came the reply.

The question the friend had posed was a good one, one that was being asked by numerous people when they learned of their quizzical pregame goings-on. And so, in the pursuit of journalistic thoroughness, a journey was made to Yankee Stadium, this mecca and symbol of all that is virtuous and pure in American life.

At the beginning of the ceremonies, the attention of the 40,000 or so fans was directed to the Diamond Vision screen in center field. There the fans were treated to a filmed collection of selected scenes from Billy Martin's baseball career, as player and manager. Here he makes his diving catch in the 1953 World Series to save the day, and there he is at bat (he was a career .257 hitter), and there he's arguing with an umpire, and here he's arguing with an umpire, and there he's kicking dirt on an umpire, and here he's got his baseball cap turned sideways and he's screaming in an umpire's face, and there he's chasing an umpire and waving his arms madly, and now he's kicking more dirt on an umpire, and more, and more. A lot of people, who got lost on their way to *Rambo*, cheered.

Billy Martin had kicked up so much dirt, in fact, that he dug his own grave numerous times in baseball. The film didn't say that Martin was let go by the Yankees four times. It didn't say that he was booted out as manager of the Twins and Tigers and Rangers and A's, too.

It didn't say that he was always being picked on in bars—his version—and forced to fight with, here, a reporter, and, there, a marshmallow salesman. Oh, and in this corner, a pitcher. Last year, when both were drinking one late night in a hotel bar— Martin was then the Yankee manager in Tour No. 4—he fought Ed Whitson. In one of the marvelous quotes of the season, Martin shouted at Whitson, who was coming at him with a look of wild hatred in his eyes, "What's wrong with you, can't you hold your liquor?"

In the film clip, not a word about calling George Steinbrenner a convicted liar, and Reggie Jackson a born liar, and then saying he didn't say it when it was reported, and implying that the reporters were liars. And then later admitting he had said it, which put into question who the on-the-record liar was.

He has his fans, to be sure. In 15 years as a manager, he won five division titles, with four teams, and took the Yankees to two World Series, winning one and losing one. He was aggressive, if not always tactful. Some players liked him very much, some would rather have taken cod-liver oil for a cocktail than play for him.

Now, Martin's family came out and gathered around home plate and met Billy, who stood with a quiet smile and tan suit and striped tie and a carnation in his lapel. His mother greeted him, and his brothers and sisters and son and daughter, and two grandchildren, followed by a lot of people showering Martin with gifts, from a set of four tires to a convertible automobile to something else presented him by a lady wearing a hat dripping with bananas, who was representing, surprisingly enough, a banana company.

There was stuff about his "distinguished" career and how he did it "with dignity" and was a "credit on the field as well as off."

Now, more film clips of him kicking dirt on umpires. And then a real live former umpire, Ron Luciano, came out and brought a gift and prominently mentioned the sponsor and then tossed down a box of dirt—from each infield in the American League, he said—and gave Billy "a free kick at a lousy umpire." Martin rolled up his pants leg and kicked meekly. Everyone on the field got a big guffaw out of this.

It was kind of strange, but fascinating. Overdone? Yes. But much of Billy has been overdone. Compelling? Well, in the way that watching a traffic accident is compelling. You rubberneck despite yourself.

In a news conference afterward, someone wondered why he had been given this honor.

He mentioned that, well, maybe it was his managing, mostly, and a little of his baseball playing.

But there had to be more, someone suggested. "I guess," said Martin, "that some of the fans relate to me as a piece of every one of them—the guy in the street being aggressive, fighting their boss. I fought for what I thought was right, and couldn't worry about what City Hall thought."

George Steinbrenner, whose brainstorm this Day was, said that he felt Billy deserved it because "being a Yankee has never meant more to anyone than it has to Billy Martin."

Is that a reason to enshrine him?

"I felt he deserved it," said Steinbrenner. "I'm tired of flowers for the dead. I like flowers for the living."

Did you notice, he was asked, that many fans were stirred most by the scenes of him kicking dirt on umpires.

"You've got to have a sense of humor about this," he said. "I mean, there are really serious things out there—there's hunger and unemployment and wars. . . ."

And so Billy Martin Day came to a close and a Yankee ball game, without Billy Martin managing the local team, began.

Later, at home, the phone rang. It was the friend.

"Well, did you find out why they honored that man?" he asked.

"Because of flowers," came the reply.

"Flowers?"

"Sure, flowers for the living. Got it straight from Steinbrenner."

The Master Bargainer

New York, January 1, 1983

At 7 o'clock one morning in early March 1966, the phone rang in Marvin Miller's home in New York.

"I can't sleep," said Robin Roberts, then a pitcher with Houston and a member of the players' committee to find an executive director for their union, calling from Florida. "I was up all night thinking about this."

"What?" asked Miller. "What are you talking about?"

"I mean, do you think you should shave your mustache? Maybe it doesn't do much for your image."

Miller laughed it off (the suggestion, not the mustache).

Miller was then a nominee for executive director of the fledgling Major League Baseball Players Association. He was preparing to visit the big-league spring training camps to meet the players, who would then vote on him.

The baseball owners, their traditional and absolute authority threatened, spread the impression that Miller was a kind of strong-arming, goon-squad character who was going to whip people into line with henchmen and steel pipes. After all, management reasoned, hadn't he been a labor negotiator and assistant to the president of the United Steelworkers of America?

"The contrast to what we were told and what we saw was laughable," Steve Hamilton, then player representative for the Yankees, would recall. "The owners hadn't even met him."

What the players saw was a gray-haired (and gray mustachioed) 48-year-old man who stood 5 feet 8½ inches, weighed about 150 pounds, wore black-framed glasses and had a right arm shorter than the left because of an injury at birth. His manner was soft-spoken but not oily. He was direct and informative. He gained the confidence of the players and was elected.

July 1, 1966, was his first official day as executive director of the Players Association. Yesterday was his last. Miller, at age 65, is retiring, and will be replaced by Kenneth Moffett.

In Miller's 16½ years in office, he helped change the face of professional sports in this country. He did so by organizing the players and striving for and attaining collective bargaining, free agency, impartial arbitration, salary arbitration and markedly increased pension, disability and health benefits.

All this in the face of a completely monopolistic enterprise, a status resulting from a 1922 Supreme Court decision in which the Court ruled in effect that baseball was a sport, not a business.

Someone suggested not long ago that he should be in baseball's Hall of Fame.

"The only way Marvin Miller will ever get into the Hall of Fame," said someone in baseball management, "is through the janitor's entrance."

For the players' part, Marvin Miller could enter through the chimney. In the last several years, the players' stockings have been stuffed largely because of Miller's talent for organizing them into a strong unit and his ability not only to convince the players that they were being underpaid and undervalued but also, in some cases, to appeal to reason on the part of baseball commissioners and owners.

He led the players on a 50-day strike in the middle of the 1981 season, which brought an expected barrage of criticism on him, with management contending that he was causing the ruin of the game.

It was nothing new. He had been giving owners headaches for years.

"He's a mustachioed four-flusher," intoned Paul Richards, when he was vice president of the Atlanta Braves.

And Frank Dale, while president of the Cincinnati Reds, offered to rearrange his nose.

But while executive director, Miller has seen major-league baseball expand by 30 percent, going from 20 teams to 26, providing 30 percent more jobs and growing by an even greater percentage in revenue.

The commissioner's office has announced that last season was a record-breaker in attendance, the fifth time in seven seasons that a record has been set. And, according to Miller, even though players are getting a greater share of the profits—from about 12 percent when he took the job to 35 percent now—teams are making more money in dollars than ever before.

Teams are also highly valued in the marketplace. When the Mets came into baseball in 1962, for example, the price of the team was $2.6 million. When Nelson Doubleday bought it a couple of years ago, it went for $21.1 million.

It was feared that free agency might destroy the competitiveness of baseball, but it hasn't. Last season, for example, each of the four divisional races was close and exciting virtually to the last drop.

The changes in the financial life of the players that Miller helped institute have been remarkable.

In 1967, the median salary of a major-league player was $17,000; now it's $170,900. The minimum was $6,000; now it's $35,000. Granting the effects of inflation, those changes are nonetheless striking.

Another improvement has come in pension benefits. When Miller was hired by the union, a five-year veteran would, at age 50, receive $125 a month. Now a five-year man at age 50 gets $745.

In a way, Miller even influenced a better game on the field, as he gained improvements for the care and safety of life and limb.

When the new ball park was built in Kansas City, the outfield warning track was inadequate and potentially dangerous. Willie Horton ran into the wall while chasing a fly ball and was injured. The track did not have a different sound or feel from the rest of the outfield. "Well," the architect said, "it's a different color." After Miller put up a fight, the warning track was improved.

At one time, some clubs refused to put in a whirlpool to salve the sore muscles of their rival players. No more.

Teams would sometimes play a twi-night doubleheader, then fly to a distant city for a game the next afternoon, sometimes getting two hours' sleep. No more.

An early criticism by owners was that Miller knew nothing

about baseball. One team's publicity man asked him if he was a fan. Miller said that he had grown up in Brooklyn in the 1930s and was a Dodger fan.

"Dodgers, huh?" said the p.r. man. "You probably can't remember anyone who played on those teams."

"Normally I might have remembered a couple of players," Miller said recently. "But I said to myself, 'The hostile so-and-so.' I dredged my memory and came up with the whole damn starting team."

The Courage of the Gentle

New York, August 31, 1986

The recent news that Jerry Smith has been suffering from AIDS for eight months was met with what, on the surface, might seem an unusual reaction from his former Redskins football teammates.

Smith, who has discussed his illness but not his life-style, played tight end for the Redskins for 13 seasons, from 1965 to 1977. He caught so many passes, and in such clutch situations, that George Allen, who coached him for more than half his pro career, called him Home Run Smith.

Smith, who is 43 years old, is seriously ill in Holy Cross Hospital in Silver Spring, Md. He has dropped from 210 pounds to 150.

"Certainly I'm not going to judge someone else's life-style as it affected them," Calvin Hill, the former all-pro running back, told the *Washington Post*. "In terms of how Jerry affected me, both on and off the field, it was very positive. He was an effervescent, helpful guy who was concerned when other guys were down."

"I liked him then and I like him now, AIDS or no AIDS," said Dave Butz, a Redskins defensive tackle.

"If you love a guy," said Bobby Mitchell, a National Football League Hall of Fame receiver and now assistant general manager of the Redskins, "you love him. That's all there is to it. Jerry has been a very dear friend for almost 20 years."

Those reactions might have come from some less brawny community. But football players? Hardnosed tough guys? The image of American masculinity?

One of the players who was asked his reaction to Smith's illness, the former free safety Mark Murphy, said, "What Jerry has done, coming out and talking, takes a lot of courage, I think he's right. It will heighten the public's awareness about the disease."

But courage was demonstrated by those who were football friends and teammates of Jerry Smith's. It's a courage greater than plunging for a first down, or chasing down a breakaway runner. It's the courage of character, the courage not to accept stereotypes. It's the courage of true virility. Perhaps it is true, as Leo Rosten wrote in *Captain Newman, M.D.*, that "it is the weak who are cruel, and that gentleness is to be expected only from the strong."

A spokesman at Holy Cross Hospital said that every third phone call there has been for Jerry Smith. There were "lots of Redskins, ex-Redskins and friends" calling, he said. "It's been phenomenal."

Smith never said he was a homosexual, but it could have been easy for friends to reject what they readily believed to be a life-style that may not have been consistent with their own, and not consistent with the image that they have fostered, or had thrust upon them.

And there will surely be some who in fact will now shy away from an association with Jerry Smith. The concern was expressed by his mother, Laverne, at his hospital bedside. Smith is scheduled to be inducted into the Washington Hall of Stars at RFK Stadium this fall. "Do you think when they find out," she asked, "they'll change their minds?" No, her son whispered. The hall committee has confirmed that there will be no change in plans.

The awareness grows that AIDS, which primarily afflicts homosexual men, can reach into the world of the arts, of law and law enforcement and industry and international business and politics and garbage collecting and sports, even football.

Will there be increased research from increased awareness of the disease, due in part to Smith's public acknowledgment?

Possibly, and it might begin in the most unexpected of places, the NFL Charities, which in the last 10 years has committed $7 million to numerous causes, but none to AIDS research. Commissioner Pete Rozelle says it's now a possibility.

Beyond that, there is another important aspect to the Smith case. And Sam Huff, a former star linebacker, said it clearly: "I think it's time that people view football players as people. Because you can play football, what makes you a celebrity? Because you can block and tackle and run? We're people. Sometimes I think people forget that."

And there is a variety of people born with athletic talent. Nowhere is it written that only heterosexuals are allowed to be coordinated.

Dr. Bruce Ogilvie, a retired professor of psychology at San Jose State, is a consultant to three National Basketball Association teams, the Portland Trail Blazers, the Milwaukee Bucks and the Golden State Warriors, and has been a consultant to half a dozen NFL teams over the last 20 years. "Incidents of homosexuality— or, at least, bisexuality—have been known, of course, in athletics," he said. "But that shouldn't be surprising. About 6 percent of the male population in America is homosexual. I think it's safe to say that that same percentage of incidence would appear in any field you could name."

He said that some players have asked him about "coming out of the closet." He advised them that it was hazardous, given the potentially negative reaction by teams, the community and religious leaders. "You cannot anticipate how others would respond," he said. "The possibility is great that they would treat it as a threat to their idealized concept of masculinity, and what sports represents to them—the essence of manhood. It would fly in the face of the projected needs of the public, their fantasy of what a man should be."

Dr. Ogilvie had recommended that they retain a private life-style. Those few athletes—such as the former NFL running back Dave Kopay and the former Dodger outfielder Glenn Burke—who did acknowledge their homosexuality did so after their playing career was over.

Dr. Ogilvie said that he was heartened by the response of Smith's teammates.

"It indicated how much we've grown as a people, and are willing to accept a diversion from ourselves," he said. "And that we don't measure the acceptability of a human being on the basis of a single dimension such as sexual orientation, one tiny, tiny segment of the totality of the human being.

"I think the response of these football players to Jerry Smith is a beautiful thing."

A Bevy of Bruises

New York, December 24, 1983

A thigh. A neck. A leg. Is it an anatomy class? A butcher's inventory? It's the National Football League's injury report!

Each week readers of many newspapers across the country are treated to a long list of the limp and halt among the 28 teams. On the report for any given weekend, there may be more than 300 players, catalogued with more than 400 injuries.

To some fans, it's a way of finding out to which of their favorite players they should send chicken soup. To other readers, it's indispensable information for betting games. (In part because it is seen as simply a gambling tool, some newspapers don't print the information.) To yet others, the list reads like an accident report from an emergency ward.

The roster of the ailing mentions the team, the player and his position, his disability and his status: "Probable" means likely to play, "questionable" means it's 50–50 whether he'll play, and "doubtful" means he'll most likely not play.

For example, a random look at the wounded for two first-round playoff games included: "Broncos S Mike Harden (ankle), probable."

"He's got an ankle," said Mike O'Brien, an assistant in the Broncos' public relations department, using the parlance of football in describing the injury. "He's actually got two ankles, but only one is sore."

Some time ago, Rick Upchurch, a wide receiver for Denver, had a pinched nerve on the left side of his neck, and it was listed as "left neck."

"We got some calls from people wondering how his right neck was," said O'Brien.

Some guys are hurting in more than one place. For Monday's game, Vince Ferragamo, the Ram quarterback, is listed with "right hand/flu," though "probable."

"Our record for one person with the most listed hurts," said Merrill Swanson, the Vikings' public relations director, "is our cornerback, Rufus Bess, this season. We put him down for ribs, ankle, shoulder and wrist."

But Tony Dorsett of the Cowboys may be the all-time leader for multiple injuries. We'll never know. At one point this season, he was listed with "general all-body soreness."

Sometimes the ailments aren't related to football. Ed Croke, the Giants' p.r. man, mentioned that Chris Foote, a center, recently had "a stomach"—food poisoning.

Croke was asked about the rest of the player: "Does Foote have a foot?"

"I'm sure he does," said Croke.

Croke recalled that there was a player named Arms with the Cardinals years ago.

Anyone else in the NFL with an anatomical name? Croke thought a moment. "Leonard Tose, but he's an owner," Croke said.

One may read of players suffering from "tibia" and "fibula" and "Achilles" and "clavicle," but the reports by the NFL try to keep things simple.

"A stretched left brachial plexus," said Greg Aiello of the Cowboys' public relations department, "comes out 'neck.' "

There is also a covey of concussions dotting the injury-laden landscape. "It's the most common injury," said Joe Gordon, publicity director for the Steelers, "with knees second."

In the NFL, a player is considered to have a concussion when he has taken a hard blow to the head—and the head remains on his shoulders, even though, to the player, it may not always seem that way.

Steve Dils, the Viking quarterback, was banged in the head during one game and suffered a memory loss. "He couldn't even remember where his locker was," recalled Merrill Swanson. "We listed him as questionable, but he played the next game."

Sometimes players will play when one would think they couldn't get out of bed.

In January 1975, the Steelers' Dwight White, with viral pneumonia, tackled the Viking quarterback Fran Tarkenton for the first safety in Super Bowl history. Jack Youngblood played for the Rams in the 1980 Super Bowl with a broken leg, and a specially fitted cast. Keena Turner, the 49er linebacker, played in the 1982 Super Bowl with chicken pox.

These are players who will go through walls to play football—hospital walls.

The phenomenon of injury lists in newspapers is a relatively new thing, no more than six or seven years old. Its primary function, it seems, is to be fair to gamblers.

"Before the reports were in the papers, you'd have to scramble around to try to get inside information on injuries," said Rocco Landesman, Broadway producer, financial consultant and regular sports bettor. "There were guys making money by selling the information that they somehow obtained. Now the NFL provides it as a service.

"The betting line follows the injury reports. If there's an injury to a key player, the whole complexion of a game might change."

Landesman cited the San Diego-Denver game of October 23. "San Diego was a 2-point favorite until it was reported that Dan Fouts, the Chargers' quarterback, was injured and wouldn't play," said Landesman. "Upon publication of the information, the betting line changed, and Denver became a 2½-to-3-point favorite.

"The NFL doesn't like it if some gamblers have an advantage over others. So they give us all an equal shot. It's kind of them."

According to Jim Hefferman, director of public relations for the NFL, "the injury list insures the integrity of the game."

There is an argument. Some people believe that it insures the integrity of the bet.

Why should one team tell its rival about injuries? It doesn't tell the other team about game plans, does it? Injuries are none of the other team's business. But NFL officials seem to understand that gambling is a reason for the tremendous interest in their sport, and they are wise enough to make the games sporting for gamblers.

Meanwhile, the injury lists tumble along—with their array of ankles and legs, hamstrings and sternums, arms and fingers, and hips and heads.

Pro football is a game that requires, on one level, a speculator's spirit, and, on another, good health insurance.

Death of a Young Star

New York, June 21, 1986

Len Bias was born November 18, 1963, four days before John Fitzgerald Kennedy was shot to death at age 46. On Thursday morning, Bias died suddenly at age 22, with no clues or alarms or history of any physical problems.

Hearing of the death of Bias—he was gloriously in the headlines just the day before as the Celtics' first pick in the National Basketball Association draft, and the second selection overall—was as shocking in its way as hearing of the murder of President Kennedy as he rode in a motorcade while thousands cheered him.

This in no way is meant to compare the global impact of a world leader with that of a basketball player. But Bias, like President Kennedy, was youthful and vigorous and talented and charismatic.

Each was glowing in the national spotlight. Each had attained great heights in his respective world, each envisioned reaching even greater heights.

The first news reports said that doctors had not yet determined the cause of Bias's death. Was it, some wondered, a congenital malfunction, like Marfan syndrome? Later, there were unconfirmed reports of cocaine use Wednesday night as Bias stayed up late celebrating his good fortune with friends in a dormitory room at the University of Maryland. Some cardiologists have said that cocaine can cause cardiac arrest.

If Bias had indeed been indulging in drug use, then he was not the kind of victim that Kennedy was, but had played with fire and got burned in extremis. He may have believed he could safely use a dangerous drug, that he could handle it. Look how much more he had handled on the basketball court. Others, not even basketball stars, had believed the same, and come to the same end. But now, in Bias's case, that was still a rumor.

Len Bias was born in Hyattsville, Md., just a few miles from where, in 1962, I was stationed with the 150th Armored Cavalry, at Fort Meade, Md., and about 30 miles from 1600 Pennsylvania Avenue, where Kennedy was then in residence. It was at Fort Meade that I first learned of something President Kennedy said that I would never forget.

I was part of a call-up of the National Guard during the Berlin Crisis. Many reservists were unprepared when they were uprooted from family and business and school. I was in the last semester of undergraduate school at Miami University in Oxford, Ohio.

Thousands of letters of protest were sent by reservists to their congressmen, to their senators, to the President, asking for just a little more time to get their houses in order before they picked up their rifles, or shovels, or pencils, depending on their Military Occupational Specialty. I remember that the great young forward for the Lakers, Elgin Baylor, was also recalled.

To the many who complained that the speedy call-up was unfair, President Kennedy made his famous reply: "Life is unfair."

How ironic, how enraging, how tragic that within the space of about a year, life would be so unfair to John Kennedy.

This came to mind when a story, clicking on a wire-service machine in the office of the *New York Times* Thursday, reported the reaction on the death of Len Bias from the Celtics' star, Larry Bird. "It's horrible, I'm too shocked to respond," said Bird. "It's the cruelest thing I ever heard."

In it were echoes of John Kennedy's words.

"Len would've been a star," Red Auerbach, the president and general manager of the Celtics, said Thursday. "He was highly competitive. He could shoot and rebound and run."

The last time I heard Auerbach's voice over the phone, a few weeks ago, he was returning a call. For some reason, I didn't recognize the voice at first. He asked if this was me, I said it was, and he said, "Big deal." Then he laughed heartily, laughing, it was easy to imagine, through a cloud of cigar smoke. Now, the laughter was gone. His voice sounded weary and grave.

"What kind of player was he?" said Auerbach, about the 6-foot-8-inch, 210-pound Bias. "I'll tell ya. He had a little Michael Jordan in him, not quite as acrobatic as Michael but a better shooter. And he had a little Dr. J. in him, too."

Auerbach had known Bias for several years, since the young man had been a counselor in his summer camp. Auerbach had met with Bias's family several times, and affection had developed all around.

Bias dreamed of being a Celtic, and had said to Auerbach, "Please draft me."

On Tuesday in a Manhattan hotel, Auerbach did. According to one observer, Auerbach "looked like he had just drafted his nephew."

Bird had also urged Auerbach to draft Bias. "Larry told me," said Auerbach, "that this was all we needed. He said, 'If you get him, I'm coming to rookie camp to play with him.' "

Auerbach told Bias last summer that if he played for the Celtics, he would, of course, have to play behind Kevin McHale, the power forward, and Bird, the everything forward.

"Len said fine," recalled Auerbach. "He said, 'Those guys can help me learn.' He was humble. He was well-mannered. That's the kind of kid he was."

After two days in New York and Boston, Bias returned Wednesday night to College Park, Md., somewhat irritated, a friend recalled, by the heavy media attention he had received. But he still was so joyous at the prospects of playing for the Celtics, of the huge amount of money that was certain for this son of working-class parents—he would have signed for millions of dollars over the next few years—that he had sprinted to his car at 2 o'clock Thursday morning.

At about 6:30 A.M., Bias was in convulsions, struggling to breathe, and was rushed in an ambulance to Leland Memorial Hospital in nearby Riverdale. He was pronounced dead at 8:50 in the morning.

As this is being typed, a press kit from the NBA draft is on the desk. On the page about Bias, it tells of his "soft jumper" and his being "an explosive leaper." It relates that he finished his career as the Terrapins' leading career scorer, and was named first-team all-America by the Associated Press and United Press International.

Lower, there is a quote: " 'Every day I do things I didn't know I could do,' Bias says. 'I'm nowhere near my potential.' "

Why Lefty Got Fired

New York, November 5, 1986

Lefty Driesell said the other day that he's still not sure why he no longer is the University of Maryland's basketball coach.

It is less than a week after Driesell was, in the words of the chancellor of the University of Maryland, "reassigned." What he meant was that Driesell was fired. Not reassigned, not dismissed, not any of the other euphemisms that have been employed. Charles Grice Driesell was unequivocally fired.

He is now an assistant athletic director and not the basketball coach simply because Len Bias, the star at Maryland, died of "cocaine intoxication" on June 19.

When Bias died, the system at the University of Maryland came under intense scrutiny by the news media.

What was learned was that five members of the basketball team—including Bias—were failing all their courses in the final semester, which encompassed the end of the basketball season. They weren't attending classes. And when they were, they were taking dopey courses that allowed them to major only in "eligibility."

With this in the open now, the university was forced to do something in the wake of public outrage. The scandal had left the university embarrassed.

Embarrassed that such things were going on at this institution of higher learning?

Doubtful. The university was embarrassed that such information had been revealed.

And if Driesell continues to be confused as to why he was fired, then so are a number of other people.

After all, Driesell was only doing his job. His concern was not to get students through their academics. Driesell was hired by the university 17 years ago to win basketball games.

He did. He elevated the won-lost record of the University of Maryland—if not the integrity of the program—to 348–159.

When Driesell took the job at College Park, the lackluster team was drawing about 3,000 fans a game, at about $4 a head. It came to a couple of hundred thousand dollars a year, including some small television and radio contracts.

Driesell, a showman who rants and rips off his jacket and stomps on it on the sidelines, was also an expert recruiter. At first people came out to see Lefty play the clown. Then they came to see his triumphant teams.

Now, Cole Field House regularly has sellout crowds of 14,500 for each game, at about $9 per person, for about $2.5 million a year. Add to this the Terrapins' going to National Collegiate Athletic Association tournaments and sharing in lucrative television network contracts, and the university comes away with some $3.5 million a year.

The university had been so happy with this that just last December, the school's chancellor, Dr. John B. Slaughter, signed Lefty to a new 10-year contract. Lefty was delighted, for, with a salary of about $85,000 and a summer camp and a television show and a sneaker endorsement, he came away with about $300,000 a year.

A long way from Lefty's original salary of $16,000 at the university.

So Lefty had to be encouraged that this pillar of academia believed he was doing a swell job. And if the academic adviser to the basketball team quits because, she said, Lefty didn't care much for his players' schoolwork, and if he makes a midnight phone call to a woman who accused one of his players of sexual harassment and tells her to back off, and if he is applauded by the board of regents for his successful basketball teams, and if the governor and various political satraps sit in special boxes during games, and if the chancellor proudly shows off this winning team to these guys who might in fact get him a raise, and if he turns around and renews Lefty's contract to the tune of 10 more years at a raise, then one can certainly understand how confused Lefty is today that he can no longer take part in the sweaty hoop exercise at Cole Field House.

The chancellor recently said that his task force has investigated the quality of education that the basketball players were getting, and he has now found it wanting, and, he adds, he has "for some time."

How much time? Before Bias's death? As far back as, say, December, when he gave Lefty the new contract?

To the argument that Lefty's players have a higher graduation rate than the rest of the school population, the chancellor now counters with, "I'm much more concerned with the quality of education students receive than the graduation statistics."

When did he become more concerned? And if it was before December, then why didn't he tell Lefty to find another place where he can throw off his sport jacket and jump on it to show his disapproval of the referees?

Remember, this is the chancellor of the school. Chancellors normally have access to the records. And he is not just any chancellor, who allows the athletic department to go its own way. Dr. Slaughter is the head of the Presidents' Commission of the NCAA, a group that is supposed to clean up the excesses and hypocrisy in big-time college sports. His nose is supposed to be sniffing in the right places.

"Leonard Bias's death brought out the in-depth look at the university and its athletic program," Dr. Slaughter said. "There's a coupling there we can't avoid."

And, if Lefty is still wondering, that's why he was fired.

The scapegrace became the scapegoat.

The Edwin Moses Case

New York, January 24, 1985

Edwin Moses, onetime honor student and holder of a bachelor's degree in physics from Morehead College, two-time Olympic gold medal winner, world-record holder and a man who has not been defeated in a 400-meter hurdles race since August 26, 1977 (109 races), has been shown to be vulnerable.

Edwin Moses, at age 29, is one of the most respected athletes in the world. The word "dignity" is mentioned as often in discussions about him as is the word "gifted." He is a man chosen to represent his country and his sport on the boards of the International Olympic Committee and the United States Olympic Committee, as well as being a spokesman for the United Way and the American Cancer Society and numerous commercial enterprises. But Edwin Moses has been shown to be vulnerable.

For one thing—at least once—Moses fell down at the job of tying his shoelace. This was in the 1983 track and field world championships held in Helsinki, Finland. He won his race despite a flopping shoelace that had come untied as he bounded over the hurdles.

But the world wasn't looking on at that, or at least the audience was nothing like the second time Moses's vulnerability became apparent. This occurred during the opening ceremonies of the 1984 Olympics. Moses had been given the distinct honor of reciting the competitors' oath before a crowd of more than 100,000 at the Los Angeles Coliseum and for an international television audience of nearly 2 billion.

Partway through the 43-word oath that he had memorized, he stumbled. Suddenly it was painfully obvious that he had forgotten the words. Moses, a lean 6 feet 2 inches, stood ramrod straight. The look in his eyes was—calm? worried? It was hard to say. Then he gathered himself, clutched the rest of the oath as he had been clutching the white Olympic flag, and finished faultlessly.

To many, this was an indication of the inner man, a prideful man who had taken the trouble to memorize the oath—however short—and had the confidence to recite it before this unprecedented audience without benefit of notes. It seemed to speak also of his meticulous training habits, and of the enduring qualities that have made him an exemplary athlete.

Only he and Paavo Nurmi, the Flying Finn of more than half a century ago, have won individual Olympic gold medals in the same running event eight years apart. Moses's current winning streak is believed to be a record for any runner in any event.

Quietly, patiently, gently, Edwin Moses had continued to go about his business. Advertisers had flocked to him, wanting to associate their products with his name and impeccable reputation. He earned an estimated $1 million last year—legal under current amateur guidelines—and it was expected he would top that this year.

He also made time to visit schools and speak to youngsters about the necessity not to drop out, and to tell them that athletics should play a secondary role to academics. He talked of clean living and the harm that drugs can do to body and mind. He was also a spokesman for athletes, particularly those lesser known who were getting shortchanged by some promoters.

He was a family man, married, and the son of educators from Dayton, Ohio.

Edwin Moses was a role model of the highest order.

Last year, he won the prestigious Sullivan Award for amateur athlete of the year. This year, among other awards, he was named *Sports Illustrated*'s Sportsman of the Year and ABC's "Wide World of Sports" Athlete of the Year.

Then, suddenly, the incredible world of Edwin Moses collapsed— or seemed to. At 3:17 January 13, a Sunday morning, he was arrested in Los Angeles. According to a charge filed later, he had solicited an undercover policewoman who was posing as a prostitute. The charge is a misdemeanor, and those found guilty are often fined around $50. Moses was given a date for arraignment and released.

Moses had been returning from a meeting of the USOC that ended around 1:30 A.M. He and a few others went to a discotheque, and after a while he left. On his way home, Moses, in his gray Mercedes, stopped at the corner of Sunset and Genessee. He said he stopped for a red light. He says that the woman came over and he turned down the window "eight inches" and "joked" with her. The police contend that he solicited her. He contends that there was no such intent.

The undisputed fact is that he never got out of the car. He never unlocked his door. He drove away. The woman was wired and the conversation was heard by two policemen in a car nearby. They followed Moses and two blocks later picked him up.

Now, Moses was hardly incognito. His license plate reads "OLYMPYN." During the Olympics, he was on billboards throughout the Los Angeles area, hurdling at passersby in his red tracksuit. When he was picked up, one of the officers recognized him.

"The officer was dismayed that it was Moses," said Lieutenant Dan Cook, a spokesman for the Los Angeles Police Department.

"When they saw it was Edwin," said Gordon Baskin, Moses's business manager, "I think they felt 'This is a nice fish to fry.'"

Whatever, word of the arrest got out—Lieutenant Cook says he has no idea how—to a local television station. It was soon a big story, and growing. "It became," said Lieutenant Cook, "international."

Moses called his wife, Myrella, who came to his side. And almost immediately Moses began receiving numerous calls and telegrams of support, said Baskin.

One caller was Peter Ueberroth, former head of the Los Angeles Olympic Organizing Committee and now the baseball commissioner. "Edwin," said Ueberroth, in New York, "is a giving, decent human being. If he says he's innocent, I believe him. I told him that if there is anything I can do to help—if I have to go back to Los Angeles—I'll do it."

Moses goes to trial February 8. He has pleaded not guilty.

"I have done nothing wrong, and that will be proven," Moses said Sunday, accepting his trophy on "Wide World of Sports." "This has hurt me deeply," he added in his straightforward manner, "but I'm going to be a champion no matter what."

A jury found Moses not guilty.

Commentators or Patriots?

New York, August 3, 1984

It is titled "Rebirth of a Nation" and stars America with a supporting cast of thousands.

The subtitle is "The Games of the XXIII Olympiad," but it has proved to be wanting in marquee value.

Out in Los Angeles, where "dreams come true," as we have been told by ABC, which is televising this epic, United States athletes are either winning gold medals, are close to winning them, or have just missed winning them and there will be a next time.

In the most hallowed tradition of Hollywood, ABC is bringing us from out of the Old West the dusty tale of the good guys against the bad guys. The good guys is "Us," the bad guys is "Them."

Maybe this isn't what Baron de Coubertin had in mind when he conceived the Modern Olympics, and sought to bring the finest athletes of the world together to compete without chauvinistic fervor, and as individuals, not as nations, and saying that "the most important thing in the Olympic Games is not to win but to take part."

And maybe the telecasts aren't the kind of objective journalism that John Peter Zenger had in mind.

But it's Show Biz, and it's what D.W. Griffith, who made the original *Birth of a Nation* in 1915, and apparently what Roone Arledge, president of ABC News and Sports, who is making "Rebirth" nearly 70 years later, had in mind—that is, flag-waving sells.

"What do you think our chances are in this event?" asks Chris Schenkel, the sportscaster, to Bill Steinkraus, one of his equestrian experts.

When a decision was reversed and a medal taken away from one of the United States' Greco-Roman wrestlers, the commentator Russ Hellickson said, "But not all is bleak here; Steve Fraser still has a chance for a medal." The Canadian who benefited by the reversal probably didn't think things were bleak at all.

Bill Flemming, at the cycling venue, said, "There's a lot of excitement at the velodrome, and it all surrounds the two Americans." The West German who would win the bronze might have saved just a dollop of excitement for himself.

But the most breathless display of patriotism was reserved for the triumph of the men's gymnastics team on Tuesday night.

ABC, hungry for star quality in the fashion of an Olga Korbut or Nadia Comaneci or, best of all, the 1980 United States hockey team, has lit, for the time being, on the United States men's gymnastics team. These six handsomely developed, exceptionally coordinated athletes indeed deserve praise for their unexpected accomplishment. They lifted our spirits for the moment, and that is a contribution; but the announcers have made it seem that they have done something beyond, like discovering a care for athlete's foot.

The afternoon anchor commentator, Kathleen Sullivan, described the gymnasts' victory as a "historic accomplishment." Her co-anchor, Frank Gifford, said, "They'll be talking about it for decades to come."

On Wednesday evening, Jim McKay, the evening anchor, asked, "Ever think a country could go so wild for a group of men's gymnasts?" Like how? Well, Rita Flynn, an ABC reporter, said that "after the miracle win, everyone was begging the gymnasts for their autographs." She didn't amplify whom she meant by "everyone."

Jim McKay said, it's "making us all wonder what marvels are yet to come."

And Jack Whitaker, at the site of the women's gymnastics team final on Wednesday night, asked, "Will history turn another page in Pauley Pavilion tonight?"

When the men's gymnastics team won the gold, there was luxurious television coverage of their smiles and tears on the winner's stand as the national anthem was played, with, superimposed, the Stars and Stripes fluttering.

When the Rumanian women gymnasts beat the United States, the Rumanians were not seen on the winners stand, their flag was not shown being raised and their anthem not heard. ABC cut to a delayed newscast.

There are 139 nations in the Olympics besides the United States, but they are at the Olympics only to compete against the United States. Witness the television coverage: rarely is there an event that does not include an American. And when there is, such as a light-welterweight boxing match between a Kenyan and a Thai, "it is interesting," Howard Cosell tells us, "because both were trained by Americans."

After an American boxer named Jerry Page won his match, Cosell interviewed the trainer, Pat Nappi, and, after a short interview, told him, "Get back to your youngsters. You're doing a great job." Cosell, the only ABC play-by-play announcer who does not work with an "expert analyst," is also cheerleader and mentor for the American team.

Meanwhile, there is the emphasis on "our" being involved in the "rush for gold," and "we" who are "striking it rich."

"Tim, Bart and Mitch," said Frank Gifford to three of the men's gymnasts, Daggett, Conner and Gaylord, who had come to the ABC studio, "we won it. They didn't think we would, but we did!"

Who is "we"? Frank Gifford? This viewer? Frank was seen only in his chair in the studio and this viewer got off his couch during the competition only to investigate the refrigerator. Neither of we got within a mile of a pommel horse.

Hockey As It Oughta Be

New York, May 23, 1987

A lot of people have it wrong. The problem with hockey is not that there's too much fighting and not enough hockey. The problem with hockey is that there's too much hockey and not enough fighting.

The Philadelphia Flyers are one of the few teams around who truly understand this. They had the foresight, the creativity and the guts recently to do something about it. They took the future of their game into their own fists and sticks and tried to show how to save it from the bleeding-heart critics.

The Flyers didn't even wait for the game to begin—they were in Montreal playing the Canadiens in the Stanley Cup semifinals—and one of their players, the ever-expendable Ed Hospodar, was obviously recruited to pummel Claude Lemieux.

Then everyone got into the act. Oh, what a lovely war.

This all took place in the pregame warm-ups, the prelims.

The only problem was that it didn't last long enough. Pretty soon, as the saying goes, a hockey game broke out. The fighting abated, with only the occasional and routine four-rounder, which was hardly anything to shout about.

There wasn't even a brawl at the final buzzer; there wasn't a scuffle, with one of the players charging into the stands to maul a patron; there wasn't a mano-a-mano on the way to the dressing room. Nothing.

The players went off to take a shower. Some hockey game. Some encore.

What would Eddie Shore, known as the Babe Ruth of hockey, have said about this? Shore, who played from 1926 through 1940, incurred fractures to his hip, collarbone and back, had a jaw that was broken 5 times, a nose broken 14 times, an ear that was virtually chewed off, and was a guy who witnessed all of his teeth being knocked out, and who needed 978 stitches in order to get through his 14-year career.

What would Eddie Shore, for heaven's sake, have said about these guys going quietly like sheep to the shower?

He would probably have hit his head against the wall, that's what.

And a lot of hockey fans would have cheered.

They cheer at any sign of someone getting his head dented.

Many hockey fans, by the way, are easy to spot in civilian life. They are invariably the ones holding up traffic when there's an accident on the highway. They're the greatest rubberneckers in the world.

And that's why I say that there's not enough mayhem in hockey today. Sure, the games are often sold out, but the people there are generally those who vent their spleen at the players for being pussycats. And so they pay good money to relish telling the players off. You don't really get the same satisfaction by screaming at the TV set.

And that's why hockey can't garner a major-network TV contract. They've had to settle for the smaller bucks on cable. And the people who watch on cable are only waiting for a good fight to break out. Meanwhile, they're sitting with a fistful of beer and lapful of pretzels and watching people ice the puck and cross the blue line and they grow more and more disappointed and despondent.

Oh, sure, there are a few fights, but that's mostly for the benefit of the film clips that will be sent to the television news shows and played on the sports segment.

A number of sportscasters like to say that this is hockey, and play those clips all the time. Their rationale is not that they're pandering to prurient interests, but that this is news. A hockey fight is news? Which shows you the news judgment of these sportscasters. And dog bites man is news, too.

Actually, the majority of hockey fights these days are a sorry excuse for a brawl, little more than guys going around and snapping each other's suspenders. The sportscasters should be arrested not only for dumb sportscasting but also for fraud and deception in advertising.

Referees allow the combatants to tangle as long as they stay standing. The professed notion is that a fight is good for the players, lets 'em release some tension in a healthy way. Only in hockey, in fact, is so brilliant a psychological concept accepted by players and officials.

But when one player slips, or falls intentionally, the refs jump in to break it up. They say one player then has an unfair advantage. Call this a fight? C'mon, let 'em roll around and really lay some bumps on each other.

Now, yes, there are hockey fans who like a clean, well-skated game. But what many hockey fans lust for is unfettered ill will. The president of the National Hockey League and the team owners would surely agree. Otherwise they wouldn't tolerate it for a minute, as other sports don't. Unfortunately, these gentlemen have been caught in a conflict between what they know is right and what the bleeding-heart critics think.

So they've made some wishy-washy, superficial efforts to clean up the fighting just a little bit in order to be able to say, "See, we're trying to do something about it."

Forget it. Hockey needs something more—and the Flyers and their brainy operatives comprehend this. It needs something like a huge, wild wrestling extravaganza. It needs violence. It needs the sound of bones cracking. It needs the sight of blood being shed. It needs Hockeymania.

Only then will sports fans take a greater interest in the game. Only then will hockey come out of its minor-sport status in this country. Only then will it get the television audience it covets, and only then will it shoot up in the ratings, to somewhere, say, around "Miami Vice."

No Hoosegow for JoJo Guerra

New York, April 9, 1987

It was a couple of hours after the middleweight championship fight in Las Vegas, Nev., Monday night and a woman who had attended was condemning the decision as an unmitigated disgrace, a blatant miscarriage of justice, and a rotten, lowdown call, too.

"How could they have stolen the title from Hagler?" she said to a guy who happened to be a reporter. "Didn't they see the points he was scoring with his infighting? He did damage. And Leonard spent the whole night on his bicycle. How can you win a fight when you're running and hiding all night?"

The reporter listened.

"And one judge, he gave it 10 rounds to 2 for Leonard!" she said. "Only a moron could have seen it that way. By the way, how did you have it?"

"Nine rounds to three," he said.

"Of course," she said, "precisely, had to be."

The reporter cleared his throat. "Uh, nine rounds to three for Leonard," he said quietly.

"You're kidding," she said, adjusting her glasses, and searching the room to converse with someone with half a brain.

It was an intriguing fight—the one between Marvelous Marvin Hagler and Sugar Ray Leonard, that is—and controversial. Veteran reporters at ringside were as divided in their scoring as the judges, or as the judges seemed.

Some reporters had Hagler winning decisively, some Leonard. Others saw it close for one or the other. At least one scored it a draw.

Fight judging is purely subjective. The extent of appreciation is often in the eye of the beholder. The judging of this fight by the three ringside officials, in terms of rounds, had it 7–5 Hagler, 7–5 Leonard, and 10–2 Leonard.

The judge whose card read 10–2 was JoJo Guerra.

"Guerra was way out of order," said Goody Petronelli, one of

Hagler's two managers. "They should remove the man. He was inept."

Pat Petronelli, Hagler's other manager, kept a cooler, more reasoned, more judicious posture than his brother. "This here official, JoJo Guerra, should be put in jail," he said.

The Petronellis admitted, however, that when they asked around about Guerra before the fight they heard only good things from respected sources.

The Petronellis also didn't dispute Dave Moretti, the other official who scored Leonard the winner. "I can understand that," said Pat Petronelli. "It was a close fight."

Breaking down the scoring, it appears that in regard to the other officials, including Lou Filippo, who scored for Hagler, Guerra wasn't out of line after all.

In fact, Guerra agreed with one or both of his brethren in 9 of the 12 rounds, or 75 percent of the time. In only three rounds—the seventh, eighth and ninth—when he went for Leonard in each, was he a lone dissenter (nonetheless, as they would in every round in the fight, each of the judges scored these three rounds close, too, 10 points to 9 points).

The other two officials, Moretti and Filippo, weren't exactly Siamese twins with their scoring pencils, either. They disagreed with each other on 4 of the 12 rounds, or once in every 3 rounds.

Over all, there was disagreement among the officials in 7 of the 12 rounds.

Judges, when evaluating a bout, generally analyze boxing artistry, effectiveness of punches and who is carrying the fight.

The Petronellis turned down one proposed judge, Harry Gibbs of England, because they thought that English officials "favor the boxers. . . . And we knew Marvin would be fighting a rough, tough, swarming style." They wanted, ironically, a Mexican official because Mexican boxers are often aggressive fighters.

They believed that on Monday night their fighter wasn't rewarded enough for his aggression.

But a bull is not rewarded for aggression against a matador. And that's the way much of the Leonard-Hagler fight appeared.

There were 792 punches thrown by Hagler, and he missed on

501. Leonard wasn't exactly standing around and enjoying the breezes. He threw 629 punches, and missed on 323.

None of that means much, however, if the 291 punches landed by Hagler and the 306 punches that connected for Leonard were effective.

The Hagler people said that Leonard's punches generally came in flurries—"he only fought for 20 seconds a round"—and were, in effect, powder puffs. Moretti, for one, saw it differently: "The hardest punching was by Leonard." Thomas (Hit Man) Hearns, who fought and lost to both Leonard and Hagler, said that Leonard hit him harder than Hagler did.

To these eyes, Leonard was the master of the ring on this night, and that's what mattered in the end. It is still the sweet science, not a barroom brawl, at least according to the textbooks. Once, Willie Pep, the clever Will o' the Wisp, informed officials sotto voce that he was not going to throw a single punch for an entire round. He didn't. He weaved, he twisted, he ducked, he slid. His opponent swung and missed and tumbled into the ropes, and fell all over himself. Pep even slipped around him, and for a moment the other fighter couldn't find him. The officials scored the round for Pep.

Could scoring be more objective? Could it be done by machines? Several years ago, a computer title fight between Rocky Marciano and Muhammad Ali was arranged. Angelo Dundee, trainer for both Ali and Leonard, recalled it.

"In the States, Marciano won," said Dundee. "But in England, Muhammad won. It's all what you put in the computers. It still comes down to the human element. Muhammad said the reason he lost here was that the governor of Alabama then—Governor Wallace—ran the computer."

A Loquacious King

New York, August 19, 1987

This wasn't simply a news conference announcing yet another world heavyweight championship fight—in this case, Tyson-Biggs—this was a Donald King news conference, with a dais of about 20 straight men, all with the astonishing ability to stay awake, as neologisms, solecisms, hyperboles and references, half-references and tortured literary, historical and biblical allusions from John Paul Jones to the Bard of Avon were flung about by King at a dizzying rate.

This stunning display took place yesterday at lunchtime in the grand ballroom of the Grand Hyatt, where each table was striving to go aloft with a batch of red, white and blue balloons that read, "Don King: Only in America."

King, the promoter with the understated hairdo, announced that "HBO is telecasting this to the whole universe of this nation."

He said that Mike Tyson had come "360 degrees around, and that's the triangle of life."

He saved his most lavish encomiums for Donald Trump, with whom he has entered into a partnership for this fight. The contest will take place at Trump Plaza in Atlantic City on October 16.

King mentioned the great "Oedipuses" that Trump the real estate magnate had built. He started off about "that guy in Russia, what's his name?" King turned to Trump, who said it softly. "Gorbachev!" said King. "That's right. He asked Donald to redo Russia personally. Oh, wooo! Leningrad is spinning in his grave!"

"Lenin!" someone shouted.

"Lenin!" repeated King, triumphantly.

He next spoke about "touching the hem of the great man"—Trump—and that he was so lost for words to define this man that he had to make up a new one—"telesynergistic"—"that will go into the lexicons and dictionaries and what have you."

What does telesynergistic mean? It has something to do with a kind of genius that, said King, "can make 2 and 2 add up to 10."

A number of the boxers—and sportswriters—in the audience looked at each other. That's how *they* did arithmetic in school and no one ever wanted to touch *their* hem.

As here and there heads in the audience began to fall into their potatoes, Mike Tyson showed why he is the heavyweight champion of three alphabets—the WBA, the WBC, and the IBF.

Tyson is undeterred regardless of the obstacles. As King's tongue rolled, so did Tyson's mouth. He ate his roast beef and creamed potatoes and broccoli with left-handed aplomb. In fact, even when he was first introduced, he stood up, fork still in hand, then sat back down and continued his assault on the vittles while King continued his assault on the language.

Eventually, the two fighters were asked to say some words.

This fight might even be more interesting than King's oration, but history will be the judge of that.

Tyson and Tyrell Biggs are undefeated. Biggs, the Olympic gold medal winner in the superheavyweight division in 1984, is 15–0 with 10 knockouts. Tyson, 31–0 with 27 knockouts, won a decision from Tony Tucker for what this promotion calls the undisputed heavyweight championship of the world.

Earlier Lou Duva, Biggs's trainer, had talked about his fighter's heart and courage, how he came back from a broken collarbone suffered in the fourth round against David Bey and went on to win. And there were allusions to some "troubles" Biggs had had the last few years. Those included drug and alcohol dependency, and treatment at a rehab center.

Now Biggs, in gray businessman's suit, discussed fear, because people have called Tyson "invincible," he said.

"I fear God—he's the only being I fear. Mike Tyson is 5-8, 220. I'm 6-5, 225. From the way it looks, I should be the favorite. As far as being invincible, on October 16 I'll prove that wrong."

Now King breathlessly introduced Tyson, "the king, the ruler, the trumpets should be blaring," and mentioned something about his being the new elixir of life, or was it ambrosia? Anyway, Tyson dragged himself from his own plate. He wore a painter's cap with the name Taurus on it with the bill turned up, a T-shirt and black training pants—this is his businessman's suit.

"It's amazing how much disrespect I get since I won the championship," he said. "Everyone's talkin' about how they're gonna beat me up." He suggested that this was not good for those people's health.

A question came from the audience pertaining to Michael Spinks. How can this be an undisputed heavyweight title match when he has yet to be beaten.

"Spinks has no belt," said Tyson. "If he fights Tony Tucker and beats him, I'll have the fight."

Biggs had said Tyson was 5-8—he's actually listed at 5-11½. Did Tyson think he was tall enough?

"Tall enough to be the champion of the world," Tyson said.

Won't a tall fighter like Biggs give you trouble?

"I beat Green, I beat Ribalta, I beat Tucker, they were all about Biggs's size. Maybe I haven't done my homework, but I don't see him being any different."

There was more give-and-take before King could stand the shadows no more. He recaptured the microphone, and added some concluding remarks, at some length, to be sure.

Suffice it to say that there was one word put into practice by the fighters that is not in Donald King's teeming vocabulary.

The word is terse.

The Twin Temples of Boxing

New York, November 20, 1982

Duk Koo Kim was the youngest of five children born to the H.Y. Kims, rice and ginseng farmers in the Kan Wan-Do province of South Korea, 100 kilometers east of Seoul.

When he was 14 years old, Kim left school to seek his fortune in the capital city. He worked as a shoeshine boy and sold chewing gum and newspapers before he took a factory job two years later.

In 1976, at the age of 17, tough and willing, Kim began an amateur boxing career. After a 29–4 record, he turned professional in 1978. He won the Orient and Pacific Boxing Federation lightweight title last February. Sometime afterward, he signed to fight Ray (Boom Boom) Mancini for the World Boxing Association lightweight championship.

His take would be $20,000, the largest purse he had ever earned. For the son of Korean farmers, it represented a king's ransom.

Last Saturday, in an outdoor ring at Caesars Palace in Las Vegas, Nev., in a bruising fight, Mancini scored a technical knockout of Kim in the 14th round. Kim, though he took tremendous punishment, struggled to his feet after the knockdown that prompted the finish of the fight. But he was carried from the ring on a stretcher and taken to a hospital. Shortly, he underwent a 2½-hour operation for a blood clot on the brain. He never regained consciousness. On Thursday, at the age of 23, Duk Koo Kim died.

The ring, as often pointed out, has always been the refuge of the underprivileged. It is a law of economics that the banker's son does not become a prizefighter. From Kim's history it seems that boxing was the only way he could strive to attain in material advantage what he could not as a rice and ginseng farmer, a shoeshine boy, a factory worker.

There was danger, he understood, in fighting. A couple of days before the Mancini fight, it was reported, Kim had written "Kill or be killed" in Korean on a lampshade in his room. When he entered the ring, he was considered in excellent physical shape. He was obviously prepared for what he considered a risk worth taking.

Boxing is the most primitive, forthrightly animalistic sport there is. It is filled with horror and beauty and the most fundamental simplicity.

Hemingway treasured a remark by Jack Britton, which he thought "summed up the metaphysics of boxing." Britton beat the stylish Benny Leonard in 1922 for the world welterweight championship.

"How did you handle Benny so easily?" Britton was asked.

"Benny's an awful smart boxer," Britton said. "All the time he's in there, he's thinking. All the time he's thinking, I was hitting him."

The hitting can be vicious. Norman Mailer was at ringside at Madison Square Garden on March 24, 1962, for the welterweight championship fight in which Benny (Kid) Paret lost his title and his life from the blows of Emile Griffith. "As he went down," wrote

Mailer, "the sound of Griffith's punches echoed in the mind like a heavy ax in the distance chopping into a wet log."

Yet poor kids with great dreams are still rapping the bags and skipping rope in boxing gyms in America and elsewhere. They see no way to become a doctor or a lawyer or a corporation president. But it's possible—however unlikely—that with talent and muscle they can become a fight champion of the world and get rich and famous.

It is a truism, sometimes reduced to a cliché, that boxing draws from members of the underclass until they reach accepted status. In America, Irish immigrants at the turn of the century were often excluded from school and job opportunities, and they produced the greatest fighters, followed in time by Jews and then Italians and blacks and Latins.

Many years ago, Whitey Bimstein, the fight trainer, was talking to A. L. Liebling about the disappearance of Jewish fighters.

"When the kids didn't have what to eat, they were glad to fight," said Bimstein. "Now that any kid can get a job, they got no ambition."

On the other side of boxing are the spectators, who pay the money for which the boxers fight.

To them, knowing or not, the basic one-to-one conflict demonstrates, perhaps, primeval courage.

"Now," says Aeneas, in Virgil's *Aeneid*, "whoever has courage, and a strong and collected spirit in his breast, let him come forward, lace on the gloves, and put up his hands."

The fight, as seen by Albert Camus, is the practice of a sacrificial rite by "low-brow gods."

Attending a small club fight in Oran, Algiers, Camus, once an amateur fighter himself, observed how even the fans were "sweating ferociously." He wrote:

"Every dull thud on the gleaming chests echoes in enormous vibrations through the very body of the crowd, who, along with the boxers themselves, give the fight their all."

He added, "These rites are a bit trying, but they simplify everything. Good and evil, the winner and the loser: At Corinth, two temples stood side by side—the Temple of Violence and the Temple of Necessity."

A Cluster of Stars

The Night Rose Passed Cobb

Cincinnati, September 12, 1985

Ten miles from the sandlots where he began playing baseball as a boy, Pete Rose, now 44 years old and in his 23rd season in the major leagues, stepped to the plate tonight in the first inning at Riverfront Stadium. He came to bat on this warm fall evening with the chance to make baseball history.

The Reds' player-manager, the man who still plays with the joy of a boy, came to bat with the chance to break Ty Cobb's major-league career hit record, 4,191, established in 1928.

The sellout crowd of 47,237 that packed the stadium hoping to see Rose do it now stood and cheered under a twilight blue sky beribboned with orange clouds.

Now he eased into his distinctive crouch from the left side of the plate, wrapping his white-gloved hands around the handle of his poised black bat. His red batting helmet gleamed in the stadium lights. Everyone in the ball park was standing. The chant "Pete! Pete!" rose higher and higher. Flashbulbs popped.

On the mound was the right-hander Eric Show of the San Diego Padres. Rose took the first pitch for a ball, fouled off the next pitch, took another ball. Show wound up, threw, and Rose swung and hit a line drive to left-center.

The ball dropped in and the ball park exploded. Fireworks being set off was one reason; the appreciative cries of the fans were another.

Streamers and confetti came floating onto the field as though the skies were raining paper.

Rose stood on first base and was quickly mobbed by everyone on the Reds' bench. The first-base coach, Tommy Helms, one of Rose's oldest friends on the team, was closest to him and hugged him first. Tony Perez, Rose's longtime teammate, then lifted him.

Marge Schott, the owner of the Reds, came out and hugged Rose and kissed him on the cheek. At about the same time, a red Corvette was driven in from behind the outfield fence, a present form Mrs. Schott to her record-holder.

Meanwhile, the Padres, some of whom had come over to congratulate Rose, meandered here and there on the field, chatting with the umpires and among themselves, waiting for play to resume. Show took a seat on the rubber.

Rose had removed his batting helmet and waved with his gloves to the crowd. Then he stepped back on first, seemed to take a breath, and suddenly turned to Helms, threw an arm around him and threw his head on his shoulder, crying.

The tough old ballplayer, his face as lined and rugged as a longshoreman's, was moved, perhaps even slightly embarrassed, by the tenderness shown him in the ball park.

Then from the dugout came a uniformed young man. This one was wearing the same number as Rose, 14, and had the same name on the back of his white jersey. Petey Rose, a 15-year-old redhead and sometime batboy for as long as he can remember, fell into his pop's arms at first base, and the pair of Roses embraced. There were tears in both their eyes.

Most people in the park were familiar with the Rose story. He had grown up, the son of a bank cashier, in the area in Cincinnati along the Ohio River known as Anderson Ferry. He had gone to Western Hills High School here for five years—repeating the 10th grade. "It gave me a chance to learn more baseball," he said, with a laugh.

He was only about 5 feet 10 inches and 150 pounds when he graduated, in 1960—he is now a burly 5-11 and 205—and the only scout who seemed to think he had talent enough to make the major leagues was his uncle, Buddy Bloebaum, a scout for the Reds.

Three years later, Rose was starting at second base for the Reds, and got his first major-league hit on April 13, 1963, a triple off Bob Friend of the Pittsburgh Pirates.

Rose was at first called, derisively, "Charlie Hustle." Soon, it became a badge of distinction. He made believers out of many who at first had deprecatory thoughts about this brash young rookie who ran to first on walks, who slid headfirst into bases, who sometimes taunted the opposition and barreled into them when they were in the way.

But never was there malicious intent, and he came to be loved and appreciated by teammates and opponents for his intense desire to, as he said, "play the game the way it's supposed to be played."

He began the season needing 95 hits to break Cobb's record, and as he drew closer and closer, the nation seemed to be watching and listening and wondering when "the big knock," as he called it, would come.

Tonight, he finished in a most typical and satisfying fashion. He got two hits—he tripled in the seventh inning—and walked once and flied to left in four times at bat. It isn't just the personal considerations that he holds dear. He cares about team accomplishments, he says his rings for World Series triumphs are his most cherished baseball possessions. And this night he scored the only two runs of the game, in the third and seventh innings, as the Reds won, 2–0.

After the game, in a celebration at home plate, Rose took a phone call from President Reagan that was relayed on the public address system.

The President congratulated him and said that he had set "the most enduring record in sports history." He said that Rose's record might be broken, but "your reputation and legacy will live for a long time."

"Thank you, Mr. President, for taking time from your busy schedule," said Rose. "And you missed a good ball game."

A Matter of Miracles

New York, September 23, 1986

On a day in which both the Giant and Jet quarterbacks were engaged in miracles of sorts—Phil Simms had thrown a go-ahead touchdown pass that bounced off two defenders and into the arms of Lionel Manuel, and Ken O'Brien had rifled a touchdown pass to give the Jets an overtime victory—the most venerable miracle-worker of all was summoned to do his stuff, too.

Jim Plunkett, who hadn't played in a regular-season game since early last year, was seeking now to rally his team in the last quarter Sunday, to bring it back from a 14–9 deficit against the Giants.

He had thrown two passes that might nearly have done the fantastical deed. But the first went for disappointingly short yardage when the receiver, with open field ahead, barely touched the out-of-bounds line, and the other to a rookie receiver who, a few yards from the end zone, couldn't quite hang on.

And now in the final seconds of the game, from about his 35-yard line, Plunkett raised back and heaved a long, high pass that seemed to travel forever through the clouds and then to drop toward an eager receiver at the goal line.

One more time, he was hoping. One more time? spectators were wondering.

Jim Plunkett is to football what Indiana Jones is to crashing boulders and toppling buildings and gluttonous crocodiles. Just when it looks like it's curtains, when the hero will finally be devoured, some incredible thing happens to save each from his seemingly inevitable and forlorn fate.

Followers of Jim Plunkett have come to expect miracles from him, for this Los Angeles Raider has proved the consummate Raider of the Lost Ark.

And so, after having missed most of last season because of a shoulder injury, and not having played the first two games of this season—the Raiders lost them both—Plunkett was called on to start against the Giants when his team's now first-string quarterback, Marc Wilson, had suffered a slightly separated right shoulder.

At age 38 (he will be 39 in 10 weeks), and the oldest quarterback in the National Football League, Plunkett has prevailed over so many disasters that he makes the estimable Mr. Jones appear a mere neophyte in the escape business. So the aged miracle-maker—the one with the helmet, not the fedora—was summoned to do it once again.

Plunkett was older than any player on the field, and slower, surely, and rustier.

Never mind. Plunkett had grown up believing that overcoming handicaps was as natural as scratching your ear.

Thinking back, one had to appreciate the tortuous road Plunkett had traveled to arrive at this moment, with the ball floating through the Los Angeles smog.

He was the son of Mexican parents in San Jose, Calif., and one of his earliest memories was that of his mother cooking. A lot of us remember our mothers cooking, but Mrs. Plunkett was different. She was blind. "She never thought twice about cooking," Jim had said. "She would reach for the utensils as though she had sight. In later years, her fingertips had become so calloused from touching the pots and pans to see if they were hot enough to put food in, that she was losing her sense of touch. It was then that my father insisted she quit cooking."

Meanwhile, his father, also legally blind, supported the family by running a newsstand.

In his neighborhood, Plunkett recalled, he was usually the last one picked in games. "I was always determined to prove that I belonged," he said, "that I was anyone's equal."

The dark-haired kid improved mightily in games. The only way young Plunkett could get to college would be on a scholarship—and he received one for football from nearby Stanford.

He emerged as one of the best college football players in the land, and in his senior year won the Heisman Trophy.

The Cinderella story seemed nearly complete as he became a first-round draft choice for the New England Patriots, started in the first game of the season—highly unusual for a rookie quarterback—and then threw 19 touchdown passes for the season and was named rookie of the year.

But in the next four seasons, neither the Patriots nor Plunkett got better. And the harder he tried, the worse he seemed to get. He was traded to the 49ers. He stumbled through two more seasons.

In 1978, the 49ers tried to trade him, and failed. He was placed on waivers; no one claimed him and he was released. He was 30 years old, and though he felt he had more victories in his arm, apparently no one else did.

He said the bottom had fallen out for him. He made calls to teams, and no one even wanted to give him a tryout. Finally, he implored the Raiders to look at him. They did, and liked what they saw, and signed him. He didn't play a down that season, and appeared briefly in four games the next season.

But in 1980, the Raiders' first-string quarterback, Dan Pastorini, suffered a broken leg in the second game.

"Plunkett," called Tom Flores, the Raider coach.

With Plunkett at quarterback, the Raiders would win 13 of their next 15 games, including a 27–10 victory over the Eagles in the Super Bowl, when he passed for all three of Oakland's touchdowns. He was named the most valuable player in the game.

In the seasons following, he lost his starting position to Wilson, won it back, lost it, and now was returning to it.

And a camera closeup of Plunkett saw a steady, unruffled look as he viewed the game Sunday from the sidelines, or in the huddle. One time, the camera stayed with Plunkett, still in the pocket, and saw him lean to the right, as though imploring the magic genie to guide the ball into the receiver's hands. The genie was on a coffee break.

And now, that last pass of the game, the one that would make all the difference, dropped from the skies and into a crowd of white Giant shirts and black Raider jerseys, and was knocked to the ground.

Plunkett walked off the field, back straight, head unbowed.

He had run out of miracles, but it was early in the season and likely the condition was only temporary.

A Fresh Start

New York, March 6, 1981

Suddenly the music stopped. Nadia Comaneci turned, her body frozen still as a park statue, arms extended, balletic toe dipped, and looked over her shoulder to see what was the matter.

"Oom," explained Ghesa Pojar, choreographer for the Rumanian gymnastics team, "yuh." He thrust his arms back and his bearded chin up.

"It must be like a bird, soaring, like wings," Pojar said, in Rumanian. "Not like a scared woodpecker."

He stood at the edge of the blue gymnastics carpet in the Felt Forum yesterday while his star pupil practiced her floor exercise routine. She was preparing for "Nadia '81," an exhibition at Madison Square Garden Sunday afternoon that includes the Rumanian women's Olympic team and selected members of the United States men's national team, the start of a six-city tour.

As Pojar spoke, a little smile appeared on Miss Comaneci's small, pouty mouth—a surprise to those observers who remembered her as the intense 14-year-old with brooding eyes who rushed into fame at the 1976 Olympics in Montreal, scoring the first 10 in Olympic history, then went on to achieve six more 10s and three gold medals.

She grew serious again when the tape of "Ciocirlia," a popular Rumanian symphonic work, again filled the relatively empty auditorium.

In a simple black warm-up uniform, her ponytail tied in a shimmery blue ribbon, wearing eye shadow and with red polish on the fingers of her calloused hands, Miss Comaneci elegantly, buoyantly, wingedly whirled through a series of flips, spins and leaps.

"Bravo," Pojar said. "Perfect."

Perfect. The word was hers well before it was Bo's.

It was her glory—she gained instant international celebrity—and it was her despair. A year after the 1976 Olympics she had gained 25 pounds, going from 85 to 110, and had grown from 4-11 to 5-3½ (she is now 5-4). Changes in body size were inevitable in a girl, but the added weight seemed excessive. And shocking.

She had received great attention—from the covers of magazines to the Hero of Socialist Labor Medal, the highest award granted in Rumania—and she was obviously buckling. Rumanian officials, often tight-lipped about such things, admitted to intimates that Miss Comaneci might be suffering an emotional breakdown.

And she discovered that she could no longer do things in gymnastics that, since age 6, had seemed to come to her as naturally as waking up.

"I couldn't look at myself in the mirror," she recalled yesterday, sitting in a chair in the Forum. Her once exquisitely muscled legs and arms had then grown beefy. She had cried to her coach, Bela Karoli, who discovered her in a first-grade recess class, "I cannot do anything right anymore." Gently, he had assured her she would.

"I had to go to the seashore for a rest," she said. She also canceled several performances and lost in meets that she was expected to win.

Gradually, she regained her form. She went on a strict diet of milk products, even abjuring her beloved Mars chocolate bars, and dropped to her present weight of 90 pounds.

"But her enthusiasm for the sport, and her concentration—that is the key—it was still there," Karoli had said.

Miss Comaneci won a gold medal in the 1977 European Championships and won the all-round title in 1979. In the World Gymnastics Championships in Fort Worth in December 1979, she suffered an infected left wrist. Despite doctor's orders not to compete, she dramatically entered the stadium, and, with one hand, scored a 9.95 on the balance beam to provide the margin of victory for her team.

In the 1980 Olympics in Moscow, she won three gold medals and again scored 10s, but her experience was tainted by a long argument among the judges that tilted the decision for the all-round gold medal to the hometown Soviet entry, Yelena Davydova.

"I don't want to remember Moscow," she said.

At 19,there is no reason for her to look back. She expects to compete in three world-class tournaments this year and, possibly, the 1984 Olympic games in Los Angeles, but she maintains a wait-and-see posture on that.

As a first-year student at the University of Physical Education in Bucharest, she is working as hard in her studies, which include English, French, geography and mathematics, and she plans to be a trainer of gymnasts.

She is a young woman now, and not the child of Montreal. Her lithe body, still slender, is endowed with graceful feminine curves. She is no longer the narrow, all-consumed gymnast. She jokes with teammates, clowning through routines in casual moments, and is involved in a social life that she never had before.

"No special boyfriend," she said. "I have many friends—boyfriends and girlfriends."

Boys, though, intrigued her even in Montreal. At the time, she was asked who her hero was.

"Alain Delon," she said, without hesitation.

At the Forum yesterday, she was asked if the French actor was still her hero. She scrunched her nose, apparently suggesting such things were for starry-eyed little girls.

"No," she said. "It's Robert Redford."

The Old Man's Game

New York, July 3, 1987

We root for old guys. We root for them not to leave us too soon—and many times, any time is too soon. They've been around and have become familiar and we've come, if not always to love them, to understand them, or appreciate them, or enjoy them.

The sadness of the end of the career of an older athlete, with the betrayal of his body, is mirrored in the rest of us. Consciously or not, we know: There, soon, go I.

So we cheer when the old guy does not go gentle into that good night.

The stunning comeback of Jimmy Connors the other day had many rooting for him as he struggled in that tennis tourney across the pond.

For a long time Jimmy Connors was a champion—winning Wimbledon twice, among other achievements. But he hasn't won a tournament in nearly three years. The tennis cognoscenti understood that Jimmy Connors, if not completely eclipsed by now, was certainly in his sunset.

And it seemed that Mikael Pernfors, in the round of 16 at Wimbledon Tuesday, was sending him swiftly and finally to oblivion. But remarkably, Connors rose from his lowest, darkest depths, at 1–6, 1–6, and 1–4 in the third set, to beat Pernfors, finishing 7–5, 6–4, 6–2.

On the following day in the quarterfinals, Connors knocked off Slobodan Zivojinovic of Yugoslavia in straight sets.

Jimmy Connors is a virtual antique, by tennis standards. Thirty-four years old—35 in two months. Pernfors is 23, a French open finalist; Zivojinovic is also 23, and also on the rise.

When Connors was a consistent winner, he was an unreconstructed one. He was heavy-handed in humor, blunt in personal relationships, sometimes a brat, but forever a fierce competitor, with his gut-deep grunts when striking a tennis ball echoing in the cavern of the tennis stadium.

And against Pernfors, in what was surely going to be an embarrassing defeat, it seemed the inevitable, the ultimate disintegration of the champion was occurring right there at Centre Court.

No amount of grunts, no amount of digging from the springs of his muscles and psyche could stay the irrevocable.

Red Smith wrote after watching the old Joe Louis be knocked out by Rocky Marciano, "An old man's dream ended. A young man's vision of the future opened wide. Young men have visions, old men have dreams. But the place for old men to dream is beside the fire."

But the fire was burning inside Connors. Even when he was far behind, he grunted and groaned and labored desperately to counter the classic topspin forehands and wickedly slicing backhands from the strings of Pernfors.

Another battler, Hector, in combat with Achilles at Troy, also knew he was in a vexatious predicament. Hector said, "At least I will not die without a struggle, but in some great deed of arms which men yet born will tell each other."

And no matter the outcome at Wimbledon—Connors had done the improbable and won the third set, and the fourth—this was a match that many would retell to their descendants. "At two sets each," Connors said later, "it was all willpower."

In the fifth game of the fifth set, Connors fell to the grass, grimacing in pain. His right thigh was knotted in cramps. He was later asked if he thought he would not be able to continue. "I was always gonna finish," he shot back. "Even if I had to crawl."

Memory resurrected another tennis match between an old man and a young man, and when one suffered cramps. It was in March of 1975, at Caesars Palace in Las Vegas, Nev., and billed as The Heavyweight Championship of "Tennis": Rocket Rod Laver, 36, the old champ, versus the bombastic young bulldog, Connors, 22 years old.

Connors won in four sets, and as he left the court, he suddenly collapsed, as if shot. He writhed and held his leg. People hurried to him.

"What happened?" someone asked.

"Cramps," came a reply. "Probably from a draft."

"No," someone else said, "tension cramps."

That someone else was Pancho Gonzales. "It's from the pressure," he said. "And tonight he'll have cramps all night. We've all had it."

Five years before that, in January 1970, Gonzales, then nearly 42, a grandfather, an old lion whose long mane was turning gray, was playing Laver in Madison Square Garden. Laver, in his prime, had just won the Grand Slam. He was acknowledged as the best tennis player in the world.

Gonzales dropped the first two sets, yet battled to win the next two. He was sensational, evincing that old-time ferocity. At one point he glared at courtside photographers. "You vultures," he snapped.

He went on to beat Laver in the fifth set, for the match.

He was great, someone remarked to a female companion, but those tantrums are still immature.

"I like them," said the woman.

"That's appealing?"

"That's passion."

These days the relatively antique Connors is, like Gonzales before him, still passionate, still capable of tantrums (he walked out on a match a few months ago). At Wimbledon against Pernfors, though, he needed every ounce of energy.

At the end, Connors said he wanted Pernfors to lead the way to the royal box for the ceremonial bow. "I didn't want him to see me pass out as we walked out," said Connors.

The old man was vulnerable, but still of championship mettle, and maybe next time—it must be one of these times—he will not come back. But it wasn't Tuesday, it wasn't Wednesday, and maybe it won't be today, or Sunday, in the final, either.

Reviling the Wind

New York, August 26, 1986

John McEnroe firmly believes that he is more sinned against than sinning. This is not new, for the tennis star with the hair-trigger temper has reviled linesmen, cameramen, reporters, fans, ushers and vendors for, as he supposed it, their noise, their rudeness, their ineptness. On Sunday, he took to task the wind at Jericho, L.I., where he lost in the final of the Hamlet Invitational to Ivan Lendl.

At 27 years old, and no longer the king of the court, he has returned from a self-imposed seven-month exile looking slightly diminished. His hair is receding, his weight has dropped from 170 pounds to 155, and his skills are not quite as deft as we, or he, remembers them. But he still rages, and, in this sense, is the closest approximation we have in sports to King Lear.

Though his shots were often uncharacteristically wide of the mark Sunday, he complained that the wind affected him. Once, his strokes were so sure that a hurricane wouldn't have affected him.

But on Sunday, the same wind that Lendl played in hurt McEnroe. And after the match he complained, though with not quite the vituperation of that old king before him who stood in tatters on a heath and railed at the fretful elements, "Rumble thy bellyful!"

McEnroe this week returns to the United States Open, which he won four times between 1979 and 1984, finally losing to Lendl in the final last year. McEnroe comes to the National Tennis Center in Flushing Meadows, only a relatively few miles from where he grew up in Douglaston, ready to be booed.

"They are New Yorkers and maybe they saw themselves in me," he said. "Maybe they said, 'We can be obnoxious, too.' It might have struck too close to home. But I always get a good hand before my matches at the Open. I think people like to see me play."

They do like to see him play. He plays the game with all his heart and, when he was the champ, with a wizardry that we associate with Blackstone making a light bulb float in the air.

But he's wrong about why they boo him. It seems that while McEnroe, the last half year or so, was resting for fatherhood and husbandhood, he was devising theories, or excuses, on why he wasn't loved by the fans the way, he says, he wishes to be. It's like he was poring over philosophical tomes and coming up with answers to explain himself. He looked everywhere, it seems, but in the mirror.

New Yorkers aren't afraid to look at McEnroe for fear they will see themselves. What draws the boos—after the initial cheers—is the kind of behavior that they do *not* ascribe to themselves. He acts like a child. New Yorkers view themselves as sophisticates, cosmopolites and persons dripping with savvy.

In London, a long way from New York in many ways, he is called "McBrat." And thus it was, here or there or elsewhere. It was the way he acted on calls by the linesman or the chair umpire that earned him that sour sobriquet. The tantrums, the rantings, the whining, the stomping, the peevish look, the acidic look, the swig-of-cod-liver-oil look.

He says that he see other tennis players doing what he does, and the crowd casually accepts it. No, they don't do it quite the way he does, or as consistently, or as long.

The other day, Bill Talbert, the former tennis champion, was saying that McEnroe also may be unfair to his opponents. Talbert believes that some of McEnroe's acts are tactical, to try to throw off the concentration of his opponent: "Where does gamesmanship end and cheating begin?" asked Talbert.

There may be a sense of that in the crowd's reactions to McEnroe. A few weeks back, in Stratton Mountain, Vt., McEnroe returned to tennis after his long layoff.

He was cheered that Tuesday and then, unaccountably, in his view, booed Saturday, when he played and lost in the semifinals to Boris Becker. The easygoing New England crowd found him untroublesome until he became abrasive to Becker, the 18-year-old phenomenon. McEnroe, to some courtsiders, bullied Becker. McEnroe shouted and snarled at the young German, obviously trying to intimidate him. It was this that made the laid-back crowd sit up and hiss.

McEnroe, anticipating the worst, has decided that some of the bad calls he gets at the Open are due to something other than incompetence. "I think some of the people on the lines are jealous," he said at Jericho. He explained that some of them were calling lines when he was a junior player. "And some of them saw me advance while their kids weren't good enough." And so, they take out their failure to hatch a tennis champion on him.

Is there some truth to this? If there is, then these same people have donned disguises and called lines in Paris and Perth and

Pittsburgh, because he has fulminated at calls in those suburbs of New York, as well.

There was a time, a few years back, when it seemed that we truly were about to see a new and gathered McEnroe. After he blew a two-set lead to lose the French Open three sets to two to Lendl, he realized that his fuming cost him energy.

But he didn't change. In the end, he wasn't about to alter the style that made him the champ. There is still within him the athlete's deep sense of insecurity. "No matter how much I've won," he has said, "I still don't know when I walk out on the court if I can do it again."

In the end, he felt that he could whip Lendl. Only against Bjorn Borg did he believe he must regularly conserve strength by marshaling his emotions.

And, in the end, regardless of how much it has hurt his feelings, the antagonism of the fans stoked his competitive zeal, and aided his tennis.

And so he will continue on, and little will change. As the man on the heath said long ago, The art of our necessities is strange.

To Another Level

New York, June 13, 1987

Maybe, mine were lying eyes after all.

Maybe, during these last eight years, the old cerebrum was distorting the images that were making their circuitous way through the lens and optic nerve and canal of Schlemm.

Maybe I only thought I saw Larry Bird playing basketball at least as well as it has ever been played. Maybe it wasn't happening at all.

Could it be that William Sampson, a sociology professor at Northwestern University and a twice-a-week columnist on the opinion page of the *Chicago Sun-Times*, was correct in his column of last week?

"Mr. Bird is a great jump shooter. That is his only asset!" wrote Mr. Sampson. "He is slow, cannot jump, cannot play defense and would never get his jump shot off if the referees didn't allow him to take three steps (as opposed to the legal one and a half steps) every time he touches the ball. Further, his teammates are allowed to set illegal picks for him all the time.

"What's more, a defender had better not think of playing Mr. Bird closely. The refs simply will not allow it. All this goes on while the fawning announcers dummy up and act as though Mr. Bird is the greatest thing since sliced bread.

"It's part of the plan. The plan to have a Great White Hope in a sport that is dominated by blacks. Indeed, even the players come to believe Mr. Bird's press clippings, and that stuff the announcers spout about how he is the best and smartest player in the game. He is nowhere near being either."

In a column in *Newsday* last week, Les Payne, also on the opinion page, wrote that Bird was "overrated." "Simply stated," Mr. Payne wrote, "Bird has been marketed, for reasons more psychological than commercial, as the Irreproachable White Hope." Mr. Payne added, though, that Bird, "who is a very fine forward, is not as great as sportswriters would have us believe."

No rational person can dispute that there is racism in this country, and that it ought to be condemned and obliterated. But these two writers, both black, picked the wrong target. Anyone who truly knows basketball—anyone who knows sports, for that matter, and is thinking and seeing clearly—can appreciate Bird.

Sugar Ray Leonard was in Boston Garden Thursday night after the Celtics beat the Lakers in Game 5 of the NBA finals. "I look at Bird," he said, "and I see that special aura—again, that certain something—that gives everyone around him the impression, 'Damn, we can do it!'"

The columns of Sampson and Payne stemmed from remarks some two weeks ago by Isiah Thomas and Dennis Rodman of the Detroit Pistons after their team was eliminated by Boston in the seventh game. Rodman, a rookie, said that Bird was overrated and that the only reason he won three straight awards as Most Valuable Player was that he's white. Asked to comment right afterward, Thomas said he agreed, and that if Bird were black, "he'd be just another good guy."

Thomas later contended that he was kidding about Bird being

just another "good guy" if he were black. "Larry is a magnificent player," Thomas said. Bird said he believed Thomas's initial remarks were made "in the heat of battle," under great frustration and disappointment.

The feeling here is that Bird was right. Thomas meant them just as he said them at that moment. But Bird also knew the respect that Thomas has for him. "I went out of my way last summer to seek out Larry and Bill Russell, to ask them how they win, and how I can help make the players around me better players," Thomas said privately.

Thomas has also discussed this topic with Magic Johnson, one of his best friends. It is Johnson, in fact, who Bird says "is the best right now."

Johnson is of like mind toward Bird. "When I play against Larry," Johnson said. "it takes my game to another level. . . . It's so much fun. It's like, if he goes before I go, and retires, I'll probably leave right after that, because it's not the same with nobody else."

Magic Johnson and Larry Bird, both 6 feet 9 inches tall, entered the National Basketball Association in the same year, 1979. Johnson is a guard, Bird a forward.

Both have meant an enormous amount to their teams, including their unselfish play, team leadership, "passion for winning," as Johnson calls it, along with their superb passing, shooting, ball-stealing and rebounding.

Johnson joined one of the great players in the game, Kareem Abdul-Jabbar, and they've been in the finals for six of the last eight years, winning three. Bird joined the Celtics, who had the second-worst record in the NBA the season before (29–53) and, with no other change in the starting lineup, he led them to the best record in the NBA in 1979–80 (61–21). The next season Boston won the league championship. They've since won two more.

Magic Johnson, this year's Most Valuable Player, is black. If he and Bird were turned into photographic negatives, it is conceivable that charges of "overrated" might, in a moment of frustration and disappointment, be leveled at Johnson.

After all, he has physical limitations, like Bird. He has never had a jump shot, for example, but, like Bird, has endeavored to improve. In this playoff series, Johnson has been deadly from outside.

And the hook shot that he learned from Abdul-Jabbar this season won Game 4.

Bird, meanwhile, has labored to make his left hand so good that he's as quick to shoot with it around the hoop as he is with his right, his natural shooting hand.

Leaving Boston Garden after Game 5 and holding a cup of soda in his right hand, Bird was asked to sign autographs. He casually signed with his left hand.

"Do you always write left-handed?" he was asked.

"No," he said, shrugging, "but I've got something in my right hand."

Sampson's Long Day

Boston, June 9, 1986

Boston history is replete with villains of different sizes and offenses, from George III to the Boston Strangler, but this afternoon they were forgotten, and the rancor of the multitude centered on a new one, a young man in size 17 sneakers.

He was here, a month short of his 26th birthday, to play a basketball game in Boston Garden, an antique barn that looks like it was built around the time of the tea party.

One of the newspapers in town featured on the front page of its sports section a caricature of him in wide-brimmed hat and brandishing a blackjack.

Inside the Garden, as the sellout crowd of 14,890—not counting the beefed-up security—filed in, signs were held aloft, most of them impugning his heart and soul. One of them, scripted by a would-be biblical scholar, read, "Sampson you fight like Delilah."

When Ralph Sampson came out to warm up before the game, in red sweats, trim mustache, serious mien and only a basketball in his large hands, he was met by howls of execration. Boo, boo, boo. And the sound would reverberate when he did or did not do something throughout this long afternoon for him and his Houston Rockets.

"We're gonna kill ya, Ralph," shouted one man in a cap with cloth lips and a cloth cigar protruding above the bill. "Dat's what we t'ink about you!"

This was before Game 6 of the four-of-seven game NBA finals, following the one Thursday night in which the Rockets in Houston had rallied to beat the Celtics. It was in the second period of that game that the 7-foot-4-inch Sampson had got into a scuffle with one of the Boston players, Jerry Sichting, who stands 6-1.

Perhaps it was only a momentary thing with a smaller man on him that set Sampson off. Sampson elbowed Sichting to get position, and Sichting said, "I'll get you for that elbow."

Perhaps it was a matter of pressure building during the championship playoffs, and Sampson not performing the way he, or others, had expected. He had been set off once before, and did precipitate an exchange with Kevin McHale, the Celtic forward, in an earlier game in the series. McHale shrugged it off.

Perhaps it was a lifetime of things, of proving that he isn't just a gawky guy, but a talented athlete. After all, Sampson seems to love to lead the fast break—a job for 6-1 guards—and to shoot perimeter jumpers.

Whatever the reasons, Sampson turned and slugged Sichting in the face, and all hell broke loose, with Sampson being ejected.

"Get the gloves on, Ralph," another fan shouted just before the national anthem.

And when the phrase ". . . And the rockets' red glare . . ." was sung, the fans booed some more.

Through all this, Sampson's only reaction was a tightly furrowed brow. He had said he was sorry about the incident, that that wasn't basketball, wasn't the NBA, and he hoped it would be put in the past.

Of course it was not.

And when, in Houston's first possession, Sampson got the ball at the top of the key, the crowd booed lustily. When he shot and missed, it booed with glee.

It was not going to get much better for Sampson.

In the first quarter, he missed the three shots he took, threw one pass away and was for the most part held off the boards. M. L. Carr, the retired Celtic forward, would note the scrappy Boston defense on Sampson.

"They knew he had to be thinking," Carr said, "and so they hounded him and made him give up the ball."

The fans, with the home team ahead by 29–23, seemed to take little notice when, before the start of the second period, Coach Bill Fitch removed Sampson from the game in favor of Jim Petersen.

Sampson returned to the game, missed a lay-up, missed a hook shot, then with about two minutes to go slammed home a dunk shot, his first points of the game. Immediately after, he committed his first foul. It was that kind of game for him.

The score began to mount in favor of the Celtics, and the Rockets and Sampson began to recede. The passing, the shooting, the steals and vibrancy of Larry Bird and McHale and Dennis Johnson and Danny Ainge were, as one of the Garden's neon notes put it, making for a "Parquet Picasso."

By the middle of the fourth period, the Celtics were ahead by 30 points.

It was only then, Sampson said later, that he had got that "sinking feeling" that it was over, and the dreams of the Rockets to come back from a 3–1 deficit and go home with the championship trophy were squashed.

With about six minutes left in that period, Sampson was removed from the game. As he sat on the bench, a white towel covering his high knees and his left fist held at his temple, he watched the rest of the destruction. "We want Ralph, we want Ralph," mocked the crowd near game's end.

Sampson wound up with only 8 points on 4 of 12 shots, 10 rebounds and 5 fouls. Another line, the final one, read: Celtics 114, Houston 97. Sixteenth championship flag for the Celtics of Beantown.

"Sure, I heard the crowd, and, yeah, I saw the signs. But I only saw the name Sampson—I didn't read anything else," said Sampson in the locker room after the game. "But none of it bothered me. When I got on the court, I took the phone off the hook and went to play."

Carr later said, "I've been in situations like that, where the entire crowd is booing me. What happens is, you get afraid to make a mistake. You want to play the perfect game, instead of the instinctive game you ought to be playing."

Sampson ducked no questions, though sometimes gave a curious look when he considered one obvious or impertinent.

"Were you trying too hard, Ralph?" someone asked.

"No."

"Was the atmosphere threatening?"

"No, I thought the security did a great job. Maybe some things were said or written that would make my mom feel bad, but I can take care of myself. I just played bad."

"What next?"

"Gonna have to work to improve my game. My outside shot, my inside game, my strength."

"When are you going to start, Ralph?"

"Tomorrow," he said.

That Old Magic

Monticello, New York, August 11, 1983

Oscar Robertson, retired as a player for nearly 10 years and with a touch of gray in his sideburns, stood beside the empty court in the near-empty arena at Kutsher's Country Club Tuesday evening. He was waiting to be brought a basketball.

Someone soon showed up with a ball. Robertson took it in his broad hands and then shook his head.

"It's rubber," said Robertson. "No leather balls around?"

They were on the way, he was told. He wouldn't use the rubber ball. Too light, the feel isn't proper. "It scoots off the backboard," said Robertson.

Robertson, in a yellow sweatshirt that read "25th Annual Maurice Stokes Benefit Basketball Game," looked out at the court.

Robertson had come early, "just to see that things are right for the game," he said. "I did it all the time when I was playing." It was 6:45, an hour and 45 minutes before the old-timers' game, the first game of a doubleheader. The second matched current players.

Robertson, now 44 years old and the head of a construction company in Cincinnati, noticed that the rim at the far end of the court was slightly tilted to the right. Have to make an adjustment there, and shoot with a higher arc. And the gray bleachers were pulled too close to courtside under the hoop. Have to watch my step, he observed.

In a while, a leather ball appeared, and so did some of the other old-timers:

Bob Cousy, who can still handle the ball with magical dexterity. And still-smooth Dolph Schayes. And Dick McGuire with red hair thinning and a large blue knee brace, and Bobby Wanzer, bushy eyebrows and seasoned legs, and Ossie Schectman, white-bearded, 63 years old, the captain of the first Knicks team in 1946, and still in good shape. These three men also came with antiques—their two-handed set shots.

And there was Jack Twyman, sloping shoulders, warm, sloping eyes. Twyman and Maurice Stokes had come up as rookies in 1955 with the Rochester Royals in the National Basketball Association. Twyman was a 6-foot-6-inch good-shooting forward. Stokes a strong 6-7 center. Each had become an all-star with the transplanted Cincinati Royals.

After the last game of the 1958 season at Detroit, Stokes lapsed into a coma on the plane ride home. He had been stricken with encephalitis, an inflammation of the brain, and would come out of the coma but remain virtually speechless and immobilized in a wheelchair until his death in 1970.

During the Stokes's illness, Twyman became the legal guardian for his teammate.

"This was before there was a pension plan, and Maurice had no insurance and little money," said Twyman. "Becoming the guardian was no big deal. Someone had to do it. And no other player on the Royals lived in Cincinnati."

Twyman, though, worked hard to get Stokes the proper medical attention. And he was instrumental in developing the Stokes benefit basketball game.

"It brought in about $250,000 for Maurice," said Twyman. But Stokes's medical bills totaled about $1 million. "The rest came from donations," said Twyman.

The benefit game continues to contribute to the study of encephalitis and to help indigent former pro players.

At Kutsher's Tuesday night, the arena was nearly packed, with kids from the resort's sports academy and with older folks who had been drawn away from the bingo game.

More players had arrived: Tom Gola and Jumpin' Johnny Green and Larry Costello and Max Zaslofsky and Adrian Smith and Connie Simmons and Kevin Loughery and Marques Haynes, the dribbler with the Globetrotters and now with the Harlem Wizards.

A roar went up. Wilt Chamberlain was making his way through the crowd. Smiling, waving, huge, triumphant as a monarch. Someone remembered that he was the most valuable player in the first Stokes game, and accepted the trophy at center court with a bedspread wrapped around him. He had split his shorts while blocking a shot on the last play of the game.

Shortly before game time, Billy Cunningham, the 76ers' coach, came hurrying into the arena. He threw down his duffel bag, tossed four cigars into it and ran out to take a couple of shots.

Wilt Chamberlain got the opening tap. Robertson hit the first shot of the game, a jumper with an arc on the slightly tilted hoop.

There was some creaking, some laughs, but the players began to break a sweat, and the beauty of the way these men played the game began to come back. There was obvious pride, and teamwork. A little behind-the-back flip pass by Cousy, a shovel pass to the left while looking to the right by McGuire, a scoop hook by Cunningham. A slam dunk by Wilt that brought another roar.

In the stands, another old player, Ray Felix, with bad knees, watched. His companion saw Twyman take an odd push shot and miss.

"What kind of shot is that?" the friend said mockingly.

"Hey," said Felix. "Pro. That's his move. Gets his man off balance. Wait."

Next time Twyman got the ball, he scored.

"Oh," said the friend.

At the press table, Twyman had another fan, his daughter, Lisa, a reporter for *Sports Illustrated*.

"It was funny in his room before the game," she said. "Some guys still work out, but he's only shot around a few times in 10 years. Dad, though, was kind of getting up for it. On his toes, a little flick of the wrist."

Twyman, who scored 12 points, was voted MVP by the reporters. The referee, Wally Rooney, asked Lisa, teasingly, if one ballot was marked "Dad."

The current players came onto the court while the old guys departed.

Johnny Green rode back to the hotel in a Kutsher's van. Teri McGuire, Dick's wife, was a passenger, too.

"I hope Dick's knee is O.K.," she said. "He got kind of a bad knee."

"Well, every one of us has a bad something," said Green, gently. "But Dick looked good."

"A little chunky, I thought," said Mrs. McGuire. "I guess the shirt was a little too tight." She laughed. "But he had a lot of fun. He loves it. He still really loves it."

"Yeah," said Green, nodding. Then it grew quiet as the van bumped and made its way down the dark road.

The Slugging Professor

Winter Haven, Florida, March 23, 1985

In his open-air classroom here among the swaying palms and noisy bats, Prof. Theodore Samuel Williams was expounding on the virtues of getting one's belly button out in front of the ball.

"It's that little magic move at the plate," he was saying recently, beside the batting cage on a field behind Chain O'Lakes Stadium. He wore a Red Sox uniform and a blue windbreaker with little red stockings embossed at the heart and stood on ripple-soled baseball shoes. It was late morning, cool but sunny as he spoke to a couple of young players. "Hips ahead of hands," he said in a deep, ardent baritone, "hips ahead of hands."

And the onetime Splendid Splinter—he is a Splinter no longer— demonstrated with an imaginary bat and an exaggerated thrust of his abdomen. "We're talking about optimum performance, and the optimum is to hit the ball into your pull field with authority. And getting your body into the ball before it reaches the plate—so you're not swinging with all arms—that's the classic swing. But a lot of batters just can't learn it, or won't."

Dr. Williams—and if he isn't a bona fide Ph.D. in slugging, who is?—is author of the authoritative textbook *The Science of Hitting*. He also is the last professor or hitter or anyone else to bat .400 in the major leagues (he hit .406 in 1941) and had a scholarly career average of .344. This spring, he is serving the Red Sox as batting instructor with minor-league players.

Ted Williams on hitting is Lindbergh on flying, Picasso on painting and Little Richard on Tutti Frutti.

Professor Williams is now 67 years old and drives around the Red Sox complex in a golf cart, stopping now at this field, now at that. And though he says he's "running out of gas," it hardly seems so to the casual visitor, and there are many who come just to see him in the leathery flesh. He arrives before 9 A.M. at the training site and spends a long, full day under the Florida sun observing the young players.

He knows that there are as many theories on hitting as there are stars in the sky. "Like I've heard somewhere they tell a batter to keep his head *down*," he said. "No way you can open your body and carry through with your head down that way." He says that he may not be right for all the players, but he urges them to "listen— you can always throw away what you don't want, and keep what works for you."

And, like the good teacher, he *listens*, too. An image returns of him in the clubhouse, sitting on a storage trunk and nodding in understanding while a minor leaguer quietly talks to him.

In the batting cage now was third baseman Steve Lyons, a 6-foot-3-inch, 190-pound left-handed batter who bears a physical resemblance to the young Ted Williams. Lyons, after four seasons in the minor leagues, has a chance to make the parent club.

Williams watched him swing. "He's improvin' good," said Williams, "improvin' good. Has good power and good contact."

Last season, Lyons's batting average jumped to .268 in Triple A ball, 22 points higher than the previous year in Double A. He credits some of that improvement to Williams.

"He's not quick to criticize or change you immediately," Lyons said. "He watches, and then when he talks, people listen. He tries to be positive in his approach. He'll say, 'You've got a good swing, but there's not enough action into the ball. Cock your bat back farther."

When Williams was young, he sought advice. Before his rookie year with the Red Sox in 1939, he met Rogers Hornsby and asked, "What do I have to do to be a good hitter?" Hornsby said, "Get a good ball to hit."

"That's not as easy as it sounds," said Williams. "If the pitcher throws a good pitch, low and outside or high and inside—in the strike zone but not in the batter's groove—you let it go with less than two strikes. With two strikes, you move up a little bit on the knob of the bat. But too many hitters aren't hitters from the head up, and never become as good as they can be."

Sometimes the best advise is no advice at all. "When I was comin' up," said Williams, "Lefty O'Doul said to me, 'Don't let anybody change you.' And when I saw Carl Yastrzemski, I thought pretty much the same thing. He had a big swing, and I thought he should cut down his swing just a little. But I never came right out and said it. I'd say, 'Gotta be quicker, a little quicker.' And I think it took him longer than it should've to get his average up. Look at his record. He batted under three hundred his first two years in the big leagues. Then he hit .321. Same guy, same swing, same everything. But he got a little quicker, got a little quicker."

It was Paul Warner who told Williams about getting the belly button out in front of the ball. "And I saw the best hitters doing it. Cronin did it, and Greenberg did it, and York and DiMaggio," he said. Of current-day players, Pete Rose and Rod Carew hit that way. "Reggie Jackson doesn't, but he's so strong that he can get away with that arm action. Now, Al Oliver isn't the classic hitter—a swishy, inside-out hitter—but he's gonna get 3,000 hits because he makes such good contact.

"Guys like Mantle and Mays—great, classic hitters—could have been even better if they had thought more at the plate. They struck out too much—and they'll tell you that, too. You got to concede a little to the pitcher, even the greatest hitters have to. Look at DiMaggio, he struck out only a half or a third as many times as he walked . It meant he was looking for his pitch—he was in control, not the pitcher."

Williams no longer teaches by example, and said that the last time he stood in the batter's box was in last year's old-timers' game in Fenway Park.

"I hit two little ground balls to the pitcher," he said. "I was so anxious up there, I couldn't *wait* for the ball, and hit them both at the end of the bat."

Was he embarrassed? "Was I?" said the professor. "I didn't want to run to first base."

Bronko Appears

Tampa, Florida, January 21, 1984

"**I**f Bronko Nagurski shows up," said Sid Hartman, sports columnist for the *Minneapolis Tribune*, "it'll be a miracle."

Hartman said that over the years a number of feature writers had traveled to Rainy Lake, Minn., four miles from International Falls at the Canadian border, where Nagurski lives, to interview the old football player. "But they all come back without a story," said Hartman. "He's refused to see anyone."

Last Thursday afternoon, Hartman and about 70 other journalists gathered in a room in a downtown hotel here, waiting for Nagurski.

Bronislau (Bronko) Nagurski was scheduled to appear at a news conference for him at 2:30 P.M., called by the National Football League. He was supposed to have been flown in from his home to be the honorary coin-flipper at the Super Bowl tomorrow.

Nagurski is famous as one of the best, if not the best, football players ever. His strength and prowess as a fullback, end, tackle, and linebacker in the 1920s, '30s, and '40s, for the University of Minnesota and the Chicago Bears, have created an aura about him that rivals that of another from his region, Paul Bunyan.

"They used to say that Bronko was the only man who could run interference for himself," said one reporter.

Someone else mentioned that Grantland Rice wrote, "Eleven Bronko Nagurskis could beat 11 Red Granges or 11 Jim Thorpes."

Another remembered the legend that he was recruited by Minnesota when the football coach, Doc Spears, saw Nagurski lift a farm plow.

Nagurski did not show up for the news conference at 2:30. At 2:45, no Nagurski. People checked their watches.

At about a little after 3, the double doors opened and an elderly man, accompanied by a few others, entered the room. The man walked with an aluminum cane and a steel elbow-brace. He wore very thick glasses and the cane seemed to have a dual purpose, to aid his balance and to help him feel where he was walking. He was rather hunched and his legs were broadly bowed.

"Hello, Bronk," someone said.

Nagurski, who is 75 years old, craned his neck and looked at the seated reporters. "What am I in here for?" he asked with a smile. It drew a nice laugh from the journalists.

Nagurski moved slowly to a desk on a little platform in a corner of the large room and sat down. His gray hair had receded on his forehead, and his face was lined, but his cleft jaw was still promi-nent and looked firm. He wore a white knit shirt with a brown unbuttoned sweater over it, patterned gray slacks, white socks and brown corrective shoes, size 13.

He seemed surprised that there might still be such interest in him, and he appeared a little shy.

By today's football standards, he would not seem particularly big, but in his time he was a huge player at 6 feet 2 inches and 235 pounds.

"I'm still about the same weight," he said in a husky voice. But he stands only about 6 feet tall now. "I've shrunk some," he said. "From the arthritis. I've got arthritis in about every joint, in my shoulders, legs, ankles. They're from the football injuries and the wrestling."

Nagurski took up wrestling in 1938, after eight seasons as a pro football player, when the Bears' owner, George Halas refused to pay him a requested $6,000 for the season.

"People told me I could get into wrestling and make millions," said Nagurski. He wrestled many of the standouts at the time, like Jim Londos and Strangler Lewis. "I did it for about 12, 13, 14 years. It was tough work, and I didn't make millions."

In 1943 the Bears asked him to return, and at age 35—after having been out of the game for five years—he helped them win a championship. Then he quit again. "I had other interests," he said.

He would eventually open a filling station, and for many years pump gas in International Falls. "It's great tourist country, and that was good," he said.

For the last several years, however, he said he has spent most of his time sitting at home because moving about is too painful.

Later, he would say why he hasn't seen many people. "I wanted people to remember me the way I was," he said, "and not the way I am. I became sort of a recluse. But I come out on special occasions."

In his house there is a reminder of the old days: photographs of him in his Bears' uniform, wearing No. 3, hang on a wall.

"Is it true, Bronko, that you hit a wall in Wrigley Field so hard you cracked it?" someone asked.

"I hit a wall right behind the goal line because I couldn't put the brakes on in time after scoring a touchdown. I don't know if I cracked the wall. I have a feeling it was cracked before, but I did hit it pretty hard."

"Did you really lift up a plow?"

"If I did," he said, "it would have to have been a small one."

He said that he thought the teams of old were more "close-knit" than they are now. "We had 18 players on a team and then 22," he said. They have 49 today.

Nagurski also said that in his day players didn't jump up and down after scoring a touchdown as they do now. "We were too tired," he said, "we used to play on offense and defense."

He does watch some football on television.

"I'm very impressed with, oh, what's his name, the great back with the Redskins—I'm a little slow on names," he said.

"Riggins?" somone suggested.

"Who?"

Louder, respectfully: "Riggins."

"Yes, Riggins," he said.

From the audience, Augie Lio introduced himself. Lio, a onetime football player, is a reporter for the *Herald-News* in Passaic, N.J.

"Bronko, I played against you in New Jersey, when I was with the Lions," said Lio. "I was a guard on the right side and you were on the right side on defense. When I saw the size of your neck, I was glad I was on the opposite side of you."

When the news conference ended, some of the reporters gathered around Nagurski.

"Hello, Bronko, I'm Sid Hartman," said Hartman.

Nagurski looked at him.

"You're not Sid Hartman; I've known Sid Hartman a long time," said Nagurski.

"No, I'm Sid Hartman."

Nagurski looked closer. His glasses glinted from the lights in the room.

"You are Sid Hartman!" Nagurski threw his arm around him. "Good to see you, Sid, good to see you! It's been years."

The Toughest Man in the World

New York, June 4, 1983

It was a cool fall Sunday afternoon a couple of years ago, and an elderly man was walking down Second Avenue near 53rd Street in Manhattan.

He walked with his left hand holding a cane and his right hand in the crook of the arm of his companion, a woman who may have been his wife or daughter.

It was a windy day, and the man wore a black topcoat with the collar turned up and a gray fedora pulled low on his shadowed face. He walked very slowly.

A young couple came up the street from the opposite direction.

"Do you know who that is?" the young man said quietly, motioning toward the man with the cane.

The young woman looked and, after a moment, said, "No, who is it?"

"He was once the toughest man in the world," the young man said as they drew nearer. "That's Jack Dempsey."

Dempsey was then about 85, and his hands looked thin.

They were and were not the hands that, in 1919, some 60 years before, had savagely pounded Jess Willard to win the heavyweight championship of the world. Willard, known as the Pottawatomie Giant, stood 6 feet 6½ inches and weighed 245 pounds. The challenger, Dempsey, at 6-1 and 187, was the decided underdog. But the 24-year-old Dempsey, swarthy and sleek, with swift, powerful fists, finished Willard in the third round.

The old man's hands on that fall day on Second Avenue a couple of years ago were and were not the gloved hands that were painted by George Bellows in his famous oil titled "Dempsey and Firpo."

In that painting, which depicted the garish setting of fight night, Dempsey, the defending champ, is seen flying backward through the ropes and into the first row of ringside seats from a blow by Luis Firpo, known as the Wild Bull of the Pampas. Dempsey, dazed and enraged, would climb back into the ring and knock out Firpo in the second round.

The hands of the aged Dempsey were and were not the hands that dropped Gene Tunney in 1927. That was the historic "long count" title fight, in which Dempsey neglected to go immediately to a neutral corner—he stood over Tunney—and allowed his opponent enough time to recover and rise, and go on to win a decision.

"I remember Jack Dempsey's hands," said Theodore Mann, artistic director of the Circle in the Square. "I was a boy of about 8 years old, and his hands seemed huge, the biggest hands I had ever seen. My father had taken me to his restaurant on Broadway. This was years after he had retired from boxing. He shook my hand. Funny, I remember that they were not menacing hands. They were kind of comforting."

For years, Dempsey sat in the window of the restaurant that bore his name, on Broadway near 49th Street, waving at friendly passersby and shaking hands with his legion of admirers. He was called on countless times to strike playful poses with his fist tapping the jaw of a fan.

Dempsey could also take a punch.

He would recall the time when he was a young fellow working in the mines of Colorado and fighting on the side for a few bucks. "I was knocked down plenty," he said. "I wanted to stay down, but I couldn't. I had to collect that $2 for winning or go hungry. I was one of those hungry fighters. You could hit me on the chin with a sledgehammer for $5. When you haven't eaten for two days, you'll understand."

Dempsey is remembered outside the ring as a gentle, amiable man, but he was not to be trifled with. And when two muggers attacked an old man one afternoon, he knocked one down with a right and the other with a left. They had no idea the old man was Jack Dempsey.

*   *   *

"I don't know why I did that," Dempsey told me one day. "I guess it was just instinct. But later I thought to myself, 'My God, they could have shot or stabbed me.' "

This was the only time I ever spoke with him. It was 1970, and he was at Madison Square Garden to watch Jimmy Ellis in training for his heavyweight title bout with Joe Frazier.

Dempsey was then 74 years old. His dark hair had turned gray but was still combed straight back, and his hazel eyes were somewhat rheumy. He looked dignified in his dark suit and red sweater.

I asked him how he would fight Joe Frazier, who had a crouching style.

"Gotta get the man up," said Dempsey, pleasantly. He did not raise his right arm off the armrest, but he made a quick fist and gave an upward snap of the wrist. A slight movement, but it carried an electricity of brute power.

After three rounds, Dempsey got up to depart. On the way out, he shook hands with an old friend, Lester Bromberg, the former boxing writer for the *New York Post*. Then Dempsey lifted Bromberg's hand and bit it. Just like that.

"Caveman," Bromberg said later. "He's always been that way. A peach of a guy. And, oh, those hands, dynamite.

Last Tuesday, about 4 o'clock in the afternoon, Jack Dempsey died. He was 87 years old. The following day, in the corner of a funeral home on Madison Avenue, a coffin was draped in an American flag, surrounded by flowers and under a spotlight. In it lay the body of the former heavyweight champion of the world, his hands at rest.

Memorial for a Slugger

New York, December 24, 1985

Amid the Christmas wreaths hanging on the tall white columns along the nave and the bright poinsettias placed on the altar, a mass was said in St. Patrick's Cathedral yesterday afternoon for Roger Maris.

The former Yankee right fielder died a week ago. Saturday, at age 51, of lymphatic cancer. He died 24 years after he hit 61 home runs in a single season to break one of the most hallowed records in sports history: the 60 struck by another Yankee, the legend-enshrouded Babe Ruth, in 1927.

A standing-room-only crowd estimated at 3,000, which included numerous political and sports figures and baseball fans and those who interrupted their Christmas shopping on Fifth Avenue, jammed the cathedral as John Cardinal O'Connor celebrated the mass.

Robert Merrill, the opera star who sings the national anthem before Yankee games, sang "The Lord's Prayer." Howard Cosell, who delivered words of tribute, called him "a man of guts." This referred not only to Maris's ability as an athlete but to the courage with which he fought cancer for the last several years.

Maris was buried Thursday in Fargo, N.D., where he grew up. George Steinbrenner, the principal owner of the Yankees, requested that the Cardinal hold the special service. A mass in New York, where Maris "sprang to his great fame," the Cardinal told the congrega-tion, "certainly seems fitting." He added that the intention was "to honor Roger Maris as he was honored in the world of sports."

Maris wasn't always honored in sports, to be sure, though he was always an excellent player. Twice, in 1960 and 1961, he was named Most Valuable Player in the American League. After breaking the record, Maris would recall that "with the Yankees I was booed for 81 games at home and 81 games on the road. You say it doesn't affect you, but it does."

But he played hard, "the only way I knew how to play," he said, years later. He still suffered pains in the rib cage from his hard slides, and pained knees from banging into outfield walls, and he had no feeling in his little finger after he broke his hand playing in 1965. "Every day," he said, "my body tells me I used to be a baseball player."

He was traded from the Yankees to the Cardinals after the 1965 season, played two years in St. Louis, both with pennant-winning teams, and then retired at the relatively young baseball age of 33. It ended his 12-year big-league career. Maris moved to Gainesville, Fla., where he was given a beer distributorship by August Busch, the owner of the Cardinals, and worked at that until his death.

Maris, who continued to wear a crew cut even when it was decidedly unfashionable, was a man of simple tastes, a frank man, who didn't enjoy the bright glare of the limelight.

"It would've been a helluva lot more fun to play the game under one mask," he once said, "and then leave the park wearing another mask. Some guys loved the life of a celebrity. Some of 'em would have walked down Fifth Avenue in their Yankee uniforms if they could have. But all it brought me was headaches. You can't eat glamour."

When permission for the service was granted, Steinbrenner invited by telephone or mailgram the notables who were on hand.

Among those in attendance were former President Richard M. Nixon, former Governor Hugh Carey, Mayor Koch, Peter Ueberroth, the baseball commissioner, and his predecessor, Bowie Kuhn. Also there were Sonny Werblin, the former president of Madison Square Garden; Roy Cohn, an attorney for the Yankees; and ballplayers and former ballplayers, including Phil Rizzuto, who read the prayer of the faithful, and Yogi Berra, Gene Michaels, Jim Bouton, Roy White, Sparky Lyle, Jeff Torborg, Ed Lopat, Ralph Branca and Willie Randolph.

In two front pews was the family of Maris: his wife and childhood sweetheart, Pat, and their six children, ranging in age from 28 to 10, and a grandson, Steven, 7, the son of Maris's eldest daughter, Susan.

The Cardinal recounted how his father had been a die-hard Babe Ruth fan and had disparaged Maris's feat, as did many older fans, because of "shortened fences" and a "lengthened season"— Maris played a 162-game schedule, Ruth 154 games. The Cardinal said that he took his father to a Yankee game and "he took one look at Roger Maris and said, 'Well, you must admit, he does look like a fine young fellow.' Coming from my father, that was practically canonization."

Cosell depicted Maris as not just a home-run hitter but a "complete ballplayer player," one who would sacrifice himself to the team and advance runners. "He would make key plays that were an integral part in victory," said Cosell.

Cosell went on to discuss some of Maris's "heartache" after he broke Ruth's record. He not only toppled the idolized Ruth, but he also surpassed in homers that season "the adopted successor to the legend, Mickey Mantle." Mantle and Maris, in 1961, kept breath-takingly close to each other in homers as they pursued the ghost of Ruth. Mantle finished with 54 home runs.

Maris had difficulty with some elements of the press, and he admitted later that he was sometimes surly. He also harbored some ill feelings toward the Yankees in the years before Steinbrenner took over ownership. He felt that at the end of his Yankee playing days he had been treated unfairly. He said he felt the Yankees had been particularly unfair in telling him he could play and hiding the fact from him that X rays taken by the club indicated he had broken his hand.

For a long time, Maris had nothing to do with the Yankees, and turned down invitations to attend Old-Timers' Day games. But in recent years he had come back. Last year, Steinbrenner surprised Maris and erected a plaque in center field of Yankee Stadium, beside those of such Yankee greats as Ruth and Mantle. The plaque, shown on the back of the program for the mass at St. Patrick's, read in part, "In belated recognition of one of baseball's greatest achievements."

At the conclusion of the mass, Cardinal O'Connor recalled the cheers that sometimes reverberated through Yankee Stadium for Maris, and asked the congregation "for one last burst of applause to honor this man."

Everyone in the cathedral rose, including the dozen or so priests at the altar, and gave Maris an enthusiastic ovation. It lasted for about a minute.

"Steven," Cardinal O'Connor said, looking at Maris's grandson, who wore a gray suit and a red tie, "you were not around to hear your grandfather applauded in the Stadium, but you'll remember this, O.K.?"

The Cardinal smiled gently. Steven, seated in the second row, his feet not touching the floor, nodded solemnly to the Cardinal.

Early Stages

For Jackson, What Choice?

New York, May 24, 1986

Put yourself in Bo Jackson's shoes. How could you not choose baseball over football? In this case, the outfield for the Kansas City Royals over the backfield for the Tampa Bay Buccaneers.

Baseball is a pleasant pastime, a genial undertaking, a civil essay. Football is war.

Baseball is a kid's game. You put on a beanie and knickers to play it. In football, you don armor.

When you put on a baseball cap, it shields the sun. When you tug on a football helmet, it burns your ears.

When it rains in baseball, you seek shelter. People usually have the good sense to go indoors and eat hot dogs. In football, people sit outside in thunderstorms, in lightning, in snow and sleet. Of course, they must come equipped with medicinal jugs to get them through the struggle.

Football crowds are like the battle crowd that sat on cliffs and watched the charge of the Light Brigade "Into the valley of Death":

> *Theirs not to make reply,*
> *Theirs not to reason why,*
> *Theirs but to do and die.*

When the field gets muddy in baseball, they stop the game. When the field gets muddy in football, the players roll around in it like boar hogs.

Boar hogs? That's the nickname of Mr. Jackson. "When I was a boy comin' up," he has said, "I was a real bad kid, the bully of the neighborhood. My older brothers said I was mean as a boar hog. 'Bo' is short for boar hog. My real name is Vincent, but nobody calls me that anymore. Even my mother calls me Bo."

Understandable that a young man might tire of even his mother referring to him in a barnyard terms.

Which brings up another difference between baseball and football. In football, down on the line, insults are an expected part of the banter, insults that relate to family and birth.

In baseball, there is much less of that. And if you get close to the field, you'll hear the fielders speaking only to the pitcher. "Humma, humma, baby, c'mon, humma." Or sentiments to that effect. It's a kind of lullaby, in fact, which is why the catcher or infielder or manager makes a periodic trip to the mound, to make sure the pitcher remains awake.

The same for outfielders, like Vincent Jackson. Sometimes there is so little activity out there that they begin to doze in the summer sun.

That's why you see infielders turning and holding up one or two fingers, in order to alert the outfielders as to how many outs there are. And sometimes you'll see a manager in the dugout waving to an outfielder, trying to get his attention before he falls into deep slumber.

Baseball is leisurely, if not in fact soporific. Football is, well, as the great Red Grange said, "Football is work. Baseball is fun." Besides playing football in college, Harold Grange, like Vincent Jackson, also played outfield on the baseball team.

Reached at his home in central Florida, Grange said, "People who go to games on Saturday or Sunday don't realize how much practice is involved on Monday, Tuesday, Wednesday, Thursday, and Friday. You're running plays over and over again, running up and down the field, and the coach is always giving you hell about something."

Football does have its quiet moments, and they can be confusing, especially to one not familiar with the game. P. G. Wodehouse, the English-born humorist, became a United States citizen but said, "I have never really taken to football, not continuous enough for me. They make a play, then they discuss it for a while."

Vincent Jackson says that he would rather play games than practice, and that's what baseball is all about.

There are 16 games over a four-month period in a regular professional football season. There are 162 games over about six months in baseball. Sure, there's batting practice in baseball, but it's before a game, and guys usually kibbitz with each other and play things like pepper and chase the hat. If you're caught kibbitzing in football, they think your nuts.

In football, you must be glum, and the crazier you are, the more serious you are seen to be. You prove this by hitting your head against a locker before a game. This is fact.

Some years ago, Jim Parker, the all-pro lineman for the Colts, said, "In the locker room before a game I'd get to thinking real hard about what was going to happen, and I'd get to rocking, from one foot to the other. I didn't know what the hell I was doing, and guys have told me that I started knocking tables over and crashing into lockers. Jim Mutscheller, he was an end for us, he used to say that he wouldn't come near me before a game because he was afraid I'd kill him."

In baseball, when somebody jumps on you, it's usually out of elation, like Yogi Berra bounding out and hugging Don Larsen after the Perfect Game. In football, they pile on top of you with the possibility, if not the hope, that you may never walk a straight line again.

It even happened to a Galloping Ghost. "You come to expect it," said Grange. "And if they don't jump on you, then you think they're bad football players."

Most running backs learn to read X rays the way they learn to read defenses. "I never had my legs cut on," Jackson said. "And I plan never to go in the hospital as far as my knees are concerned."

In baseball, there is a certain lightness of spirit about the language that doesn't exist in football.

What can you say about the "blitzes" and "bombs" in football, other than to try to avoid them? But not so baseball. On a recent game-of-the-week telecast, Vin Scully noted that something was buzzing around the head of a batter, who then stepped out of the box to swat it. "That," said Scully, "must be the dreaded infield fly."

And like many mothers, Jackson's, Mrs. Florence Bond, would rather her son not play football. "My mother was against it," Jackson said a few years ago about his taking up football. "She was afraid I'd get hurt. And she'd sometimes lock me out of the house when I came home from practice."

Baseball was different. And now Vincent can always go home again.

The Dempsey-Díaz Affair

Baltimore, October 12, 1983

Ten years ago, during winter ball in Maracaibo, Venezuela, Rick Dempsey saved the life of Bo Díaz. Last night they were the starting catchers on opposing teams in the World Series, Dempsey for the Orioles, Díaz for the Phillies. But back then, Dempsey was the first-string catcher for Caracas, and Díaz was his backup catcher.

What happened that night, in November 1973, is a curious tale, and for each, of course, unforgettable.

Dempsey, then as now, was a combative player, and in days gone by rather quick to take umbrage. If there was a fight on the field, Dempsey was usually its centrifugal force.

Once, he got into an argument with a player much larger than he. The other player weighed about 220 pounds, Dempsey 170. The umpire stepped between the two. The players pushed against the umpire, trying to get at each other. Then Dempsey hollered, "Duck, ump!" The umpire ducked, and Dempsey threw a punch that flattened the player.

"It took about 35 guys to restrain him," said Dempsey, "but I had plenty of people between me and him by the time that fight slowed down a little bit.

"Now, one night not long after, we were playing Maracaibo and their pitcher threw at me. I took off after him and chased him around the field, and then around third base, and then he ran into the dugout. I never really got any blows in, but he was a very popular pitcher who was a hometown boy. The fans got very upset at me, and got even nastier because we came back with four runs in the ninth inning to beat them.

"After the game I came out of the park with two of my teammates. We were about to go for a cab and I noticed there were about 2,000 people out there. We're still in uniform because we change at the hotel, so we're pretty conspicuous. I was with two big guys, a big first baseman and a big pitcher. I said, 'Well, you guys make sure you stick close to me because these people look a little unhappy. I think they want to attack me. But if you big guys are around they won't do anything. Let's go for that cab over there.'

"And as soon as I pointed to the right, they both went to the left. I looked around and about 2,000 people were coming my way. One guy hollered, 'Dancy, Dancy.' that's how they said Dempsey.

"So I tried to jump in the cab, but a little guy about 5-2 came up and kicked me in the ribs, and so I turned around and smacked him and then I jumped into the cab. I locked all the doors. People converged on the cab. They started trying to break the windows.

"Then they started to rock the cab back and forth and they were going to turn the thing over. Talk about being scared!

"Then, suddenly some police ran out, thank God, and they pushed people back and tried to escort the car out of there.

"Well, then Bo Díaz jumped into the front seat and a couple of my other teammates jumped into the back seat with me and we started to drive out the front gate.

"Then I saw that little guy who had kicked me. He was running up to the car with a brick, and he threw it through the windshield, and hit Díaz. The broken glass cut a vein in Bo's neck.

"There was blood coming out of this guy's neck like you couldn't believe, I mean, in spurts, and nobody in the car could see it because the glass was in their eyes, all except me. I was hidden behind the cabdriver. Bo lost consciousness and slumped in the seat. I took my catcher's pad from my back pocket—I still had my glove with me and I was still wearing my batting glove—and stuck the pad on Bo's neck to stop the bleeding. It kept him alive.

"The cabdriver is in the middle of this riot and he doesn't know what to do. I don't know what happened to the police. But the cabdriver panicked, and ran into the car in front of us, and locked bumpers. We couldn't get loose and we're in the car screaming for him to get loose. I mean, the crowd is going berserk and a man is bleeding to death in the front seat. I told the cabdriver, 'We've got to get this man to a hospital!'

"Then the cabdriver throws the car into reverse and tears off the front bumper. But he breaks free and is trying to get out through all that traffic and the people from the end of the game. And he's driving over the center dividers and on the wrong side of the street and finally he gets Bo to the hospital.

"When we get there, we carry him into the operating room, and set him down on the table. And it looks like they're going to save Bo. So everything's fine, except when I walk out of the operating room three Venezuelan police are coming through the front door and they've got sabers drawn. I know who they're after—the guy who started the riot. So I cut back around to the back door and they've got three more of 'em with sabers coming at me. So I went peacefully, and they put me in jail.

"At about three in the morning, Oscar Prieto, the owner of our ball club, comes and gets me out of jail because we had to be in another town the next day.

"Well, Bo would turn out to be fine, of course, but if you see him today he still has the scars on his neck from that night.

"And so I went back to the hotel to get some sleep. I figured I'd get in about two or three hours of sack time. It's now about four in the morning, and I'm thinking, What an incredible night. I'm glad it's over. Well, it wasn't quite over.

"I had a roommate who drank a lot. I don't know who he thought I was, but when he came in at around five in the morning, he crawled into my bed and put his arms around me and said, 'Oh my darling, oh my darling.' I jumped out of bed and turned the light on and said, 'Hey, fella, what's going on!' He was so tanked up he didn't know who I was.

"I had been in the ball park, I had been in the hospital and I had been in my hotel room, and I realized that the only safe place I had been all night was in the jail."

The Big Surprise

New York, January 14, 1984

It was the summer of 1955 and the Landon School in Bethesda, Md., a suburb of Washington, was having its annual Father-Son Alumni Softball Game. Bob Wolff was asked to announce the event on the public address system. Wolff, now a sports commentator for the Madison Square Garden Network, was then the main radio and television announcer for the Washington Senators.

"I've got an idea that could really liven up the affair," Wolff told one of the fathers. "I'll ask Harmon Killebrew if he'd like to come and pinch-hit. We won't tell anyone, and then when he promptly knocks the ball out of the lot and is coming around the bases, I'll tip off that he is the great slugger of the Senators."

"That sounds great," said the father.

"Sure," said Killebrew, when Wolff suggested it, "I'd be happy to go."

Killebrew was then 18 years old, the Senators' publicized "bonus baby," having signed the year before for $30,000. He had gone directly from high school in Payette, Idaho, to the big leagues.

"The Senators," Wolff said, "were probably in last place at this time—actually, I don't ever recall them *not* being in last place—and Harmon was being hailed as the big hope for the Senators. You know, Killer Killebrew, maybe the greatest home-run hitter since Babe Ruth. He was going to be like Joe Hardy and take the Senators to a pennant.

"But outside the ball park, few people would recognize him. He looked a lot older than he was. His hairline had already receded a great deal and he was barrel-chested and quiet, and in a sport jacket and tie. I was going to pass him off as one of the fathers."

The game was played in the afternoon. Wolff drove Killebrew to the field and would take him back for the Senators' game that night at Griffith Stadium.

"I became friendly with Harmon from the time he came off the train and joined the team in Chicago right out of high school," said Wolff. "He had never seen a big-league game before this. I used to write a column for all the newspapers in towns that carried the Senators' broadcasts. And I had Harmon write something in it. He wrote it on hotel stationery, and it was really quite nice.

"He told about this dream come true for a kid, and that it was also his father's dream for Harmon to make the big leagues, and he wished that his father, who had died the year before, could be alive to see this. And he wrote, 'I know I must make good and not let my family and friends on the ball club down.' "

When Wolff and Killebrew arrived at the boys' school, Wolff

noticed that a microphone had been set up behind a little backstop. He looked at the diamond and noticed that the outfield was ringed by woods—it looked like a snap for Harmon to belt one into the trees and really give the folks a show.

There were a few hundred people there, and as each father or alumnus came to bat, Wolff gave him a fluffy send-off, "So-and-so, a sparkling line-drive hitter," etc. "I made it sound like a game I was announcing for the Senators," said Wolff.

"I remember there were men on base and I decided this was the time for Harmon.

" 'And now, folks, a pinch hitter for the fathers' team,' I said, 'John Thomas.' Or something like that. No one recognized him. He took off his sport jacket and loosened his tie.

"He tipped the first pitch, then took a big swing and missed the second pitch. This had to be a fluke. The ball was as big as a watermelon and it was being tossed in real slow. I wasn't worried. The next pitch came in looking bigger than ever. Harmon cranked up and took a mighty swing, and missed. Strike three. Oh, God! 'Wow,' I said, 'he just barley tipped the ball. He's got another swing coming.' Nobody seemed to really take notice. He was just another father up there.

"The next pitch he topped easily to the pitcher and was thrown out. I said, 'Well, fans, I've got a surprise for you. The man you've just seen at bat is not one of the fathers but the great Harmon Killebrew, who undoubtedly will become one of the most feared home-run hitters of all time.'

"I said, 'Harmon, would you give the fans a demonstration of your might?' Now everyone perked up. Harmon goes back to the plate and proceeds to miss some pitches, pop some up and hit grounders. He can't get the ball out of the infield.

"Now the hole's getting even deeper. Now, you can feel that the natives are getting restless. Either I'm lying or they want the game to go on.

"So I finally say, 'Harmon, why don't you just fungo some out yourself.'

"They give him the ball and he swings at this elusive object. He manages to hit some line drives and a couple of hard ground balls, but he never gets under one to really lift it up in the air.

"The gimmick has about run its course now, and I say, 'Harmon is always a great sport, fans, and he doesn't want to break up the game by losing your softball. So let's give him a hand!'

"There was polite applause and pretty soon we got out of there.

"Poor Harmon. All the way back I had to console him. 'Don't worry,' I remember telling him, 'you hit a hardball real well. This is just a different sport,' And he nodded his head.

"Of course, Harmon went on to hit 573 home runs in the big leagues, and only four guys ever hit more, Ruth, Henry Aaron, Willie Mays and Frank Robinson. I was reminded of all this last week when Harmon was elected to the Baseball Hall of Fame.

"But I can kid Harmon now about that game at the Landon School nearly 30 years ago. I remember telling him once that he's going to make the Baseball Hall of Fame one day, and he deserves to. But he'll never make the Softball Hall of Fame. He looked at me and smiled. He said, 'You're right.' A honey of a guy."

From Dante to Darling

New York, June 11, 1986

A. Bartlett Giamatti once described himself as a household name only in his own household. An apt description, perhaps, for someone who just six years ago was teaching college kids a course in Myths and Mythography in Renaissance Cultures.

In the nation's households, he may never be up there with names like Twinkies or Drano, but A., or "Bart," as he prefers to be called, may soon be making inroads.

Yesterday he was introduced in the Starlight Room of the Waldorf-Astoria to members of the news media as the 12th president of the National League, a unanimous selection by the owners of the 12 National League teams.

For the last eight years he toiled in what he apparently assumed was virtual obscurity as another kind of president. He was the head of a school in Connecticut that, most recently, is famous for having produced a pitcher for the Mets named Darling.

It is natural to wonder why a man who led the cheers for Eli

Yale's scholars would decide to join the sweaty forces of the cleated and knickered. Was his leave-taking of academia reminiscent, in any way, of a scene he once recalled in a baseball article he wrote for *Harper's* magazine? The scene was "The Expulsion of Adam and Eve" in the Brancacci Chapel.

He was asked, in other words, why a man of letters would gravitate to sports.

"Men of letters have always gravitated to sports," he said. "Witness yourselves."

If ever a gravitator wished to ingratiate himself to a gathering, Dr. Giamatti found the perfect method.

This professor of Italian literature had swung smoothly and swiftly from Dante to Dale Carnegie. Dr. Giamatti has gray hair and a gray mustache and goatee, grayish eyes, and wore a gray suit, but his approach to these inquisitors was as many-hued as a Petrarch sonnet.

When he made his reply to this assemblage of lettered men, the 48-year-old scholar smiled a gentle and knowing smile. He conceivably was resisting the temptation to quote a line from dear Dante, who once remarked that "He listens well who takes notes."

But Dante was in the air. When asked what the author of *The Divine Comedy* would have thought about his move, Dr. Giamatti said, "He would have been delighted. He knew very well the nature of paradise, and what preceded it. After all, baseball was first played in the Elysian Fields—in Hoboken, N.J., in 1845, if I'm not mistaken."

He added that he was looking for changes and new challenges in his life, and it is no secret that he is a great baseball fan, and has been since he first began following the Red Sox in the middle 1940s.

It had been said that he was often seen wearing a Red Sox cap around the New Haven campus. Would he continue to do so?

"No," he said, "I'll be wearing a lot of other hats in my new role."

He was asked about his own participation in baseball. "I had dreams of becoming a second baseman," he said. He paused, and then, as if to reveal a deep secret, he said, "O.K., I wanted more than anything to be Bobby Doerr. There, and that's the last time I'll say it."

Dr. Giamatti said he played second base, as did his Red Sox Doerr, but he played it because "the throw was the shortest to first base."

The highest level of baseball he reached, he added, was as student-manager for the South Hadley (Mass.) High School team. And how did the team do?

"As well as it could," he said. "But maybe that was the beginning of my desire to be part of management."

He said that a president of a league does a number of chores that are not much different from that of a president of a university. There's keeping a hand in the financial end of the game, and surely in the public relations end. And though he has had no previous contact with professional organized sports, he said that he has had a lot to do with organized sports. "I had the ultimate responsibility for 33 varsity sports for undergraduates at Yale," he said.

He was asked if, in fact, he didn't attempt to de-emphasize sports at Yale. "No, I tried to affirm Ivy League principles," he said.

He did have strong opinions on certain elements of baseball.

On the designated hitter: "I'll soften my answer by just saying that it's appalling."

Interleague play? "I favor the fundamental grid, the geometrical beauty, the fundamental structure of the history of baseball, and I think it ought to be tampered with very gingerly. I support the current autonomy of leagues, except of course for All-Star Games and World Series play, as exciting and meaningful."

On expansion: "I'm not instinctively proexpansion. I'm for making strong and vibrant the franchises that exist. I'd first want to shore them up."

He added that "the challenges and issues that affect baseball to an enormous degree affect the country." He added that part of his job would be to maintain this "institution, this form of a public trust."

It seems to some casual observers, though, that a league president might be nothing more than a well-dressed figurehead.

Dr. Giamatti believes this will not be so. He must oversee the screening of ownership transfers and represent the league in legislation with television and lawsuits, and be responsible for the approval of player contracts.

None of which sounds particularly enthralling to at least one of the assembled flowers of American sports journalism. But there is no accounting for tastes. After all, a Renaissance man whom Dr. Giamatti studied once spent four years painting the ceiling of a church.

Refrigerator's Thanksgiving

New York, November 29, 1985

Last Thanksgiving, William (The Refrigerator) Perry was unconcerned about his weight, which was zero on some scales. That is, he stepped on the scale and when the needle zoomed past the maximum, 350, it came to rest back on zero.

Last Thanksgiving, Refrigerator Perry enjoyed dinner at his in-laws, the Broadwaters of Aiken, S.C. And what, Refrigerator Perry was asked by phone yesterday, did they serve?

"You name it—it was there," he said.

What did you eat?

"A little of everything," he said.

A little of everything, he was asked, or a lot of everything?

"Both," said Perry.

This Thanksgiving at home in Chicago, it was, in fact, only a little of everything—a little of the turkey that his wife, Sherry Perry, cooked, and a little of the trimmings and the stuffing and the broccoli and the cauliflower and the brussels sprouts and the two sweet potato pies and the two coconut pies.

Some philosophers theorize that Refrigerator Perry, who stands 6 feet 2, has a 22-inch neck and sports a 52-inch waist, has suddenly become a beloved national phenomenon because he is not only galloping for touchdowns for the Chicago Bears—Coach Mike Ditka imports him from the defensive unit when the team has the ball close to the goal line—but is flouting our madness for thinness, and doing it with gusto.

Actually, Refrigerator Perry is on a diet and watches his behemoth's weight like a hawk. He is down to 308 and holding steady.

The Bears, who drafted him as a defensive lineman in the first round out of Clemson last April, decided that his best playing weight was between 305 and 310. He was up to about 380 pounds last year, but reported to training camp in August at 325. It took him only a matter of weeks to slim down to his present poundage.

Twice a week now, on Tuesdays and Fridays, the team weighs in. It is in Perry's contract that at each weigh-in during the season he receives a bonus of $1,000 if he comes in at 310 or under.

He's thrilled about it. "I haven't missed on a thousand dollars but once," he said.

Mrs. Perry considered holding off Thanksgiving dinner until after the weigh-in on Friday, but decided against it. "William is careful at the table," she said.

What then are the diet secrets of Refrigerator Perry?

"For one thing," said Sherry Perry, "he doesn't eat as fast as he used to. I remember at a Wendy's when I first saw him eat a hamburger. He ate half of it in one bite. I said, 'Gosh, William, slow down.'

"And at dinner, I'd be amazed at him eating and eating and eating. I'd say, 'William, isn't that enough?' "

The Perrys have been married for three and a half years, and in the beginning, Mrs. Perry said, "cooking for William was very hectic."

"You have to remember," she added, "that I wasn't used to this kind of eating. I'm 5 feet 5 inches and weigh 120 pounds and I've always eaten small portions.

"To keep William's weight down now, I put the food away after dinner, and don't let it set out. He used to love to finish dinner and then help himself to whatever was left over.

"And William used to sit in front of the television and drink cans of beer and snack the whole time on potato chips and cookies and what have you. There was no weight limit when he played for Clemson. Now William is showing a lot of control. I'm proud of him. He doesn't snack at all. He says it doesn't bother him, and it seems to be true."

So popular is the Bears' hefty rookie that in Chicago many people have a picture of The Refrigerator on their refrigerator. Do the Perrys?

"All we have on our refrigerator," said Mrs. Perry, "is the door."

William says he has a lot to be thankful for this Thanksgiving. "I thank the Good Lord for giving me health and strength and my little girl"—the Perrys have a 3-year-old daughter, Latavia— "and my wonderful wife and a good family.

"I've been blessed. I'm thankful that Coach Ditka gave me a chance, and I'm grateful for all that's happened to me. It's crazy, and sometimes my wife and I sit down at night and look at each other and laugh about the whole thing. Do you really believe this? But it's been great. I mean, all the popularity, all the endorsement opportunities, all the good feelings. And I'm not going to change just because I got this and I got that. I'm still going to be the same old William Perry. It's me, as I am, same personality, same kid who grew up with a family of 12 brothers and sisters, same kind of character."

He was reminded that he wasn't quite the William Perry of old. There is a little less of him.

"Weightwise," he said with a laugh, "yes. But that's all."

The other change, of course, is that on occasion Ditka installs The Refrigerator in the backfield.

"I don't know all that much about football," said Mrs. Perry, "and when we were in college I used to say to William, 'I'd love it if you ran with the ball.' And he'd say, 'Sherry, don't even say that. It's something I'll never do.' "

At first this season, he was put into the backfield to plow holes for the lean running backs. Then, in a startling development, he was given a chance to carry the ball and ran for two touchdowns, each was for 1 yard—on the last, a week ago, he dived over the line like Walter Payton, or Walter Mitty. He has also caught a 4-yard scoring pass, and leaped up with glee and spiked the ball.

"To tell you the truth," said Mrs. Perry, "I'd love for him to run a long one with the ball. I'd like to see him run through a whole team, meet 'em and knock 'em down flat and keep going.

"I love to see number 72 go in the game. I just wait to see what William's going to do next."

She is not alone. A goodly number of football fans, and other members of an intrigued and delighted citizenry, watch and wait with her.

An Afternoon in Gleason's Gym

New York, December 15, 1984

There is the old man, and the young man. The old man is teaching the young man the skills that made him so proficient when he was young. "He's catchin' on real good," says the old man.

They are in Gleason's Gymnasium on West 30th Street just off Eighth Avenue. It is a small gym, with two boxing rings, and the young man is alone and shadowboxing in the ring farthest from the door. In the adjoining ring, there is the thump and grunt of boxers sparring. In a corner of the gym, a rope is being skipped with a slap-slap-slap. The smell of sweat clings to the old blue-gray walls of Gleason's

The young man wears a red sweatshirt, black boxing trunks, and his hands are taped to the knuckles. The old man at ringside keenly observes the young man move about on the squeaky canvas. The old man, as lean as the young man but no longer as muscular, wears a blue turtleneck sweater, jeans, and has wisps of gray in his hair.

The young man is Ricky Wallace Young, age 24, a professional prize-fighter for 19 months. The older man is Bobby McQuillar, age 61, who quit fighting when he was nearly the same age as the young man, at 25 years old.

The old man was a contender in the lightweight division, at 135 pounds. The young man is slightly heavier, at 140, and is a junior welterweight.

The old man had dreams of fame and fortune when he turned professional, just as the young man has now. The old man, though, didn't realize those dreams.

He quit after he killed a man in the ring. It was the night of September 29, 1948, at Chicago Stadium, and Bobby McQuillar, who was, he says, "fixin' for a title fight" with the champion, Ike Williams, floored one Kid Dinamita, a fighter from the Dominican Republic. Dinamita is Spanish for dynamite. McQuillar hit him with a crushing right hand that sent Kid Dinamita to the canvas. The bell saved him. But he was unable to come out for the ninth round. He was carried out of the ring, and five hours later, on a hospital operating table, died of a cerebral hemorrhage. Kid Dinamita was 22 years old.

"I had no desire to fight after that," said McQuillar. He said his record was 72–6, and he had beaten three men who went on to hold world titles, Joe Brown, Jimmy Carter and Sandy Saddler. With a smile now, the old man said, "I was washed up at 25."

He returned home to Detroit, earned a degree from the Detroit Institute of Commerce and started work in a pharmacy. Not long afterward, he accepted an offer to help train a fighter, Johnny Bratton. McQuillar would also help train Sugar Ray Robinson and, as he calls him, "Muhammad"—Muhammad Ali.

"There is a thrill," said the old man, "in helping a talented youngster make the good moves, watch him improve. It's inspiring. Boxing kinda gets in your blood."

The young man, Ricky Young, is disciplined, says the old man; he takes this profession seriously. He has won 11 of 12 professional fights. As an underdog to the veteran Angel Cruz last August, in a bout for the New York State junior welterweight championship, Young lost a close decision in 12 rounds. "I'm an up-and-comer," he said. "Definitely."

Ricky Young is a high school graduate, and lives in a housing project in Harlem. He lives with his parents—his father is a bookkeeper, his mother works as a trimmer in a clothing factory—and with his two younger sisters. It is a tough neighborhood, he says, but has a lot of good people in it, but some bad ones, too. He would like to move away, to make enough money to buy his family a home "on Long Island or upstate New York."

Young had been employed as a carpenter's assistant when he decided to go to a gym "just to get in shape." He found he had a talent, and began to nurture it.

"Boxing gives me a chance to maybe be rich," said Ricky Young. He wasn't interested in any kind of street life in pursuit of wealth, because "you always have to be lookin' over your shoulder," he said.

"People told me when I went into boxing, "Hey, Ricky, you're going to get brain-damaged,' " he said. "My mother, especially, was worried when I started training. But then she came to my first fight—and it's the same reaction from the others. They were surprised how good I was, and they got behind me. And they cheered. Oh, that makes you feel good. 'Hey, Ricky,' they say, 'you fought beautiful. You fought smart.' It's a feeling like you're on a cloud.

"I always liked boxing and boxers. They used to talk about Joe Louis, a great fighter and a great person. They said that a lady couldn't pay her rent and had no place to stay. Joe Louis went into his pocket and gave her not one month's rent, but three months' rent! Stories like that overwhelm you.

"I'd like to have that kind of respect and prestige as a champion, too, to be looked up to in the community."

He understands how dangerous boxing can be. "You have to be a scared fighter—one that doesn't want to get hit," he said. "The best fighters are scared, and great on defense, like Sugar Ray Leonard."

Ricky Young is aware that the American Medical Association and others have condemned boxing and want it banned. "I don't think it should be," he said. "It should be monitored closely. But it's a beautiful sport, an art and a science. You're not out to hurt anybody. It's the slippin', duckin', blockin' and scorin' that makes it so nice.

"There are dangers in other sports, and people die and get hurt in football, hockey and car racing, too. As athletes we know the risks when we step into the ring."

The old man said, "There's gonna be dangers but you can do all right if you learn the skills, stay in shape, leave the ladies and drugs alone, and take boxing as a profession and not as a game. It ain't nothin' to play with."

Ricky Young, wearing black boxing gloves now, was at the heavy bag, and began to pound it. The old man was nearby. "Stick it to it," he urged, "stick hard."

Fighting Family Gets Together

New York, October 29, 1983

The setting for the news conference for the television film "We Are Family," about the fighting Frazier clan, was held yesterday afternoon in an elegant, chandeliered room in the St. Regis Hotel.

As befitting the occasion, the patriarch of the family, Smokin' Joe Frazier, the former heavyweight champion of the world, showed up in stylish apparel—a gray pinstriped suit, a gray pinstriped vest and no shirt.

That is, his chest was bare, except for two gold pendants that nestled among the bristles.

"How come no shirt today, Joe?" someone asked.

"Too warm out," he said. Now that he mentioned it, it was an unseasonably clement day.

Besides that, Joe Frazier needs fewer habiliments than in former times. He is thicker of neck and heftier of breadbasket than when he was the champion 10 years ago.

He now weighs about 250 pounds and fought at around 215. He is, though, still active in pugilism.

He is the manager and trainer for six members of the family, all but one of whom are undefeated. The best known of them, Marvis, his 23-year-old son, with a 10–0 record, is fighting Larry Holmes for the heavyweight championship November 25 in Las Vegas.

Marvis resembles his father in the face, though he's taller and leaner. Like his father, Marvis appeared in modish attire, with a pinstriped suit, a brown one, and two gold lavalieres. But Marvis wore a shirt, for some reason.

The other Fraziers hadn't yet arrived.

Mike Cohen, who was running the news conference, said, "There's going to be a lot of Fraziers on the undercard with Marvis, but how many, I don't know."

Someone asked which of the other fighting Fraziers were expected at the St. Regis.

"Three others," he said. "There's Mark, a junior welterweight, who is 4–0 and Joe's nephew; Rodney, a heavyweight, 10–0 and Joe's nephew, and," said Cohen, "Hector and Joe, Jr."

"That's four," it was mentioned.

"Hector's fighting name is Smokin' Joe Jr.," said Cohen. He is 4–0. Hector is Joe's other son; Joe has five daughters.

As it turned out, Mark and Smokin' Joe Jr. showed up, but Rodney didn't, and no one knew where he was.

Perhaps Rodney was still celebrating his victory last month over Smokin' Perkin. No relation.

"But he ain't smokin' no more," said Frazier. "We took the name back."

Rodney is kin because he is the son of Joe's sister Rebecca, one of Joe's 12 brothers and sisters, and Mark is the son of Joe's brother Tommy.

The two other Frazier fighters not in attendance are Bernard—son of Martha, Joe's sister—who is 4–1, and Joe Smith.

"Smith? Who is Smith?" someone asked Joe Frazier.

"An in-law," replied Joe. "He hasn't made his pro debut yet."

Marvis Frazier was being questioned about his credentials—only 10 pro fights—in challenging a veteran like Holmes for the heavyweight title.

"People don't understand what the Frazier camp is like," said Marvis. "I've boxed some tough fighters, like Mike Dokes and Tex Cobb and Jimmy Young and Pinklon Thomas—and Joe Frazier. Yeah, Pops gets in the ring now and then.

"And I know how to fight Holmes. Pops showed me. I'm gonna stick him and move on him and whirl him and stick 'im again. My time has come."

Did he get this chance because he's Joe Frazier's son?

"I'm his son, all right, but he don't punch for me and he don't get hit for me and he don't get up at 4 in the morning for me," said Marvis.

"But he does keep me pumped up. One time I was having a tough go of it and in my corner after the seventh round he says, 'Want me to take the three rounds for you?' I laughed and said, 'No, I got it, Pops.'"

Someone from Total Video, the syndicate that will show the film that is scheduled for television in January, put his arm on Marvis's shoulder and said to a few of the newspeople, "Can we borrow Joe Jr. for a few minutes?"

Shortly after, Marvis was asked if people often call him Joe Jr.

"Sometimes they do," he said.

What do you say?

"I say, 'How ya doin'?'"

Nearby, Joe Frazier said of Marvis, "The kid is smart. He hits you from any position, any angle."

What does Marvis do best?

"Hurt people," said Joe. "With either hand."

Frazier, who is in the corner for each of his fighting sons and nephews, said that, no, he wouldn't send any of them into the ring if he didn't think they were capable of winning.

Does he ever feel the punches when the lads are hit?

"Nah," said Frazier. "I don't feel nuthin'."

In another part of the room, Smokin' Joe Jr. said, "We don't have disagreements with my father. He's the master. That's what we call him. He's not only been the heavyweight champ of the world, he's been the Olympic gold medal winner. He wasn't a guy who just came and went. He's been and stayed."

Mark Frazier said, "He always tells us, No matter what you do, be the best at it. If you're going to be a fighter, be the best fighter. If you're going to be a bum, be the best bum. And we listen to Uncle Billy."

You mean Uncle Joe, it was suggested.

"No, sometimes we call Uncle Joe Uncle Billy."

Well, there are a lot of people in the family, it's easy to confuse. . .

"We've always called him Uncle Billy."

Why?

"I don't know, but we have."

Joe Frazier was asked about it.

"I was called Billy since I was a boy," Joe said, "You see, Daddy had an A-Model Ford. And it was dependable. And I was dependable."

But what does that have to do with the car?

"The car's name was Billy."

The Wimbledon Finalist

Jericho, Long Island, August 27, 1983

It was in the first round in the Hamlet Challenge Cup Tennis Tournament. He was warming up for his match and wearing what has become in the last eight weeks one of the more recognizable symbols in tennis, his wide bandanna tied round his forehead.

His hair is shoulder-length and his face distinctive—high, lean cheekbones, firm jaw, closely knit eyebrows and dark eyes.

Often now, even when he is not wearing the bandanna, people come up to him on the street in New York, or Cincinnati, or Paris, or Stuttgart, and say, "I'm sure I know you from somewhere."

There was a crackle now from the public address system, and the announcer at the Hamlet tournament was about to introduce the players. First the opponent, Andrés Gómez of Ecuador. And then the player with the bandanna:

"From Auckland, New Zealand, 1983 finalist at Wimbledon, Chris Lewis."

That's where they saw him.

It was just eight weeks ago, on Sunday, July 3, that Chris Lewis was at Centre Court at Wimbledon, playing John McEnroe in the final. And television cameras focused closely on his face, and caught the bandanna that is worn thicker than that of any other player.

A television audience of millions throughout the world viewed, and many, surely, rooted for the scrappy 5-11, 180-pound Lewis. For his presence in the Wimbledon final was startling, and warming.

He seemed to have come out of nowhere—an unseeded 26-year-old New Zealander who was No. 91 in the world ranking. He was going against the No. 1 player for the championship of the most prestigious tennis tournament in the world.

Before the Wimbledon final, Lewis had received more than 5,000 telegrams wishing him well. It was choking the communications section at Wimbledon, he would be told, and it seemed impossible to get a telegram to anyone else.

The reaction was not just because of Lewis's dramatic possibilities, but also a statement about McEnroe, who has rankled many, especially the English, with his sometimes churlish court behavior.

The crowd of 14,500 at Centre Court gave Lewis a moving ovation, and he says that if ever a crowd could will someone to win, this would have been it. He felt, he says, "that the world was behind me."

There had been seven other unseeded players to make the final, but none had been ranked so far down as he. Each had lost in the final. He would recall that at that moment his mouth was very dry.

Lewis's story would end not like Cinderella's. McEnroe dominated the match and won easily, 6–2, 6–2, 6–2.

Now, at the Hamlet Cup tournament, there was a polite round of applause from about 300 or so spectators at the introductions. This was the last match in the day; earlier, the stands had been filled with about 1,500 people.

It is a small, makeshift tennis stadium, with bleachers set up in the middle of a condominium development. The court was illuminated by several light poles and by the full moon that, at the beginning of the match, shone through a nearby fir tree.

The sparse crowd was quiet. At times, all that was heard was the smack of the ball, the grunt of the players, and the crickets with their small mariachi bands.

The match was played on a hard surface, the kind that somewhat inhibits a player like Lewis, who, on grass, spends a good part of the time flying and sprawling after shots.

"But on a hard court," he said, "sometimes I find myself in midair, and then crunch."

"I'm very aware of having been the Wimbledon finalist," said Lewis, after his 6–4, 6–4 victory. "I think it puts a little more pressure on my opponent when they announce it before the match. He's got to be thinking, 'This guy's a player.'

"What it did was actually confirm for me what I thought about myself since I won the junior championship at Wimbledon."

That was in 1975, when he was 18. He and others expected a great deal of him when he left the junior ranks and joined the pro circuit full-time. And although he made the semifinals and finals of some Grand Prix tournaments, and won a tournament at Munich in 1981, he remained a player ranked in the range of 30s to 60s.

Early this year he grew discouraged, sloughed off in his practice schedule and fell to 91. Then he got angry with himself, and about six or seven weeks before Wimbledon decided to practice harder than ever.

"At Wimbledon things began to drop right," he said. "I went through the round of 16, then the quarters, and semis, and suddenly I was going to face McEnroe in the finals. Incredible. A dream. Well, for the next 48 hours I didn't listen to a radio or TV, or read any newspapers. I didn't want to put any added pressure on myself. But I got so many telegrams, and the Prime Minister of New Zealand, Mr. Muldoon, called and told me that whether I won or lost, the whole country was proud of my achievement.

"I won the first service, but then John just took over. It was like someone had let air out of my balloon. He's an amazing player. He seems to know by instinct where you're going to hit the ball, and where you're not going to be on his return. And he keeps the ball on the racket longer than anyone else. It's a gift you're born with, like a great artist is born with something special."

Since Wimbledon, Lewis has played six of the last eight weeks—including in the Davis Cup. His best individual finish in a major tournament was reaching the quarterfinals in the United States Clay Court Championships at Indianapolis. Yesterday, he defeated Guillermo Vilas to reach the semifinals here. Lewis is entered in the United States Open, which begins Tuesday.

"I saw John recently," said Lewis, "and he thought I'd been playing too much. Maybe he's right. Wimbledon and the Davis Cup right after took a lot out of me. But I feel now I can play at that highest level again. I have confidence in myself. If I made it to the top once, why not again?"

Thomas Makes a Decision

New York, April 27, 1981

It was Draft Day in the ghetto. That's what everyone there called it. On a few days each year, chieftains of the notorious Vice Lords street gang appeared at certain homes on the West Side of Chicago to take recruits.

On this summer night in 1966 about 25 Vice Lord chiefs stopped in front of the home of Mary Thomas. She had nine children, seven of them boys, ranging from Lord Henry, 15 years old, to Isiah, 5. The Thomases lived on the first floor of a two-story red brick building on Congress Street, facing the Eisenhower Expressway.

One of the Lords rang the bell. Mary Thomas, wearing glasses, answered the door. She saw behind him the rest of his gang, all wearing gold tams and black capes, and some hand guns in their waistbands that glinted under the streetlamps.

"We want your boys," the gang leader told her. "They can't walk around here and not be in no gang."

She looked him in the eye. "There's only one gang around here, and that's the Thomas gang," she said, "and I lead that."

"If you don't bring those boys out, we'll get 'em in the street," he said.

She shut the door. The gang members waited. She walked through the living room, where the rest of the family sat. Isiah, frightened, watched her go into the bedroom and return with a sawed-off shotgun. She opened the front door.

She pointed the gun at the caped figure before her. "Get off my porch," she said, "or I'll blow you 'cross the Expressway."

He stepped back, and slowly he and his gang disappeared into the night.

Isiah Thomas never joined a gang, and was protected from the ravages of street life—the dope, the drinking, the stealing, the killings—by his mother and his brothers, even those who eventually succumbed to the streets. Two of his brothers became heroin addicts, one was a pimp, a couple would be jailed, and one would become a Vice Lords chief.

Isiah, though, was the baby of the family, and its hope.

He became an honor student in grade school and high school, an all-American basketball player in high school and college, and a 6-foot, 1-inch point guard, led Indiana University to the National Collegiate Athletic Association championship last month. After only a few weeks out of high school, he was a standout in the United States team that won the gold medal in the 1979 Pan-American Games, and was a starter on the 1980 United States Olympic team.

The pros liked what they saw. "He's a terrific talent," said Rod Thorn, general manager of the Chicago Bulls. "Not only physically—and he seems adept at every phase of the game—but he has a charisma, an ability to inspire confidence in his teammates that only a few players have, like Larry Bird and Magic Johnson and Julius Erving."

Last weekend, Isiah Thomas, a 19-year-old sophomore and B student majoring in forensics, with an eye toward law school, made an important decision. He passed up his last two years of college basketball to declare his eligibility for the National Basketball Association's draft on June 9. Thomas said that three teams—New Jersey, Detroit and Chicago—had been told he could expect an offer of at least $1 million to sign.

Thomas had wrestled with his decision all season.

"Don't do it," said Bobby Knight, the Indiana basketball coach. "You can still improve in basketball. You could be worth more."

"Stay in school," said Quinn Buckner, a former Indiana player and now with the Milwaukee Bucks. "The college experience at your age is valuable and can't ever be repeated."

"What's left for you to prove in college?" said his brother Gregory.

"Go only if the price is right," said his former high school coach, Gene Pingatore. "Don't sell yourself short."

"Son," said Mary Thomas, "do what makes you happy."

The idea of turning pro had been with Isiah for as long as he can remember, instilled by his brothers, who had their own basketball dreams squashed.

"There was a lot to consider," said Thomas. He sat on the arm of a couch in his small apartment in the Fountain Park complex on the Indiana campus in Bloomington. He wore a red baseball cap, a blue U.S.A. Olympic jacket, jeans and yellow sneakers. He speaks softly, thoughtfully, with careful articulation. Sometimes he'll flash that warm, dimpled smile that has become familiar from newspaper photos and national magazine covers. Behind that smile is also a toughness and intensity—twice last season he was involved in fights in games.

"I know I'm a role model for a lot of people back in the ghetto," said Thomas. "Not too many of us get the chance to get out, to go to college. If I quit school, what effect would that have on them?

"And I had said I wanted to be a lawyer, and one day return there and help the people. They need it. I've seen kids who stole a pair of pants and they get a five-year prison sentence. Literally. Because there was no adequate help for them. I know that I'll get my law degree. I know you can only play basketball for so many years. Then you've got the rest of your life ahead of you.

"And I have to think of my family. My mother worked hard all her life and for not much money. My father left when I was three years old, and my mom kept us together by herself. She worked in the community center, she worked in the church, she did whatever she could. She's got a job with the housing authority in Chicago now, and she shouldn't be working. Her eyes are bad, and her heart's not good. I'd like her to quit."

He feels that with the connections he makes in basketball he can help his brothers. He has already opened a few doors. Larry has a job with the city housing and Mark is with the police department.

"I can always go back to school," Isiah said. "But I can't always make a million dollars. I won't always have a chance to provide stability for my family. And I'm doing it at basketball, a game I love."

Isiah Thomas was a prodigy in basketball the way Mozart was in music. At age three, Amadeus was composing on a harpsichord; at three, Isiah could dribble and shoot baskets. He was the halftime entertainment at the neighborhood Catholic Youth Organization games. "We gave Isiah an old jersey that fell like a dress on him, and he wore black Oxfords and tossed up shots with a high arc," said Ted Kalinowski, who was called Brother Alexis before he left the order. "Isiah was amazing."

By the time Thomas was in the fourth grade, he was a standout on the eighth-grade team at Our Lady of Sorrows.

His mother and brothers watched him closely. Mary Thomas made sure that he went straight home from school and did not dawdle in the streets. "If I did," he said, "my brothers would kick my butt."

From the time he was in grade school, his brothers lectured him. The seven of them sat in a bedroom and closed the door so that their mother and two sisters would not hear the horror stories of the street. They would take him for a walking tour and point out dangers. "They told me about the mistakes they had made, so that I wouldn't have to make them," said Thomas.

Lord Henry, for one, had been an all-city basketball player at St. Phillips; people in the neighborhood contend that he was the best basketball player in the family. He still holds the Catholic League single-season scoring record. But he had problems with discipline and grades and was thrown out of school. He went into the streets, and became a junkie. Isiah could see for himself the tortures his brother went through and the suffering it caused his mother.

As an eighth-grader, Isiah sought a scholarship to Weber High School, a Catholic League basketball power. The coach turned him down—too short. He was 5-6. "Look, I'm 6-4," Larry Thomas argued to the coach. "My brother will grow just as tall."

Gene Pingatore, the coach at St. Joseph's in Westchester, a Chicago suburb, was convinced. "He was a winner," said Pingatore. "He had that special aura."

At Westchester, a predominately white school in a white middle-class neighborhood, Thomas endeavored to learn textbook English. At one point, his brother Gregory was confused. Isiah recalls his brother saying, "You done forgot to talk like a nigger. Better not come around here like no sissy white boy."

"Hey," Isiah said, laughing, "pull up on that jive."

But the brothers, like Isiah, understood the importance of language, and the handle it could provide in helping to escape the ghetto, a dream they shared.

"What I was doing," said Isiah, "was becoming fluent in two languages."

Isiah would rise at 5:30 in the morning to begin the 1½-hour journey by elevated train and bus to Westchester.

"Sometimes I'd look out the window and see Isiah going to school in the dark and I'd cry," said Mary Thomas. "I'd give him grits with honey and butter for breakfast. And felt bad that I couldn't afford eggs and bacon for him, too. He sure did like to eat."

Although he excelled in basketball, Isiah neglected his studies and nearly flunked out of high school after his freshman year.

"You're a screwed-up kid," said Larry. "You can go one of two ways from here. I had a choice like this once. I chose hustlin'. It's a disgustin' kind of life. You got the chance of a lifetime."

Pingatore emphasized that without a C average he could not get a college scholarship, under NCAA rules.

"From that point on," recalls Isiah's sister Ruby, "he was a changed kid." He made the St. Joseph's honor roll in each of his next three years.

He also led his team to second place in the Illinois state high school tournament, and was chosen all-America. He had his pick of hundreds of college scholarships. He chose Indiana because it was close and because Bobby Knight played it straight. "He didn't try to bribe me," said Mary Thomas. "Other schools offered hundreds of thousands of dollars. One coach promised to buy me a beautiful house. Another one said that there'd be a Lear jet so I could go to all Isiah's games. All Bobby Knight promised was he'd try to get Isiah a good education and give him a good opportunity to get better in basketball. He said that I might not even be able to get a ticket for a basketball game. I liked that." She also got tickets, and went to all of Isiah's games, sometimes traveling to Bloomington by bus.

He made all-Big Ten as a freshman. Last season he was a consensus all-America. Despite this, he and Coach Knight had conflicts. Thomas appreciated Knight's basketball mind, and knew that the coach relied on his ability as a floor leader, but Thomas had trouble swallowing what he considered Knight's sometimes insulting behavior.

Once, Thomas, who had been appointed team captain, decided to talk with Knight about the team's poor morale. Thomas believed that Indiana—going poorly at the beginning of the season—had some of the best players in the country, and could win the championship if they could pull together and not fight the coach. "There's a problem here, coach," said Isiah.

"There's no problem here," replied Knight.

Indiana, however did improve and made it to the final of the NCAA tournament against North Carolina at the Spectrum in Philadelphia on the night of March 30.

Amid the blaring of the school bands and the waving of pom-

poms and the screams from the crowd—the Indiana rooters were sectioned on one side of the court in red and white, the school colors, and the North Carolina fans on the other side wearing blue and white—the game was tightly played. North Carolina led by 26–25 as Isiah Thomas took the ball from under the Tar Heels' basket and dribbled slowly upcourt. There were only 12 seconds to go in the half and tense Indiana fans wondered if the Hoosiers would get another shot off, especially with Thomas's casualness.

"I didn't want the team to press, I wanted them to relax, and if they saw I wasn't rushing I hoped they wouldn't rush, either," Thomas said later. With two seconds to go, he hit Randy Wittman with a pass in the corner, and Wittman connected, giving Indiana its first lead of the game, and a terrific lift as it went to the locker room.

Starting the second half, Thomas stole two straight passes from North Carolina and scored. Indiana went ahead by 31–26 and went on to a 63–50 victory. "Those two steals," said Dean Smith, the North Carolina coach, "were the turning point of the game." Thomas scored a game-high 23 points, and had five assists and four steals. He was named the outstanding player of the championship tournament.

As soon as the game ended, Indiana fans rushed on the court. One of them, Thomas saw, was a black woman in a red suit jacket with a button on her lapel. The button read, "Isiah Thomas's Mom. Mrs. Mary Thomas." Near the center of the court, they embraced. She was crying and it looked as if Isiah was holding back tears.

"Thanks, Mom, thanks for everything you've gone through for me. I hope I can do something for you."

"You done enough, honey," she said.

Reporters and cameramen were all around them. And Isiah whispered in his mother's ear, "Well, you can do one more thing for me," he said.

"What's that, baby?"

"I heard you in the first half when I threw a bad pass. You hollered, 'What the hell are you doin'?' Don't cuss at me on the court. I was fixin' to get it together."

Then Isiah was scooted off to receive the winner's trophy. And the woman who wore the button proudly saying she was Isiah Thomas's mom took out a handkerchief and wiped her eyes.

Bumpy Roads

One More Chance

Omaha, June 29, 1981

Dusk was settling over Rosenblatt Stadium here and the sinking sun lit the light towers in the outfield red. It was humid, but a wind had picked up—an ill wind, very ill, bringing the unmistakable odor from the sewage plant a half-mile away.

Jim Buckner hardly noticed. He sat in the corner of the home team's dugout while most of the other Omaha Royals were on the field randomly warming up for the game against the Springfield Redbirds. Buckner slapped a gnat on the blue stirrup stocking of his uniform, and then discharged a stream of tobacco juice from under his furry red mustache.

A reporter sat down beside him. "Heard anything yet?" Buckner asked.

"No," said the reporter.

"Just thought you might have a pipeline," said Buckner, with a little smile.

This was last Tuesday night, possibly the last night of Buckner's last best chance in professional baseball.

For 10 years Buckner, a left-handed outfielder, has bounced around the minor leagues, always with the dream to make the major leagues—and join his older brother, Bill, a first baseman-outfielder with the Chicago Cubs and last season's National League batting champion. Bill Buckner has been a major leaguer for 12 seasons.

Jim Buckner is 28 years old, long in the tooth for a minor leaguer. He had been brought up from Jacksonville to Omaha, Kansas City's Class AAA affiliate, to replace an injured player. He was told that the stay would be two weeks, or until 23-year-old Pat Sheridan, a hot prospect, returned to health. The two weeks were up, and Sheridan had recuperated. But Buckner thought—hoped—he had a chance to stick with the club. And imagining that if he did well and the major-league player strike ended and Kansas City needed help . . .

If he got the ax now and was returned to Jacksonville, the

Double A club, he might never get this high in organized ball again. This was his third time around in Triple A.

"Joe said he'd tell the decision after the game," said Buckner. He referred to Joe Sparks, the Omaha manager. "Why the suspense? Why don't they just come out with it?

"It's like the time I played with Toledo in a doubleheader against Tidewater. I was traded to Tidewater sometime during the afternoon but no one told me. I found out in the fifth inning of the second game. Ray Smith, one of the Tidewater players, said to me, 'Our manager just said, "Boys, don't ride Buckner too hard, he's on your team now." ' After the game I just changed locker rooms." Buckner laughed, and shook his head.

He has played with 12 teams and 7 major league systems in every part of the country, and in Mexico and South America. He estimates his career batting average is .295. He's had some outstanding years, including his first, 1973, when he hit .355 for Lewiston, Idaho, and was named best player in the Rookie League. "I was unbelievable," he said. But he was relatively small for an outfielder—5 feet 9½ inches tall, 160 pounds, compared with his brother Bill's 6-1, 185. Jim does not hit for power consistently, but has a good arm and good range and decent speed.

However, there has always been someone just ahead of him on the ladder.

"This could be the end, but I just don't know," he said. "You hate to quit when you're so close." And Sparks had told him that he liked what he saw—that Jim hustled, that he was patient and that he'd eventually start to hit (he was batting only .150 as a part-time player), and that even if he was sent down there was always a distinct chance he would return.

But one day it would have to end. Buckner knows that. So does his wife, Jayne.

When Jim was called up to Omaha, Jayne, three months pregnant, moved from Jacksonville with their 18-month-old son back to her parents' home in Asheville, N.C.—to wait out the decision with the Royals.

They had married in 1977, and she has traveled all around the minor leagues with him, working as a waitress, secretary or temporary help. Three times she has driven cross-country alone, following him after he was traded or cut.

They had met in 1975 at a ball game while Jim was playing for Asheville, and they fell in love. Before the last game that season, Jayne said she couldn't bear to go because he'd be leaving afterward. Jim considered that, then suggested she return home with him to Napa, Calif. On the spur of the moment, Jayne, then 19, said yes to Jim, who was 22. That was her first cross-country trip, and she made it hanging onto Jim as they roared along the highways on his motorcycle.

"It was all an adventure then," Jayne says, "and we were young and everything was new. We hardly had time to get bored. But now, well, we've got a family. It's different. It's a grind now. To say the least."

But Jayne has never suggested that Jim quit. "In 20 years I don't want him to blame me because he felt he didn't give his career the full chance," she says.

Buckner doesn't want regrets. "I know I can play up there," he says, "but there does come a time when you have to make a final decision. And I'd like to do what's right for my family."

The biggest problem as a minor leaguer is not so much the day-to-day uncertainty, or the fierce competition, or the dreary 20-hour bus rides, or the parks with lights so bad an outfielder needs a lantern. The biggest problem is the money, especially for a family man.

Buckner earns a $1,600 a month for six months. The $9,600 a year doesn't go far, and he's always hard-pressed to meet his bills. In contrast, Bill Buckner earns $400,000 a year with the Cubs.

"Sure, I'd be lying if I said I haven't been envious—his money, his success, the glamour, but I'm not jealous of Bill," says Jim. "He deserves everything he's got. He's the hardest-working, most-disciplined guy I know. I'm proud of him. He has such a hunger—even more than me. I'll never forget the time he played against the Vacaville Prison team. It's a maximum security prison. They're dangerous people in there. And the umpire, an inmate, called a third strike on Bill. Bill hates to strike out more than anything. He started hollering. It was scary. He didn't care where he was. I wouldn't have done that. I'm aggressive, but I'm a little more mellow than that."

He may be now. But Jim had a wild streak in him that got him in trouble early in his career, and he admits that, though he played hard on the field, he may have played too hard off it. "And I got a reputation," he says. "But I've turned that around."

Buckner was signed in 1973 by the Orioles after his freshman year at Yavapai College, a two-year school in Arizona. He was a 38th-round draft choice, out of 39 rounds. He was cut by Baltimore in 1976, but he was determined to make baseball a career. At one point, he paid his own way to the Cubs' training camp, and was dropped, but several weeks later they called and offered him a job with their Midland, Tex., team. He was visiting a friend in Lake Tahoe at the time. "I jumped into my Volkswagen and raced down the mountain," he said. "I got a speeding ticket going 90."

In the last few off-seasons Jim has worked as a hand on Bill's 1,000-acre cattle ranch near Boise, Idaho. Their oldest brother, Bob, manages the spread. "When I finish playing, I could go up there," he said. "Bill would like me to. We're a close family. But I want to do something on my own. Maybe sell sporting goods—eventually own a store."

Bill, though, has always refrained from advising Jim. "The more I worry about him," said Bill, "the more things seem to happen. But I respect his decisions. I know he's going to have to give up baseball soon—unless something unexpected happens. When the strike hit I was thinking about seeing him play, but I didn't have the heart. I want him to do well so bad it makes me nervous."

There were times for Jim when being Bill's brother was difficult. People asked him why he never made the big leagues, and sometimes he wondered if the team was keeping him around just because he was Bill Buckner's brother—and maybe they were missing something.

"Then one day I ran across a baseball card of Bill," said Jim, "and on the back it said, 'Brother of James Patrick.' It made me feel real proud that I was his brother. I know it sounds stupid, but it really made me feel good."

Now, at Rosenblatt Stadium, Jim started in the right field against the Springfield Redbirds. The game wasn't an inspiring one for him. He went hitless in four times at bat. The Royals lost, 7–5.

After the game, Jim slowly removed his dusty uniform and then dropped his personal equipment into his canvas baseball bag, just in case he would be shipped out: three pairs of spikes, three gloves, two pairs of cut-off long underwear, three sleeveless T-shirts, one jockstrap and two garters.

Still no word from the manager. "When do they tell people around here?" asked Buckner.

Just then, the clubhouse man came by. "Joe wants to see you," he said.

Wearing only his shower clogs, Buckner disappeared into Joe Sparks's office. A few minutes later he came out. Several players watched him out of the corner of their eyes. Buckner is a popular player because he's loose and a hustler, and he's respected, being an elder statesman. Several had told him they hoped he would stay, and because he batted in the winning run in two games, they said, "They can't let you go now."

Buckner sat down on the stool in front of his locker. The player next to him looked up. Their eyes met.

"I'm gone," said Buckner, directly, quietly. "Jacksonville."

Boy of Summer, Briefly

New York, January 30, 1985

In just a few weeks, Dick Teed will pack his bags and leave his home in wintry Windsor, Conn., for wintry Orlando, Fla. Teed will include among his travel items a list of high school and college baseball schedules, prospects' forms, a stopwatch and—despite the recent frost down South—a bottle of suntan lotion.

Dick Teed, age 58, gray-haired and trim at 5 feet 11, is a scout for the Los Angeles Dodgers. He once played for the Brooklyn Dodgers—*once* is the correct word, since he appeared in just one game, as a pinch hitter in 1953, and struck out.

Now, Teed will make his annual six-week tour of training sites of bookish baseball players, for many college and some high school teams, even those from the North, take at least a week or two in Florida to play games.

What he won't pack is a chemical he purchased not long ago that he uses for his own purposes. He calls it "Dri-It."

"It's a chemical that can dry a wet baseball in 40 seconds," he said. "It's a gritty solution in a can. You put the wet ball in, shake it around, and it comes out dry. I try to sell it to schools and the minor leagues, who want to save on baseballs. The major leagues don't need it."

The chemical business is for the off-season. When Teed dons his scouting togs, he puts away the stuff that—who knows?—might one day make him rich.

Even baseball scouts do not abhor wealth, though sometimes it seems that way. They are known to go about their work with uncommon zeal, and yet are among the lowest-paid people in baseball. An average scout's salary is only about $23,000 a year. When there is a budget cut, the scout's head is the first one lopped off.

Over the weekend, when the New York area scouts got together at Shea Stadium for their annual awards dinner, a question was raised: What is missing in the Hall of Fame? Well, at Cooperstown there are ballplayers, of course, and umpires and team executives and league presidents. What's missing are scouts. None are enshrined.

"That's an injustice," said Teed, who received the "good guy" award at the dinner. "I mean, somebody's finding those players that are on the field."

Some legendary scouts, Teed recalled, include Tom Greenwade of the Yankees, who beat the bushes and came up with, among others, Mickey Mantle and Bobby Murcer; Paul Krichell, who happened upon Lou Gehrig as a collegian; and Joe Cambria, who once scoured Cuba and signed many fine Latin players for the Washington Senators.

Teed has been a scout for 17 years, first with the Phillies and then with the Dodgers, for whom he is the chief scout in the New England, New York and New Jersey areas.

"You still look for pitchers who have good movement with their fastball, and you still look for batters who can make the ball fly off the bat," he said. "But the big change is with fielders. You look for speed. It used to be all arm. But with the artificial turf, the ball bounces so fast, you want agility.

"And since the Major League Scouting Bureau began in 1975, it's getting harder to make the secret discovery. Now most of the information is pooled among all the clubs. And what I do mostly is cross-check, to look over a prospect that one of our scouts has recommended and that had been recommended to him from a bureau report."

But Teed must still be careful. He can look good if, as has happened, someone he recommends makes it to the big leagues, or he can look bad. The classic story is of the unfortunate Yankee scout who didn't think a certain plump Mexican pitcher was worth, it is said, a $50,000 bonus. The pitcher is Fernando Valenzuela. The scout is no longer with the Yankees.

"Then you can recommend a player," said Teed, "but your team has to be lucky to draft him before someone else does."

But when a scout gets behind a player who makes it to the majors, that's pure delight. One such recent Teed prospect is John Franco, a relief pitcher signed by the Dodgers and then traded to the Reds. "I was a little disappointed we traded him, but I guess we needed something else."

Teed has not yet come up with the superstar, a player, say, like the one Herb Stein found in a Bronx sandlot a number of years ago, and signed for the Twins. The signature on the contract was Rodney Cline Carew.

But Teed hopes, and is patient. He is used to that. It took him seven years as a catcher toiling in the minors to make the big leagues.

He came up to the team that would be memorialized as "The Boys of Summer." He still has the Dodger yearbook of that year in a scrapbook. The roster is lustrous with famous, though formal, names: Edwin Snider, Harold Reese, William Cox, Jack R. Robinson, Elwin Roe, Gilbert Hodges. . . .

Teed came up from Mobile, Ala., as a backup to Roy Campanella, after Rube Walker suffered a bruised thumb. "Everything seemed different in the big leagues—magnified," he recalled. "The lights were brighter, the crowds were larger. I even thought the sound of the pitches hitting Campy's glove was louder. And it was. I learned he always wore a new stiff glove because he always wanted the pitches to sound faster."

On the night of July 24, after a week with Brooklyn, he got a call in the bullpen to pinch-hit for Jim Hughes. "I ran—I didn't jog—I *ran* to the dugout, I was so excited," he said.

It was the seventh inning, he said, and the Braves were beating the Dodgers, 11–1. Max Surkont was pitching. Teed fouled off several pitches, worked the count to 3–2, and then swung and missed at a low sinker on the outside corner.

"I wasn't down, I figured there'd be another day," he said.

There wasn't. He was sent out 12 days later, never to play again in the big leagues.

"What I'll always remember," he said, "is that I was up there challenging Surkont. I struck out, but I went down taking good cuts."

Lookin' to Get Lucky

Saratoga Springs, New York, August 27, 1984

The early morning sun came streaming through the cool pine and oak trees in the stable area adjoining the Saratoga Race Track, and stippled the broad neck and head of the 2-year-old bay gelding, Doubly Clear, moving around the walking ring. On his back was a yellow blanket that brightened with the shifting pin-pricks of light. Doubly Clear was escorted by his trainer, Steve Rowan, a white-haired man in a blue windbreaker with the collar up.

A quiet Sunday morning and, to the casual eye, hardly porten-tous: The dew shimmered on the grass. The heavy sound of hoof-beats was heard from the training track across the road. Steam billowed from a trash drum over a fire where the water was being heated for Doubly Clear's bath and where his oats are cooked.

This was the morning of the late afternoon in which Doubly Clear, from humble origins, would race against the horses from, literally, the other side of the track.

He was stabled in the hundred-year-old "Horse Haven" area, which may be torn down soon; meanwhile, many of the richest horses, those purchased for a million dollars and up, and whom he would be running against, like Chief's Crown and Tiffany Ice, were residing in the new area behind the backstretch.

Doubly Clear had been purchased for $1,500, the son of Two a Day, whose stud fee is a modest $500, and Clear Mistery, who has never produced a winner, and was sold last year for $600.

Doubly Clear's first two races were claiming races. But he went on to win his last three races, all stakes, and now would be racing here in the 6½-furlong Hopeful, the first time 2-year-olds are asked to go this far in a stakes race.

The Hopeful—with past winners including Secretariat, Foolish Pleasure and Affirmed—generally determines the early favorite for the following year's Kentucky Derby.

For Rowan, who trains horses primarily at the small Penn National Race Course in western Pennsylvania and has been at his business for more than 40 years, it is also a chance, at age 61, to emerge from relative obscurity.

"Me and him, we're titled 'Tobacco Road,' lookin' to get lucky," said Rowan.

Suddenly, Doubly Clear reared up and kicked. "Hey, ho!" shouted Rowan, stepping lively, working the reins. "C'mon, ya big lug. Ho! Ho!" The horse threw back his head, blowing, and reared again. "What's the matter with you!"

The horse returned to earth on all fours. "He's just bein' playful, but I ain't never seen him this playful before," said Rowan. "He's mellow, mellow as Costello." Rowan led him off out of the ring. "But I better take him into his stall—before his jaw gets broke."

"I've been here a week," said a security guard, "and I never seen him do that."

"He never done it before," said Rowan. "He's primed. He wants to go. Maybe he heard he's 8 to 1 and don't like that."

Rowan now watched his large horse—better than 16 hands and about 1,050 pounds—dine on a fare of hay tacked on the door of his stall.

"Look at him, got an awful good look in his eye," said Rowan. "He's healthy, there's no excuse if he don't do good.

"You know, before the Mayfair at Suffolk, he was havin' an awful time with shin splints. Nowadays they got all these whirlpools and stuff, but I thought if we take him in a van up to Boston, the vibrations would do him good. And it did. Ever get a bad hip, try it sometime. And he wins the race by a length and a quarter.

"Couple weeks later we go in the Tyro and he's got trouble with his teeth—he's in pain. Well, about 4:30 in the morning the vet comes and we cut him under the gums. I think, 'Oh my God, he won't eat.' But then he takes the hay and dunks it in his pail of water. Judy Bujnicki, his owner—she's afraid he's gonna be a dunker. That's bad—means he eats only 50 percent of his food, like a baby. But no, he eats all the oats and hay. And he wins the Tyro by three lengths."

For the Sapling, less than two weeks later, on August 11, he was fit, and won by a length.

This could be the best horse Rowan ever saddled. "I've had some good horses, I'm not allergic to the winner's circle," said Rowan, "but I don't know if I ever had one as good as this fella."

In the 1950s, Rowan trained War Fable. "He was good, lost to Social Outcast," said Rowan."Then I had a horse named Gangland about 30 years ago. Won a handicap at Atlantic City. but he broke his leg. We put him in a cast, and I stayed up with him a lot of nights and we saved him.

"I had a terrific young horse a few years ago that we called Swoopy. A real rank thing. I got on him one morning and he broke on me. He was coming to a six-foot fence and I thought, 'This ain't for me,' and he went sailing over the fence and I sailed right into a manure pile."

What was that like?

"Very soft," said Rowan, "very soft."

Rowan watched Swoopy leap two more fences. "He wound up," said Rowan, "jumpin' on the United States equestrian team.

"It's been fun, though. Never met a horse I didn't like. One day a long time ago my mother saw me with a hole in my shoe. She said, 'I thought this is the Sport of Kings.' I laughed, but you know, you don't have to be a Vanderbilt or duPont or Whitney to win. There's always a last minute in this game."

Now he watched Doubly Clear nap after his feed. "If he gets beat, we have nothin' to be ashamed of. We can both leave here with our heads as high as when we came in."

The bell clanged, and nine horses broke from the starting gate in the Hopeful. Doubly Clear, going off at 5 to 2 and the second choice among the bettors, took the lead. But at the quarter pole, Vindaloo moved in front while Doubly Clear dropped to fifth.

At the halfway mark, the jockey, Joe Garcia, urged Doubly Clear into fourth position and he remained there as the horses turned toward home. Chief's Crown, the even-money favorite, went to the lead.

Now the horses pounded down the stretch. Chief's Crown pulled farther ahead and swept across the finish line 3¾ lengths in front of Tiffany Ice, in second place.

Double Clear, in the dust of the leaders, finished sixth.

Giving Up the Tour

New York, August 17, 1982

On Saturday Dana Quigley, waking and suddenly finding himself in another world, shot a 61 in the Greater Hartford Open, one short of the Wethersfield (Conn.) Country Club's course record. "It's the best I can ever imagine shooting," he said, "unless I cheat."

On Sunday he completed his best tournament in the five years he has been a touring professional golfer, finishing in a tie for ninth and earning a check for $8,400, the largest of his career.

It wasn't enough, however, to keep alive the embers of the dream he once held of being a renowned tour pro. He's retiring. By October, the 35-year-old Quigley, a strapping 6 foot-2-inch blond known for his smile and forbearance, hopes to have a steady job as a club pro—9 to 5, or thereabouts, and a lunch pail if he can't bargain for dining-room privileges.

Unlike Arnold Palmer, Quigley has had no personal Lear jet transporting him from one tournament to another; there is a bus, a plane and another bus. With suitcases and golf bag and a wife, Charlotte, and an 11-month-old daughter, Nicole.

And unlike Jack Nicklaus, Quigley has had no national television commercials to appear on. In fact, he generally plays to a gallery of one. "My wife," he said. "And since our baby was born, even she usually stays away. Besides, people might think it's a little dangerous following me down the fairway. I've been known to hit a few balls wide."

There are no Grand Slams for Quigley to pursue. His effort to qualify on Mondays often leads to disappointment, and during those weeks when he does qualify, making the cut on Friday is another worry. "It's frustrating, and the pressure is inhuman," he said. And if he does make the cut, it's improbable that his check—when the top players are raking in thousands—will be more than three figures on Sunday.

The most he has ever earned in a year was $32,000, in 1980, and it costs about $40,000 to play and travel on the tour. "If you're going to make a decent profit, about $30,000 after taxes, what any normal guy on the outside makes, you've got to take home $100,000 from the tour," he said.

Before the tournament last weekend, Quigley had played in 12 tour events this year—earning a total of $954, for finishing 45th in the Tucson Open. That was the first tournament of the year for him. He then failed to make the cut in the next 11 tournaments, until Hartford.

"The hardest thing about being a mediocre golfer," he said, "is that your bag gets heavier. Just once I wanted to win so that I could go to an airport and holler, 'Porter, porter.'

"No, the tour's not nearly as glamorous as a lot of people think—geez, not as glamorous as I thought."

Quigley, who had been a club pro at Sun Valley in Rehoboth, Mass., played in the early 1970s on the Florida minitours and competed evenly with golfers he saw faring well on the tour.

"So I decided to give it a shot," he said. "I went through the qualifying school, and I started out on the tour. When I began, I was broke. And I'm just about finishing up broke.

"I've played with some of the best players in the world—Nicklaus and Raymond Floyd—and the difference between their game and mine is about four putts a round. Nothing else. But it's everything. There are 156 guys teeing up who are all great ball strikers, but if you don't knock the holes out, you might as well go home.

"You've really got to believe in yourself to be a great putter," he added. "And golf comes down to that. It's entirely a game of mental approach. You've got to be thinking the ball's going to go in. The great golfers *think* the ball's going in.

"Sometimes I do, like when I shot that 61. But then there are days when I'm completely negative.

"My wife gets mad at me. She says, 'Think in.' I try to, but when you've seen your ball go past the cup a million times, it's hard."

Missing the tour, he says, will be like missing a broken arm, but he does have some fond memories, especially the camaraderie he has developed with other players.

"My greatest thrill in that regard was playing with Arnold Palmer," he said. It was in a twosome in the third round of the 1979 United States Open at Inverness in Toledo, Ohio.

"Here I am playing with The Man," recalled Quigley. "There must have been 10,000 people waiting for us at the first tee. I was scared to death. I was thinking, 'My God, what if I miss the ball?'

"So I went back to the basics. Where the club is, and how to get it on the ball. But I striped it dead solid down the middle. I even went on to beat Arnold in the round. I shot a 74, and he scored 75.

"It was unbelievable. I had never experienced a gallery as huge as that one. All those eyes watching every shot I took. I was so nervous I spent most of the afternoon gasping for air."

Cowboy from the Bronx

New York, September 29, 1983

The first time Bobby DelVecchio, the Bronx cowboy, rode off into the sunrise, it was on a bus headed for North Washington, Pa.

"I was leavin' home to try to make a livin' at rodeoin'," he said, "and I was wearin' a black leather jacket and construction boots. But I had me a riggin' sack which I bought and inside I put my cowboy boots and a stupid cowboy hat, but I folded the hat real neat-like. I didn't wanta look like no hillbilly. I mean, where I was from—around Fordham Road and University Avenue—cowboys was unheard of.''

That was 8 years ago, when DelVecchio was 18 years old. Now, at age 26, he is the leading money winner among bull riders on the professional rodeo circuit—with $55,000 in prize money—and was runner-up in his event in the national championships of the last two years,

He was sitting in an office in Madison Square garden, where the rodeo arrives tomorrow, and wearing, as though born in it, a black cowboy hat that occupied a substantial part of the room.

DelVecchio himself is not especially big. He stands 5 feet 7 inches and weighs 160 pounds, but he is strong. His shoulders are broad, his waist is only 29 inches wide, and his thighs are 21 inches thick.

He is a cowboy now from an urban background—making the long and unlikely transition from East to West in dress and life-style and language. "When I first came around, the cowboys useta make fun of me 'cause I'd say 'youse guys' instead of 'y'all,' " he said. "Now their way's completely natural to me."

But he is no Urban Cowboy on the order of the Hollywood film.

"You got no idear the difference between ridin' one of them real thousand-pound bulls to a mechanical bull," he said. "In a rodeo you're on a bull whose back is as wide as these two chairs, and steam is comin' off him and he's nasty. He's got these horns and he just wants to bite ya and buck ya and stomp on ya.

"The worst that happened to me was about three years ago when I got my back broke. The doctor said it'd take me a year before I was rodeoin' again. I said two weeks." DelVecchio laughed. "It was six months.

"In rodeoin' you don't get no salary, like the ballplayers do. So it's costin' you money every day you're not ridin'. One time in a rodeo in Colorado Springs, this rank bull jerked me down right outta the gate. He kicked me and gashed my eye. Blood was gushin' out. But there was a nice chunk of prize money and I went to the paramedics and said, 'Can you stop the bleedin' for just a few minutes so's I can reride that bull?' They put a patch on and I got back up and really took aholt of that bull, and I won the rodeo.

"There was 10,000 people in the stands. And my head started gushin' again. I'll never forget it. I was wearin' a baby-blue shirt and it was red with blood. I bowed to the crowd and they gave me a standin' ovation. They went crazy. I blowed 'em a kiss. And they went a little wilder. It was a way of thankin' the people, and now whenever I win I blow 'em a kiss. It's become sorta my trademark."

DelVecchio's parents were divorced when he was 8 years old, and he went to live with his father, Frank. He quit school after the eighth grade. "I had long hair and I was a real derelict, a hood, you might say, runnin' through the streets all night," said DelVecchio.

It happened that he sometimes hung around the stables at Pelham Parkway, and began riding. When he was 14 he met a man there who took him to Cow Town, in Woodstown, N.J., where there were rodeos.

"The first time I saw the bull-ridin'," recalls DelVecchio, "I said, 'That's me.' It looked exciting. They let me ride one. It was a yearling, a little bigger than a calf. And I got dusted in a second, just sort of rolled off. I was supposed to be a tough guy—and you can't show that you're hurt. And when you lose a fight you act like you coulda won. I said, 'I wanna try again.' This time I stayed longer. I started comin' back regular."

By the time he was 18, he thought he was good enough to earn a living at it.

"I entered a bunch of rodeos and I wasn't winnin' nothin'," he said. "I do mostly bull-ridin', with a little steer rasslin'. Well, I'd get discouraged, and was ready to pack it in several times. I had some cowboy friends on the circuit now, and they'd say, 'If you can't take it, then go home, Yank.' They knew that would make me mad. And I started to win some."

A turning point came in the month of July, 1980, when he competed in 37 rodeos in 31 days and won $30,000. "I was learnin' how to squeeze the bull, how to dig in my spurs to his flanks, and how to keep my chin down proper when he's buckin'."

DelVecchio has earned more than $300,000 over the last three years—though traveling expenses cut into that deeply. He now pilots his own single-engine Cessna Skylane and sometimes in one day flies from events in, say, Red Lodge, Mont., to Cody, Wyo., back to Livingston, Mont.

The adjustment, however, from the Bronx to home on the range is still not complete.

"Chicken fried steak is not my favorite food," he said. "I can't wait to get back to New York for baked ziti."

And his parents—who still call him Robert—are proud of him but haven't completely adjusted either.

"I remember I called my mother a while back and said, 'Hi, this is Bobby,' and told her that I was rodeoin' up in Portland, Urgin, and I asked, 'And how y'all?'

"She said, 'Don't y'all me. Talk like Robert.' "

Of Cabbages and Rings

New York, October 24, 1984

One gentleman was wearing a zebra costume that fit tighter on him than it did on the zebra.

Another fellow wore feathery earrings on each ear and one on his left cheek.

A third man, who called himself Moondog Spot from "parts unknown," carried a thick bone about a foot in length. What kind of bone was it? "A dinosaur bone," said Moondog Spot.

This is the world of professional wrestling, and into it has stepped David Bruno Sammartino, son of Bruno Sammartino, the retired champion.

The scene is the dressing area under the stands of Madison Square Garden, where the wrestlers are preparing and primp-ing for the evening—wiggling into their outfits, taping their fingers and toes and grunting through desultory warm-up routines.

From a distance, from inside the arena, comes the sound of a bell being rung.

David, in black T-shirt and black wrestling shorts, looks like the boy next door, if the boy next door is 5 feet 10 inches tall, 252 pounds—with a 52-inch chest, 20-inch biceps, an incipient cauli-flower left ear—and walks like he's carrying two heavy suitcases.

How did he get that big? "Ate a few cabbages," he said, "and did some exercises."

Sammartino is bulky, but he is also baby-faced, even at age 24. After five years of the wrestling circuit, performing in small towns and high school gyms and fairs and armories as well as large cities and large arenas, he was making his debut in Madison Square Garden.

Before the matches began, David was brought into a small room to be interviewed on television for the wrestling show. An interview was already in progress.

". . . and my man will wipe him off the face of this planet and there will be the greatest celebration in the history of Manhattan and champagne corks will be popping and I masterminded the whole—"

"Hold it, cut," said the cameraman. "The tape broke."

The interviewee was Bobby (The Brain) Heenan, the agent for Big John Studd, who this night was challenging Hulk Hogan, the champion, for the World Wrestling Federation title.

The tape was fixed and The Brain repeated his spiel without missing a single fulmination, and even added a finger in the mouth to imitate the sound of a cork popping.

Now it was David Bruno Sammartino in front of the camera. The tuxedoed interviewer, Gorilla Monsoon, welcomed him and praised him and said, "So much of you reminds me of your father." He predicted a great future for David. David said he was "living a dream, a fantasy" by appearing in the Garden, "the mecca of wrestling, where my father had so many great matches."

"Thank you, David."

"Thank you, Mr. Monsoon."

When David left home in Pittsburgh for the world of wrestling, five years ago, he did so despite the continuing protests of his mother and his father. "My mother wanted me to continue in school, and Dad said the wrestling life was too hard," said David.

"In fact, when I was 5 years old he took me to my first wrestling match so that I would get discouraged. He was wrestling Gorilla Monsoon. I'll never forget it. Gorilla Monsoon was much bigger in those days—he weighed about 400 pounds. He's only about 280 now. But I thought the matches were thrilling. I got chills up my back. And decided that that's what I wanted to do."

His parents, though, emphasized the dangers. His father, who is somewhat larger than David, had his nose broken 12 times, suffered innumerable concussions, back sprains and a broken neck. He took one year off from wrestling in 1971 and spent it as an outpatient at Allegheny General Hospital.

"Dad and I also wrestled a lot, we were like brothers," said David. "I admire my father tremendously. And when people compare me to him, I'm honored. It's like someone comparing you to Joe Louis or Babe Ruth. He's a legend."

Yet David may have flinched slightly from it, for until a year ago he was billed as Bruno Sammartino Jr. "I put the David in front because I thought it was time to establish my own real identity," he said.

He was ready for the Garden, he said, because he was now good enough and strong enough for the competition. "My head," he said, "is in the right place."

A somewhat remarkable occurrence, especially after a recent bout with Larry Szbysko in which his treacherous opponent hit him over the head with a chair from ringside. It resulted in David's face being weaved with a bunch of stitches.

Shortly now, he would be in the ring against Moondog Spot, who wore fringed jeans, a rope for a belt, and who howled on occasion at a light in the rafter that he apparently mistook for the moon.

When David was introduced, the crowd of 22,000 that packed the Garden gave him an ovation. The name Sammartino rang bells—though it doesn't take much for wrestling fans to hear bells.

Moondog wanted to wrestle with his dinosaur bone in hand. The referee tried to take it away from him. Moondog climbed onto the ropes in a huff, but finally was persuaded to hang the bone—it had a string attached—to a ring post.

The combatants now bounced and pounced and grappled and groaned. Moondog engaged in expectedly nefarious tactics, like eye-gouging, hair-pulling, scratching and strangling. David lifted him over his head—Moondog was listed at 287 pounds—and then flung him to the canvas with a great thud. At length David pinned him.

The crowd roared with delight. But Moondog wasn't finished. David's back was turned and the crowd hollered to David, "He's got his bone! Watch the bone!" David turned to see Moondog stalking him with bone brandished. In a moment, though, David cleverly snatched the bone from Moondog and Moondog left the ring like a hangdog.

Now David raised his arms in triumph as the crowd cheered and bells—they were bells, weren't they?—rang some more.

Miles of Ovations

New York, October 28, 1985

For almost the entire circuitous route of the 26-mile, 385-yard New York City Marathon yesterday, it was standing room only along the sidewalks, with a healthy scattering of leaning-out-of-windows, propped-up-against-storefronts and entwined-around-lampposts.

A few others were observed entwined in each other's arms, undistracted by the hordes tromping by on this blissfully sun-kissed day. The wooers were a fitting symbol, though, for an event—the Marathon—in which the people of New York embraced the runners, opening their arms to these legions with sore feet.

On Fourth Avenue in Bay Ridge, Brooklyn, only about a mile or so into the race, the runners passed a store with a large brown and white sign reading "FOOT DOCTOR." A man in a white smock stood in the doorway, with a look of barely suppressed glee. "Here come some live ones," his eyes said.

The race had begun when The First Spectator, Mayor Koch, pulled the string that shot off the cannon and—unlike the circus, where only one man issues forth—16,705 people poured out and over the Verrazano-Narrows Bridge.

The First Spectator had been asked if he ever runs. "Yes, for a mile or five minutes," he said, "whichever comes first. If a mile comes first, I quit. If five minutes come first, I quit." Apparently, neither came first yesterday because he was not among the hoofing multitude.

In the narrows, a flotilla of boats gathered and Sunday sailors gazed at the gaggle of legs passing on the bridge above.

On the westbound approach to the bridge, long lines of cars were stopped, and drivers and passengers rubbernecked at the sight of so many people in such a hurry.

But along the streets, people waved flags and signs of encouragement and brought out glasses of water for the runners.

"Let's Go Uncle Mickey," read one sign.

"The tiger has nothing on the lion—Run, Leo, Run."

A practical sort held up another sign: "Watch Out for Potholes."

Spectators cheered the runners in front of the Pilgrim Covenant Church and the Iglesia De Dios and the Salem Gospel Tabernacle. They clapped for them in front of the Polska meat market, the No Pork Chinese Restaurant and the Socrates Coffee Shop.

People in front of the Oritz Funeral Home solemnly viewed the assortment of trudgers trudging.

So did many Hasidim on Bedford Avenue in Williamsburg. In black hats and black caftans and white beards, they scrutinized this odd frivolity. Some smiled, several scratched their heads, but one had a camera out.

Young basketball players at Classon and Lafayette stopped their game to pump a few arms of encouragement to the runners. A man in a T-shirt leaned out of his window and toasted the lopers below with a bottle of beer. A couple of kids leaned on a sill and blew whistles of exultation, while in the window over their heads, a Halloween skeleton danced, one which bore a striking resemblance to one of the bony runners.

The inviting smell from the DeSimone Bros. bakery on Vernon Boulevard greeted runners as they crossed the Pulaski Bridge into Queens. In Long Island City, a nonconformist in Bermuda shorts ran on the sidewalk in the opposite direction of the oncoming marathoners. Two guys on bicycles stopped, looked and disdainfully peddled away down 10th Street.

No matter. Up 10th Street a man and woman came running to see the runners.

A high school band in green uniforms and yellow plumed hats tootled pop hits; somewhere else, a band of bagpipes played and, farther along, salsa music from apartments kept the beat for the runners.

The stationary crowd was six-deep to greet the ambulatory throng coming off the 59th Street Bridge at First Avenue.

This is the cynosure of the singles scene, and many in the crowd wore high-fashion running outfits in order to stand and watch the runners run.

The runners just touched a tip of the Bronx at 138th Street, and then came sweeping back into Manhattan at Fifth Avenue in Harlem.

Ahmed Saleh of Djibouti was in the lead and he received a huge welcome from the folks lining the streets. One young woman in red boots ran in place with such excitement that it appeared her feet were moving quicker than Saleh's.

Several patrons of the Friendly Bar at 115th Street strolled out and shouted with expectation as Orlando Pizzolato of Italy began to challenge for the lead.

A white-haired lady with a walker halted and watched the scene come and go in front of the Terence Cardinal Cooke Health Care Center on 105th Street.

The runners turned into Central Park at 102nd Street and stayed on the road near Fifth Avenue, observed by the braided doorman of a chic apartment building and by residents high up in penthouse gardens. Art lovers at the Guggenheim peered from windows, and, a while later, red-jacketed waiters in the Plaza Hotel glanced from behind heavy curtains to follow the action.

Pizzolato passed Saleh at 85th Street, and Grete Waitz was uncontested among the women, as the crowd in the park, standing on curbs and boulders, hanging from tree limbs, and nestled on knolls among the fall leaves, cheered the pooped and plunging runners home.

A Loud Crack in the Night

Philadelphia, November 5, 1984

A shout from below her window awakened Charlotte Smith. She had been sleeping in the bedroom of her second-floor apartment at 131 North 15th Street, a three-story red-brick building, in Center City here early Friday morning, October 26.

She heard, "Back against the wall! Back against the wall!"

It was still dark outside, around a quarter to three, and Charlotte Smith climbed out of bed. Her window was partly open because it was an unseasonably warm and humid night, and she pushed the window higher and leaned out.

On the sidewalk, she saw a large black man—she is also black—and the man was wearing a dark jacket or sweater and tan pants, she would recall. He was moving toward a policeman. The policeman, a white man and considerably smaller than the other, was hollering "Back against the wall!" and slowly retreating from the advancing man.

She didn't notice a weapon or anything else in either one's hands. An empty police cruiser with a flashing blue light rotating on the roof was alongside the curb. The two men were now stepping into the yellow light on the sidewalk that spilled through the window from the night light in the closed luncheonette. Several yards away, at the corner of 15th and Cherry, two young black teenagers on mopeds watched. Otherwise, the street was deserted.

Charlotte Smith has on occasion been roused in the dead of night because, she told a reporter, "derelicts" come around that area—there are mostly office buildings, but the "derelicts" drift over from the bus terminal a few blocks away—and sometimes cause problems. Her immediate worry was that her boss, Murry Auspitz, might be in trouble. Murry Auspitz owns the luncheonette on the ground floor, where she works as a counter attendant. He arrives early to open the store.

When she saw it wasn't her boss, she said she "didn't pay it no attention," and got back into bed. A moment or so later, a loud crack rang out. "It was a gunshot," she recalled. "I've heard gunshots before."

She jumped up and looked out the window again and now saw the black man lying on the ground, bleeding. The policeman was at the squad car and, she recalled, "radioing in for help."

"I was hysterical in the window," she would say, "screamin' and cryin'."

She did not learn who the black man was until the following day, Saturday, when she saw the headline in the *Philadelphia Daily News*. It read "Cop's Bullet Kills '50s Grid Star."

The dead man was Charles Fletcher Janerette Jr., age 45, an English teacher at the Daniel Boone School in Philadelphia and a former all-America lineman at Penn State and onetime player in the early 1960s with both the New York Giants and the Jets. For the last 12 years, Janerette had suffered from what was described by his parents as manic depression.

His killing would raise numerous questions and inflame passions, particularly in the black community of Philadelphia. In the official police statement, the officer would say that Janerette had gotten into the marked squad car when the policeman had stepped out to talk to the two youths on mopeds. Then, the policeman stated, he pulled Janerette from the car. He said that a scuffle ensued and his revolver went off. Janerette was shot in the back of the head. Janerette was taken to a hospital and died about 12 hours later.

Was Janerette, in fact, up against the wall? Was this a case of police brutality in extremis, or an accident, or did the policeman have no recourse in order to protect himself? How was it, if there was a scuffle, that he was shot in the back of the head? Had Janerette taken the medication that helped control his mental problem? Toxicology reports, which should show whether he had been taking the medication, will not be available for several weeks.

The police officer, Kurt VonColin, age 33, who reportedly stands about 5 feet 7 inches tall and weighs about 160 pounds, bears a well-known last name in Philadelphia. In 1970, his father, Police Sergeant Frank VonColin, age 43, was shot to death while alone at his desk in the Cobbs Creek Park guardhouse by a group of black men, members of a radical organization known as the Revolutionaries. The killing was considered by the police to be part of a conspiracy by the group to kill whites.

That crime touched off the largest manhunt in Philadelphia history. All but one of the assailants were caught. The only one still free is the one who is said to have pulled the trigger.

There are other questions that the story of Janerette raised: some deal with the adjustments of life after football, some with racism in American society, and others with the problems of manic-depression, a psychosis from which, according to his family, Janerette had been suffering the last 12 years.

Charlie Janerette grew up in Philadelphia, first in the Richard Allen projects, and later in a better neighborhood in West Oak

Lane, and became an all-city and all-state high school lineman. He went on to Penn State, where he was chosen a second-team all-American by the *Sporting News* in his senior year, and he played seven years in professional football. He was with the Los Angeles Rams in 1960, the Giants in 1961 and 1962, the Jets in 1963, the Denver Broncos for the next two years, and finished his career in 1966 with the Hamilton TigerCats in Ontario.

In 1956, Charlie Janerette became the first black class president of Germantown High School. He was popular, gregarious and exceedingly bright. By the time he was a senior, he had reached his full height, 6-3, though, at about 240 pounds, not quite his full weight, which would go as high as 270 pounds with the Broncos. "Charlie," said a longtime friend, Garrett Bagley, "was a gentle bear."

Two of his boyhood friends were Harold Brown, now a North Carolina businessman, and the comedian Bill Cosby. Brown is believed to be the model for Cosby's comic invention Weird Harold, and another Cosby character, Fat Albert, is believed to have been loosely based on Charlie Janerette.

Brown smiled when he recalled Janerette. "He was funny and he could take a joke," he said. "We said his shoe size kept up to his age."

Brown was asked if Janerette was in fact the inspiration for Fat Albert. "The guys have always thought he had a lot to do with it," said Brown. "He was round, robust, as a kid," said Brown. "Not fat sloppy, but robust sloppy."

The boyhood friends kept in touch through the years. Last year, said Charlie's sister, Hope Janerette, when Bill Cosby opened a show in Lake Tahoe, he sent Charlie Janerette a round-trip first-class ticket to Nevada. Cosby told Charlie he'd have a Rolls-Royce waiting for him to use there.

Charlie told Hope, "I can't drive that thing. What if I had an accident? I could never pay for the repairs."

One of the many bouquets of flowers sent to the Janerette home bore this note to the family: "I'll see you later." It was signed, "Bill Cosby."

Charlie Janerette was the oldest of five children, and the only male, born to Charles Janerette Sr., now a retired postal office supervisor, and his wife, Lillian Ernestine. The five children—the other four are named Carol, Faith, Hope, Charity—would all earn doctorates. Charlie had dreamed of becoming a physician, and he enrolled as a premed student at Penn State.

But, he would say, the requirements of football didn't give him enough time to pursue the rigorous discipline of medicine, and he instead earned a bachelor's degree in science, and later a master's in educational counseling.

When he first went to Penn State, recalls Joe Paterno, now the head coach but then an assistant coach, they thought there might be a problem. "He was a sensitive, shy kid and we wondered whether he was aggressive enough to be a good football player," Paterno said. "But he was very committed, and he wanted to make something of himself. He was very quick and had a lot of explosiveness, and he got tougher and tougher."

Janerette was thrilled to receive a scholarship from Penn State, but, he said in a newspaper interview a few years ago, "they didn't tell me I'd be the only black on the team. I didn't worry about that, though. I saw all the huge freshmen, and I just wanted to survive."

In the mid-1950s, blacks were just beginning to be recruited on a large scale for college athletic teams at major state universities around the country. It was no different at Penn State, the school tucked away in an area known as "Happy Valley." Janerette, though, seemed to make adjustments.

Janerette was drafted in 1960 on the fifth round by the Los Angeles Rams. His contract called for $7,500, and he received a $500 signing bonus.

It was enough for Janerette to put a $3,000 down payment on a house for his parents and sisters, a brick semidetached four-bedroom house on a street lined with spruce and cedar trees in the quiet East Mount Airy section of Philadelphia.

He started some games for the Rams, but at the end of the season was picked by the Minnesota Vikings in an expansion draft, and then traded to the Giants.

In two years with the Giants, he recalled for the *Philadelphia Tribune*, a black newspaper, he played "a lot of defensive tackle when Rosey Grier was hurt, and I played on all the special teams. I even played with a broken hand. I had to."

Andy Robustelli, a defensive end on the team, remembers him as a "happy, jovial, always upbeat guy. But the Giant teams were so strong then and it was tough for anybody to break in."

In 1963, Janerette was cut by the Giants and picked up by the Jets. Weeb Ewbank, then the Jets coach, remembers him as a "nice person, never caused any problems, but we let him go because he was on the downside of his career, and we were building."

Janerette went to the Broncos as part of a nine-player deal with the Jets. "I remember Charlie getting up at a club we used to go to, called 23rd Street East, and doing great, funny imitations of James Brown," said Cookie Gilchrist, a teammate of Janerette in Denver. But there was another side. "He didn't play enough, and he and I both thought he should have," said Gilchrist.

Denver, where Janerette earned his highest salary, $17,000, cut him and he played for a year in the Canadian Football League. He was 27 years old and finished as a professional football player.

He had married in 1965, and he and his wife, Joan, soon had a daughter, Dariel. There seemed no evidence of problems. He spent five years in the marketing department for general Electric in Syracuse, and it was in August of 1972, said Joan Janerette, when difficulties developed.

"He began acting strangely," she recalled. "Very hyper. His movements were very quick at times, and he began to say strange things. Like he was going to solve all the problems of the world."

He began to leave without telling her where he was going, and wouldn't return for days. She urged him to go to a psychiatrist, and he was eventually admitted to a Syracuse hospital and stayed there 10 days, she said.

She wondered about the source of his problems.

His wife believed he was suffering from manic-depression, in which there are sudden mood changes, surging from euphoria to deep depression.

The problems intensified. She went to a therapist, and she was told that he could be dangerous. "He was a big man, and I found it hard to restrain him," she said. In October of 1972, she left him, taking their daughter to Pennsylvania.

On October 18, 1972, he was charged with driving while intoxicated when he was involved in a car accident in which a pedestrian was killed. He pleaded guilty to a reduced charge and, as a result his driver's license was suspended for three months.

"Charlie was so broken up by that accident," said Hope Janerette, "that every October 18 he would not go out of the house."

Following the accident, there were days of unexplained absence from work, and he lost his job.

Paterno, who stayed close with Janerette and knew of his problems, hired him as a graduate assistant. Janerette stayed at Penn State for two years and earned his master's degree.

But Paterno saw times in which Janerette would not be "acting right." And when Janerette next went to Cheyney State in Pennsylvania as an assistant coach under Billy Joe, there were more problems. "He was a good assistant," said Billy Joe, "and then on occasion he would do something completely out of character." At a football dinner, Janerette, the guest speaker, rose and soon "began yelling out and cursing," said Joe. Janerette had to be led away.

He moved to Washington, where he sold computer software to federal agencies. He told a friend that one day he had been picked up off the streets by the police for no reason and jailed for four days.

He returned home to Philadelphia, where he got teaching jobs.

After his death, a student whom he had taught named Angela Hurst wrote a letter to Janerette's parents: ". . . I really do miss Mr. Janerette. He could joke with us, but he was also serious about his students getting to work, because he wanted us to learn. Even when I said, 'Mr. Janerette, I can't do this,' he would say, 'Yes, you can. Try it.' "

Although he took several jobs teaching in the Philadelphia public schools, he would continue to talk to friends about his dreams. "He wanted some kind of entrepreneurship," said Garrett Bagley, a friend, "or he wanted to get back into football. He missed football a lot, and he missed being a star. There were no more locker rooms, no planes to catch, no more autographs to sign."

Janerette was aware, of course, of his mental problem. "He always thought that the last episode—he called them episodes—would be his last," said his sister Charity. "He didn't really want to admit that he had a problem. And when he took his medication—lithium carbonate—he was fine. But when he didn't take it, and sometimes he didn't want to, he would be out of control. He was never violent, that we saw, but he'd be blinking his eyes and moving the furniture and talking fantasies."

He lived for the last three years in the house he had bought at the corner of Boyer and Horttler. But Charity said he considered it "only temporary."

"We knew he was in pain because of the illness, and he suffered with it and we suffered to see him that way," his sister Carol said. "But it was pretty well hidden. Almost no one outside the family knew about it."

His parents worried, too. "I hoped he wouldn't be a street person," said Mrs. Janerette, "and when he was out late, we waited for him, and when I finally heard the key in the lock, I could go to sleep."

He was working then at Boone, a remedial disciplinary school for boys. "He really related well to the boys," said the principal, Willie J. Toles, "and we had absolutely no problem with his performance or his attendance. And he always looked nice—suit and tie."

On Thursday, October 25, he did not report to school. The school called his house. He had not been home the previous night.

That afternoon, a student had seen Janerette in Center City, and the teacher gave him a few dollars, even though the boy hadn't even asked for it. Later, Janerette was reported to have asked a storekeeper he knew to lend him some money, and the storekeeper said Janerette berated him vulgarly for giving him so little.

At around midnight, Paul Jones, an old friend of Janerette's, and now a cabdriver, saw him near the bus terminal.

"He didn't seem right," said Jones, who said he did not know of Janerette's mental problems. "He talked O.K. We spoke about guys from 30 years back, but his movements seemed too quick, and his jacket and pants were disheveled.

"I said, 'Charlie, can I drive you home?'

"He said, 'No, but can you let me have a few bucks?'"

Jones did, and told him he had to get a fare and would come back in a little while.

He never saw him again.

It was a couple of hours later that police officer VonColin was in his cruiser near 15th and Cherry.

He stopped two teenagers on mopeds for a possible traffic violation. During the ongoing investigation of the death, VonColin is not speaking publicly. According to the formal police statement, however, one of the teenagers told him that someone was trying to steal his squad car.

According to the statement, VonColin moved toward Charles Janerette.

"Charlie once told me," said Hope Janerette, "that he had heard that if you ever have trouble, or don't have money, and need help, then you should get into a police car. He said, 'They have to take you home.'

"When Charlie was in a bad state, he always had some presence of mind. He was never totally out of control. And I wonder if his getting into that police car wasn't a kind of plea for help." It was just about this time that Charlotte Smith heard shouts, and, soon after, the gunshot that killed Charlie Janerette.

Hundreds of people milled outside the gray-stone Berean Presbyterian Church on Broad and Diamond Streets last Wednesday at noon, before the services for Charlie Janerette.

People were angry about the way he died.

Willie J. Toles thought it was a "classic case of misunderstanding."

Inside, in a gray steel casket strewn with flowers, lay Charles Fletcher Janerette Jr.

"I'm glad for one thing," said Hope Janerette. "I'm glad that now Charlie is out of that little private hell he was living in."

Charlie Janerette was eulogized by the Reverend J. Jerome Cooper, and then Cookie Gilchrist read a poem he had written for the funeral. Next, Faith Janerette, a dramatic soprano, shook the church with a moving gospel song, "Ride on, King Jesus." Some of the congregants moaned and sobbed.

The mourners then filed out, and some of them sang along with the church choir, accompanied by an organist, to the "Hallelujah Chorus."

As the funeral procession was about to leave for Northwest Cemetery, Harold Brown spoke to someone beside him. "When Charlie and I used to sit in church, and they played the 'Hallelujah Chorus,'" he said, "on the last 'Hallelujah,' Charlie, under his breath, would add a '50s rock group ending, a little doo-wop. And today it was there. Damned if I didn't hear it. He was speaking.

And it made me think, 'Charlie's O.K. now. Even with all the tears here, he can still play jokes.' "

In August of 1985, the district attorney's office in Philadelphia said that it had decided not to prosecute police officer VonColin, because "there was not enough evidence that the officer had acted improperly" in the shooting of Charlie Janerette.

Those Yesterdays

The Glory of Rhodes

New York, October 20, 1981

It was around 11 o'clock on a recent morning, and in Ginger's Tavern, beside the docks on Staten Island, a baldish man with a wide-creased face sat on a bar stool stirring his pick-me-up. Alongside him were a few of his fellow tugboat men.

"Oh, I'm still in touch with some of the old boys," he was saying. "Hey, a week or so ago I called Art Fowler when Oakland was in town to play the Yankees." Fowler is the A's pitching coach.

"I said, 'Art, buddy, how you doin'?'

"He said, 'Who is this?'

"I said, 'Dusty.'

"He said, 'Dusty who?'

"I said, 'Is there any other?'

"Then he just about shouted, 'Rhodes!' "

Dusty Rhodes threw back his head and laughed hoarsely.

In fact, there has never been another like Dusty Rhodes, particularly in World Series history. No batter has ever quite dominated a Series the way Rhodes did in 1954. His key pinch hits in the first three games galvanized the New York Giants' four-game sweep over the favored Cleveland Indians.

As World Series interest grows keener with anticipation of tonight's opening game at Yankee Stadium, Rhodes's feat remains a paramount delight in the memories of many fans.

Rhodes, now 54 years old, was a country boy out of Alabama who enjoyed hitting so much he generally swung at the first good pitch. He had learned to play the outfield in bare feet, had picked cotton and was fun-loving.

In the first game of the 1954 Series, his pinch home run with two men on in the bottom of the 10th inning—it just cleared the wall 260 feet from home plate in the Polo Grounds—provided the Giants with a 5–2 victory. (The Cleveland pitcher, by the way, was Bob Lemon, current Yankee manager.) Rhodes hit important pinch singles in games 2 and 3—he stayed in the second game and homered in a subsequent time at bat. He did not play in Game 4.

"It was just as well," he said, grinning. "After the third game, I was drinking to everybody's health so much that I about ruined mine."

His three pinch hits in that series still tie him for a Series record, and his six runs batted in as a pinch hitter stand alone as a Series mark.

"I was watching television a few years ago and Howard Cosell was saying that if the wind hadn't been blowin' out, my home-run ball in the first game would never have carried," Rhodes said. "It got me mad. A home run's a home run. Anyway, we can all use a little help now and then, right?

"You know, that home run stayed in the air longer than Howard's variety show stayed on the air. But Howard's a big deal now. I remember when he first started in 1962, and he walked around with a little tape recorder and I don't think his socks even matched."

The remarks drew laughs from the men at the bar and a wry smile from one of the two women behind the bar. Gloria, dark-haired and wearing a black business suit, is Dusty's wife and the owner of the establishment.

Someone mentioned to her that the line about Cosell "sounds like an old story."

"Real old," she replied, untroubled.

"Hey, Dusty," said one of the boatmen, "tell me something. If you go to the World Series, you get free tickets?"

"No way," he said. "For the Series, everyone pays. No Annie Oakleys like in the regular season."

Two of the men had got up to leave. They picked up suitcases at their feet. "Take it easy," one of them said. The other nodded. Like Rhodes, these men work one week on the tug and then are off one week. Rhodes is a steerer, deckman and cook—depending on how he is needed—on the *Peter Callahan*, a tugboat for the Manhattan Oil Transportation Company out of Mariners' Harbor on Staten Island.

He rises every morning at 5—a habit he is used to after 17 years as a boatman—and on off-days, as this one was, he accompanies his wife to open the tavern. This is his third marriage—they were wed a year and a half ago and seem to have an easy, affectionate relationship.

On off-days he generally discards his boat dungarees for a natty suit. He wore a tan one this particular morning, with a light tie held with a red cat's-eye tie clasp. He finished his second drink and then pulled out a packet of chewing tobacco and took a plug. He wore a wedding ring and a Masonic ring. But no World Series ring.

"I got mugged on the subway in 1963 and they took it off my finger," he said.

It was during a difficult period for Rhodes. His baseball career was over—his seven-year major-league career, in which he had a career batting average of .253, had ended in 1959 and he had played three more years in the Pacific Coast League. "It was a little tough to give it up," he said, "and when the sun comes up in the spring and you're not playing baseball, you're kind of lost."

Eventually, he caught on working tugs. "I like it," he said, "otherwise I wouldn't be doing it. It's a challenge. You pull a barge to alongside a ship and you unload the cargo. If the crew don't do it right—with the waves moving and the wind blowing—you can clean house. Everything goes into the ocean. You have to have good timing and work with good people who know what they're doing. And I do, that's the fun of it."

Though he must, of course, hold his own on the boat, Rhodes remains a celebrity. "I can't go anywhere without people coming up and remembering the old days," he said. "Sometimes it's no fun because you can't be yourself." He looked up. "Right, hon?"

Gloria said, "Absolutely not. He loves it."

They both laughed.

Rhodes, though, does not live in the past. And he hasn't been to an Old-Timers' Day game in several years. "The last one I went to," he said, "they announced my name and I came out of the dugout and I got a little woozy. I guess it was a combination of my high blood pressure and the excitement of the big crowd. I couldn't play. I had to go back and sit down in the dugout.

"Imagine that. And I used to go up to bat in clutch situations before 80,000 people and never blink. When the pressure was on, I couldn't *wait* to grab a bat and get to the plate."

He was a country boy, but he was serious about his game, and he said he never failed to get to the park early to work on his hitting. He says he works just as hard on the tugs. "Whatever I do, I try to do as best I can," he said.

Gloria and Dusty were planning to leave the tavern. Rhodes put on his brown snap-brim felt hat with a tuft of feather in the band and stopped at the pool table along the wall.

"You play pool?" he asked a visitor.

"Not much," the visitor replied.

He took a cue stick and casually banked a beautiful shot into a corner pocket.

"I don't know much about this game neither," he said, with a wink.

Gloria waited at the door.

"Comin', darlin'," he said.

Thirty-Year Nemesis

New York, October 3, 1981

It happened 30 years ago today, but remains curiously alive. And every single day in those 30 years someone has mentioned it to Ralph Branca, or he has expected someone to.

At worst, he admits, he was in shock. But soon he could talk openly about it, and eventually even joke about it. He would make talks to various groups, and he had a running gag. "After two questions from the audience, I'd say, 'Isn't somebody going to ask me how I felt?' It is always the third question."

It was called "the shot heard round the world" and "the miracle of Coogan's Bluff." It happened around 3:30 on a beautiful fall afternoon in 1951, in the Polo Grounds, and the essential details are to baseball fans what the movements of the War of the Roses are to history buffs:

In mid-August, the Brooklyn Dodgers were leading the second-place New York Giants by 13½ games in the National League pennant race. The Dodgers seemed uncatchable. But the Giants embarked on the most dazzling comeback in baseball history and tied the Dodgers on the final day of the regular season. A three-game playoff ensued. The Giants won the first game, the Dodgers the second.

It came down to the bottom of the ninth inning of the deciding game. The Dodgers led, 4–1. The Giants seemed finished. But with one out they scored one run and now had two men on base and Bobby Thomson striding to the plate. Manager Charlie Dressen went to the plate. Manager Charlie Dressen went to the mound and replaced his starting pitcher, Don Newcombe, with Ralph Branca, a dark, husky, 6-foot-3-inch right-hander.

The crowd of 34,320 was roaring, and the old ball park shook. Branca, walking in from the bullpen, passed Jackie Robinson and Pee Wee Reese on the infield grass. "Anyone have butterflies?" Branca asked. The remark was meant to ease the tension.

Branca's first pitch was a strike. The next, a fastball, was high and tight, and Thomson, leaning away, swung and lifted a high fly ball to left field. Branca remembers watching the ball and wishing, "Sink, sink, sink."

The ball dropped into the stands just 30 inches past the 300-foot mark, for a three-run homer and the pennant. The place erupted. Giant fans poured onto the field even as Thomson circled the bases. Dodger fans wept.

"Ralph Branca turned and started for the clubhouse," wrote Red Smith. "The number on his uniform looked huge. Thirteen."

Ralph Branca is now 55 years old, an insurance broker in Westchester. He retired as a pitcher in 1956, but he has maintained ties with the game. Until a few years ago, he enjoyed throwing batting practice on occasion for the Mets. He still attends some Old-Timers' Day games. He still wears No. 13.

"The number never bothered me," Branca said. "I got it when I was a rookie in 1944. The clubhouse man said it was the only uniform my size but that if I was superstitious he could change the number.

"Well, I thought it might be lucky. I'm one of 13 kids in the family. And I was always the kind to defy superstition. I'd walk under a ladder or step on a sidewalk line. But when I arrived in training camp after we lost the pennant in '51, the team management had changed my number to 12. I was livid."

The number was no factor in Branca's early years.

"I won 20 games in a season when I was 21 years old—people don't remember that," he said. He was 21–12 in 1947. "Not many other pitchers ever did that."

In his 12 major league seasons, Branca won 88 games and lost 68. But after 1951 he was only 12–12. The Dodgers traded him to Detroit in 1953. He played with the Yankees and then the Dodgers again briefly before retiring at the young age of 30.

Despite his respectable record, the one pitch to Thomson dominated Branca's career. "People looked at me as if something awful—some horrible incident—had happened," he once said.

At one point, Branca was so troubled that he asked a priest, "Father, why did this have to happen to me?" And the priest said, "God gave you this cross to bear because he knew you'd be strong enough to carry it."

Most people were well-meaning. "It's amazing," Branca said. "They're always coming up and telling me where they were when the homer was hit. One guy was walking on 187th Street, another was listening on the radio in Korea."

In business, Branca talks about the homer with clients who are curious about it, before getting down to insurance. "It doesn't hurt to do that," he says.

A year ago April, on the day before the opening of the baseball season, the Mets, running an ad campaign with emphasis on nostalgia, used the famous photograph of Branca after the Thomson homer, his head buried in his hands, sobbing on the clubhouse steps. The ad copy recalled the moment. Branca saw it and was upset. No one had asked his permission to use the photograph, even out of courtesy. Bobby Valentine, his son-in-law and the former Met infielder, called the Mets' office to voice the family's indignation.

The reaction disturbed Fred Wilpon, the Mets' president. Wilpon immediately withdrew the ad and called Branca and apologized. "I told him," said Wilpon "that we simply tried to represent that picture—and others, like Jackie Robinson stealing home—which symbolized the drama of baseball in New York history. I also told him I had a special interest in him. He was a kind of idol of mine.

He was used as an example by my parents. I had big-league aspirations when I was growing up in Brooklyn. Ralph had gone to New York University, and my parents said, 'See, there's a fine, intelligent young man who went to college before he entered baseball.' I had wanted to follow in that path. He said he appreciated the call."

But it is one thing, apparently, for Branca to bring up the subject of the home run and quite another for him to open a newspaper and see a full-page ad of himself in that desolate moment.

"I've lived with this thing for 30 years," he said the other day, "and, really, I think it's about time it died."

The Missing Banks

Chicago, June 14, 1983

Ernie Banks smiled. It is perhaps the most famous smile in sports.

Once, he would greet someone with, "It's a beautiful day today, let's play two."

That was in a different life. Banks' hair is thinning now and he wears steel-rimmed spectacles for reading some of his business papers. He had on a dark tie and a vest from a blue business suit as he sat in his office at Equitable Life Assurance on Michigan Avenue.

He was a standout infielder for the Chicago Cubs for 19 years, and was elected to the Baseball Hall of Fame in 1977. He had a career average of .274 and hit 512 home runs—and became the greatest power-hitting shortstop of all time. Twice he was named the Most Valuable Player in the National League, in 1958 and 1959.

He was called "Mr. Cub." And that was the title of his autobiography.

No more. Retired for 12 years, Banks, now 52 years old, has stayed with the Cubs during that time in one capacity or another. Most recently, it was on a part-time basis in the team's promotional department.

On Saturday the Cubs announced that Banks will no longer be a member of the "Cub family."

The reason is that Banks, according to Cub management, had missed several scheduled appearances over the years, and that he was "unreliable."

Is that true?

"I had missed some," said Banks. "Not a lot, but two or three in a hundred. And when I did, I'd send a note of apology afterward, and maybe a Cub cap and a ball. I didn't want them to think I ignored them intentionally."

Was this the first time he had been the subject of negative remarks from the Cub office?

"No," he said. "In 1980, they had said similar things about my not showing up."

Was it justified?

"I had missed some engagements, yes."

The Chicago papers used words like "Cubs snub Mr. Cub," and a story castigated the Cubs for treating an idol in such a "callous" manner. A statement issued from the Cub office today said in part, "There are always two sides to every story. The Ernie Banks story also has two sides, and he apparently has chosen to let the newspapers do his talking for him."

Banks has said the split was amicable.

"They said that they had to make budget cuts," said Banks. "And they did make me an offer, but then my attorney made a counteroffer, and the next thing that happened was that Dallas Green wrote me a letter." Green is the Cubs' general manager.

"He said that the Cubs just couldn't afford what I was asking, and that he hopes there's no hard feelings. I told him that I was getting deeply involved in the insurance business, and he wished me luck."

Banks has not had a particularly easy time of it since he retired. He was a coach for two years, and he was in the marketing department of the Cubs, and then he tried the banking business, going to work for the Bank of Ravenswood in Chicago.

"They put me through an entire program starting with teller," said Banks. "And I enjoyed it. I love people, love being around them, and I could have been even a teller for the rest of my life. But

I hoped to rise in finance, and took courses at several colleges. But sports always seemed to take me away from it.

"They always thought of me as Ernie Banks, the ballplayer. It was hard to make a new identity. There was always the company softball team, and racquetball with the bank president, and functions to attend.

"I think I had a fear of failure in doing something outside of sports, like a lot of athletes do. And people don't help, because they keep talking to you about your past. They are trying to be nice, but they don't understand the problems an athlete has in adjusting to a new career.

"The bank had a social psychologist, and employees go to see her. I told her my problem, and she said, 'You can't change what you were, and you can't change the way people look at you. So why don't you just enjoy it?' And that's what I try to do now."

Banks retired after the 1971 season, just before free agency, when the truly big money for baseball players began. The most he ever earned in one season was $65,000. He was, though, able to save a substantial amount. But much of that is gone.

"But I spent it the best way you can," he said. "I put my three kids through the best private schools, and then helped them each go to college."

Money remains a factor, however.

"Wherever I go in Chicago," he said, "people are always coming up to me—just like a woman this morning in the drugstore—and saying, 'Ernie, I'm still a big fan of yours. I want to thank you for all the pleasure your playing ball gave me.' I think that's great, that they still remember me and wish me well after all these years. But, you know, that doesn't put any money in my pocket.

"I have no regrets, though, and I hope to make a success now in insurance. I have a temporary salesman's license, and on the 24th of this month I take the test to be certified as an agent. It's tough, and there's a lot of studying to do, but it's something I like and want to succeed in."

And the Cubs?

"I feel I'll always be a Cub. And I feel if there's anything I can do for them, I'll be happy to do it. They've been a part of my life for 30 years. I'd be happiest, probably, if I could stay with them for another 30 years."

Executing the Potato Play

New York, September 3, 1987

In a minor league baseball game in Williamsport, Pa., the other night, the catcher threw a potato wildly in an apparent attempt to pick a runner off third base.

When the base-runner reached home plate he was surprised, as was the umpire, that the catcher had the ball and tagged him out.

The runner and the umpire were surprised for good reason. They thought that the thing thrown by the catcher and still being retrieved by the outfielders was the ball in the game. It turned out to be only the potato in the game. A white potato, as it were, which had been shaved cleanly by the catcher, Dave Bresnahan of the Williamsport Bills, a Cleveland Indians team in the Class AA Eastern League.

It was a costly play for Bresnahan, who had sneaked the potato into his glove before the pitch. It cost his team a run, cost him a $50 fine, and also cost him his job. The Indians' director of player development, Jeff Scott, released him right afterward.

"I had checked the rule book a few days ago," said Bresnahan yesterday by phone from Williamsport, "and found nothing in it that says you can't throw a potato in a game." Which is absolutely true. The rule book also has no ruling against throwing a watermelon in a game. But that's another issue.

Before the pitch, Bresnahan had told the plate umpire that he had a problem with a string on his glove, and went back to the bench to get a new glove. In that glove was the now notorious white potato.

Back behind the plate, potato in glove, Bresnahan gave the pitcher the signal, then just before the ball was thrown, Bresnahan deftly switched potato to bare hand, caught the ball in the glove, and threw the potato intentionally wild to third.

"When I tagged the runner," said Bresnahan, "the umpire looked stunned. He realized that the potato was in the outfield, and called 'time out!'

"I didn't know why he called time out, but he said the runner was safe. I really thought they'd say, 'Do it over,' like a net ball in tennis, and get a laugh out of it. But the umpire didn't have any sense of humor about it at all. Maybe in a week he might. I think he thought I was trying to show him up, but I wasn't.

"I was just trying to put some fun into the game. I mean, it's not like it was the seventh game of the World Series. We're in seventh place, 26 games out of first. It was the 137th game of a 140-game season.

"The ump said, 'You can't do that!'

"I said, 'Why not? Where's the rule against it?'

"He said, 'You just can't, that's all.' I guess he was referring to his personal rule book."

Bresnahan makes a distinction between what he did and the recent outbreak of corked bats and scuffing of balls to get an edge.

"What I did was just to liven up a dull end of a season," he said. "The Phillies, they thought it was funny. My teammates thought it was funny—and had encouraged me to do it. The fans and management thought it was funny. You know, they're having a Potato Night at the ball park. Come to the park with a potato and you get in for a buck. I think tickets are $2.50 or $3 otherwise.

"Everybody thought it was funny except the umpire, and the Cleveland management."

The "prank or practical joke," admitted Scott of the Indians, "was kinda funny, but I think the game, once you get on the field, is sacred. You can't tamper with the integrity of the game. It disrupted the flow of the game, and I can't accept that."

Bresnahan, 25 years old, holds a business degree from Grand Canyon College in Phoenix, his hometown. This is his fourth year in the minor leagues and it appears, with a .149 batting average in 52 games this season for Williamsport, that this might be the end of the line for him.

It is a long way from the career of his great-uncle, Roger Bresnahan, the Hall of Fame catcher for the Giants and the Cubs, among others, in the early years of this century. It was great-uncle Bresnahan who introduced shin guards in 1907, and who, following a severe beaning, is credited with being the first to experiment with a batting helmet.

"I guess ingenuity is in the Bresnahan blood lines," said Scott.

"All I knew about my great-uncle," said Dave Bresnahan, "is that he was called the Duke of Tralee—that's in County Kerry where my grandparents are from—and he used to catch Christy Mathewson."

Dave Bresnahan said he couldn't believe that he would be released for this. As for the fine, he said his teammates wanted to pay it for him. What he did the next day was come to the park with a sack of 50 potatoes and a note pinned to it and put it on the desk of his manager, Orlando Gomez, who had removed Bresnahan from the game immediately after the incident.

The note read that he couldn't pay the fine, but that he hoped the manager would be satisfied with the potatoes. The note concluded, "This spud's for you. Bres."

Well, some thought the idea of throwing a potato in a game was half-baked, others expectedly weighed in with its being sweet.

Whatever, the result was that Dave Bresnahan was going back home.

Did he have any plans for the future?

"Sure," he said. "Run for governor of Idaho."

Tom Gorman's Final Call

New York, August 17, 1986

When Brian Gorman, son of Tom Gorman, the former major-league umpire, was in grade school in Closter, N.J., a classmate asked Brian one day what it felt like when his father missed a call.

"I don't know," said Brian, "he's never missed one."

That is how the offspring of baseball arbiters often go through life. Like their fathers, they know that he's always right, at least in his heart, if not specifically on the diamond.

When Tom Gorman died last Monday night, Brian still knew that his dad had never missed one.

It is an uncommon and difficult life being an umpire. In the autobiography that his father wrote with Jerome Holtzman, *Three and Two!*, published in 1979, Gorman recalled how the Hall of Fame pitcher Ed Walsh responded to umpiring. He worked at it for two months after having retired from the Chicago White Sox.

"It's a strange business," he told Billy Evans, the umpire. "All jeers and no cheers. You can have it!" And Walsh quit.

But there are rewards. Brian understood from his father what satisfactions can accrue to a man who calls balls and strikes, and safes and outs, and can tell a man earning $2 million a year to go take a shower, and right now.

Brian is now an umpire in the Southern Association, with dreams of making the major leagues, and he learned to love the life of an umpire when, as a boy on summer vacation, his dad would take him for two weeks on a trip through the National League towns. His dad also took his two brothers, Tom Jr. and Kevin, and their sister, Patty Ellen. "He took us each separately, so he could give us each undivided attention," recalled Brian.

He did it before their mother died, suddenly in 1968 at age 46, and the children were then ranging in age from 9 to 14. And Tom Gorman kept the household together—with help from neighbors and relatives—even as he continued clocking 100,000 miles or so a year in his travels as an umpire.

With the kids grown, and Gorman retired as an umpire after 27 big league seasons—he was most recently a supervisor of umpires for the National League—he married again six weeks ago. He was 67 years old, and life seemed to hold out continued joys.

A few weeks ago, in fact, he traveled to Memphis to watch Brian work some games there, and then sat up at night with Brian's colleagues. "He loved to talk umpiring," said Brian. "And he never gave me secret advice. If he had something to say about the techniques of umpiring, he told us all, and did it in a way that was kind of indirect. But you got the picture."

Brian recalled that three years ago, umpiring his first game, in the Class A New York–Penn League, in Oneonta, N.Y., he absently looked around the stands between the third and fourth innings, and there, right behind home plate, was a familiar strong-jawed, white-haired gentleman. "He gave me a nod," said Brian, "and I gave him a nod back. I didn't know Dad was coming. He surprised me. And it didn't make me nervous at all. It felt great to see him."

When Tom Gorman would tell his kids stories of days as an umpire, he told them with delight, and with none of the pain of the jeers, the travel, the lowly days of when he was a young umpire, and the pay. In 1950 in the National League, it was $5,000 a year and he had a nail on the wall for a locker.

He told of the five no-hitters he worked behind the plate, the five World Series, the five All-Star Games and the great games he was involved in. His favorite was the 1968 World Series opener in which Bob Gibson of the Cardinals struck out 17 Tiger batters.

"He'd correct people on that," said Brian. "He'd laugh and say, 'Gibson only struck out 10—I struck out 7.' There were seven called third strikes."

Tom Gorman recalled a time when Henry Aaron had two strikes on him and the pitcher threw a pitch right above the knees, on the outside corner. "Nobody," he wrote, "could hit a pitch like that. Nobody. And so I yelled, 'Strike three!' The next thing I knew, the ball was sailing into the seats.

"Aaron trotted around the bases and the catcher turned to me. 'Tom,' he said, 'what the hell are you doing?'

" 'I'm practicing,' I said."

Brian Gorman recalled that the most important thing for an umpire is to keep control of the game. An umpire must "keep an even keel," and try to calm the irate manager or ballplayer who is arguing a call.

Sometimes Gorman accomplished this in the oddest way. He told the story of when Leo Durocher, a nemesis of his, raced out of the Cubs' dugout to argue that he had missed a call on Don Kessinger, who tried to beat out a hit at first base.

"How the hell can Kessinger be out?" Durocher hollered, his eyes large.

"Leo," said Gorman, "he tagged the base with the wrong foot."

Gorman recalled that Durocher "stopped and looked at me, like I was a nut. He didn't know what to say. I had him stumped. . . . He turned and walked away." Gorman could see Durocher, when he got back to the dugout, talking to some of his players. Gorman could tell they didn't know what he was talking about.

"The game ended an hour later. Our dressing room was behind the Cub dugout and Leo was in the runway waiting for me. As I came in, he said, 'Hey, Tom, I want to talk to you.'

"What is it, Leo?"

"How long have you been in this league?"

"Twenty years."

"I want to tell you something, Tom," Durocher said. "And I'm only going to tell you once. They can tag first base with any foot."

Yesterday, in a cemetery in Paramus, N.J., Thomas David Gorman, born in Hell's Kitchen in Manhattan, was laid to rest. "When I go," he had told his children, "I want to be buried in my umpiring suit, and holding my indicator."

His wish was granted. His suit was buttoned, and his blue cap with the white letters "NL" was at his side. In his right hand was an indicator. The numbers read "3" and "2."

The Pied Piper

New York, January 4, 1986

Some will remember how Bill Veeck threw a post-leg-amputation party for himself—he was not about to wallow in self-pity—and danced the night away on his new wooden limb. That was in 1946, more than a year after he was injured. He had been a marine on Guadalcanal during World War II when an antiaircraft gun recoiled into his leg, and the leg became infected.

Others in recent years will remember—who can forget?—that wrinkled old face with that bright, boyish look in his eyes. And you had to remember his laugh, a deep, hoarse, genuinely delighted laugh, with head thrown back and stein of beer gripped solidly.

Others will remember him as the greatest hustler since Jack

Falstaff. And perhaps it was no coincidence that when he was the owner of the Chicago White Sox he named the press quarters "The Bard's Room." He understood that it couldn't hurt business to con the reporters some, too.

Bill Veeck will be remembered by many as the guy who brought midgets and orchids to baseball, or exploding scoreboards to the ball field, and signed the first black to play in the American League, Larry Doby, and put old Satchel Paige into a big-league uniform. And he'll be remembered by some as the guy who never wore a tie but who made starchy baseball owners so tight around the collar they got bug-eyed.

And some will remember how much he loved baseball. And some will remember how much he loved people. And some will remember both. "The most beautiful thing in the world," he once said, "is a ball park filled with people."

I have my own memories of William Louis Veeck Jr., who died Thursday of a heart attack at age 71. I remember him covering the Philadelphia-Baltimore World Series in 1983 for the *Chicago Tribune*. And in the outdoor press box in Philadelphia I noticed him at game's end set up his turquoise portable typewriter and begin to hit the keys.

He had been forced for financial reasons to sell the White Sox three years before, but his heart was still in the game—it always would be—and now he would write about it. On deadline. He was no phony. This former big-league baseball owner wrote his own stuff. I remember reading one of his pieces afterward and enjoying it very much. He knew the game, had original insights and stuck the adverbs and adjectives in all the right places.

I remember the first time I heard Veeck speak. It was in a hotel in Chicago in 1959—the first year that he ran the White Sox. He had placed billboards all around the city proclaiming, "We will bring a pennant to Chicago." I remember that the hall in the hotel was filled. Veeck at the lectern fidgeted and he seemed to list because of his leg, but he spoke without notes and told stories—old stories, but fresh to my then-fresh ears—about how poorly the Browns in St. Louis drew: One day he asked someone to come to a Browns game. The person said, "What time does it start?" Veeck replied, "What time's convenient?" The crowd loved him.

So did the rest of the city. True to his word, he brought a pennant to Chicago that very first year, and set another attendance record. He made Comiskey Park—often a dreary joint—a swell place for a few hours' entertainment. He not only cleaned up the old park, and had it painted, he even installed washrooms and an outdoor shower for the people in the bleachers. For the nearly 50 years that Comiskey Park had been in existence, those who had been treated as the underclass in the bleachers had simply been inconvenienced. Veeck cared enough about them—and his promotion—to do something about it.

One of the people he brought with him to Chicago was Hank Greenberg, the Hall of Fame ballplayer who became Veeck's general manager there. Greenberg was also his assistant when Veeck owned the Cleveland Indians in the middle 1940s. Greenberg lives in Beverly Hills, and on the morning when it was learned that Veeck had died, I called him.

"I've lost a great friend and great partner—he was the most unusual man I ever met," Greenberg said. His voice was a little shaky. As we spoke, there were moments when Greenberg stopped to gather himself.

"Bill brought baseball into the 20th century," he continued. "He sold baseball not just on the field, but off the field. Before Bill, baseball was just win or lose. But he made it fun to be at the ball park. Even if it was a lousy game that day, a lady could go home with an orchid he had handed out. Of course, he always wanted to win, and knew he'd draw more if he did.

"I remember the 1948 season in Cleveland when we set the attendance record for the major leagues with 2.6 million. I'd look out the window of the stadium and see these great crowds of people coming out over the bridge and heading for the ball park. I told Bill, 'You're like the Pied Piper.'

"Bill wasn't just a guy trying to make a buck by running promotions. He really enjoyed people enjoying themselves. He was color-blind and race-blind and religion-blind. I first met him in 1947 and he talked to me about the Indians—I mean the ones in Oklahoma and Texas—and how unfairly they had been treated. I never knew from such things. This was so far advanced for me. I was a guy who was concerned with base hits and how to win a ball game. It opened up my eyes.

"When he brought Satchel Paige into baseball, a lot of people said he was making a mockery of the game, because Satchel was 48 or something. Remember, this was a day when a ballplayer was really old at 32 or 33. Well, Satch was 6 and 1 for us down the stretch and we won the pennant."

Though Veeck was out of baseball for the last six years, he couldn't stay away, and was frequently seen in the bleachers in Wrigley Field. Greenberg recalled: "The last time we talked was on Monday when I called him in the hospital. Bill said, 'You know, I think I can get the Cleveland club.' I said, 'You're crazy. Why don't you go someplace where you have a chance to make some money? Why don't you go into the stock market, or some other business? With your talents you can make a lot of money at anything.'

"He said, 'Wouldn't it be great, Hank, to get the old gang together again?'

"He was hopeless. I said. 'You still want to sell peanuts at the ball park, don't you?'

" 'Yeah,' he said, 'I do.' "

With a Hole in His Head

New York, January 5, 1985

The talk was about hardnosed and hardheaded football players, and the name of Dick Plasman naturally came up. Not only was Plasman hardheaded when he played, he was bareheaded, too.

Dick Plasman was the last man in the National Football League to play without a helmet, as late as 1947. He also coached without a helmet in the National Football League, but that is beside the point.

In the early days of football, at least into the 1930s, playing bareheaded was not rare. But such historical players have been taking a bad rap in recent times. Perhaps the unkindest cut was made by Lyndon Johnson about Gerald Ford: "He played one too many games without a helmet."

Ford, in fact, wore a helmet—a thin leather covering, but a helmet nonetheless—as a center for Michigan in the 1930s. Plasman wore nothing on his head but a shock of blond hair, part of which covered a hole in his head, a result of a gridiron mishap.

Plasman, who died in retirement at age 67 in 1981, played for the Chicago Bears and the Chicago Cardinals, and later became an assistant coach with the Green Bay Packers and the Pittsburgh Steelers. With the Bears, he was, at 6 feet 4 inches and 220 pounds, an offensive end, linebacker and occasional kicker from 1937 through 1941, during the team's glory days as the Monsters of the Midway, and in the 1944 season.

Plasman served in the military during World War II, then joined the Cardinals and played with them for two seasons, 1946 and 1947. In the time he was away, the NFL had instituted a rule that made wearing a helmet mandatory, much to Plasman's dismay. He protested that this would cause a hardship for him, that this was an unfair labor practice. The league reconsidered and issued a special dispensation to Plasman, comparable to baseball's exempting the old spitball pitchers when rules were changed while they were still active.

Plasman was primarily a kicker with the Cardinals, and so didn't get much involved in head-to-head confrontations. Not so in his earlier days, when he received the hole in his head which was actually a deep indentation in the acreage around his left temple.

It was obtained one fall Sunday in 1938 at Wrigley Field. Skull untrussed and hands outstretched, Plasman raced into the end zone for a pass, following the flight of a ball he would not catch. He never considered the outfield wall that jutted two feet into the end zone. In later days, the field would be resituated, and mats would be hung on the wall. Too late, though, for Plasman's pate. He crashed headfirst into the bricks.

When he woke up, a few days later, his head was finally covered, but with bandages. He lay in a hospital bed.

Sometimes there are indeed blessings in disguise. This was one of those times. An attractive nurse was ministering to him, and if there was something wrong with Plasman's head at this point, there was nothing wrong with his eyes. When he left the hospital, he took the nurse with him, and married her.

Plasman soon returned to the football field, but still with no helmet, opting for more skull drudgery. But he had a reason: The leather chapeau of those days would drop disconcertingly over his eyes like the broken visor of a knight's armor. Besides, Plasman never liked to wear hats of any sort, and in the Army—he made the rank of captain—was nearly court-martialed once for strolling about the base with a denuded cranium.

Plasman was visited a few years ago while living in Arlington Heights, Ill., a Chicago suburb. At the time, he was selling optical equipment, and he seemed to have weathered his days of playing without a helmet quite nicely. He said he thought of the crevice in his head only when he touched it. (Still, he did have a few other aches and pains. For one thing, he couldn't sleep on his right side, because of old football injuries—one of which was due to his never having worn hip pads.)

It seemed that his wife, June, considered the crash into the wall more than he did. When they had a disagreement, she explained to him, "You know something, you never recovered from that head injury."

Plasman recalled that only one opponent ever took advantage of his unhelmeted head. This was a defensive end with the Redskins who "kept bashing me with his elbow," said Plasman. One day the guy lay on the ground after a play, and Plasman stepped on him. "It worked," said Plasman, "and the guy stopped his antics." Plasman smiled, showing the bridgework that had replaced his football-lost teeth.

Hadn't Plasman feared injury as a player? He said no: "If you hustled and weren't lazy, you wouldn't get hurt." He added that if someone gave you a "real good shot," it wouldn't matter whether you were wearing protection or not. "The bells would be ringing," he said.

During his years as a coach with Pittsburgh, he was a favorite on the team, recalls Art Rooney, owner of the Steelers. "He was smart and had the touch with the ballplayers," Rooney said.

As a coach, Plasman still refused to wear headgear. And on the sidelines once he suffered frostbite of the ear.

Even though all modern players wear helmets, Plasman said he respected them. And he believed that they were bigger and smarter and faster than those in his day. Did that mean he'd have worn something on his head if he had played today?

"Yes," he said. "Earmuffs."

"Candlelight" Goes Out

New York, August 1, 1986

In the fall of 1974, a funny thing happened on the Harvard campus. A scout representing a National Football League combine was seen walking through the square. NFL scouts don't normally appear on Ivy League campuses. Was he confused? Was he lost?

In fact, he had come to test Pat McInally, a Harvard senior. The scout carried a standard list of questions that is given to all potential draftees, and he would administer it to McInally, a wide receiver and punter.

Now, the Harvard football program had described McInally as "a 6-6, 210-pound marionette, who looks as though he were strung together by some football-crazed Gepetto. [He will break] from the Harvard huddle and toddle off to the sideline with his wooden, herky-jerky gait. The pumping of his long, bowed legs will cause his shoulders to jiggle at crazy angles.

"The shirt-tail of his crimson jersey will be dangling, and the stockings, pulled tight and taped, will still leave three inches of shin exposed. The helmet will be askew."

Forget appearances. He was fast, he had slippery moves, he was sure-handed, and he nabbed enough passes that he was a consensus all-American.

It had been determined that, physically, McInally was pro football material. But mentally? Sure, he was an excellent student who would soon be earning a degree in American history. Yet the question remained: Could he pass the rigid NFL intellectual requirements?

McInally took the scout to Widener Library and they found a quiet corner.

"The first question he asks," recalled McInally, "was, 'Is 11 P.M. before or after midnight?' I looked at him, and he looked at me. I said, 'I can't commit myself.' He said, 'What?' I said, 'It depends on the day. It's after 11 P.M. on one day, but before 11 P.M. another day.'

"He marked down, 'wrong answer.' " Later, McInally would learn why 11 P.M. was so important to football people. "That's the curfew hour," said McInally, with a chuckle.

The scout had 17 more questions, and apparently McInally did much better on those, for he was drafted in the fifth round by the Cincinnati Bengals.

And although his brains were suspect in the beginning, McInally overcame the obstacle and did well enough to play 10 years in the NFL, sometimes as a wide receiver, but mostly as a punter. He twice led the league in punting average, was named to the NFL all-star team in 1981 and was the kicker on the Cincinnati team that lost to the 49ers in the 1982 Super Bowl.

Last Sunday, at the Bengals' training camp in Wilmington, Ohio, John Patrick Joseph McInally retired from football. There was a rash of young receivers with the Bengals now, and McInally was relegated to punting only.

He had been the fourth-leading punter in the American Conference last year, and the 10th in the NFL, with a 42.3-yard average. He was still very good, but the challenge for him had dissipated. It was harder for him to concentrate on such lofty subjects as hang times when he was wondering what he would do with life after football.

He was viewing classmates from Harvard now in the early part of good careers, while he was coming to the end of his. He decided that he had opportunities he wanted to explore—such as in broadcasting or writing (he had written a once-a-week syndicated column for a few years for 90 newspapers).

And he had felt his age. At 33, he was now one of the old men of the team.

"Suddenly I was feeling more on the outside," said McInally. "Some of my longtime friends on the team had gone. And as a specialist, you're not in there on a regular basis, and so you're not really a part of the game."

So now it has ended, and he says it has been a great deal of fun. At Harvard, he proved he wasn't just "a jock," but "a person, too." He had come out of Villa Park, Calif., where, he said, "People admired athletes. They called us 'studs.' But at Harvard you were considered a kind of Neanderthal."

He recalled his college girlfriend, Lisa Mann, a Radcliffe English major, who introduced Pat to her father, Robert, who is first violin in the Juilliard String Quartet.

There was tension when McInally and Mann—men from two different worlds—first met. But that subsided. Once, Mann was working a crossword puzzle and asked McInally for help.

"Do you know a six-letter word for a strategic football kick?" Mann said.

"Onside," replied McInally. They've been friends ever since.

Pro football was tougher than the crossword puzzle, though.

In McInally's first game as a pro, in the 1975 College All-Star Game, and on his first play, he caught a pass for a touchdown, was tackled in the end zone and broke his leg. He was out for the year.

He came back the following season, and on his first play in a scrimmage caught a pass and was hit with a vicious clothesline tackle by Ron Pritchard.

"The next thing I knew, I was in a hospital with a concussion and a shoulder injury that would lead to surgery," recalled McInally. "That's when Bob Trumpy began calling me 'Candlelight.' One blow and I was out."

But he would show that in the Ivy League they didn't just play flag football, as some had supposed. He'd get out of that hospital bed and go on to play superbly that season, and the nine more following.

"I remember Pritchard visiting me in the hospital," said McInally. "I had gotten along fine with Ron, considering he was a linebacker. Well, he came into the room with his head hanging down. He explained that he had mistaken me for Chip Myers, who was built like me. He didn't like Chip. But when he saw that it was me he had hurt, he felt awful. He said, 'I felt so bad that I went to Chip and made up with him.'

"How did I feel when he said that?" McInally said. "I wanted to raise up and hit him, but I couldn't move."

The Fire Inside Ali

Los Angeles, April 28, 1985

The sprawling three-story house was quiet, except for the tinny too-wa, too-wee of birds in a small aviary next to the office room on the first floor. It was early on a recent morning and the cool, shadowed office was dimly lit by two antique candelabras that had a few of their small bulbs burned out. An antique lamp was also lit and with its slightly crooked shade peered over the large black mahogany desk scattered with letters and an Islamic prayer book. Nearby were several open boxes stuffed with mail.

Behind the desk, three large windows opened onto a backyard, half in sunlight, with cypress trees and pruned bushes and a swimming pool. Along another wall in the office, a pair of black men's shoes stood by themselves in the middle of a brown-suede couch. In another corner, a television set, with another on top of it, rested on the Oriental rug that covered most of the floor of the room. On the wall facing the desk was a marble fireplace without a fire.

Suddenly, a torch appeared in the doorway. The fire, burning at the end of a rolled-up newspaper, was followed by a large man in black-stockinged feet who trotted into the room. "Hoo, hoo," he said as the flame burned closer to his hand, and he tossed the torch into the fireplace. Quickly, the logs in the fireplace crackled with the flame, and Muhammad Ali, the torchbearer, watched them burn. Then he sat down in an armchair in front of his desk and in a moment closed his eyes.

He said something, indistinct, in a gravelly mumble, and the visitor, in a chair facing him, asked Ali if he would repeat it.

"Tired," he said, with a little more effort, his eyes still closed. It was 8 o'clock in the morning and Ali had been up since 5:30 saying his daily prayers.

He stretched his legs. He wore a light blue shirt, unbuttoned at the cuffs, which was not tucked into his dark blue slacks. At 43, Ali's face is rounder and his body is thicker than when he first won the world heavyweight championship by knocking out Sonny Liston in Miami in February 1964. The 6-foot-3-inch Ali weighed 215 then and is now about 240 pounds.

In the ensuing years, he would weigh as much as 230 in the ring as he lost and regained the title two more times—an unprecedented feat in the heavyweight division. Ali, who was stopped in a one-sided bout by Larry Holmes while attempting to win the title yet a fourth time, retired five years ago, but he is hardly forgotten.

A few days before, he had been at ringside at the Hagler-Hearns middleweight title fight in Las Vegas. Numerous ex-champions were introduced before the bout. Ali was saved for last.

He was asked now how he felt about that moment. He said nothing, and it appeared he was sleeping. Then: "A-li, A-li, A-li," he said, opening his eyes and mimicking the chant that arose among the 16,000 fans when the ring announcer introduced him.

"I had to go like this," he said softly, raising his right index finger to his lips, "to calm the people down.

"A lot of fighters, when they quit no one ever hears of them again. But I've gotten bigger since I quit boxin'. Look at this," he said, nodding to a box in the corner, "people from all over the world writin' me. Thirty-one boxes full of fan mail in four years."

One was from Bangladesh, sent to "Loos Anjeles" and calling Ali "my unknown Uncle." Another from West Germany asked "Mr. Ali" for his autograph. A third was from Drakefield Road in London and sent to the New York Presbyterian Hospital, where Ali had gone late last summer for a checkup. He has been diagnosed as having Parkinson's syndrome, a nerve disorder.

Ali asked the visitor to open the letter and read it aloud.

"I am very sorry to know of your temporary problem," wrote the Briton, "and wish you most sincerely a rapid recovery. Many of my friends who are fans of yours are thinking the same, that you will in a very short time be back to your old poetic self and come and see us in dear old London. . . ."

Do you still write poetry? the visitor asked Ali.

"No," he said, "no more. That was in a different time. Eighteen times callin' the round. 'That's no jive, Cooper will fall in five.' 'Moore in four.' "

The visitor recalled a personal favorite, when Ali predicted how his first fight with Liston would go. It turned out that Liston didn't answer the bell for the seventh round. Did Ali remember the poem?

"Mmmmm," he said. It wasn't clear what he meant by that.

But he began, his voice still very low:

"Ali comes out to meet Liston,

"And then Liston starts to retreat.

"If he goes back any farther, he'll wind up in a ringside seat."

He paused thoughtfully, then continued.

"And Liston keeps backin' but there's not enough room,

"It's a matter of time—There! Ali lowers the boom.

"Ali lands with a right—what a beautiful swing!

"The punch knocks Liston right out of the ring. . . ."

Just then the phone rang. "My phone's ringing,' " he said. "Hold on." He reached over to his desk. "Yeah, naw, naw," he said sleepily into the phone. "I wouldn't try that for no $5,000, you crazy?" He nodded. "Check ya later." And hung up. "Where was I?"

He was reminded that he had just knocked Liston out of the ring.

"Who woulda thought," he continued, "when they came to the fight,

"That they'd witness the launchin' of a hu-man satellite.

"Yes, yes, the crowd did not dream when they laid down their money,

"That they would see a total eclipse of the Sonny."

Ali's voice was fading again. "I wrote that 22 years ago," he said, his words getting lost in his throat. "That was a long time." He is taking voice lessons from Gary Catona, who had come into the room during the recital of the old limerick. Catona is a voice and singing teacher who three weeks ago had come to Los Angeles from Austin, Tex., to try to help Ali speak more clearly.

Ali began to speak more slowly and less distinctly over the last several years. There was much speculation about him suffering a variety of illnesses. During his hospital visit in New York last September, doctors determined that he had Parkinson's syndrome.

Catona believes that the only problem with Ali's voice is that his vocal muscles are weak, that they lack resonance.

Ali was asked what was wrong with his voice.

"I dunno," he said, "somethin'."

"Muhammad never really had strong vocal muscles," said Catona. "He used to scream out his words. His normal speech was never a normal speech."

Ali and his voice teacher schedule a one-hour lesson every day, but Ali travels a lot and they don't always connect. "But he's good when we do it," said Catona. "It's like building body muscles, you've got to work at it. He sings the sounds of the scales. 'Ah! Ah! Ah!'" Catona sang, his voice rising at each "Ah."

Catona and Ali had already had the session at the piano in the living room, and beyond this Ali was asked what he's been doing with himself lately.

"People are interested in you," he was told. "You're one of the most popular figures—"

"Popular niggers?" he interrupted.

"Figures," the visitor repeated.

Ali looked at him playfully out of the corner of his eye.

"What am I doin' now, oh, I'm so busy," he said, growing serious. "I'm busy every day. I've got all this mail to answer—they're startin' fan clubs for me all over the world, in Asia, in Europe, in Ireland, in China, in Paris. But my mission is to establish Islamic evangelists, and to tour the world spreadin' Islam."

He converted from Christianity to the Islamic faith 21 years ago, changing his name, as the world knows, from Cassius Clay to Muhammad Ali.

On the shelf above the fireplace stood a *Sports Illustrated* cover from May 5, 1969, laminated on a wooden plaque. The cover showed the young boxer wearing a crown, with the caption, "Ali-Clay—The Once—and Future?—King."

What's the difference between Cassius Clay and Muhammad Ali? he was asked.

"As much difference as night and day," he said. "Cassius Clay was popular in America and Europe. Muhammad Ali has a billion more fans all over the world. Cassius Clay had no knowledge of his self. He thought Clay was his name, but found out it was a slave name. Clay means 'dirt, with no ingredients.' Cassius—I don't know what that means. But Ali means 'the most high,' and Muhammad means 'worthy of praise and praiseworthy.'

"Cassius Clay had Caucasian images of God on his wall. Muhammad Ali was taught to believe that there should be no image of God. No color. That's a big difference."

He rose and got a large briefcase from under his desk. He withdrew several religious pamphlets with pictures of Jesus Christ. All but one was white. Then he took out a Bible and opened it to Exodus 20:4, and asked the visitor to read it. "Thou shalt not make unto thee any graven image, or any likeness of any thing that is in heaven above. . . ."

"Ooohh," said Ali. "Powerful, isn't it? But what are all these? Man, you thought boxin' was powerful. Boxin's little. These pictures teach supremacy. The Bible says there should be no pictures of God, no images, he should be no color. But you see that God is white. Tarzan, King of the Jungle, was a white man. Angel's food cake is white, devil's food cake is black. Man, ain't that powerful?

"Cassius Clay would not have the nerve to talk like this—he'd be afraid of what people might say or think. Ali is fearless, he's hopin', prayin' that you print this. Cassius Clay would not have the courage to refuse to be drafted for the Vietnam War. But Muhammad Ali gave up his title, and maybe he would have to go to jail for five years."

He rose again and this time brought back a plastic box, flipped up the latches, and opened the lid. It was a box of magic paraphernalia.

He took two red foam rubber balls and made them become four right before the visitor's eyes, then turned them into a box of matches, then made them disappear altogether. His eyes widened in mock shock. He still has the fastest hands of any heavyweight in history. It was a very good trick.

How did he do it?

"It's against the law for magicians to tell their tricks," he said.

"It's a tricky world."

He next transformed three small unstretchable ropes of varying sizes into the same size.

He made a handkerchief disappear, but, on the second showing, he was too obvious about stuffing it into a fake thumb.

"You should only show that trick once," he said, a little embarrassed.

He redeemed his virtuosity by putting four quarters into the visitor's hand, snapping his fingers, and ordering the quarters to become two dimes and two pennies. The quarters obeyed. He snapped his fingers again and the quarters returned; the pennies and dimes vanished.

"It's magic for kids," he said. "It's my hobby. See how easy they can be deceived? But these aren't childish things. They make you think, don't they?"

It was mentioned that perhaps Ali's best magic trick was transforming the small house he lived in as a boy in Louisville into this 22-room house with expensive antique furniture. He made more than $60 million in ring earnings and endorsements. "But the Government took 70 percent," he said. He says he is financially secure. He doesn't do commercials, for example, because, he said, "I don't need the money."

He lives here in Wilshire with his two children by Veronica Ali, 8-year-old Hana and 6-year-old Laila. They employ a live-in house-keeper. His six other children live with his two former wives.

"My wife likes antiques," he said, walking into the living room. He pointed to a tall clock against the wall. "It's 150 years old."

Gary Catona now took his leave, and arranged for a session the following morning. Ali led his visitor for a tour of the house. "I'm not braggin'," he said, "just showin'. I don't like to talk about what I have, because there's so many people hungry, homeless, no food, starvin', sleepin' on the streets."

In the dining room is a long dark table with 12 tall carved chairs. On the second floor are the bedrooms. In the kids' rooms, toys and stuffed animals tumbled across the floor. There's an Oriental sitting room, a guest room.

The phone rang. "City morgue," he answered. He spoke briefly and hung up.

Ali and the visitor ascended the carpeted staircase to the third floor. On a wall are a pair of red boxing gloves encased in glass. One glove is signed, "To the champion of champions—Sylvester Stallone." On an adjoining wall is a robe with multicolored sequins that bears the inscription, "The People's Choice." In the corner of the case is a photograph of a man with his arm around Ali. It is Elvis Presley, who gave Ali the robe.

In the adjoining room is a large pool table with a zebra skin lying over it. Trophies and plaques and photographs line the wall and cover the floor.

He was asked about recent efforts to ban boxing.

"Too many blacks are doin' well in it, so white people want to ban it," he said. "But how do I live here without boxin'? How would I ever be able to pay for all this? Look at Hearns and Hagler. Two poor black boys, but now they help their mother and father and sisters and brothers. It's from boxin'.

"There's more deaths in football than boxin'. Nobody wants to ban football. You see car races. 'Whoom, whoom.' Cars hit the wall, burn up. Motor boats hit a bump. Bam! Don't ban that, do they?"

Going back down the stairs, the visitor is met by a nearly life-size painting of Ali in the ring wearing white boxing trunks. He is on his toes and his arms are raised in triumph. The signature in the corner of it reads, "LeRoy Neiman. '71."

Did Ali miss fighting?

"When the fight's over," he said, "you don't talk about it anymore."

The visitor asked about his health.

"I don't feel sick," Ali said. "But I'm always tired."

How did he feel now?

"Tired," he said, "tired."

A doctor friend, Martin Ecker of Presbyterian Hospital, has said that if Ali takes his prescribed medication four times a day—the medication is L-Dopa, which in effect peps up the nervous system (the disease does not affect the brain)—then Ali's condition would be improved substantially. The medication does not cure the disease, but it increases alertness.

Ali is inconsistent in taking the medication. He believes it doesn't matter if he takes the medication, because he is in the hands of Allah, and that his fate is sealed. Days go by when he doesn't take the medicine. But when friends urge him to, or when he is going to make a public appearance, then he is more inclined to take his dosage.

Did he feel that after 25 years of amateur and professional fights, of countless hours of sparring, that he had taken too many punches?

He stopped on the second-floor landing. He rubbed his face with his hands. "Uh-uh," he said, softly. "Look how smooth. I very rarely got hit."

As the visitor turned from Ali and opened the door to go, he heard an odd cricket sound behind his ear.

The champ smiled kindly but coyly. There was either a cricket in the house or something that sounded like a cricket in his hand.

Walking to his car in this quiet, elegant neighborhood, and then driving out past the security guard at the gate, the visitor realized he would not plumb the mystery of the cricket sound in Muhammad Ali's house. It's a tricky world, he recalled, and he would leave it at that.

A Soupçon
of Savvy

Sage Advice from Solly Diamond

New York, July 31, 1983

Solly Diamond went through life at his own pace and with his own wisdom. Once, for example, he sized up a former golfing partner this way: "If you put his brain in a canary, it would fly backwards."

Solly Diamond came to certain convictions. "Money isn't everything," he once said. "Health is five percent."

And he was no sentimentalist: "My grandfather in Russia used to go out with a rope and come back with a horse."

Solly Diamond's name came up recently in regard to the shot Hale Irwin missed in the recent British Open. It was a 3-inch putt that Irwin thought he'd nonchalantly tap in backhanded. He missed the ball.

That one stroke was the difference between Tom Watson's winning the Open and Irwin's finishing second. With the PGA Championship in Los Angeles beginning Thursday, Irwin could probably profit from advice by Solly Diamond, who, despite being dead for the last several years, still lives in memory.

"If you look back," Solly said, "you die of remorse."

And perhaps of somewhat less consolation for Irwin, Solly noted, "Just remember, every shot makes someone happy."

Solly was an avid amateur golfer. Amateur in a fashion. Golf was no game for him unless it was played for money, not prize money like the professionals but side bets, and of an inventive nature. His club brimmed with people like him.

Solly played at Tam O'Shanter Country Club, just outside of Chicago. It was the sight of one of the most famous golf shots in history. Lew Worsham sank a 130-yard wedge shot for an eagle on the final hole to win the 1953 World Championship of Golf by one stroke.

A particular shot by Solly, though, is recalled for being as remarkable in its way as Worsham's. At least, it caused quite a stir.

Solly was a baldish, stocky man who favored a cap and knickers when he went on the course. "Solly loved golf because it gave him a creative outlet," surmised his son, Terry Diamond, an investment broker in Chicago, "and sometimes added generously to his wallet. And sometimes took away from it.

"You have to remember that Solly left school when he was 9 years old to make his way in the world. He used to ride the rails. He went all over the country except Florida. The only way to get there was through Georgia, and if they caught you on a freight train in Georgia, they'd throw you on a chain gang. So no Florida.

"Solly went to Hollywood and was an extra in the old Tom Mix westerns. Sometimes he played a cowboy and sometimes an Indian, and sometimes both."

When Solly was a young man he stopped in Louisville, Ky., and met a short man who suggested a business deal that appealed to Solly.

"They went to the racetrack," said Terry, "and Solly picked up the losing tickets for the first two races and ran through the stands shouting 'I won, I won.' He did it again after the third race. People began to gather round him. Then this short man who looked like a jockey came by and he and Solly whispered to each other. People watched. Soon people began paying my father for tips.

"Not long after, Solly's partner happened to pick nine winners in one day. And he said, 'I'm not going to give those suckers winners.' End of business. The guy believed his own lies."

Solly would return to Chicago, find his way into the linen business and do so well that he could eventually spend considerable time on the golf course. He couldn't hit long, but he developed a "commercial swing," as it was known at the club. His shots were invariably straight down the fairway. And his short game was superb.

Solly's round that caused the controversy, Terry recalled, was played against Julius. Julius was one of the club's more clever golfers.

Julius had a 10-stroke handicap, Solly a 6. Julius sought to work a deal. Julius wanted Solly to spot him eight strokes. That is, four more strokes than the handicap would suggest.

Julius, as Solly knew, was no fool. "Money goes through his pockets like cement," Solly once noted of him. They wangled and cajoled. Terry recalled: "Finally, Solly said, 'O.K., I'll give you the strokes if you let me place the tee anywhere I want on a hole of my choosing.'

"Julie agreed, but on one condition. 'You have to hit from the same place,' he told Solly. Agreed.

"And of course they put a nice bit of change on the outcome. It was a close match. Coming up to a tee on the last nine, Solly was three strokes down. He noticed the thick woods to the right. This was the time to take advantage of Julie's tendency to slice.

"Solly placed the tee markers right beside the woods. He drove first and hit his characteristic straight shot, narrowly missing the woods. Julius's shot scattered birds as it ripped through the trees."

From the 11th to the 14th, they remained neck-and-neck. On the 14th, Julius went into a sand trap.

"Now," Terry said, "Julius made another offer to Solly. He said, 'If you let me throw my ball out of the trap instead of hitting it, then I'll give you a throw when you want it.'

"Solly said fine. Julius threw his ball a few feet from the hole for a gimme putt.

"Now they're at the 18th hole. The score is even. They both drive well. Because Solly was away, as usual, he would hit first. The second shot must carry over a water hazard. Solly, remember, has a throw coming. And he walks over to Julius's ball, picks it up and flings it in the water.

"Julius is hopping mad. He shouts it's not fair. Solly says, 'It's only a one-stroke penalty. You're lucky I didn't throw it in the woods. That's two strokes.'

"Solly takes the lead, the match and the dough.

"Julius is not only mad about losing but he says, 'How come you had to throw a brand-new ball in the water?'

"Julius appeals to the club for a ruling on the throw. And Solly is upheld. Then Solly goes to the pro shop and buys a dozen new balls and gives them to Julius.

"Solly," recalled Terry, "always said, 'There's room for a bull, there's room for a bear, but there's no room for a pig.' "

Such Sweet Thunder

New York, February 27, 1982

For the first time in history, two Kentucky Derby winners have been brought together to play the horse breeder's version of spin the bottle.

To be sure, the mating of Secretariat and Genuine Risk was a hard business decision with a commercial eye focused on the auction of yearlings in the spring following next. But for those inclined it also had symbolic overtones.

The assignation occurred, happily enough, shortly after Valentine's Day. And if only for the 180 seconds it took to consummate their match in the breeding shed at Claiborne Farm in Paris, Ky., it demonstrated that romance, despite the cynics, is still a part of sports.

It also brought to mind one of the most unlikely love affairs known in horse-racing circles. It involved Mike the speculator and Leonore the cellist.

Mike was a regular at the tracks around a certain large midwestern city. Leonore played cello in the city's renowned symphony orchestra.

They met at a wedding, and right from the start there was a definite chemical reaction between them.

It is true that birds of a feather flock together, but it also happens—as it did now—that opposites attract.

Leonore liked Mike's dark good looks and his light, smooth, uncerebral approach to life. He took her to the track. She was impressed with his stature. People came over to him frequently and asked, "Mike, who do you like?"

The races themselves also appealed to her. She was reminded of the words of the Bard: "I never heard so musical a discord, such sweet thunder."

Mike responded to Leonore's willowy elegance and her good breeding. He had decided that she was definitely the class of the field.

She took him to concerts. It was different for Mike; in fact, just being indoors for such a long period of time was different. He often found the music soothing. And Mike took pleasure in watching Leonore play; the fact that a cellist's bow is made of horsehair was incidental for Mike, but charming nonetheless.

Eventually, he could compare the artistry of some jockeys to those of some conductors—how one could bring out the best in a horse, while the other could bring out the best in the woods and strings.

Hartack had a forceful, hard-driving manner, like Solti; Shoemaker was all hands, and patient, and waited for the opening along the rail and then gently eased the horse through, like Maazel.

Mike and Leonore set up housekeeping. They enjoyed candlelight dinners in fine restaurants when Mike was flush, and traveled together when Leonore toured in states that allowed horse racing.

But even in the best performances there are sour notes struck, even in the best races there are wrong steps taken. And Mike and Leonore encountered these in their relationship.

They also had a certain incompatibility in their respective spheres.

Mike enjoyed her companionship at the track, but Leonore often had to practice.

Leonore wanted Mike to take more of an interest in music, and not fall asleep at the concerts.

"I doze," he said, "because I'm enjoying it. It's a compliment to the musicians. If they played scratchy, it would keep me awake."

After performances, she'd ask Mike his opinion. He said it was nice or it wasn't nice. He thought that should suffice. Leonore didn't. "She wanted 'marvelous,' or 'dynamic,' or 'moving,'" Mike recalled. "The movements I cared about were during the post parade. What else could I say?"

It hurt Leonore to see the "squalor and poverty," as she termed it, of some of his fellow speculators. And it disturbed her to see people losing who, she understood, couldn't afford it.

Mike said gambling had its compensations. It gave people hope that maybe tomorrow the world would be a better place for them.

"And it's so freeing there," he said. "The fresh air, the grass—I even love the smell of manure."

Sometimes they'd quarrel over domestic matters, and at home the sound of Leonore's mellow cello would be replaced by the crashing of dishes she threw, and the door he slammed.

And by now the romance between Mike and Leonore, once a triumph of love over the severest obstacles, was foundering.

Leonore left for Europe with the symphony, and, as a kind of last-ditch effort, Mike joined her in Vienna, as planned.

They toured the cathedrals and drank espresso in atmospheric cafes, but Mike was getting homesick. One afternoon he sat in the great concert hall and listened to the orchestra rehearse Mahler. It was melodic, but he still longed for the rhythms of the hooves back home.

After the rehearsal, Mike went up on the stage.

As he approached, Lenore asked, "Mike, how did you like our Mahler?"

Mike, whose mind had been elsewhere, quickly caught himself and replied passionately, "All for Mahler, stand up and holler!"

Now, several years later, Mike recalled that time.

"I never saw Leonore again," he said. "She was pretty mad. But we had a happy ending—as endings go." He paused. "She's still playing, and so am I."

Maybe it was the lighting near the mutuel window, but it did seem that in Mike's gambler's eyes there was moistness.

Living and Dying by Horses

New York, June 5, 1982

Ever since Al died, about a year ago, Annie hasn't gone to the racetrack quite as much as she once did. This year, she won't be going to the Belmont Stakes—she attended regularly—but she'll be involved. Annie's got a gig.

She and her husband used to go to tracks in New York during the day, and then again at night. His occupation was professional cardplayer, and he was so good that sometimes people in the game made him wear gloves to deal, just to make sure his hands wouldn't move quicker than their eyes. But he played cards only in order to play the horses.

He didn't play the horses nearly as well as he played cards. And sometimes after losing at the track, he didn't have enough change in his pocket to pay the toll on the expressway, so he signed a voucher and the attendants let his Cadillac pass. Annie remembers when Al and their two kids drove to Florida on a vacation, and instead of first dropping their luggage at the hotel, Al headed straight to Hialeah to make it for post time.

Their son grew up to be a professional horse player and their daughter still reads a form chart quicker than she does a menu.

To keep her hand in the action after Al passed on, Annie would visit an old family friend at his business, a bookmaking parlor in one of the boroughs. He is a mustachioed entrepreneur known as Manhattan Tommy.

There is a lot of activity at his place of business, a second-floor apartment that looks as if a broom would be as welcome as the fuzz. There are two rooms, a kitchen and another room with a round green table in the center. There are two portable TV sets, half-pulled Venetian blinds on the windows. There are also three phones. They ring a lot. Soon, Annie was answering them, taking bets on the slips and carrying on conversations in her spirited way.

She was good, and Manhattan Tommy said, "As long as you're hanging around so much, I might as well pay you for it." Since she was passing a certain amount of money to Tommy, she figured, why not have a little of it returned?

"Hi, Charley, give me that horse, again," she said now, the receiver of the phone nestled inside her curly red hair. The rattle of the nearby elevated train shook the room. "Got it." She jotted the bet onto a yellow legal pad. The caller asked how Annie was doing. "Came in second in the third." she said.

An elderly lady named May in a knit hat came through the door. "I went on a hunch last night," May said to Annie. "Picked Empress Marge, because that's my sister's name."

"How'd it do?"

"Nothin'," said May filling out a slip. "Didn't even scratch."

May is a regular, and goes out for coffee for Annie and puts quarters in Annie's parking meter downstairs on the avenue.

"Who do you like in the Stakes tomorrow?" May asked.

"Cut Away looks good," said Annie.

"I don't think it can go a mile and an eighth. I like Gater Del Sol." She meant Gato Del Sol.

They've been taking bets for the Belmont at Manhattan Tommy's for several days. "The sooner you take the money, the better," said Manhattan Tommy. Lately, Manhattan Tommy has been standing around the corner from the Offtrack Betting shop downstairs—to make it easier for customers who don't like to climb stairs. An employee named Sammy used to be at the OTB for him, but Sammy has since changed his address.

"Sammy," said Tommy, who had come upstairs between races, "made himself a little too conspicuous. He sat on a milk carton, eating hot dogs and doing business—right in front of the OTB, always kibitzed with customers. If he was busy and someone tried to get his attention, he'd say, 'Just a minute, officer, be right with ya.' This time, it *was* an officer."

At the apartment, there is a regular procession of people coming in to make bets. They prefer the bookie to OTB because there is no surcharge with Tommy, they can have credit with him, and he sends each one a turkey on Thanksgiving—last year, $1,200 in turkeys. The bettors trade information, trade tips.

"I don't go for tips," said Annie. "If a tip is good, why would anyone want to tell anyone? You bet it yourself. Besides, tips are supposed to go like this: from the owner or trainer to his wife to her cousin to the cousin's friend to you. By then, my God, they've probably got the horse's name wrong.

"I learned that from my husband, Al," she said. "But he didn't follow his own advice—but you can't help it, it's human nature to want to go with a tip. It almost didn't matter. We loved those horses, couldn't get enough of 'em. Al always said that he'd want to have his ashes scattered on the track.

"Well, when he died, I went to Yonkers racetrack with his ashes in a container. It was like 2 in the morning. Raining so hard you couldn't believe it. There's one guard there. But I snuck around him and, even though it was dark and rainy, I found my way down to the track. It wasn't hard. After all, I had been there before.

"I climbed over the railing and in the rain and mud spread Al's ashes across the finish line. It was sad, but it was nice. It's what he would have wanted." The phone rang, but before picking it up, Annie said, "You know, I'd like the same myself."

A Bad Time for Queenie

New York, November 14, 1983

It's hunting season around Rochester N.Y.

"I know they're hunting something because I hear the guns going off all day," said Mr. C., a resident of Fairport, N.Y., a suburb of Rochester. Behind his house is a woodsy area. "They're not supposed to be shooting back there. It's posted, but they don't care. Maybe it's pheasant they're after. I'm pretty sure it's not deer because I haven't seen any guys coming around here with trees on their heads.

"Some of my relatives drop by for coffee before they go out to try to kill the deer, and they wear the trees on their heads. Not actually trees, but branches. They can't get through the door.

"Now, my watchdog, Queenie, she attacks them when they come in. Oh, a walking tree! Trees are the only thing she's not afraid of. She's the biggest coward in the world. And she doesn't like hunters at all. When she hears the hunters shooting, she falls on the floor, and lays there.

"July Fourth is a terrible time for her, with all the firecrackers. She thinks it's the middle of hunting season. She tries to run into the vacuum cleaner to get safe.

"Now, any kind of noise and Queenie goes sliding across the floor. When people come over to visit, they see Queenie acting this way and they think it's because we beat her. I try to explain that it's just because she's a nervous wreck from the hunters.

"But the people don't believe it. And for some reason Queenie really gets scared when my wife, Molly, walks into the room. The dog whimpers and falls down. So they think Molly is the real cruel one, the one who kicks the dog all the time.

"But Molly's just as concerned about these hunters as Queenie is.

"One day Molly's outside and an arrow just misses her head.

"It's one of those hunters and I guess when he heard footsteps coming around the house he thought it was a deer. All Molly was doing was hanging up clothes in the backyard.

"Queenie's not as brave as Molly. Queenie won't go out of the house."

Mr. C. never cared for hunting himself. "The deer freeze when they see a man, they're so frightened," he said. "I went deer-hunting with my brothers-in-law one time. You go out all day and it's cold and you're shiverin' and shakin', and then a deer came by and he stopped and just stared at us. He was scared out of his wits. And they started shooting.

"Where's the contest? It's murder. Maybe the lion is a sport, or the rhinoceros. They'll charge you. But not pheasants and turkeys, and not deer. And the hunters say, 'Well, we've got too many deer around here and they cause accidents by running in front of cars on the road.' Maybe. But I think there's got to be a better way to handle that problem. Especially when these bow-and-arrow guys don't hit the deer right, and he escapes, and he's running around suffering with an arrow in his side for the rest of his life.

"My brothers-in-law, they love it. They're always bragging about how good a shot they are. One time one of 'em comes by with a dead deer on his pickup truck and he's real proud. I go to the truck and look it over and look the animal over. He said, "What are you looking for?' I said, 'The dents.' He said, 'What dents?' I said, 'The only way you could kill a deer was if you ran over it with your truck.' He got all flushed.

"But I could say that because I was letting him hang up the deer in my garage. It's all right if the blood drips on my car, he doesn't want it to drip on his.

"I have one relative, he eats everything he kills from hunting and he lives on the meat all year long. It's all he eats. It's like he's living in the 1800s.

"He sits in a tree for two or three days waiting for the deer to walk underneath. He thinks the deer has a fair chance. He's dressed like someone in a war.

"So it's raining, it's freezing, and he's sitting up in the tree. And then he shoots the animal in the back. He thinks this is great sport. That's his vacation, sitting up in the tree. He's got two sons and they sit up in a tree all day, too. He's got them broken in good. His wife sits home. But she must really love it because they've been happily married for 15 years.

"I had another brother-in-law, he didn't hunt, but he liked hunters a lot. And fishermen. He made a lot of money from them. This is my brother-in-law, Jim. He was a very good cardplayer.

"Now, some of these hunters they'll go shooting and then they'll go to a cabin and play cards. It was the same with deep-sea fishing. They'd kill fish and then they'd gamble on the boat the rest of the day.

"Jim would tell these people what kind of great deep-sea fisherman he was, and when he went hunting, how he was a great shot, the great white hunter.

"One time he went with these hunters, real rich guys who didn't know him too well, and they were laying there in the woods for hours and he was getting extremely tired and cold and bored. Finally, they saw a deer. He got so excited. He jumped up. 'There it is! There's one!'

"The deer ran away. Nobody got a deer that day. Instead of getting mad at Jim, the other guys had a big laugh out of it, and went off to play cards.

"Jim was no athlete at all. He could hardly even walk. But he had a nice personality and everyone enjoyed kidding him.

"They laughed about how he scared off the deer the whole time they were losing their money in cards to him. And he had saved a deer. He was happy about that, too. It turned out to be not such a bad day after all."

The Gobblers' Last Stand

New York, November 23, 1984

The turkey is an endangered species among sports nicknames, a most miserable and undeserving fate for this noble fowl.

There is only one college that has ever carried the banner of the gobbler, the male turkey, and brought its distinctive gobble-gobble-gobble cry into the athletic arena, and that is Virginia Polytechnic Institute, in Blacksburg.

At Virginia Tech, as the school is commonly known, the nickname Gobblers has been virtually superseded in the last few years by another—Hokies—a calculated if wrong-headed effort on the part of the athletic department to alter the image of its teams.

The name-lift began in earnest in 1978, when Bill Dooley arrived as athletic director and football coach. His feathers would flare at certain insults, such as when opponents referred to the team as "a bunch of turkeys." He felt the sting from rival schools when their bands struck up "Turkey in the Straw." And when his football team scored a touchdown and a device inside the Gobblers' own scoreboard rapturously sounded a turkey mating call, he considered it undignified, or at least unfootball.

Above the entrance to Lane Stadium, the Tech football field, a legend still reads, "Home of the Fighting Gobblers." Since Dooley arrived, though, the sports information department and reporters covering the teams have been asked to refer to them as the Hokies.

What's a Hokie? Good question. The story at Tech goes that many years ago a contest was held in Blacksburg to choose a new and exciting cheer. The winning chant went:

> Hokie, Hokie, Hokie, Hi,
> We're the boys from V.P.I.

The inspired lyricist was later asked what Hokie meant. "Nothing," he replied. "It just seemed to fit in with what I was trying to say."

So the Gobblers in the past were occasionally also called the Hokies, an endearing if meaningless name among Techites. But now the complete turnover to Hokie is a full-fledged campaign, and succeeding. With it goes the last vestige of a turkey nickname.

This is a dolorous notion to contemplate, but it points to the fact that we often take the turkey for granted, as well as with cranberry sauce.

Benjamin Franklin thought so highly of the toothsome turkey that he proposed it as the national bird. That it lost out to the bald eagle, a fish-eating scavenger, a plundering, craven, nasty-tempered bully, says little for the ornithological background of the general run of Founding Fathers.

*   *   *

The wild turkey in particular, with its brilliant plumage, is a most estimable bird. It is strong—it can spring into flight without a running start. It is fast—it can race along the ground at up to 25 miles per hour and fly at 55 m.p.h. And it is sharp-eyed—it can spot the glare on a hunter's cheek from an impressive distance. (Which, hunters say, is why they put on greasepaint or wear masks when lying in the brush in wait for their prey, though it is widely known that hunters like to wear greasepaint, masks and other fittingly oddball stuff any time they can.)

It is also true that the wild turkey's domesticated cousin is a dimwit and probably the source of the pejorative "turkey" in our idiom. But, says Gene Smith, editor of *Turkey Call*, a slick magazine devoted to the wattled fowl, the domesticated turkey "has been bred over many years to grow fat and foolish and palatable."

The wild turkey, meanwhile, has all the virtues that a sports team would want for a nickname—and more than many other schools' team nicknames or mascots.

Besides the normal plethora of fauna, such as Wildcats and Tigers and Lions, there are Hogs (the Arkansas Razorbacks), Horned Frogs (at Texas Christian), Gorillas (at Pittsburg State in Kansas), Terrapins (at Maryland) and, at California-Irvine, Anteaters.

Turkeys may not offer a tough and battling image, but neither do the University of Hawaii Rainbows, the Stetson Hatters of Deland, Fla., the Whittier Poets in California, the Scottsdale (Ariz.) Community College Artichokes or, in our own backyard, the New York University Violets.

Birds in general provide popular nicknames, including Cardinals, Falcons, Hawks, Orioles and, of course, Eagles. But none of these are so much a part of our lives as the turkey.

Another advantage to the nickname Turkey for Virginia Tech would be that the women's teams there, now called the doubly meaningless Lady Hokies, could have an easily and naturally adaptable and perfectly respectable name, which is Hens.

If they did, they would be spared having to perform the linguistic gymnastics that other schools have undertaken so as to fit contemporary needs. Schools with the nickname Rams, for example, have called their women's teams Ramettes, Rambelles, Wrams and even the gender discrepancy Lady Rams, rather than use Ewes.

Other schools have had better luck with the sexual diction. At Northland College in Wisconsin, the teams are known as the Lumberjacks and the Lumberjills; at Duquesne, they are the Dukes and the Duchesses; and at the College of the Ozarks, the male teams are the Mountaineers, and the females teams the Mountaindears.

Meanwhile, the Gobblers are lamentably on their last legs as a symbol for a college team, victims of slander, to say nothing of a lack of appreciation.

But the turkeys have at least had a run. That's more than can be said for some others, such as oysters.

No team, as far as can be determined, has ever been called the Oysters. Too bad. For, as Jerry Kirshenbaum of *Sports Illustrated* has suggested, the pep yell would be natural, with the Oysterettes chanting on the sideline, *"Oysters, oysters! Raw! Raw! Raw!"*

The Sleuth of Baseball

New York, February 24, 1986

"No," Bill Haber was saying, "I've never been in a cemetery looking for a missing ballplayer. But I deal with cemeteries frequently."

By vocation, Haber of Brooklyn is a baseball historian and statistician. By avocation, he tracks presumably dead, obscure baseball players.

Haber is the Sherlock Holmes of baseball, the Nero Wolfe of necrology.

When Haber came across the name of one "Samuel Powell" in a baseball encyclopedia, he was intrigued. Powell pitched in two games for the St. Louis Browns in 1913. Other than the listing of his name, there was not an ounce more of background information about him.

Who was Samuel Powell? Haber asked himself.

By "incredible perseverance" over a period of years, says Haber, he found out. Samuel Powell was actually Jack Powell, who was actually Reginald Bertrand Powell. Haber traced him to a small newspaper clipping in the *Memphis Commercial-Appeal* on March 12, 1930. The headline read, "Man Chokes to Death Attempting Swallow Half Steak in One Bite."

In a "cafe on South Main Street," Reginald B. (Jack) Powell, then 38, sought to establish that he was indeed "the fastest eater" in Memphis. He ordered a large steak, cut it in half and, while customers and the proprietor watched, tried to swallow one of the halves. "After a couple of chews," said the newspaper account, "Powell began choking and grew frantic in his efforts to dislodge the piece of meat from his throat. An ambulance carried the man to St. Joseph's Hospital.

"While physicians strove vainly to remove the steak, Powell died on the operating table."

Haber, saddened to learn how Powell had met his end, was nonetheless pleased that the case was finally solved.

From 1901 through 1985, there have been 10,844 players and nonplaying managers in the major leagues, said Haber, "and of that number, as we speak, 6,038 are living, 4,734 are deceased, and 72 are missing."

There are some fairly young players whose whereabouts are not known, but they probably just haven't had their change of address recorded yet, said Haber. They include some like pitchers Joey Jay and Ed Rakow and Phil Ortega. But it's old guys, little-remembered guys who vanished without a trace years ago, like Dummy Deegan and Joseph Aloysius Peploski and Oscar C. (Otto) or (Rube) Peters, who make Haber's pulse beat quicker.

Since 1969, Haber has been searching for these old players whose deaths, according to *The Baseball Encyclopedia* and the Baseball Hall of Fame, have gone unrecorded. He has located nearly 300 of them.

Haber never leaves New York, conducting his searches from home by calling cemeteries and next-of-kin, and next-next-of-kin, writing letters and consulting libraries and old newspaper files. He also keeps in touch with a network of baseball histories and others around the nation who burn with a passion for baseball nuggets.

There is something about an unrecorded death that challenges this slender 44-year-old man whose eyes, through spectacles, gleam with a gentle but unmistakable fervor when discussing his quarry—in regard to both his triumphs and his frustrations.

In the office in the basement of his home, there are books and notebooks and files neatly and systematically lining his shelves. He takes down one hefty file bound with a thick rubber band.

"This," he says, "was probably the most baffling case I've had occasion to solve."

It is the curious tale of a pitcher who had a 1–0 record in nine games in four years—spanning 1904 to 1909—with the Dodgers, Senators and Giants. *The Baseball Encyclopedia*, first published in 1969, listed him as Louis G. (Bull) Durham, born in Bolivar, N.Y., in 1881, and the brother of James Garfield Durham. Haber would learn that none of that was true. The player's real name wasn't "Durham," he wasn't born in Bolivar, and he wasn't the brother of the other Durham. This made the first forays into the case rather difficult for sleuth Haber.

"It was a sparse trail," Haber recalls. "Our man was a very private fellow, who seemed to trust few people in his lifetime. Besides that, he had a very lively imagination, and wove stories about himself out of whole cloth."

At one point, Haber came across a note in a 1909 copy of the *Chicago Journal*, which said, "Lou Durham is one of the few Hebrews in professional baseball, his real name is Louis Klotzbach."

Not true.

Another story said that Durham one day "laid down his bat" in the Polo Grounds "and walked out to the street" and went to New Mexico, where his wife was dying. Haber determined there was no record of any such wife.

Haber happened to have a baseball card of Durham from 1909, when he played with the Giants. "I'd look at it sometimes, when I had hit a dead end," said Haber. "He had this sly grin on his face, and it was like he was saying, 'Ha, ha, you'll never find me.' That got me mad."

Haber eventually uncovered a crucial fact: a Louis Staub Durham was born in New Oxford, Pa., in 1877. Haber would learn that this Durham was really Louis Raphael Staub, that he sold patent medicines and dabbled in "mining interests in the southwest," and appeared in several silent films in Hollywood. "In some of those old westerns," said Haber, "you'd see a fight and in the background standing at the bar in a big cowboy hat was Durham." The ex-player had left a wife and daughter in Pittsburgh, disappeared, and, unknown to the first family, married again and fathered another family of nine kids in Bentley, Kan.

After a search of nearly 14 years Haber, in 1983, established that Durham Staub had died June 28, 1960, at age 83.

"I was thrilled to crack the case," said Haber, "but I didn't celebrate. No way. I had work to do."

He still pursues the trail of Otto Peters, among others. Peters pitched one year in the big leagues, for the White Sox in 1912. He was known to be working in a munitions factory in Brooklyn in 1918. He has not been heard from since.

"But something just came up," said Haber, the other day. He pulled down the Peters file. "I think I've got a hot lead, a real hot lead."

An Old-World View

New York, May 5, 1983

Ike Herschkopf was talking recently about his father, Wolf, who loved playing soccer as a youth in Poland but who has had certain problems with the peculiarities of sports in America.

Ike Herschkopf's father, who built a respected materials business in the garment center, retains old-world sensibilities. "Dignity and decorum have the highest priorities with Dad," said Ike, a Manhattan doctor. "He's a husky man who always wears a dark suit and a dark tie and a dark snap-brim hat. And when, for example, he poses for pictures at a family wedding, he never smiles. He feels it is not dignified to smile in a wedding picture."

Ike's father, now in his 70's, immigrated to the United States in 1950. Actually, Wolf isn't his real name. It was the closest the immigration officials could come to his Yiddish name. Which is Velvel. But "Velvel" was impractical for business. He never liked "Wolf," and he tried calling himself "William" and "Walter" but didn't care for those names, either.

Often in a group he is called William by some, Walter by others and Wolf by still others. Some of the group will look at the others and wonder whom they're talking to.

Ike's father introduced himself to Ike's future in-laws as "Zev." He liked the name, but as it happened, he soon forgot he had given himself that name. Shortly afterward, Ike's mother-in-law said to Ike, "Doesn't your father like me?" Ike asked why. "Because when I call him," she said, "he just walks right by." Ike assured her that his father liked her very much.

For years, Ike's father had been hearing about football in America, how great a game it was. And it was his passion for football—he had enjoyed it as a youngster in Europe—that finally persuaded him to buy his first television set. He was deeply disappointed.

"Look, look!" he shouted to his son, "They're picking up the ball with their hands! Penalty! Penalty!"

Ike explained to him that American football is not played by the same rules as European football; in fact, the Americans call that game soccer.

Ike's father gave the sport a second chance the following week. But the rules didn't improve, and he lost interest.

Basketball was another strange American game for Ike's father, especially the way Ike played it when he was young. Ike used to toss rolled-up socks into a lampshade in the living room. He found that the perfect-sized ball for the lampshade hole was three socks. Naturally, he used his father's socks.

On a business trip to Boston once, Ike's father was caught in the rain. He returned to his hotel room to change clothes before the next meeting. When he looked into his suitcase, he found only one sock; that and the two wet ones had been one of his son's lampshade basketballs.

Ike's father had to get to the meeting, and thought that one dry sock was better than two wet ones. He would just be sure not to cross his legs.

At the meeting, he kept both feet on the floor and his cuffs pulled low to cover his ankles. But as he became more involved in the sales pitch, he grew less concerned about his feet, and crossed his legs.

That immediately arrested the attention of the businessman seated across from him. The man looked at the naked white ankle, and then at the ankle with the black sock. His eyes shifted back and forth again.

Ike's father cleared his throat. "Excuse me," he said, "but you see, my son plays basketball with a lampshade."

A few months later, Ike's father was again in Boston on business. He checked into a hotel. In the room he noticed that the window was up. It was the dead of winter, but he thought that the maid had wanted to air out the room.

He went off on his business, and returned at night. He went to pull down the window and found that the pane for the lower half was gone. And the room was very cold.

He went downstairs to the desk clerk and asked for another room.

"I'm sorry," said the clerk, "the hotel is booked solid."

"Then please get me into another hotel," said Ike's father.

"There's a convention in town," said the clerk. "There's not a hotel room left."

Ike's father dragged himself back upstairs. He went to bed fully dressed. The wind was blowing, and he was freezing. He couldn't sleep.

Then he remembered something his son had told him. It was a lesson from school. Ike had told him that layers are very important if you're cold. Bulk wasn't as important as layers. In fact, newspapers on your body, Ike had said, can help keep you warm.

Ike's father jumped out of bed and hurried downstairs. He bought several newspapers. He went back up, took off his clothes off, covered his body with newspapers, then put his clothes back on, including his coat, and climbed into bed. And he fell off to sleep.

He was so exhausted from his trials that he slept through his alarm. When he got up, he realized he was already five minutes late for his meeting. He leaped out of bed, threw on his hat and raced out the door.

It happened that the meeting was with the same man who had

seen him wearing one sock. As Ike's father went into the business-man's office, he suddenly realized that he was still wearing the newspapers. The businessman asked to take his coat. "No, thank you," said Ike's father, "I'm very comfortable."

They began to discuss business. Ike's father was feeling very warm. He began to sweat.

"Are you sure I can't take your coat?" asked the businessman.

"Oh, no," said Ike's father.

He began to feel woozy. He thought he might faint. He ripped off his coat, grabbed the newspapers and tore them from his body.

The businessman stared in disbelief. Newspapers were flying all over his office.

Finally unencumbered, Ike's father wiped the sweat from his face. He was terribly embarrassed. He looked at the newspaper all over the office floor.

"I can explain," he said. "You see, my son—"

"Yes, yes," the businessman interrupted, "I understand. Your son plays basketball with a lampshade."

Look of Eagles

New York, July 10, 1983

Joe Lazarro was telling about arriving at a local golf club near his home in Waltham, Mass., and, not having come with a group, asking the starter to fill him with any threesome. The group he was put with knew nothing about Joe, but they immediately noticed something odd.

Joe had come with another fellow who placed the ball on the tee for him, then, while Joe was holding the club, the other fellow fit the club head against the ball. Joe, without the golfer's customary waggle, took the club head back slowly and then came down, whacking the ball straight down the fairway.

The same procedure was followed when Joe hit his irons and putted.

After the first hole, one of the golfers politely asked Joe, "Why do you have someone place the ball down for you?"

"I've got an awful strain in my back," he replied.

"Oh," said the other golfer.

After a few more holes, Joe decided to tell his golfing partners the truth.

"I don't have any sight," he said.

"And you know," Joe recalled, "they stopped talking to me. Some people think if you're blind you're dumb. So I had to start making some jokes to get them speaking to me again, like, "The reason I can hit straight is good mechanics—I keep my head down and don't have to follow the flight of the ball.' "

Joe Lazarro laughed. Lazarro, who seven times has won the National Blind Golfers' Championship, was walking now with his shoulder brushing his "coach," David Ferson, onto the green of the eighth hole in the one-day Connecticut Golf Celebrity Classic in Easton, Conn. Ferson is a paid assistant to Lazarro and is his "eyes."

Lazarro was playing in a fivesome with the golf pro Gardner Dickinson, and three businessmen. They were playing "scramble," in which the best shot of the group is scored.

Now Lazarro and Ferson lined up his putt. Ferson explained to him the lie of the putt and the distance, about 20 feet.

Lazarro, age 65, medium build, with short white hair, prominent nose, blue shirt, white slacks, white golf shoes and eyes that appear slightly crossed, now stood over the putt.

Lazarro tapped the ball and it rolled toward the hole. "Too much left!" he said. It missed the hole by a foot. "I felt it the minute I struck it."

Lazarro plays by feel and sound. "Muscle memory," as he calls it, is crucial. "When I'm told that the distance to the hole is, say, 170 yards, I gear my body to hit it that far. I've walked that distance and practiced hitting shots for hours and hours and weeks and months and years so that I know it in my body. My coach takes care of the direction, and I take care of the distance."

Ferson was asked Lazarro's handicap. "Right now," said Ferson, with a smile, "it's me."

Lazarro, in fact, has a 20 handicap. His best round was a 77, in 1971.

When another player hits from the tee, Lazarro leans on his driver with his head up and hunched forward, following the action. Although he has a false right eye and his left eye is, he says, "no damn good," he seems to have the look of eagles.

"Dance," he called to a partner's ball as it bounced on the green, "dance to the hole."

How does he know what to root for?

"From the sound," he said. "You can tell how the face of the club hits the ball. You play a lot of golf and you can tell. With a wood or a nine, if the ball's hit in the sweet part of the face—in the middle—there is a distinct click. Off the heel of the club, it's a dud sound. On the toe, it's like hitting a rock, to my ears."

Lazarro lost his sight in World War II, when he was a 26-year-old private first class. "It was 1944, over in Italy," he said. "I was with the Combat Engineers, 34th Division, called the Red Bull Division. We were clearing mine fields to make the Po Valley crossing. I was behind a jeep when it hit an active mine and blew up. The shrapnel ripped my right eye right out of my head on the spot, and scorched my left eye. My face was burning. They bandaged me up and I was soon shipped back to Valley Forge, in Pennsylvania.

"The medics hoped to save my left eye. There was a detached retina and a scarred cornea, and I had several operations. But one day the doctor came and said, 'Joe, look, you're not going to ever see again.' Well, something like that can make you melt like a marshmallow. It's tough, who you kidding. But you either quit or accept it."

Lazarro had met a girl, Edna Louise Basnett, in Liverpool, one month before leaving for the Africa campaign. They corresponded regularly, and talked of marriage. Now he wrote and said to forget it, "I'm blind." She wrote back, "I didn't love you for your eyes."

It was difficult getting passage on ships to America. They were booked with war brides. Edna was only a war fiancée. Desperate, Edna Louise decided to write Eleanor Roosevelt. Eleanor Roosevelt wrote back and said, "I'll see what I can do."

She would help get Edna passage to America in early April 1946. And on April 30, Joe and Edna, she's now called Skip—"I was going to need a skipper for my ship," says Lazarro—were married.

Lazarro, who caddied as a youth, took up golf regularly in 1951 because, he said, "blind people need a hobby and I like being outdoors."

"Now," he said, "I'd rather play golf than eat."

In order to eat, though, he works at Raytheon as a mechanic who dismantles machine parts for engineering analysis. "You learn to see with your fingers," he said.

Though he has obviously made adjustments to being blind, he says at times he gets "fed up" with it.

"Once a friend of mine, Paul Fahey, and I were going to a restaurant," said Lazarro. "I said, 'You be blind this time.' He said fine. I'm hanging on his coattails and I tell the restaurant people that my friend is blind. I get the menu, and order spaghetti and meatballs. And they cut up Paul's meatballs and gave him a spoon.

"When we pay the bill, the restaurant people walk out with us. Our car happened to be parked right in front. Well, Paul opens the door and gets behind the wheel, starts up the car, and we drive off," said Lazarro. "You can imagine the look on the faces of those poor people."

A Lesson From Muscles

New York, August 6, 1987

Muscles the Bookmaker was Lou Guida's first hero and taught him a lesson that the lad would carry with him the rest of his life.

Muscles was very skinny and so, naturally, everybody in the neighborhood called him Muscles. Muscles was a tenant in George's Barber Shop on Communipaw Avenue in Jersey City in 1945 when Lou Guida was 10 years old.

George was George Guida, Lou's father, and because there was a scarcity of heads to shear during that war year, George's father rented the back room to Muscles for $5 a week, and minded his own business.

Lou Guida shined shoes in his father's shop, and shined Muscles's shoes every day and received a handsome 25-cent tip. That was one reason Muscles was Lou's hero. Another was that he taught Lou, who was often being beaten up on the way to Our Lady of Victories grammar school, how to fight.

"Then one day," recalled Guida, "two suspicious-looking guys walked into the barber shop and went to the back room—all of the people who went back there looked suspicious, so I thought nothing of it. Remember, bookmaking was a way of life in those days in Jersey City, when Frank Hague was mayor. Well, these two guys carried cases, like for musical instruments.

"I'm shining someone's shoes and suddenly I hear rat-a-tat-tat. I started shining the shoes so fast that smoke came out of them.

"The two men rushed out, ran into a car that was waiting for them outside and sped away. My father hurried into the back room and found Muscles shot to death. The killers were never found. People said that Muscles got into trouble because he owed money and wouldn't pay. So my hero taught me the most important lesson of all. Cheap is expensive."

Guida, now 52, in suspenders and expansive demeanor, smiled wanly while recalling this recently. Many of the lessons learned in the barber shop in Jersey City have contributed to his becoming one of the premier owners, syndicators and managers in harness racing today. His horses have earned more than $20 million in the last 16 years.

Guida is co-owner and managing partner of Mack Lobell, one of the best trotters in the business and the 2–5 early favorite in the Hambletonian, the Kentucky Derby of trotting, to be held Saturday afternoon at the Meadowlands.

All this would have amazed Muscles the Bookmaker, to say nothing of George the Barber.

Guida's father had urged his son to become a shoemaker. "If you're a barber," George Guida told his son, "you sit around all morning doing nothing until about 11:30. Then eight guys come in and say, "How long will it be?' Then five of them walk out. If you're a shoemaker, they bring in shoes and leave them there. You have all day and night to work on them."

But neither barbering nor cobbling struck Guida's fancy. He had bigger fish to fry.

At age 12, in fact, he learned syndication. He rented three or four shoeshine boxes to kids in the neighborhood, assigned territories, and then earned a dime a day from them.

"I don't know if I made any money after buying their polish and brushes, but I felt like I was," said Guida.

School didn't challenge him, and he quit in the 10th grade. He became a television repairman, owner of a car wash, and a stock broker. He became so successful as a broker that he needed tax shelters. One that appealed to him was owning a racehorse. He bought several and, remembering Muscles, he went first-class, paying $300,000 for Lumberjack Hamde. And bought a lemon.

He bought 21 horses inside 30 days, and in about 250 races he won once. "I didn't want to be cheap," said Guida, "but I also realized that I was ignorant. I didn't know anything about what I was buying. One day I was talking with a trainer, and when he left my house I saw him get into his run-down half-truck. I thought to myself, 'I'm taking advice from a guy who can hardly even earn a living.' That's when I began studying horses—not just breeding, but conformation, and how they finished races—as opposed to simply how fast they run."

Guida would own Niatross and one of Niatross's son's, Nihilator, two of the fastest pacers—and best finishers—in harness history.

Then in 1985 he fell in love with another horse, Mystic Park, who a few years before had been a star 3-year-old. Mystic Park had come down with a mysterious horse disease known as Potomac Fever. The fever had localized in Mystic Park's feet and he lost all four of his hooves. A horse without hooves can't stand up. A horse that can't move has no circulation, and would have to be destroyed.

Mystic Park was sent to the New Bolton Center at the University of Pennsylvania, where an experiment was tried. In order to take the pressure off his legs, he was submerged in water for nearly eight months. He swam, grew stronger, and miraculously his hooves grew back. And joyfully he returned to his career as a sire.

"I was so impressed with Mystic Park's incredible will to live," said Guida, "that I was determined to buy some of his foals."

Guida bought two, Galaxy Lobell, for $80,000, who has done only fair, and Mack Lobell, for whom he dished out $17,000. Mack has now won 14 of his 24 races—4 out of 4 this year—for nearly $1 million in winnings. Guida also syndicated a half-interest in the trotter for $2 million.

Looking back after all these years Guida the Businessman fondly recalls Muscles the Bookmaker. "I was sorry to see Muscles go the way he did," said Guida. "Not only did I lose a friend, but my father also lost a very good tenant."

The Pleasure of Fleetness

New York, September 13, 1984

Fifteen years ago this October, John Cheever interrupted the taping of an interview with the *Paris Review* to watch the Mets beat the Orioles in the last game of the World Series.

At one point earlier in the interview, Cheever, the novelist and short-story writer, was asked if he had ever held any jobs other than writing.

"I drove a newspaper truck once," he said. "I liked it very much, especially during the World Series, when the Quincy paper would carry the box scores and full accounts. No one had radios, or television—which is not to say that the town was lit with candles, but they used to wait for the news; it made me feel good to be the one delivering the good news."

Cheever's reminiscence was brought to mind last Sunday, when the *New York Times Book Review* carried a moving excerpt from a soon-to-be-published memoir, *Home Before Dark*, by Susan Cheever about her father, who died June 18, 1982.

In the excerpt, Miss Cheever wrote that her father was "runty, unathletic" as a boy growing up in Quincy, Mass.

"And yet," she said by telephone the other day, "all his life he was very interested in sports as a fan and a participant. He loved the Red Sox, for example, and he was passionate about skating and swimming."

Burton Benjamin, an executive producer with CBS-TV and a close friend of Cheever's, recalls the writer's coming to Benjamin's house for a swim, and the way he'd dive in. "Never a toe in the water first," said Benjamin. "John was not a man to test the waters by putting a toe in."

In his short story "The Swimmer," Cheever's main character "had an inexplicable contempt for men who did not hurl themselves into pools." This was apparently a reflection of Cheever's admiration for those who were passionate and daring about life, as he tried to be and often was, particularly in his approach to his art.

"Fiction," he said, "is meant to illuminate, to explode, to refresh. . . . Acuteness of feeling and velocity have always seemed to me terribly important."

Throughout Cheever's work, there are quiet, isolated but revealing moments in which his keen feelings for sports, and those who participate in them are depicted.

In *The Wapshot Chronicle*, he wrote a paragraph that seems to sum up the entire careers and aftermaths of some great athletes, but he did so in unusual fashion, with a carnival as a backdrop:

"In the next booth a young man was pitching baseballs at a pyramid of wooden milk bottles. His aim and speed were superb. He stared at the milk bottles, drawing back a little and narrowing his eyes like a rifleman, and then winged a ball at them with the energy of sheer malevolence. Down they came, again and again, and a small crowd of girls and bucks gathered to watch the performance but when it was ended and the pitcher turned toward them they said so long, so long Charlie, so long, and drifted away, arm in arm. He seemed to be friendless."

Often in Cheever stories there is a melancholy air, but also a sense of hope. In *Oh What a Paradise It Seems*, the novel he wrote shortly before his death, his protagonist, Sears, tells a psychoanalyst: "It reminded me of a fourth down with something like twenty to go. All you can do is to punt but how marvelous it is to punt, that feeling of booting a ball way down the field on a fourth down is such a hopeful feeling, such a feeling of beginning that I've often wondered why football never caught on in other countries."

Cheever, as his daughter points out in the memoir, suffered from alcoholism and in 1975, at age 63, profited from a rehabilitation program at Roosevelt Hospital in New York. His feelings at that time seem to evoke a period when he was in his 20s, and worked and wrote at Yaddo, an artists' and writers' community in Saratoga Springs, near the famous racetrack. Young Cheever spent time around the track, and observed the clientele.

In *The Wapshot Scandal*, he wrote that a song continued to play in the "chamber" of his character's mind:

"It was a tune he had heard forty years ago on a crank-up phonograph and yet he could not stop singing:

> Got those racetrack blues.
> I'm feelin' blue all the time.
> Got those racetrack blues.
> With all my dough on the line."

Despite the bleakness and the desperation, there lives an odd optimism—that is, a chance to prevail.

Cheever dealt with intense feelings there. In a similar but lighter vein, he described the thrilling sensation that might accompany the simple act of catching a ball. He once saw a "pretty girl" with "fine dark gold" hair on the sidelines of a Princeton-Dartmouth rugby game.

There was, he wrote, "a muffled kick and it went directly into her arms. The catch was graceful; she seemed to have been chosen to receive the ball and stood there for a second, smiling, bowing, observed by everyone, before she tossed it charmingly and clumsily back into play. There was some applause. Then everyone turned their attention back to the field, and a second later she dropped to her knees, covering her face with her hands, recoiling violently from the excitement.

"She seemed very shy. Someone opened a can of beer and passed it to her, and she stood and wandered along the foul line and out of the pages of my novel because I never saw her again."

The pristine quality that Cheever personally felt for sport at its best, at its most beautiful and tranquil and spiritual, was described in his last novel:

"He skated and skated. The pleasure of fleetness seemed, as she had said, divine. Swinging down a long stretch of black ice gave Sears a sense of homecoming. At long last, at the end of a cold, long journey. . . . It seemed to Sears that all skaters moved over the ice with the happy conviction that they were on their way home."

Strictly Personal

Mr. Hardrock, Sir

New York, April 5, 1986

Hardrock Johnson died. He was 90 years old.

The short obituary on him in a recent issue of the *Sporting News* sent a sportswriter back in time, to a summer's day in Chicago in 1951, when an 11-year-old boy stood under the stands at Wrigley Field after a game and, along with his pals and numerous other fans, sought autographs from the Cubs who emerged from the clubhouse, looking large in slicked-down hair and wide sport jackets.

A Cub coach named Roy (Hardrock) Johnson hurried through the crowd to the nearby parking lot. He was a leathery man, gruff-looking but with a pigeon-toed walk that seemed to suggest a vulnerability below the tough exterior.

The boy followed and importuned him for his autograph. Johnson said he was in a hurry, couldn't sign. As he slammed his car door, about a millimeter or so from the boy's pencil and the boy's fingers, Johnson said, "Come to the park tomorrow, kid, and I'll give you a baseball."

Silly boy, said the 11-year-old's associates, Hardrock ain't givin' you no ball.

"He said he would," said the true believer.

The next day—or so it seems in memory, though it may have been two days later, or a week—the boy and his pals returned to the ball park. It was well before the start of the game, and the Cubs in their white uniforms were practicing on that stunningly clean green and brown field.

And there, along the first-base line, hitting fungoes to the outfielders, was Hardrock Johnson, No. 42.

The kid remembers the flight down the concrete stairs from the grandstands to the short barrier that divided the box seats from the playing field. He remembers the smell of the hot dogs sizzling on the vendors' grills, the scratchy recording on the public address system ("Goodnight, Sweetheart" always seemed to be playing) and the soggy hole—from the peach his mother had packed—that was forming in the brown lunch bag he carried. And he remembers his lofty expectations.

"Mr. Hardrock, sir," called the boy. "I'm the kid you promised a ball to."

Mr. Hardrock, sir, kept hitting fungoes. High fungoes that hung in the blue sky, and then fell. The boy called to the coach again, and again. Nothing. Some adults sitting nearby tittered. Soon a heavy hand clamped on the boy's shoulder, accompanied by the usher's dulcet tones: "Get outta here."

The boy began the forlorn climb away from the field when he heard, "Hey, kid." It was Hardrock. He tossed him a baseball.

Up the stairs the boy flew. He remembers holding the ball tightly as the other guys looked it over. Then he sat down with it, rubbed his fingers over the red stitching and inspected the dirt and grass smudges. He'll never forget the smell of that ball. There is a distinct, unforgettable muskiness to the tanned horsehide of a baseball, but this one also held the aroma of the ball field, and the kid loved it.

In the neighborhood, there were suggestions on how to get the ball clean. The most impressive argument was made for immersing the ball in a bowl of milk. This the kid did. A few days later, he removed it. The ball had turned yellow as parchment.

Nonetheless, he took it back and asked Hardrock to sign it. 'I gave you the ball to play with," Johnson said, "not to put on a shelf." He signed it, but the boy did eventually play with it. The stitching came apart, and the cover fell off and the ball was a mass of string. Then it disappeared for all time.

Through the years the incident of getting that baseball from Hardrock Johnson stayed with the boy. It enlarged possibilities for him.

And through the years, as a sportswriter, he would occasionally ask someone with the Cubs what and how Hardrock was doing.

Johnson left the Cubs as a coach in 1954—he had been struck by a baseball and suffered from a bad hip—and began scouting for the Cubs in the Southwest. Johnson lived in Scottsdale, Ariz., and the sportswriter thought one day he'd visit him and, after all these years, thank him for that baseball. But it never materialized.

Then came the news that Johnson had died, in a nursing home. He had lived there with his wife, Fanetta.

The sportswriter called Mrs. Johnson. She is 86, and her voice sounded clear over the long-distance wires.

"Some people called him 'Hardrock' because he used to work the pitchers so hard," she said, "but most people called him 'Grumpy,' including me and our daughter and even our grandchildren. But living with Roy was wonderful. We were always laughing. We had the best time our whole 70 years together. He had that grumpy look, and sometimes his temper was short, but usually it didn't mean anything."

The couple was from Haileyville, Okla. To avoid becoming a coal miner like his father, Roy first became a prizefighter. It wasn't long before he understood that this was as tough a way to earn a living as digging coal, and turned to baseball, and pitching. He was a big leaguer for one season, with Connie Mack's last-place Philadelphia A's of 1918. Johnson won one game and lost five.

He would tell about pitching to Babe Ruth, who was then still a pitcher but making a reputation as a slugger with the Red Sox. "Roy said that Mr. Mack told him, 'This guy can hit,'" recalled Mrs. Johnson. "He said, 'Don't give him anything. Make him bite. Or walk him if you have to.' Roy threw and the Babe hit the ball 400 feet into the last row of the bleachers. Roy said, 'It might have cleared the Bunker Hill monument, but at least I didn't walk him.'"

After 1918, Johnson spent many years in the minor leagues, playing, and then managing, in towns like Bisbee, Ariz., and Fort Bayard, N.M., and Ottumwa, Iowa. In 1935, he came up as a coach with the Cubs.

"Roy," said Mrs. Johnson, "loved to work. He was going out and sitting in a beach chair to scout high school and college games until just a year or so ago. And, you know, when he died he still had his teeth."

"Still had his teeth," the sportswriter repeated. "That's nice, that's very nice." And he meant it.

Pitchers Do Get Lonely

New York, July 22, 1987

With the Yankees losing 18–3, in the bottom of the eighth in Texas—even after a few days, the score still reads like a typographical error—Lou Piniella did the unusual, though not the unreasonable. Rather than waste one of his regular relief pitchers in that forlorn enterprise, he saved his sirloin and served the Rangers chopped liver.

The chopped liver was named Rick Cerone, normally a catcher.

Cerone was fetched because he sometimes throws batting practice, and gets the ball over the plate. Cerone admitted later that he was excited about pitching in a game. "It's something you always dream about," he said.

He arrived with the bases loaded and none out and, though he balked once and allowed two runners to score, he retired the Rangers on three straight batters, which included a near-grand slam by Ruben Sierra and a near-home run by Bobby Witt.

How did he feel on the mound?

"Scary," said Cerone. "It's lonely out there."

How true.

Many of us who have stood on the pitcher's hill in a ball game have shared Cerone's emotions.

This writer, before he took pen in hand, took baseball in paw and was prepared many years ago to fling it for the greater glory of Sullivan High School, located on the North Side of Chicago.

The calendar now flips back to the spring of 1954. The writer is a freshman for the Sullivan Tigers and sitting on the bench out of harm's way while the team is being soundly threshed by Waller High.

In later years I'd read where James Thurber said that "most middle-aged husbands get to sleep at night imagining they are striking out the entire batting order of the Yankees." Maybe Cerone was having just such a dream the other night about the Rangers. I may have been doing the same about Waller.

But it's one thing to dream it, and another to be sent out to do it.

In the last inning of the Waller massacre, our coach, a dark-browed, grim figure known to us as Black Nemo for his sunny disposition—"C'mon, you jokers," he'd snarl, "get a hit"—turned and called out, "Hey, you! Warm up." I looked around to see which of the pronouns among us he was referring to. "Yeah, you." It was me. "You're pitching the next inning."

I had never before pitched in a game in high school, or even seriously warmed up. I removed my overcoat and winter gloves—it gets chilly in the springtime in Chicago—and hurried to a grassy knoll and threw to the warm-up catcher.

When I entered the game, I stood on the mound and peered toward home plate. It seemed seven miles away. Not only was my heart thumping, but I discovered I had made a grave error in warming up on the sideline. I mistakenly threw from about 50 feet away, rather than the requisite 60 feet. I think I also warmed up throwing downhill.

When the Waller players came to bat, I realized that some of them had been recruited from the Lincoln Park Zoo, which was nearby. They were huge and hairy and had big teeth, and when they squeezed the bat, sawdust oozed from it.

I looked around at my fielders. All of them were backing up.

Cerone had it right. It's scary out there, and lonely.

And when I pitched, it was the Fourth of July. The Waller hitters boomed and rocketed my pitches all over the field. But miraculously this ball was caught by that outfielder in a tree, and that line drive was snared by this infielder who threw up his glove just in time to save his life, and someone else made another impossible catch, and thus the inning ended. Three up, three down.

About two weeks later, in school on the morning of the last game of the season, the coach collared me.

"You're starting against Von Steuben this afternoon," he stated.

"Sure, coach," I said. And he was gone.

Starting? Von Steuben? They're meaner than Waller.

I got to the field by public bus, and changed into my uniform in a stall in the men's room of a small brick building. As I was tugging on my baseball pants, I heard two men enter the room. It was Black Nemo and the coach from Von Steuben. I was behind the door of the stall, and they didn't see me. I overheard them talking. I didn't breathe.

"Yeah," Black Nemo said, "I don't have anyone else, so I gotta throw this freshman today."

"Yeah, sometimes it's rough," said the Von Steuben coach.

They left, with Black Nemo still grumbling.

My confidence at an all-time high after overhearing that conversation, I dragged myself to the field. After two innings, the Sullivan fielders were dying of exhaustion from chasing base hits, and Black Nemo, showing uncustomary humanity toward them, yanked his freshman hurler.

I pitched a couple more years for Sullivan and Black Nemo, and even enjoyed the occasional painless outing. That was more than 30 years ago.

Recently I called Cal Feirstein, who caught most of my games in high school. Cal owns a liquor store in Chicago. I remember him toiling behind the plate in his bulky catcher's equipment.

"Cal," I said, "what comes to mind about our team?"

"One thing is Nemo," said Cal. "Remember he used to call me Wooden Arm, because I always threw the ball into center field?"

We laughed. We reminisced some more.

"You know," he said, as we were finishing, "I always thought it would be better to be a pitcher."

I imagine that Cerone, like Cal, thought the grass around the pitcher's mound was always greener than around home plate.

It's not. I know it and so, now, does Cerone.

Old Connection to the Majors

New York, August 21, 1986

An item the other day in this sports section noted that six members of the Reds were graduated from local Cincinnati high schools, led by Pete Rose, the manager and first baseman. They all appeared in the lineup last Sunday before a crowd of

27,175 "that included numerous relatives, classmates, neighbors and friends."

Most of us have had some connection, however distant, with someone who reached a particular height. And we followed that person's career, knowing that there but for just a little more talent, a little more speed, a little more power, a little more courage and/or a little more brains, go I.

In my case, there was only one person whom I grew up with in Chicago—or played against as a kid—who made the major leagues. This was Jim Woods, listed fully in *The Baseball Encyclopedia* as Woods, James Jerome (Woody).

He played parts of three seasons in the big leagues, long enough, each time, to down the proverbial cup of coffee. When we think of long-ago heroes, the big names often come to mind, and songs are sometimes composed to them:

> *Where have you gone, Joe DiMaggio?*
> *The nation turns its lonely eyes to you.*

Jim Woods wasn't Joe DiMaggio to much of the nation, but he was a young hero on the North Side of Chicago in the late 1950s. He led Lane Tech to the state baseball title as a pitcher and third baseman in 1956, as a junior, and struck out a record number of batters in the championship game, I seem to recall, and maybe even hit a home run.

That was also the year that I came closest to immortality in relation to Jim Woods. I played for Sullivan High School, and we played Lane and he was pitching. Woods, a redhead and right-hander, was of average size—*The Baseball Encyclopedia* has him at 6 feet, 175 pounds, just about my size. But he was gifted. He threw smoke, BBs, aspirin tablets, all that stuff, and yet I hit a double off him in that game. This is true. Down the left-field line. I struck out the other two or three times, but I did hit a double, swinging, I believe, as Woods was winding up. Bob Sanders, our center fielder, also got a hit off him.

A story about the game in our school newspaper, the *Sentinel*, had the following headline:

> *Lane Beats Diamond Nine;*
> *Sanders, Berkow Lead Team*

We had lost the game 9–0, and many Sullivan students had a pretty good idea in which direction Sanders and Berkow were in fact leading this team.

There was also a time that I pitched to Jim Woods. This was in a Pony League game at Thillens Stadium in Chicago, when Jim and I were 13 or 14. Thillens is a good little park with a high left-field fence. Behind it is a canal, and then trees on the other side, and a boulevard beyond that. I threw and Woods swung.

He hit a wicked line drive to the third baseman, and just as the third baseman flung up his glove in self-defense, the ball rose. The left fielder started back to make the catch, and the ball kept rising. I've never seen anything like it. The ball cleared the high fence, went over the trees and landed in either the street or the adjoining state.

I was shaken at the time, but I came to relish that homer as my connection to the big leagues, for Jim Woods was signed by the Cubs as an infielder in June 1957—right after our senior year in high school—and went straight to the Cubs, to Wrigley Field, to the majors!

It was virtually unheard of. The only other person I knew of that this happened to was Phil Cavarretta, in the mid-'30s, who, it was said, also went directly from Lane Tech to the Cubs.

Now, Sullivan had played Lane in May, and we beat them—and Woods—amazingly, 1–0. (I grounded out twice.) And then a month later—30 days!—Woods is in a Cub uniform. It was unbelievable, and very exciting.

I remember wondering how he'd do against Spahn and Burdette and Newcombe and Drysdale. Would he blast a homer off them as he had off me? Oh, what company I'd be in!

As I recall, he sat on the Cubs' bench the whole summer. I went out to the ball park and I watched on television and read the papers, and waited for him to see action. Nothing.

Then one night, I think it was the last series in St. Louis, I heard on my car radio—I had bought a 1950 Plymouth for $200 and it came with two accessories, and an outside metal sun visor and a shaky radio—that Jim Woods was being sent in to pinch-run at third base. Finally. Oh, boy.

Woods took a lead off the base. Danced around. Suddenly, the pitcher wheeled and threw to third. "They picked him off!" shouted the announcer. "They got him!"

In *The Baseball Encyclopedia*, it says that Woods played two games for the Cubs in 1957. I simply don't remember the other game. The only thing he did was score a run, so he must have been a pinch runner a second time.

He went down to the minor leagues, and I followed him sporadically in the *Sporting News*. He was traded to the Phillies, and played 11 games for them in 1960, hitting one home run; and another 23 games in 1961, hitting two homers. He hit the last two in a span of a week, and *Sports Illustrated* did a short piece on this power-hitting rookie.

But Woods, with a career batting average of .207, was gone from the majors after that season, never to return.

I heard of him only casually years after. For a short period, I understood that he owned a tavern near Wrigley Field. Eventually, he moved to San Bruno, Calif., and then disappeared.

Not long ago, I was talking to a man in Iowa whose hobby is to track down the addresses of former major leaguers. Some he can't find. Some ballplayers disappear, for no other reason, occasionally, than they just don't leave a forwarding address.

One of those ex-players is Jim Woods.

I think about Woods sometimes, think of the homer he hit off me that may still be going, think of him as my link to the major leagues, and that he realized that boy's dream that so many of us once shared.

And I wonder, Where have you gone, Jim Woods?

The Shooting of Ben Wilson

New York, November 25, 1984

A magazine, *Hoop Basketball Yearbook '85*, arrived in the mail not long ago. It details the coming season from the pros to the colleges to the high schools. On page 86, it lists "High School's Hottest Prospects." One of them was "6-8 Ben Wilson of Chicago Simeon HS," a 185-pound senior forward who was "being recruited by most of the nation's powers."

The magazine describes Wilson as "an emotional, spirited player who sparked his team to wins in its final 26 games as it captured the Illinois AA championship and finished with a 30–1 record."

The Chicago high school basketball season has begun, but Ben Wilson is not playing, not hearing the roar of the crowd for his shots, not trying to spark his team to another state championship. There will be no more phone calls from recruiters; no longer will they be ringing his doorbell.

Last Thursday, Thanksgiving Day, a headline on the first page of the *New York Times* sports section read, "Chicago Prep Star Is Dead of Wounds." The prep star was Ben Wilson. He was 17 years old.

The wire-service story said that on Tuesday, during a lunch break, Wilson and two female friends bumped into three youths outside a store. A quarrel began and one of the youths tried to rob Wilson. He resisted and one of the youths, according to the police report, drew a .22-caliber pistol and fired two shots into Wilson.

Ben Wilson died in a hospital the day after he had been shot. The Reverend T. L. Barrett, of the Wilson family's church, said, "What happened yesterday is not new. It is glorified and celebrated because the victim was a star and a champion. But it happens day after day after day in our community."

He was talking, or course, about senseless and deadly violence. And as severe as the problem surely is there, he need not have confined it to his community.

It recalled another shooting of an athlete in Chicago under circumstances equally as grotesque. The gun blast that shattered the midnight stillness on June 14, 1949, and sent Eddie Waitkus crashing against the wall of a young woman's room in the Edgewater Beach Hotel, rocked me, too. I was then a 9-year-old fan who had enjoyed the baseball style of Waitkus, a former Cub who the winter before had been traded to the Philadelphia Phillies.

On several occasions at Wrigley Field, I had watched the lanky, long-faced, left-handed Waitkus. He had a cool and buttery style around first base. I had admired him, but I was not alone. I learned after that night of June 14 that a Chicago teenager named Ruth Ann Steinhagen was also fond of him, but in a totally different way. She must have been in some of the crowds I was in that waited an hour after games under the stands and cheered as the players emerged from the clubhouse, all hair-slicked and deific.

Who knows, who can predict the actions derived from the stirrings within some people, young or old, black or white, male or female? What kind of people were those youths who shot Ben Wilson? What kind of person was Ruth Ann Steinhagen?

"As time went on," Ruth Ann Steinhagen would tell the felony court, "I just became nuttier and nuttier about the guy. And I knew I would never get to know him in a normal way, so I kept thinking, I will never get him and if I can't have him, nobody else can. And then I decided I would kill him. I didn't know how or when, but I knew I would kill him."

Ruth Ann Steinhagen, who would be judged criminally insane, rented a room in the hotel, sent a message to Waitkus and then, when he entered the room, put a bullet hole through his lung.

The bland savagery of that shooting, the cutting down of a hero, is part of our national mythology now, and the incident was the basis for the critical scene in Bernard Malamud's novel, and the recent film, *The Natural.*

I have never forgotten that shooting of 35 years ago. The bullet ripped a hole through my boyish notion that sports were not a part of the real world, that they were impregnable to the madness around us. Although Waitkus survived four operations and lived—miraculously, he played the full 154-game schedule the next season as his Philly "Whiz Kids" won the National League pennant—I was learning of the mortality of men, which included athletes.

The shooting of Waitkus was also the beginning of a lifetime of experiencing the hollowness of senseless tragedies: the murders of the Kennedys, of the Reverend Martin Luther King; the sniper Whitman, the mad Manson; the unspeakable slaughter in Vietnam; and, also in the world of sports, the massacre of the 11 Israelis at the Munich Olympics.

"A day hardly passes, we feel, without some new threat to the ordered peace that makes life bearable," wrote Anthony Lewis in the *Times* shortly after the Munich murders. "We sense a society at risk from terrorists, hijackers, assassins—creatures beyond the familiar restraints of reason and humanity."

That appeared on September 18,1972, a day after the obituary of Eddie Waitkus.

Waitkus was 53 when he died of cancer of the esophagus in a Boston hospital. In preparing an article at the time, I called his sister, Stella Kasperwicz. She did not believe that his having been shot had directly led to his death. "But it might have taken away some of his endurance," she said.

Waitkus had played the last year of his 11-year big-league career in 1955. In the following years, he was an instructor in Ted Williams's summer baseball camp, made some speeches and collected his pension. He retained an interest in sports. His sister said that she and Eddie had talked about the tragedy at the Olympics.

"Eddie thought it was awful," she recalled, "and he said that none of us will ever be the same because of it."

To many, that echoes the sentiments for Ben Wilson, dead at 17.

Memories of Coaches

New York, August 19, 1985

Shecky Greene stopped in Manhattan briefly before traveling to Browns Resort in the Borscht Belt for a show on Saturday night. While here, we visited. We had never met, but we had a few things in common. For one, he and I—he is older by 14 years—are the only two graduates of Sullivan High School in Chicago that I know of to make it to Carnegie Hall at the same time. The date was last March 28. He performed on stage and I sat in the audience and watched.

The second thing we had in common was the Shecky Green Special—his name was misspelled on the menu—at Ashkenaz Restaurant, on Morse Avenue, a few blocks from Sullivan. The sandwich named in his honor at popular Ashkenaz was the neighborhood's ultimate tribute to a local boy made good. The sandwich consisted of a double-decker of corned beef and egg, lettuce and tomato, with a generous dollop of potato salad spilling off the plate.

That and the barbecue-beef sandwich with the special Ashkenaz hot sauce that made you cross-eyed with the first taste were favorites of mine in high school in the mid-'50s. (Stomachs, like everything else, were better constructed in those days.)

Shecky Greene and I spoke about the teams at Sullivan—we had both participated in sports there—and about some of the coaches, some of the funny stuff, some of the odd stuff. One coach he recalled, and to whom he sometimes referred in his routines, was the burly football coach, Coach M.

"He was a big, broad guy and everything he did was broad," said Greene. "I remember him talking in health class in his booming voice and pointing with his pointer: 'You punks, you, you young yout's, listen to me. I don't want any of you to drink, I don't want any of you to smoke, I don't want any of you to carouse. I never smoked a cigarette, I never drank alcohol, and I never chased after women. You hear me, you yout's.'"

The coach suspected that some of his football players were smoking. He knew some dated the cheerleaders. And so he made the cheerleaders take a vow that he composed. It went:

> *The lips that touch a cigaroot*
> *Shall never rest beneath my snoot.*

At Sullivan, there was a basketball coach named Art Scher, who came years after Shecky had graduated. Unlike the football coach,

Scher was small and thin. In the three years I was on the team, I never heard him tell a joke or attempt a witticism. He had a quiet smile, which was as much a courtesy as anything else. He had funny ways, though. And some people laughed at him.

I remember one morning meeting him in the crowded corridor between classes. I saw him coming. He was no more than 5 feet 5 inches tall. A lock of gray hair fell on his forehead, and gold-rimmed glasses rested on his thin nose. He wore his customary gray cardigan buttoned up, and white sneakers.

We stopped in the hall and I don't remember how we got into it, but he soon was demonstrating the pivot move without the ball. Amid all the students' movement and clatter, this little gray-haired man backed up a few steps and ran at me—I stood with books in hand—and he slammed down on his right foot, spun left and slipped behind me, arms outstretched, to catch the nonexistent pass. I had to bite my lip to keep from smiling.

Before sending a player into a game, Coach Scher had a habit of saying to the kneeling substitute, "We're counting on you," or "You can do it." Something that he hoped would make us soar. Once, with the team hopelessly behind and less than a minute to go in the game, he was about to send in Earl Pratt. "Think you can do it, son?" he asked. Earl looked at the scoreboard and the clock, and then at the old man. "If I don't get tired, coach," he said, straight-faced. About four guys fell off the bench laughing.

The coach had been in an awful car crash the year I was a freshman, and people weren't sure whether he'd pull through. He came out of it with a loss of his sense of smell. The gamy aroma in the locker room never presented a problem to him.

It was generally believed the accident also impaired his memory. He often got guys' names mixed up. He was always calling me someone else.

Some thought he was a flawed basketball coach. Oh, he was strong on fundamentals, and read the textbooks on basketball, but the plays we practiced hours on end rarely worked in a game. In fact, we rarely tried them, and I'm not sure he realized that. His substitutions seemed arbitrary. Yet perhaps he had his reasons, as arcane as they might have appeared to us.

He gave a basketball letter to a guy who played little in games and caused the coach grief in practice. Some time later, out of curiosity, I asked why he had given that fellow the letter. Coach Scher said, "Well, he's a senior, and I didn't want him to leave school with a bad taste in his mouth."

He told me he had been a substitute and the smallest player on his Benton Harbor, Mich., high school team. He loved basketball and practiced hard, and one time got into a tight game and won it with a last-second shot; but when graduating, the coach had not given young Art Scher a letter. Coach Scher, now, did not want this fellow to feel as deeply disappointed as he once did.

The last time I saw Coach Scher was shortly before he died. It was on an elevated train in Chicago. It was good to see him again after several years. He greeted me with that nice, quiet smile and looked up over his glasses and asked how I was doing. My stop came up. We shook hands and said good-bye. He called me by someone else's name.

The Game—and Life—Goes On

New York, August 21, 1983

I'm not going to analyze why, at age 43, I still play in pickup basketball games. What's the purpose?

Sometimes people want to know what I'm trying to prove. They ask, "Can't you let go of your youth?"

In fact, I did retire once from basketball. I was in my mid-20s and I had figured, "Well, it's time to put away childish things."

I had played on my high school team, played in college and in the Army, played in schoolyards, in gyms, all over the country, and in England, in Italy, in Morocco, in Cuba.

In the University of Havana gym, after several half-court games, one of the players asked me to compare basketball there to the game played in the States.

I told him, "The only difference is that you guys argue in Spanish."

I quit basketball to play grown-up sports. I played squash and I played tennis—I hate waiting for a court—and I jogged. Not marathon jogging—just three or four miles. Enough so that when I had my blueberry cheesecake, I felt I deserved it.

But when I wasn't playing basketball, I missed it. It took me three or four years to admit this to myself. I'm not going to say I've got a Basketball Jones—as my friend Walter Iooss used to say he had (he now has a Tennis Jones)—but I liked playing the game. It felt good to throw a head fake on a guy and go up for a jump shot from 20 feet out and have the ball drop through the net—or rim, when there wasn't a net. Once on a windy day outdoors, I threw in just such a shot and the guy guarding me fixed me with a look and said, "You damn meteorologist."

And it felt good to strip a good player of the ball when he made his move. And it felt good to thread a pass. I won't say how often such moments occurred. Rare? Possibly. Jeweled? Yes.

And it felt good to be part of a team—when it played like a team. If you could call the five guys on some of the teams I played on a team.

Always, though, when I've had a day that was not too congenial on the courts, when, for example, my baseline jumper hit the side of the backboard—disgraceful!—I wondered if it wasn't curtains for my basketball career.

But that is some dilemma. When, in fact, are you finished? And can't—won't—tomorrow be better?

Or take the afternoon at the Y not long ago when I was dribbling at the top of the key and one of my younger teammates came around and took the ball from me and dribbled off. Something like that could drive a man to introspection.

A couple of times a week I play at the Vanderbilt YMCA on East 47th Street. In summer, I'll also hit outdoor games in a park or playground.

Forty-three and still playing basketball regularly? You might be curious to know what such a person as this looks like.

Not long ago, I was talking to a woman in her 20s, who said she didn't remember the 1960s. I said, "I can remember the 1940s."

She stared at me. "How old are you?"

I told her. "Gee," she said, "you're very well-preserved."

I told this to a friend on mine. He said it's true, he said I don't look a day over 42.

In this health-aggressive society today, people don't generally question anymore why runners run or squash players squash and so forth, but basketball—"Oh," they say, "really?"

Maybe one reason is that it's not particularly chic. There are no designer shorts for basketball. There's dirt and there's sweat and there's contact.

And there are communicative sounds there that people who sail or ski don't hear.

"Hey, pal," said a guy entering the gym to one of the players waiting for the next game, "can I run witchya?"

Basketball is different from most other sports that a middle-aged man might engage in. Compare it, for example, to running. You don't hit a "wall" in basketball, unless someone rams you into one on a lay-up, which happens. Nor is there anything in basketball like the runner's so-called "euphoria." In basketball, there is no spiritual transcendence that I know of. But there can be be thrills. And there might be more than imaginative truth to the notion that a certain play or shot could have been made in the pros, as well.

Not all, but some. Who's to say it couldn't be so? And how do they know?

The full-court games I play in at the Y are with a wide assortment of people, from diverse fields, some of whose names, or real names, I don't know. People come and go at the gym, like the Foreign Legion.

There were Big Al and Little Al and Orphan Annie (he had big eyes) and Diogenes (he read a book between games) and Monster.

"Call me at home tonight and I'll trade you the tickets to the game for ones next week," Monster said to another player.

"Who should I ask for if your wife or kids answer?" the player inquired.

"Just ask for Monster," he said.

I've been playing basketball for something like 35 years, beginning when I was about 9 years old. In my family's apartment in Chicago, I ran around trying to throw a rubber ball into a paper bag that I hung above the hallway entrance. The neighbors below us said I should take up checkers.

When older, I remember playing alone outdoors at Green Briar Park at night wearing gloves in the snow. I played by the light of a streetlamp.

I played and I dreamed. I dreamed of soaring. That's the wonderful thing about playing basketball. When things are going well, there is a certain sense of soaring. Like Elgin Baylor. Or Pistol Pete Maravich. Or Earl the Pearl Monroe. Or, today, Dr. J.

Not just like them. But a *little* like them.

And when at work now, when there emerges a sentence that seems to me vivid, precise and right, it has a correlation to basketball on a good day.

And that's the part of not letting go of my youth that I don't want to let go of.

The dreaming. The soaring—well, in a fashion soaring. And feeling unabashedly good about an achievement of mind or body or both.

It was Picasso who said, "Youth has no age."

And the poet Schiller wrote, "Keep true to the dreams of thy youth."

So you ask me, "Why can't you let go of your youth?"

And I ask you, "Why should I?"

Joys and Perils of a Golf Outing

Chicago, June 16, 1985

Golf, legend has it, is a gentle game, a leisurely pastime played in a sylvan setting with amiable companions.

All of this may be true, on occasion, but sometimes golf can be dangerous.

"Last week," Pop was saying, "they dragged a lady away from here in an ambulance."

Pop and his son were waiting to tee off at the first tee, and the son had noticed that the fairways seemed a bit narrow, even to the rather inexperienced golf eye of the son.

Pop explained how the ball that was hit from one fairway wound up not only in the adjoining fairway but smack in the middle of a woman golfer's forehead. "Got her right between the eyes," Pop said. "Laid her out flat."

"You've got to keep your head up around here—except when you're about to hit the ball," added Pop. "They're coming at you from all directions."

The son thought about that, and about being in this high-risk zone to begin with. He had not golfed in nearly 20 years but decided it would be a good opportunity, especially with Father's Day coming up, to spend some time with Pop.

His father had rarely played golf until he retired a few years ago. Over the years, he had been too busy with business to give much time to sports.

In fact, except for occasionally playing catch with his son when the boy was very young, or taking him to a rare ball game, the two shared very little in the way of sports, though their relationship—despite now and then the traditional difference of opinion—has always been a warm one.

The son, who lives in a distant city and was visiting, had been pleased when he learned a couple of years ago that his father had begun to find joy in the royal and ancient game, in any game, in fact, where he could be so enthusiastic.

The father had told the son that he used to be afraid of being embarrassed about playing, and he'd make excuses that he was otherwise occupied when friends would call for a game. Then, one day after he retired, he stopped by a golf course where many of his pals go and watched them swinging at the first tee. "Lot of them were duffers," he said. "But all of them looked like they were having fun."

Tentatively, he began to play. Soon, he was hooked. "Hooked," in this case, means playing once or twice a week, reading some golf manuals and demonstrating in the living room to his patient wife, who has never touched a club in her life, how he used a 2-iron on the dogleg on the eighth hole.

She nods, and then returns to her newspaper, happy for him and happy for herself that his swing is with an imaginary club and doesn't imperil her nearby vase.

The son teed up on the first tee. First, the ball fell off the tee. Then the tee fell. Then the ball and tee fell. The image of the woman with the golf ball in her forehead was still on the son's mind. His father came over and offered help.

And soon they were off.

It was a pretty, well-tended, tree-studded course, bright and green on this sunny morning. And while the son and father were in the woods looking for the son's ball, the foursome behind were already taking dead aim at them. Plop. Plop. Two balls landed nearby. "Two weeks ago," said the old man, "a ball whizzed past my nose."

"What did you do?" asked the son.

"Ducked," said the old man.

As they went along, driving a motorized golf cart, the son discovered that golfers liked to sing. They sing one word, "Fore!" There were choruses of "Fore!" sometimes in counterpoint, sometimes in harmony. Baritones were heard, and tenors, and mezzo-sopranos. And golf clubs were held aloft like batons as the golfers warbled.

A ball cracked off a tree trunk, and another ball clanged off a nearby golf cart. The son observed a number of people walking funny, and wasn't sure if it was because they were old or because they had been conked.

At another tee, the son noticed so many people in the fairway from other parts of the course searching for their balls that it looked like a hunt for Easter eggs.

But the father seemed unperturbed. He was having a grand time. And he was good. Oh, he had his share of muffed shots, but, hey, so do Nicklaus and Watson. Once, on a dogleg, the old man hit one right over the trees. He watched it soar and land in perfect position for a chip to the green. "Oh, man!" he said with unabashed delight.

On the same hole, the old man had a "gimme" putt but didn't take it. "I like to hear the ball drop in the hole," he said.

He also was not averse to giving his son some gentle advice. "Take an easy swipe at the ball," he said. "Let the club do the work for you."

And he spoke about some of the golfers at the course: "The old guys'll beat the young ones every day in the week. The old guys hit it short, but they're consistent down the fairway. The young guys hit it eight miles, but then they can't find the ball."

Father and son moved around and through the course and the woods and the water holes, hitting shots and ducking others.

When it was over and they climbed into the father's car in the parking lot, Pop said, "It's a good time, isn't it?"

"It was great, Pop," said the son. "We enjoyed the round, and we aren't leaving in an ambulance."

The father nodded in agreement, and he drove off, the golf clubs clanking merrily in the trunk.

The Roots of the Super Bowl

Los Angeles, January 29, 1983

More than 100,000 fans will be packed into the Rose Bowl in Pasadena tomorrow to watch Super Bowl XVII, more than 100 million people will view it on television, and an estimated $600 million will be bet on whether the Miami team or Washington can push a football across a stripe of white paint with greater frequency.

The event is of such magnitude that only Roman numerals and not your garden-variety Arabic digits are used to describe it.

Football, clearly, has strayed from its roots.

I can recall what they are, at least for me.

It is the early 1950s. Springfield Avenue on the West Side of Chicago. It was a neighborhood street that, with cars parked on either side, was just wide enough for two-way traffic to squeeze through.

Primarily, though, it was a football field for two-hand touch, with normally three or four kids on a side. The goal lines were two sewers, one adjacent to where Mr. Massarelli lived with his vicious bulldog, and the other alongside Cutler's grocery store.

It was serious football, to be sure, and cars that traversed the backfield during games were deeply resented.

Certain moments come to mind. "Hey, what is this, anyway, a boulevard?" John Browne once called to a driver when a play he was diagramming in the huddle was interrupted.

"Stick it, kid," came the reply. Not everyone was a football fan in those days.

The plays were the thing. They were drawn on the street with a stone. It was not an uncommon trick for the other team, waiting for the offense, to play catch with the ball—and throw it toward the huddle and have one player try to sneak a glimpse of the play.

It rarely worked, since the offense, crafty beyond its years, hunkered down to hide it. Besides, even the players with the ball had trouble following it.

"Henry," John Browne the quarterback whispered, "You go 10 steps and banana peel right between the green Ford and the yellow Chevy.

"Pinhead, you go long. Start slow and then put on the steam. I'll hit you around the fireplug."

On every play one receiver always went long and one went short.

"Hey," shouted John Browne the quarterback, back to pass, "come back, I didn't tell both of you to go long!"

Pinhead came running back. So did Henry. "Go back!" cried John Browne. "Go back!"

Pinhead had ducked between two parked cars, not the designated ones, but he was shouting and waving, "I'm clear! I'm clear!" Henry was racing back out, hollering, "Hit me!" Two cars behind each goal line were honking to get through. Mr. Massarelli's dog was barking. Old Man Witcoff had been out late the night before and he opened his apartment window and stuck his blowzy head out and hollered for everyone to shut up.

John Browne, dodging the player coming in, finally threw long and the ball slammed into the branches of an overhanging tree, and then, as in a pinball machine, it eventually came through and dropped onto a red Studebaker, denting the hood, as Henry crashed valiantly into the car, denting the door.

The games always seemed to be interrupted for one reason or another, besides passing cars.

Harry Jaffe, in his 20s, thought he was a star. He'd come by and always want to get in the game for a few plays. One guy would have to sit out, and no one liked to.

"Aw, c'mon, Harry."

"Couple plays, that's all."

Of course, he always made himself the quarterback. He'd throw a few stupid passes, blame his receivers and then leave. People liked it when Harry Jaffe left.

Mrs. Padilla once was sweeping the sidewalk in front of her home when a coffin-corner kick hit her in the head. She shook it off, picked up the ball and marched into her house. I don't remember how the ball was retrieved.

But it took even more guts to get the ball back when it bounced into Mr. Massarelli's yard.

Mr. Massarelli was short, with a thick neck and hanging belly and eyes that burned with hatred for football. His dog looked just like him.

Now and then, just for spite, during a game Harry Jaffe would decide to wash his beat-up Dodge parked on the street.

Harry Jaffe thought he was the life of the party.

But the games went on.

One that remains clear in memory was tied at four touchdowns each and the team that scored next would win the game.

Pinhead's team was threatening, and was closing in on the goal near Cutler's grocery store.

Just then the Wonder Bread truck drove up and double-parked right beside the sewer.

Screams of protest from the players.

"Be right out," said Al the Wonder Bread driver, grabbing his basket stuffed with bread and hustling from the open door of the truck into the store.

Pinhead was struck by a brainstorm. He called a huddle. His team clapped in unison and came to the line of scrimmage.

"Let's go," he said.

The other team was delighted. The truck cut off a good portion of the field—simplifying defense.

"24-76-99-38-65-49 Hut!"

The ball was snapped to the quarterback. Pinhead streaked right for the truck, and scaled it. He scrambled to his feet on the roof, and the quarterback threw and the ball sailed softly into Pinhead's arms.

"Yeeeooowww!!" Pinhead screeched. "Touchdown!!!"

Suddenly, Al the bread driver hurried out of Cutler's, jumped into his truck and began to drive off. Pinhead, panic in his eyes, flung himself flat on the roof.

"No touchdown," called John Browne, who was on defense.

"Whaddya mean?" said Henry, Pinhead's teammate. "He caught the ball over the goal line."

"But he didn't touch ground," said John Browne.

"He doesn't have to."

"Sure he does."

The argument raged—and continues to this day.

And Pinhead? Well, what about him?

A Derby Pick

New York, May 8, 1984

About 30 minutes into the hour-and-a-half Kentucky Derby telecast on ABC Saturday afternoon, the viewer, hereafter called the Big Tuna, realized he hadn't made a bet.

Hey, *everybody* makes a bet on this race.

In his living room, Big Tuna had been listening intently to the team of Jim McKay, Jack Whitaker, Howard Cosell and Bill Hartack discuss the field and, particularly, the favorites and their jockeys and trainers. The gears in Big Tuna's upper story were cranking away as he sank deep into thought.

When the program began, it sounded like a two-horse race. It opened with what McKay called a "head-to-head battle of the sexes" between Althea, the filly, and Swale, a colt. This was just hype, Big Tuna soon learned. The field was packed with a total of 20 equines.

There was a picture of the infield, and Big Tuna was told that "this is a young people's happening ... somewhere between a tradition and a carnival." And maybe a riot thrown in, too, since the infield has been the scene of drunken brawls in the past. But no mention of that.

This was the Run for the Roses, and it was presented, for the most part, through nice and rather rose-colored glasses. A number of the horses looked or seemed good. Some of the jockeys were described as "extraordinary" and "brilliant" and "great," and several were "one of the best." Similar encomiums were bestowed upon some of the trainers.

Meanwhile, Hartack, "the unconquerable," as Cosell called him, was his forthright self. Asked about how Althea might do in a race against colts, he said he didn't think she'd have the stamina or strength to succeed. Then Lafitt Pincay Jr., who would be up on Swale, spoke confidently about his mount.

Fali Time, Taylor's Special, Vanlandingham and At the Threshold all were distinct possibilities, and Big Tuna considered them.

Whitaker interviewed Bill Shoemaker, who is 53 years old and could be the oldest jockey "by far" to win the Derby. Shoemaker was riding Silent King. Silent King is a stretch runner, Big Tuna heard The Shoe say, and definitely had a shot.

Hartack had liked Silent King to win. "And," said Shoemaker, "he picked last year's winner. So I hope he keeps his record clean.

Big Tuna pondered.

The camera scanned the grounds. In a box was a beautiful woman wearing a hat with long pheasant feathers sticking out, and in the infield was a young man wearing the shaft of a golf club that went in one ear, with the head of the club coming out of his other ear.

As the moment of the race drew nearer, McKay said, the horses would begin to feel it. Some, he said, would begin to sweat nervously, or "lather."

Big Tuna was getting a little lathered, too. O.K., he would put his dough on Silent King. There was an OTB office a few blocks away, but he didn't want to leave the television set. He asked his wife to go.

"You must be kidding," said Mrs. Big Tuna, hanging a plant in a window.

"This could mean big bucks," he said.

Her reply was the snip of scissors on a spider leaf.

*   *   *

Big Tuna had a number for a bookie, and called. The number had been disconnected. He called a friend who is a friend of a bookie. His answering service answered.

Mr. Tuna called a third friend, who said he hadn't been involved since his wife ripped the phone out of the wall because he had spent so much time getting information and making bets on it.

"Who ya pickin'?" asked his friend. "I'll squeeze for ya."

Bookies, Big Tuna thought, are like cops. They're never around when you need 'em.

He didn't have much time. He decided to lope over to OTB.

He was nearly out the door when his wife called to him: "Bet Swale for me to win." She obviously had been listening to the broadcast with half an ear.

"Do you know that a filly is one of the favorites?" he asked.

"Bet the filly," said his wife.

"You don't want Swale then?" he said. "You're changing your mind?"

Pause. "Bet the filly," she said, "and Swale. Two dollars on the filly, five on Swale. That's it!"

At OTB, he put a five-spot on Silent King, who was at 7–2, and bet Swale and Althea as instructed.

Big Tuna hurried back and made a strong kick down the home-stretch on 33rd Street and came through the door as the horses were entering the starting gate.

"And they're off!" called the announcer.

"Where's my horse?" asked Mrs. Tuna.

"Taking the lead," said Mr. Tuna, without enthusiasm.

Swale was a few steady strides off the pace. As the horses began to spread out, eight or nine got a call. Big Tuna listened for Silent King. Nothing. Big Tuna looked for Shoemaker's blue silks. He couldn't spot them in the long camera angle that showed the full field.

Midway through the race, Swale took the lead. At the turn into the final stretch, the announcer shouted, "Gaining ground on the outside!" Now, Big Tuna thought, his come-from-behind horse was making its move. "It's At the Threshold," the announcer said.

No matter. Swale won going away. Silent King was never heard from, and finished ninth. Althea pulled up and came in 19th.

"How much did I win?" asked Mrs. Tuna.

"I don't know," said Mr. Tuna. "He paid $8.80 to win at Churchill Downs, but it might not be the same odds at OTB. Different pool. It's about the same, though."

"Well, about how much did I win?"

"About two and a half times the price. Let's see, at $5 ..." His thoughts were still on the disappearing act of Silent King.

"That comes to ..." she said.

"I'm working on it," said Big Tuna.

"Isn't that $22?" she said.

"Sounds right," he said, deciding not to look for a pencil after all.

"Oh, Sweetheart, one other thing," said Mrs. Tuna. "Would you mind going over to OTB and pick up my winnings?"

To Win a Million

New York, June 25, 1987

A Mr. Boyars got to Belmont Park early yesterday, at 10 in the morning, three hours before the first race.

"Why so early? Because I'm a New York subway rider," he said.

Not all of the several million New York subway riders showed up so early at Belmont; most, in fact, didn't show up at Belmont at all. The hook for Mr. Boyars was the ad campaign by the track for its "Horse Course."

"There was a poster about it on every subway car I got on," said Mr. Boyars.

On the posters and in newspaper ads, there was this allure: "It's free and the homework can really pay off. . . . Learn to handicap to *win* in 4 FREE lessons."

So Mr. Boyars and a group of 23 other would-be horse scholars—including a newspaper reporter—took the bait and showed up with the view to learning more about how to pick a victorious nag, how to get more fun out of the race oval and, certainly, how to become as rich as a rajah quick.

This first course—three more will be held on Friday and over the weekend—was held in the film room at Belmont. The instructor was Ernie Aldi, a gray-haired man in gray suit with vest and a yellow handkerchief blooming from his breast pocket. He is a former longshoreman, a former interior decorator and a contemporary horseplayer.

Many of the scholars were so eager to get on with their studies that they were perusing the *Daily Racing Form* even before class began.

The scholars were informed by Horse Professor Aldi that at the conclusion of the four courses they would receive a diploma.

This diploma and one dollar—in paper or silver—will get the bearer on any subway in New York.

"This first course is designed to instruct you in four basic fundamentals," said the horse professor. "We'll discuss distance, form, class and running style and pace."

There was a program with past performances in which the students picked horses in past races and then watched the films to see how they did.

The professor told the students what he liked and didn't like about a horse from studying his form. "I don't normally like to bet favorites, to begin with," he said. "They only win about 33 percent of the time. And they don't pay a lot usually. So why waste your money?"

He said he liked the comments of "driving" and "rallied" to describe the previous performance of a particular equine. And when there was a possible contradiction, he noted, "On the other hoof. . . ."

"What does 'flattened out' mean?" asked one scholar.

"Tired," said Professor Aldi.

"I took it literally," said the scholar.

"I don't think it was meant to be taken literally," said the professor.

After the three race films, the professor asked his students if any had got all three right. A few raised their hands.

The reporter got one right, and won two coasters. "Sorry, but I can't give any money," said the professor.

Did any get all the races wrong? A few more hands went up. One belonged to Mr. Boyars.

"Isn't it more fun to win by picking a color, or a number, or a name?" Mr. Boyars asked the professor at the end of class.

"Not for me," said Professor Aldi. "I like digging into it. It's more satisfying. But I remember one woman in a class here last year was going, 'Eeny, meeny, miney, moe'—and she won twice."

He laughed. "In fact, one of the biggest days I had at the track was when I bet on the wrong horse," he said. "I had just lost six races by a nose, and was so disgusted I threw the program away. I kept walking and picked up another form, bet Raggedy Cat, and he lost. But I had bet the wrong number. That number won. And I won $1,800, and I still don't know the horse's name."

"You see," said Mr. Boyars, "luck just might be better than skill. I'll be going for red."

"Green's my favorite color," Professor Aldi admitted.

No hints had been offered as to how the students should bet the day's actual races. And each student went his or her separate and dream-laden way.

In the first race, the reporter carefully checked the *Racing Form* times and weather conditions and distances of past performances as well as breeding and training and jockey—then he picked a colt named Harry L.

Why? Very scientific: On the way to the window he asked a security guard whom he liked, and he said "Harry L." Never know when there's inside information.

Harry L. ran second, beaten by three lengths.

In the second race, the reporter liked Allison's Dance, who in his only other race ran second at six furlongs. But he had "rallied outside." This race was seven furlongs. More time to rally, right? Allison's Dance finished fifth, 12½ lengths behind the winner.

In the third race, the reporter bet Backslapper, his first race ever. But the astute eye caught that Backslapper's papa was the great Alydar.

Backslapper went off at 3–1. "He's getting some action," the reporter was told. "Looks good." The reporter winked knowingly.

Backslapper ran earnestly, and fourth.

Enough. The reporter decided that handicapping was for other kinds of students, probably Ph.D.'s in rocket science, and quit throwing away his life savings.

As he was about to fling his program in the trash can, he noticed the color that the winner of the third race, Wild Behavior, rode under. It was red.

Red! That was Mr. Boyars's favorite color!

Mr. Boyars, who won no races in the class, was probably calling a Brinks truck to take him home.

So much for breeding and form. So much for higher education. And hat's off to you, Professor Boyars, wherever you are.

The Wet Look

Newport, Rhode Island, May 18, 1983

The ocean was starting to get a little crowded. It was nearly 11 o'clock, and some seven miles out in the Atlantic, on Rhode Island Sound, about two dozen white yachts had gathered, bobbing in the water.

This was the spectator fleet, here to watch the first day of the finals from which would be chosen a defender of the America's Cup. The blue sky was flawless, the morning sun shone brightly, the water sparkled like seltzer. And the boats bobbed in the easy breeze.

Boats bob a lot in water. To the nonsailor, this boat-bobbing comes as something not fully expected.

But it didn't seem to bother many of the spectators. Some were already indulging in early libations. Others peered through binoculars to track the two boats soon to be racing, *Courageous* and *Defender*. Others flattened themselves on various parts of their boats and sunbathed.

Someone once described watching the America's Cup as "seeing how the other half drowns." But a first-time visitor to a yacht race was told that, although it still takes plenty of money to fool around with yachts, the "middle class" has begun to move into racing circles.

In Newport, where the summer mansions of the wealthy are called "cottages," definitions are broad.

"How much are some of these yachts out here?" the visitor asked.

"Between a half-million and three million dollars," he was told.

"And what about the racing yachts?"

"Well, Al Bond of *Australia II* has spent about $16 million in 10 years to try to win the Cup."

Yachting here is a venerated tradition. To sit in what passes for the stands at a yacht race, however, is generally more complicated and expensive than at a ball park.

You have to know someone to get on a yacht to view the event—the most prized invitation is from the Aga Khan—or be a member of the press, or pay $25 a head to get on the *Viking King*, a fishing boat, or be in the body of race executives.

A spectator has to be on his toes or the race will start without his knowing it. The race committee's boat sends up a series of flags, and the last one, in the shape of a red cylinder, signals that the race is on.

The visitor turned for what seemed only a moment to observe a sea gull when someone said, "*Courageous* is in the lead!"

The visitor looked, and saw the two boats only a few lengths apart. But it appeared that *Defender* was ahead.

"No, *Courageous* is windward," a veteran of yacht racing told him. "*Defender* looks like it's ahead, but it's only an illusion of the angle."

"Is there any perfect angle?"

"Not really, because it keeps shifting."

And so do the stands. The fleet began to take off after the racing boats.

Each of the competing yachts has two beige-and-white sails. *Courageous* has a white hull and a green deck, and the crew of 11 wears green short-sleeve shirts. *Defender* has a dark blue hull, and the crew wears dark blue shirts.

"The idea is to get on the other guy's wind," said the veteran. "You try to blanket him, or give him bad air."

"Bad air?"

"That's so the opponent has trouble getting good direction from the wind in his sails."

The racing boats zigzag up the first leg of the course, and then turn left and later left again, then up and back and up on the original first leg, and the race is over. It's about 24 miles, and takes three to four hours.

From the spectator fleet the visitor saw an outline of activity on *Defender*.

"What are they doing?" he asked.

"You can't ever see exactly what they're doing," said the veteran.

"No one can?"

"Well, maybe the selection committee."

One yacht, which had been following just behind the racing boats, carried the members of the selection committee. There are nine of them—like the justices of the Supreme Court, and nearly as formal. They are decked out in uniforms: straw hats, blue blazers, white shirts and red trousers.

"Their job is to observe the way the crew handles their jobs," said the veteran. "How do they manage the sails? How do they respond under pressure? Sometimes a boat crew loses a race, but they have a defect in the mast, or they haven't got new sails yet, or there is a fluke like a sudden wind change. And they might actually have been more impressive then the crew that won. So the committee watches the sailors' skills very closely, when they're not down in the cabin having cocktails."

Now one of the spectator boats with a good motor moved ahead to the first marker. The visitor could make out the sails of the racing boats in the distance but had no idea who was in front.

He waited on deck as the noonday sun beat down and the boat bobbed. His head was beginning to bob, too, along with his stomach.

The boats came toward the marker, an orange buoy. *Courageous* was first around, and its hull and sails seemed to be tipping so far toward the water that the visitor wondered how handy were the life preservers.

Suddenly, several crew members went scurrying about, and—puff!— up went the spinnaker, and the big blue-and-white sail billowed in the wind.

Defender was about half a minute behind, and—whoosh!—up went its spinnaker, a bright red.

And then they receded.

Another race was going on a mile or so away. This was a semifinal among challengers, the foreign competition. The boat of the visitor rocked over to see it. It resembled the first race to a great degree, except that the crew of the British ship, *Victory 83*, wore black-and-yellow-striped bumblebee shirts.

After a while, the viewing boat returned to the first race. By now, the visitor's eyes had closed, to be opened only by the splattering of a wave against the boat.

In time, the veteran said, "The race is over."

"Who won?" asked the visitor.

"*Defender*."

"Oh, good. Well, I guess we go home now."

"No, they're going to have another race, a short one."

"I see."

That one eventually ended, too, and the boats—after six hours—headed to port.

Land was soon spotted. Home is the sailor, the visitor mused with gratitude, home from sea.

It had been a glorious day.

FOR THE BEST IN PAPERBACKS, LOOK FOR THE 🐧

☐ **THE GAME**
  Ken Dryden

The veteran of eight years as goalie for the Montreal Canadiens, Ken Dryden reveals the texture of hockey—from the fundamentals to the rivalries and camaraderie—as only an athlete can.

"Extraordinarily insightful"—*Philadelphia Inquirer*
                    248 pages   ISBN: 0-14-007412-0   **$6.95**

☐ **THE LONG SEASON**
  Jim Brosnan

An inside account of the 1959 baseball season by a veteran National League pitcher, *The Long Season* presents an honest look at the game and many of its greatest stars, including Stan Musial, Hank Aaron, and Willie Mays.

"Probably the best factual book in the literature of baseball"—*The New Yorker*
                    278 pages   ISBN: 0-14-006754-X   **$6.95**

☐ **THE SHORT SEASON**
  The Hard Work and High Times of Baseball in the Spring
  David Faulkner

In a collection of anecdotes, stories, and interviews, David Faulkner captures the sunny, all-things-are-possible atmosphere, the conditioning and carousing, of the "Grapefruit League."

"A vivid, exciting account . . . David Faulkner is the most engaging baseball writer since Roger Angell."—*Philadelphia Inquirer*
                    276 pages   ISBN: 0-14-009850-X   **$6.95**

☐ **CHAMPION**
  Joe Louis: Black Hero in White America
  Chris Mead

This is a masterful biography of Joe Louis the man—more than the Heavyweight Champion of the World, Louis was the most recognized black American of his time and a dignified symbol of hope and achievement.

"A valuable addition to American social history"—Robert Creamer, *Washington Post Book World*   330 pages   ISBN: 0-14-009285-4   **$6.95**

☐ **WHY TIME BEGINS ON OPENING DAY**
  Thomas Boswell

From an affectionate and analytical perspective, veteran sports writer Thomas Boswell offers a penetrating look at the traditions, teams, ballparks, and games that make up the national pastime and inevitably the American grain as well.

"The writing is fresh, enthusiastic, and joyous."—*New York Times Book Review*   298 pages   ISBN: 0-14-007661-1   **$6.95**

FOR THE BEST IN PAPERBACKS, LOOK FOR THE 🐧

☐ **CAN'T ANYBODY HERE PLAY THIS GAME?**
Jimmy Breslin

Breslin's celebrated account of the New York Mets' first year of life—a year that produced a record number of losses and an unforgettable collection of oddballs—is a jubilant toast to the tenacity of the human spirit.

"Jimmy Breslin has written a history of the Mets, preserving for all time a remarkable tale of ineptitude, mediocrity, and abject failure."—Bill Veeck
124 pages   ISBN: 0-14-006217-3   **$5.95**